AF543021

Inheritors of Silence

Inheritors of Silence

Four generations and a forgotten homeland

Aloka Dasgupta Niyogi

NU VOICE
PRESS

NU VOICE PRESS

First published by NU VOICE PRESS 2025
An imprint of Hubhawks Pvt. Ltd
www.nuvoicepress.com

Copyright © Aloka Dasgupta Niyogi 2025

The moral rights of the author have been asserted
Database right Nu Voice Press (maker)

This is a work of fiction. Space and time have been rearranged to suit the convenience of the book. Except for public figures, hotels, and institution names, any resemblance to persons living or dead or the real events are purely coincidental. The opinions expressed in the book are those of the characters, and should not be confused with that of the Author.

All rights reserved. Enquiries concerning reproduction outside the scope of the above should be sent to Nu Voice Press at the address above.

ISBN: 978-81-988726-9-2
Typeset by Pooja
Printed at Manipal Technologies Limited, Manipal
Published by Nu Voice Press

To the cherished memory of my paternal aunt, Sisir Kumari Dasgupta.

Your stories left a deep impact.

Advance Praise for the Book

"A bundle of letters bound in twine, a family's tenuous, forgotten history, a woman on a mission to unravel the stories behind the faded ink and the lost hand, a narrative stretching from colonial Burma across countries, seas and continents, this is as much a journey to discover the past as it is a woman's journey to find herself and her purpose. Intricately detailed, richly written, and extensively researched, Aloka Dasgupta Niyogi has written a book that will draw you into the world of its protagonist, Anurima, a world that most women would identify with, one that is about finding oneself after losing oneself, and of reclaiming one's legacy after having forgotten it."

—**Kiran Manral**, author of *The Moon in the Lining of Her Skin*

"*Inheritors of Silence* is a novel that touches deep. Aloka Dasgupta Niyogi weaves a fascinating story spanning across time, human relationships and emotions. Told in lucid prose, it draws from the power of memory and the quest to fulfil a desire to belong and connect with the past and present."

—**Moin Mir**, author of *The Monastery of Solitude*

"This semi-historical story of a well-to-do Bengali family through the eyes of the protagonist, Anurima, is a most enjoyable read. It captures the essence of the evolving world of the *bhadrolok* through turbulent times. The struggles of women of such a family to find their identity is nuanced and interesting."

—**Brinda Karat**, former MP, political activist & author of *Hindutva and Violence against Women*

"I was deeply moved by Anu's journey of revisiting her past. Her experience was one a generation would yearn to undertake. My own tales, drenched in stories of Dacca, and my in-laws at Cooch Behar and Tripura, stir a deep desire to uncover my own history. *Inheritors of Silence* vividly revisits the cobwebs of a country with rich legacies alongside its own torn souls. I yearn to trace my identity four generations back to my great-great-granduncle, the legendary filmmaker Hiralal Sen. But unlike Anu, I can now never revisit the places that hold my identity. Anu's story has touched a deep chord within me."

—**Moon Moon Sen**, Indian actress, Hiralal Sen Lifetime Achievement Award 2025 & former MP

"An engrossing tale of a family's journey through the years—rising, falling, and travelling across four generations. Spanning nearly 150 years up to the present day, Aloka Dasgupta Niyogi's saga, *Inheritors of Silence*, vividly brings Bengal and its people to life."

—**Madhulika Liddle**, author of *An Unholy Drought* & other books

"*Inheritors of Silence* by Aloka Dasgupta Niyogi artfully blends the colonial and post-colonial history with the dramatic journey of Anurima, or Anu, in the present time. Anu has grown up in the background of her family's inspiring history of bravery and female emancipation. Her quest to know more about her ancestry takes her to Comilla, now in Bangladesh. What she learns there gives an intriguing insight which brings a fascinating twist in the tale. I loved reading this gripping narrative which keeps the reader on tenterhooks. Aloka's storytelling keeps one glued."

—**Aloke Lal**, former Director General of Police & bestselling author of *Barabanki Narcos: Busting India's Most Notorious Drug Cartel*

"*Inheritors of Silence*—Anurima's Story is a gripping account of colonial and post-colonial India. The focus is on East Bengal, now Bangladesh, and West Bengal. The book takes the reader on a journey of discovery, spanning continents, and a delightful collage of mindscapes of faith and betrayal, revolution and sacrifice, sweat and tears, love and longing. It all began with Anurima's dream of her aunt, minutes before the latter passed away. . ."

—**Bijoya Sawian**, author of *Shadow Men: A Novel and Two Stories* & *From Sylhet to Shillong*

Author's Note

My first love was, and remains, English. While I always yearned to pursue it during my undergraduate years, my scientific bent led my parents to encourage me toward science instead. Yet, the silent thirst for storytelling never faded. I found myself writing short stories and blogs, but the prospect of penning a full-length book felt like an insurmountable challenge.

The fire to write was first ignited by Jhumpa Lahiri's *Interpreter of Maladies.* Later, Arundhati Roy's *The God of Small Things,* a gift from my aunt, Punku-mashi, Dr. Manjusri Sen, resonated deeply. In 2006, Kiran Desai's The Inheritance of Loss further deepened this passion.

During my time as Public Relations Officer for the Governor of Uttarakhand, I frequently wrote articles and travelogues for our local daily. One day, he suggested I try my hand at writing a novel or a memoir to capture my life's experiences. I would simply nod, my courage failing me.

Life meandered on, and I often found myself haunted by childhood memories, particularly the stories told by my paternal aunt, Sisir Kumari Dasgupta (my Rangapishi). Her subsequent passing, and an uncanny dream I had around that time, stayed with me for years.

As the years unfolded, the inspiration for this novel gradually emerged. I realized I held a story worth telling, and the idea of writing a book began to solidify. My mother's short story about our family's ancestral home in

Bangladesh, which my sister Montuli had visited, provided a guiding light.

My research began with a pressing need for firsthand information. I travelled to Kolkata, where I spoke with my sister-in-law, Krishna Deb (my Krishna-boudi), the daughter-in-law of my paternal aunt, Saroj Kumari Deb (my Mejopishi). I knew she was the only living witness to certain events of that era, and I was convinced that she held the key to unlocking the family's long-lost legacy.

Armed with this information, my quest for a point of contact in Bangladesh began. My aunt, Punku-mashi, connected me with my cousin, Bubai, in Dhaka. Subsequently, my online research led me to Chandraprabha Vidyapitha—a school my ancestors founded that had withstood the test of time. After connecting with its alumni, I finally traveled to Bangladesh.

That journey became the foundational backdrop for this novel. The entire process was a true labour of love that spanned five years, weaving together memories and locations to tell this story. I also realized that nothing can be achieved without hardship. It is my sincere hope that this book offers the world a distinctive voice and a powerful message.

To the Reader

This novel is a work of fiction, albeit inspired by events that transpired in the past. While certain characters, such as Indian nationalists, are modelled on real historical figures and events, and real names of Indian leaders have been used, the names of other characters, places, and incidents are products of the author's imagination and presented fictitiously. Any resemblance to actual persons, living or dead, events, or locales, is otherwise entirely coincidental.

Contents

Prologue 1

Part I: Nainital, Calcutta (1987–1991)

Enigma 5

The Sandalwood Box 11

The Prized Letters 17

Part II: Comilla, Burma (1860–1896)

The El Dorado 23

The Land of Golden Pagodas 26

The Telegram 31

Part III: Comilla, Paksey, Calcutta (1906–1959)

The Ancient Chains 38

The Seeds of Change 43

The Inferno 47

The Revolution 50

Ye Mothers' 55

The Secret Mission 58

Ruminating Through Time 62

The Partition Saga 66

Part IV: Calcutta (1960s)

The Time Machine 73

A Fog of Nostalgia 78

The White Elephant 83

Part V: Jabalpur, Ambernath, Calcutta, Munich (1956–1974)

The Voyage 88

The Suitcase with the Name Tag 96
The Lion Gate 104
The Bungalow 111
The Cadbury Book 117
The Wood Sniffers 123
Clive House and the Seven Tanks 127
Boundaries of Life 132
The Kashmir Sojourn 138
The Cubicle of Time 142
Part VI: Calcutta (1975–1984)
The Mystic City 150
The City Speaks 157
The Melody of Belonging 163
The Shifting Tides 167
The Marriage Bazaar 170
A Dense Tangle of Choices 176
The Proposal 184
The Big, Fat Envelope 190
Part VII: Pune, Nainital, Calcutta, Tezpur, USA, Bangalore (1984–1997)
A New Home, A Hidden World 199
The Lake District of India 207
The Echo of Loss 212
An Ocean Apart 217
The Wonderland 221
The Weeping Sister 225
Married His Letters 231

Part VIII: Kolkata, Bangalore, Europe (1998–2004)

The Cursed House 239

The Solitary Postcard 244

The Shadow of Unknowing 248

The Path to Light 251

Ray of Sunshine 256

The Strange Caller 264

Tug of War 269

The Limousine Ride 280

Part IX: Nainital, England, Sundarbans, Scandinavia, USA (2005–2016)

Beyond the Hill Town 289

The Scottish Castle 294

The Charm of Stone and Whispers 299

Echoes Across the Ocean 306

Bridges Across Borders 312

The Secret of the Red Diary 318

Part X: Bangladesh (2017)

In Search of Her Roots 326

From Dust to Recognition 331

My Golden Bengal 335

The Lighthouse 342

The Legendary Bridge 348

The Fire Station 353

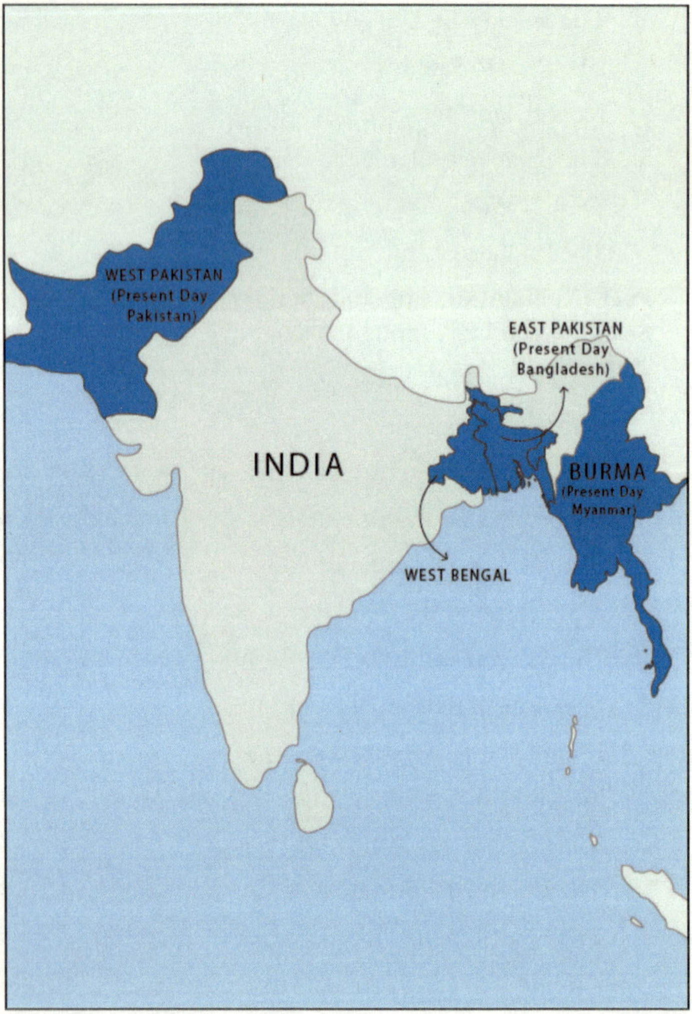
WEST PAKISTAN
(Present Day
Pakistan)
INDIA
EAST PAKISTAN
(Present Day
Bangladesh)
BURMA
(Present Day
Myanmar)
WEST BENGAL

Prologue

"A Tribute to Our Comrade Satyendra Chandra Dasgupta, May 1934, by Comrade Jatin Sen."

Anurima's gaze lingered on the newspaper clipping, its once vibrant paper now yellowed and mottled with age. It was a relic, carefully preserved within her *Thakurda*, Amalendra Chandra Dasgupta's, scrapbook.

"Look, Anu, how Baba, cherished the moments of his time," Mihir said, her voice tinged with a wistful pride.

"I must be dreaming," Anu whispered, almost disbelieving. "Thakurda truly left footprints in the sands of time."

Mihir Kumari, Anurima's Rangapishi, her paternal aunt, sat beside her. It was summer break in 1976, and Anu's father, Tathagata, had just been posted back to Calcutta.

As Mihir began weaving tales of bygone days, a face strikingly similar to Amalendra's stared up at Anu from the clipping. A sudden chill ran through her as she glanced at her grandfather's portrait, hanging high on the wall.

Mihir gently pointed to the photograph. "That's right, Anu. He was my Baba's youngest brother, Satyendra, your grand uncle Satyen. His features mirrored my father's."

Anu's gaze settled on a yellowed, crinkled newspaper article within her Thakurda's scrapbook. The headline read:

"13 May 1934. Satyendra Chandra Dasgupta Successfully Intercepted an Arms Consignment at the Chittagong Port of Comilla. He Died a Martyr's Death."

Anu, perplexed, looked up at her Rangapishi, her eyes brimming with unspoken questions.

"Anu," Mihir explained, her voice tinged with sorrow, "my uncle Satyen became a revolutionary. He tragically died while attempting to stop an arms shipment from Burma. My father was devastated."

Anurima stared at the faded photograph, a mix of pride and sadness swirling within her. She turned the page, her gaze falling upon another newspaper clipping.

"Two School Girls Shoot District Magistrate of Comilla. DM Dead."

The clipping, dated 1931, showed two teenage girls, Srimoyee and Srilata, their faces etched with defiant courage. Below the picture were lines of fierce resolve:

"Freedom's sword will strongly draw,

Freeman stand, or freeman fa',

Lay the proud usurpers low!

Tyrants fall in every foe!

Liberty's in every blow!—

Let us do or die!"

Anu lifted her head, a hesitant curiosity in her gaze as she looked at Rangapishi.

Mihir smiled gently. "Yes, Anu, this incident shook the family. One of the girls, Srimoyee Choudhury, was our first cousin. Srilata Ghosh was her friend. After the assassination, this poster was found scattered in the alleys of Comilla. Those were lines from Robert Burns' poem, 'Scots Wha Hae'. It was said to be the scotland's national anthem for many years." She paused. "Anu, it was an era of sacrifice, a time when people gave their all to free the country from foreign rule."

Anu nodded, absorbing the weight of the stories. A profound gratitude washed over her, a desire to hold on to every word, every image. Deep within, these tales planted a seed—a yearning to visit her ancestral home, a daunting yet compelling dream.

PART I
1987–1991
Nainital, Calcutta

1

Enigma

In a haze of half-consciousness, Anurima listened to the muffled sounds of the deep sea. Her heart seized, a suffocating claustrophobia crushing her as the dull thrum of the ocean pressed in. An icy palm then cut through the fear, caressing her forehead. As the pressure eased, she saw Mihir Kumari, her paternal aunt, standing beside the bed. Desperate, she tried to speak, but her voice was clogged; only an incoherent, guttural sound escaping.

Anurima struggled to see through the swirling miasma, her body leaden, resisting her efforts to rise. Then, a voice floated through the air like a warm spring breeze: "Anu, my brother, Abhinandan, has come to take me."

Anu saw the smiling visage of Mihir Kumari, her Rangapishi, illuminated by a ball of serene light amidst an eerie darkness. Her gentle smile had an absorbed, inward look. In a voice as soft and mystical, Anu heard, "I couldn't leave without seeing you, one last time." A tranquil silence filled the air when a tender voice spoke again, "Someday, you will unravel the tales of your kin, Anu, my dearest; my blessings will always be with you. Now, I must go."

Her eyes were closed, her arms outstretched, almost as if she was trying to grab onto something invisible while sobs wracked her body. Anu's fingers clenched at the empty air, her knuckles white. Each thud of her heart against her ribs echoed the frantic whisper in her mind: *No, no, don't go.*

A cold dread seeped into her limbs, making them tremble at the sight of the ethereal, dark, and shadowy mist consuming her beloved Rangapishi. A strange choking noise escaped her throat as she pleaded, "Rangapishi, you are like a banyan tree that has kept us safe under its loving shelter. How can you leave us?"

Tears burst forth as she struggled. Panic-stricken, her vision blurring, Anu watched Rangapishi's hazy form waver and oscillate in the strange dream-light. Then, as if emerging from the very mist consuming her aunt, she envisioned the dim figure of her paternal uncle Abhinandan in the distance. He was Anu's Jethamoni, floating as if in a vacuum, a translucent form, while her husband, Mrinal, slept beside her in deep slumber.

Anu, her limbs in a state of paralysis, felt strangled as she begged, "I love you, Rangapishi. Please don't go." Her voice cracked with jagged emotion and she let out an agonised cry.

Mrinal was jolted awake by Anu's heart-rending cry. His eyes snapped open, and in the dim light, he saw a dishevelled figure tangled in the bed linen. He sat up, a knot of concern tightening in his chest as he took in Anu's state: bathed in sweat, her face contorted in pain, with arms reaching out as if grasping at something unseen. He cleared his throat, his voice still thick with sleep. "Anurima?" He gently touched her shoulder. "Wake up. You seem to be having a bad dream."

Anu's eyes fluttered open, unfocused and wide with lingering fear. A ragged sob escaped her lips, followed by a hoarse and aching plea, "Rangapishi . . . please don't leave me."

Mrinal sensed the surge of emotions. This time, there was an urgency in her tone, and Mrinal felt that Anu was speaking to him. Then he heard. "Rangapishi is leaving us; she is going away!" He was surprised and rushed to Anu's side of the bed. He placed his hand on her shoulder and gently nudged her. "Anurima, wake up!"

Anu appeared unaware of her surroundings as tears rolled down, forming a rivulet from her face onto the crumpled sheet.

Mrinal tried to comfort her, speaking softly in the stillness of the night. "Anurima, go back to sleep. We can look into it in the morning."

Anu let out a painful sigh, her voice sounding hoarse and rusty. "Jethamoni is taking Rangapishi away from us."

Mrinal was astounded as he stared at his wife in confused silence. "Anurima, Rangapishi is in Calcutta, and we are in the hills of Nainital."

His words sounded empty, as deep within, he knew it was hollow comfort. He frowned. *Why such a vivid dream about her aunt, and why this . . . strange behaviour?*

*

Anu woke up abruptly from a vivid and disturbing dream. She rubbed her weary eyes and glanced at the clock. It was two minutes past four in the morning. Even with her eyes open, the hazy image of Rangapishi oscillating in the darkness flickered at the edges of Anu's vision. A dull throbbing pulsed behind her temples, a heavy residue of the night's terror. She tried to go back to sleep, only to find her Rangapishi's words still reverberating in her head. After tossing and turning, she finally gave up and welcomed the first rays of the morning sun gently kissing her face.

Anu slowly pulled herself out of bed and trudged to the balcony, where Mrinal was sitting with a steaming cup of tea and his *India Times* newspaper. Anu sat down, took the tea cosy off, and poured herself a hot cup from the pot. She then idly glanced at the shimmering lake. The sun illuminated the buildings in the valley, their heads poking through the clouds. The rays of light and shadow dappled Anu's face when she felt a sudden electric shock traverse through her body. She winced and looked at her husband, who had forgotten all about the early morning episode until he heard his wife gasp. Mrinal looked up from his newspaper, an eyebrow raised in curiosity.

Anu shook her head and said, "I don't feel good about my vision this morning."

Mrinal looked at Anurima and brusquely shrugged it off, saying, "Write a letter to your Rangapishi. I bet she is doing fine out there in Calcutta." He paused. "She must have been on your mind, so you dreamt of her. Now go on, relax."

Anu nodded slowly at Mrinal's words, but a knot of unease tightened in her stomach. Despite her desire for his reassurance, the vivid images from her dream replayed in her mind, Rangapishi's fading smile, the shadowy mist. The weight of half-forgotten tales of dreams that foretold reality settled heavily in her thoughts.

She drank her tea and got up, saying she hoped he was right and that Rangapishi was fine. Anu strolled into the study and opened the writing bureau, desperately searching for the postal file. To her dismay, she realised they had run out of stamps. However, a single postcard was peeking out of the binder pocket. She grabbed a pen, and with a quivering hand, jotted down the address.

Srimati Mihir Kumari Dasgupta

10, Golf Green House

Calcutta, West Bengal

Anu sighed, as a few months ago she had met her Rangapishi in Calcutta. She wondered what message Rangapishi was trying to give her. She could feel her eyes welling up with tears; then with a quivering hand, she quickly wrote down the date, 15 February 1991, and hastily penned down a few lines.

After finishing breakfast, Mrinal picked up his briefcase and walked down the hallway. He noticed Anurima pacing in the hallway, deep in thought. When she saw Mrinal, she paused and handed him a postcard, which he slipped into his breast pocket. Mrinal, his usual cynicism hovering, almost made a light-hearted jab about her dream. Instead, he simply nodded. "I'll post it on my way to the office."

Anu poured herself a mug of coffee and strolled to her flower-bedecked veranda. She stood leaning on the rails, just in time to see Mrinal riding away on his new Kinetic Honda. After strolling back into her bedroom, she stood in front of the oval mirror. Bright, yellow shafts of sunlight fell on her puffy countenance, while her wavy, black tresses cascaded down on either side of her oval face. Her dark, swollen eyes seemed to stare back at her.

*

The moonlight changed the landscape to a soft sculpture; its blemished face smiled sadly tonight, peeping out from behind a thin cloud. The distant hillside was touched with the glint of starlight. Anu settled into the nearby armchair, her slender form outlined by the chill February breeze, while the stellar garden shone above. She closed her eyes and tried to feel the pulse of the universe. But her mind wandered back to her childhood days, snuggled up with her aunt, Rangapishi, listening to bedtime stories. The two of them had a strong bond, formed when her father, Tathagata, allowed Anu to spend time with his Rangadi, Mihir, who was four years older than Tathagata.

Lost in her thoughts, gazing at the distant stars, Anu snapped out of her trance as a meteor burned its way across the sky. Her morning dream came back to her, wrapping its icy tentacles around her heart. Anu found herself being engulfed by a dark cloud as she envisaged the figure in her dream oscillating in the darkness. She winced as the face of her Jethamoni loomed up, waiting to take his sister away. Abhinandan had died nineteen years ago, holding on to the handrails of a railway compartment.

As Anu gazed pensively at the shimmering lake, there was a paralysing moment of sudden insight. A thought penetrated her like a probing knife: was her early morning dream a premonition or an apparition? But then, another thought sparked, chilling her even more: was Rangapishi trying to tell her something? Was her aunt, so deeply rooted in their family's past, urging Anu to begin her own search for their history, and was this unsettling dream the sign she needed to start looking for her roots?

2

The Sandalwood Box

The year was 1987, and Anurima was on her annual visit to Calcutta, spending the day with her Rangapishi and Basanta, her aunt, Sejopishi. As she reminisced about their time together, her thoughts drifted to her childhood memories and the times spent with her dear Papa. Anu had just lost her father and was still coming to terms with it.

It had been barely a month since she joined St Mary's Convent as a middle school teacher when she received news from her mother, Reena, about her father's declining health. Rushing to his side, she was there as he took his last breath, his head resting on her lap. It was as if he had waited for her. Tathagata succumbed to double pneumonia. In the aftermath, Reena had her younger daughter, Jayina, who was pursuing her post-graduate studies, for company.

Anu adored her trips to Calcutta, enjoying moments with her family and reconnecting with old friends and relatives. She was spending the day with her aunts, Mihir and Basanta. Suddenly, overcome by sadness, Anu spoke up. Her voice trembled. "I still do not understand why I was made to go through such ordeals at an age when one needs to concentrate on education. Look at me now. I even got myself a good life partner, didn't I?" She fidgeted before carrying on. "I had to go through all the torment when I was in my teens, but for all that I cannot blame my Papa.

He was a strong individual but was beaten by his illness." Anu went on to lament, "Papa even saw his son-in-law. If he had been granted a few more years, he surely would have experienced the joy of becoming a grandfather too."

Mihir and Basanta were momentarily at a loss for words. There was a moment of complete silence; they all sat with their heads hung low. Then Mihir cautiously began, "Anu, we desired the first grandchild of our family to finish her higher education. However, your father's illness made us reverse gears as we did not want to intervene in your mother's decision."

Anu's father, Tathagata, was known as "Kanu" to the family. Basanta went on to say, "Kanu's illness was alien to us, and your mother, Reena, was shaken by it."

Anu had not expected that, so this sentiment lifted her spirits, and she blurted out, "I too did not think it proper to call upon you for help."

Mihir and Basanta looked at Anu with confused adoration.

Anu quietly thought: *In your dignified presence, my problem felt too trivial.*

Then, to Anu's surprise, Basanta said, "Anu, you had the confidence and the strength to overcome the struggles that came your way. You must have inherited the resilience from your father and grandfather."

A wave of pride washed over Anu, as she recognised that her father's resilience mirrored her own. She then looked up at the large portrait hanging in Mihir's room. She was filled with admiration and respect for this remarkable man, her revered grandfather, her Thakurda.

Then Mihir looked at Anu and said, "With the passage of time, perhaps the stories we have shared with you will illuminate your path."

Anu chirped on a happy note, "Rangapishi and Sejopishi, the truth is, all the ancestral stories that I grew up hearing from both of you about my erudite family were my source of strength." But deep within, Anu wished she could go back and redo those chaotic years, as she knew they would always linger in some remote corner of her mind forever.

*

As a college student, Anu had known better than to sift through the scattered fragments of the life of her great-grandfather, Monindra Chandra Dasgupta. She sensed it would unearth a past her aunts preferred to conceal from posterity. Mihir had once revealed that her grandfather had become a cold, hollow echo. Anu felt Rangapishi had sequestered herself in a dark, emotional solitude.

One blustery day, as the wind told its own wild tale, Mihir, with a pained expression, sifted through old files. "Anu," she said, "my grandfather passed long ago. All that remained were stories of my grandmother, Ratnaprobha Debi. We heard that Baba, our father, was so determined to name the school after her that he pledged his entire provident fund to rebuild it."

Anu had braced herself and asked, "Rangapishi, do you or your siblings ever wish to go back to your native place, now in Bangladesh?"

Mihir grimaced and said, "No Anu, never, as we would be foreigners in our own home. Maybe, Anu, when you are older, you can check out the land of your ancestors. The place is steeped in history."

No matter how much stress was placed on her, Mihir showed more grace than many. However, Anu was annoyed by the way she trusted people blindly. So, she had asked, "Rangapishi, why do you trust people blindly and then get cheated in the bargain?"

Mihir's serene face had broken into a smile. "Maybe because they needed the money much more than I needed."

Anu knew people took her aunt for a ride due to her compassionate and supportive nature. She secretly thought maybe all these characteristics added to her inner magnificence. One day, she gathered her courage and asked, "Rangapishi, why didn't you get married?"

With a bashful smile, she had replied, "I had too many responsibilities, Anu, as I lost my father way too early in 1945. The partition of our country turned us into refugees. We had to leave behind our huge property which fell in East Pakistan, now Bangladesh, and my siblings were still studying. They had to be settled."

Anu, a teenager, couldn't quite understand it, but she would look at her Rangapishi's tall frame, fair and slender body, and flowing gait, along with her warm and dignified personality, and wonder if that was the only reason she had remained a spinster! In those moments of pain, Anu saw right through her soul and said to herself, *Rangapishi, my love for you is eternal.*

To Anu, Rangapishi was her pillar of strength. It took a great spirit to become the person she was. This greater-than-life personality was Anurima's guru.

Mihir Kumari exuded warmth like the summer rays, regardless of the season. An epitome of love!

*

Following Jay's marriage, Reena found herself living alone in Calcutta. Seeking purpose and engagement, she first took up a Montessori teacher's training course. Then she established a Montessori training institute and named it "Taxila Teachers' Training Institute".

Reena tried to involve her family in the institute as well. Her brother, Pradipto, who had by then retired, took care of the finances, while his wife, Aseema, taught English classes. Reena's sister, Juthi, also taught mathematics and biology. Anu, too, would teach science subjects in her mother's school whenever she was visiting. So, the school was also a family gathering, which kept Reena busy and gave her mental nourishment.

Anu and Jay made it a tradition to spend their winters with their mother during annual visits. It was December, and the sisters were once again in Calcutta.

As was her custom, Anu visited her aunts, Rangapishi and Sejopishi. Observing their increasing years, a growing sense of urgency washed over her to uncover the stories of their great-grandfather before those memories disappeared forever. Arriving at her aunt's house, Anu took a deep breath, steeling herself to broach the long-awaited topic one last time.

She meekly asked, "Rangapishi, why have you always been evasive regarding our great-grandfather?"

Mihir was taken aback by the intrusive question; her face registered hurt, speaking volumes. Anu immediately realised she had overstepped, and without another word, she left the room. As twilight deepened, shadows stretched and yawned. Anu settled into a recliner with a book, just as Mihir emerged from her room after her afternoon nap. Her face was tired and creased, as if she'd slept in her own thoughts. In her hand, she held a delicately carved sandalwood box.

Anu looked up, a sudden understanding dawning. *Rangapishi is about to reveal something hidden from her nieces and nephews.*

Mihir walked towards Anu, her shaking hand outstretched, her expression heavy with sorrow.

Anu stood up. "Sorry, Rangapishi, if I've trod on forbidden ground. I didn't mean to bring up old hurts."

"You are now grown up and mature enough to know why I had to keep your great-grandfather away from you," Mihir said in a heavy tone. "You have the right to know your family history, or what you could call a family secret." She paused. "Anu, I think the sandalwood box will answer some of your questions."

Mihir, her hands trembling, walked towards Anu.

Anu, feeling a bit overwhelmed, gingerly took the sandalwood box from her Rangapishi's outstretched hand. Her head bowed, her gaze fixed on the box, she asked in a barely audible tone, "What is in the box, Rangapishi?"

Mihir hesitantly chose her words. "It contains our grandfather's letters." After a pause, she continued, "My father preserved our grandfather, Monindra Chandra's, letters written from Burma to his wife, Ratnaprbha Debi, our grandmother."

Mihir left the room, leaving a heavy silence in her wake. Anu stared at the closed door, the box in her hands suddenly immense. For a long moment, she stood transfixed, clutching the treasure. As she opened the box, she felt the weight of the past close in, her breath catching in her throat. Inside, she found a bundle of letters bound with twine. The creamy, thick papers carried the earthy, woody scent of a bygone era. Holding the box, Anu felt a sudden sense of responsibility settle over her.

Deep in thought, she reflected, *Rangapishi is trying to break the fire-hardened chains of her past.* Clutching the sandalwood box, Anu promised to return it the following day, a thrum of anticipation running through her.

3

The Prized Letters

Upon returning from her aunt's, Anu presented the box to her mother, Reena, who was equally surprised and unaware of its existence. Anurima, Mrinal, Jayina, and her husband, Abhishek, had all assembled at Reena's. Abhishek, a doctor, had chosen the NGO sector over a traditional medical career—a path Jayina, a literature student, also followed after their marriage.

The following day, Reena carefully placed the treasured box on the dining table, a sense of mystery filling the room. The family gathered, anticipation hanging in the air, eager to unravel its secrets. Reena slowly untied the twine securing the letters, extracted one, handed it to Anu, and then another to Jay. She distributed the letters among her daughters.

Jay nudged Abhishek and said, "Look, they were all written on thick handmade paper from that era."

Abhishekh inspected it and said, "That is why they've withstood the test of time."

Mrinal, a sceptical man by nature, nodded his head as he inspected and sniffed it.

By then, Anu had opened a letter. She said, "Why don't we uncover the mystery of our great-grandfather?"

Jay excitedly chimed in, "Yes, these could be 'love letters' from our great-grandfather."

Reena smiled and said, "In those days, married men hardly had time to write romantic letters to their wives. Everything was matter-of-fact."

Abhishek's opinions often dominated, leaving little room for others. He impatiently interrupted, "Let's begin. We can do the dissections later."

Jay looked at Abhishek, her voice laced with sarcasm. "Stop, we are just discussing, not dissecting things. We all know you're a doctor and love to dissect everything."

"That's enough. Let's move on, we're digressing from the topic," Anu said, already looking at one of the letters. "Let me read the one I have."

She began:

"Shan Tea Estate, Burma 15/05/1888

Dear Ratna,

I have reached Burma. It was a long and tiring journey. You couldn't have come here with Amal and Deben. They've given me nice quarters. You won't have to work much when you come here; there are many servants. There's a cook. I'm getting used to the local food. I like this place; it's beautiful.

Yours. . ."

Jay looked excited. "That was nice, short, and crisp, eh?"

"I told you, in those days, they wrote to-the-point letters," Reena said.

Suddenly, Mrinal, usually silent in family gatherings, smiled. "I once came across some of my father's letters to my mother, written while he was finishing his studies in Calcutta." He continued, "In those days, they married so young that they left their wives in their parental homes until they came of age, when the girl reached puberty. I remember reading one of his letters. Baba sure tried to write a few romantic lines to Ma."

Reena looked at her son-in-law. "It must have been right after they married."

"Your father was young and in college?" Abhishek grinned.

Mrinal smiled and nodded.

Jay was fidgeting with one of the letters, so she cleared her throat and said, "Now listen to this one."

"Shan Tea Estate, Burma 20/06/1888

Dear Ratna,

Yesterday, I was invited to my senior's house in the 'Burra' bungalow. He is an Englishman. There is another Bengali gentleman here. I spend a lot of time with him. My bungalow, too, is very big. I have never seen a house like this. There is a big garden. Amal and Deben can play. I must go now.

Yours. . ."

"The gentlemen of that era were so drab; they had nothing to say to their wives," Abhishek said.

Everybody laughed.

"Abhishek, we've gone back a hundred odd years," Reena said.

"I'm truly excited," Anu said. "I'm discovering my great-grandfather through his handwritten letters."

Jay started reading the next one.

"Shan Tea Estate, Burma 25/12/1888

Dear Ratna,

Time flies here. It has been eight months already. I really don't know when I can come to fetch you and the boys. There is too much work here. Plus, when I think of the bumpy five-day journey, I get scared and wonder if it will be worth bringing you all here. I think you are safe with my parents, out there in Comilla. We don't have much leave here. I will try to come as soon as possible.

Yours. . ."

Jay sarcastically said, "Look at our great-grandfather. He was enjoying his freedom, leaving his wife and kids with his parents."

Reena said, "Now I understand why his name was taboo in my in-laws' house. They never spoke about him."

Anu frowned. "Look, he wrote this one, six months later."

Reena nodded. "It was common at that time for young married couples to be separated for extended periods."

Abhishek and Mrinal nodded and exchanged meaningful smiles.

Anu began reading the next letter.

"Shan Tea Estate, Burma 6/6/1889

Dear Ratna,

I really don't have time to write to you. You must forgive me. I am trying to take leave and come home. I cannot say the exact month, but I will come sometime this year. It is a long journey from my tea estate to India.

Hope the boys are not disturbing you much. Hope Amal is studying well. My father is there to help him.

Yours. . ."

Jay looked at Anu, who was her elder sister, her Didi, and said, "See, Didi, he hasn't asked about his wife in any of his letters."

Anu nodded. "Our great-grandfather was a very self-centred man."

"This is the last letter I'm reading," Jay said, unfolding the next one.

"Shan Tea Estate, Burma 5/1/1890

Dear Ratna,

It's been two years since I came to the Tea Garden. Life here is so different from India. I'm learning a lot of new things. I read a lot. Here, I mostly read English books. Which class is Amal in? Has Deben started going to school? The weather here is very pleasant now.

Yours. . ."

Jay slammed the letter down, rising abruptly. "I'm done. If you want to sift through the rest, be my guest."

"I heard he was a brilliant student," Reena said. After a pause, she continued, "Maybe that's why your grandfather and the Dasgupta line inherited his good genes and excelled in studies."

Anu nodded, a hint of bitterness in her voice. "At least one good trait survived."

Rising to her feet, Jay stated flatly, "I couldn't care less."

PART II

1860–1896

Comilla, Burma

4

The El Dorado

Monindra Chandra Dasgupta grew up in 19th century Comilla, a cantonment town in British Raj's East Bengal. He was proud of his birthplace, often citing its educated, intelligent, and prosperous populace when comparing it to neighbouring towns.

The city thrived due to the presence of the British Indian Army. As a result, Comilla became a significant centre of education and culture, with European missionaries establishing and running schools. Education was highly prioritised in the region, a fact underscored in 1837 when English became the official language of administration.

Monindra, hailing from an elite family, gained admission into an English medium school. Following his matriculation, he was sent to the University of Calcutta, the first university established in colonial India. This institution produced educated and capable Bengalis who were often sent to Burma to assist the burgeoning bureaucracy.

In 1886, after the Third Anglo-Burmese War, the British annexed all of Burma to British India. During this period of colonisation and administration, the Scots played a particularly significant role, so much so that Burma was often referred to as the "Scottish Colony".

While pursuing his college studies in Calcutta, Monindra was regaled with stories from his peers about opportunities in the newly annexed part of British India. They spoke of how intellectual men from Bengal were highly valued and sought after by the English, who showered them with jobs, money, power, and prestige the moment they touched shore. Though intrigued, Monindra eventually returned to Comilla after graduation and secured a job at the Bank of Bengal in Chittagong, a bank thriving under the Bengal Presidency.

Years after the partition of India, Anu learnt that the Bank of Bengal, where Monindra worked, merged with two other banks to become the State Bank of India.

Monindra had settled into his bank job when he began to hear tales of how ethnic Indians formed the backbone of Burma's government and economy. Stories circulated about Indians shedding traditional customs and embracing a freer lifestyle in Burma. Whenever news of this unknown land reached him, something stirred within him. He came to see Burma as a politically tumultuous yet resource-rich and labour-scarce country, providing opportunities for Indian migrants, especially those from Chittagong and East Bengal. Tales from Burma's "gold-paved" cities fueled Monindra's imagination, and he saw it as an "El Dorado".

An opportunity then arose when his old college friend, Chittaranjan, a lawyer at the Calcutta High Court, wrote to him about job openings in Burma, specifically recruitment by Englishmen. Monindra immediately travelled to Calcutta to meet him.

Monindra had grown into a tall man with a chiselled jaw, dark eyes, and neatly parted, crisply coiffed hair. When he met Chittaranjan, he noticed his clean-shaven cheeks glowed with health, and his gold-rimmed spectacles gave him a scholarly look. Both men were in their early thirties. They were meeting after a long time and began to reminisce about their good old college days.

The next day Chittaranjan took his friend to an office in Calcutta's Park Street area. They entered a room where Monindra saw a gentleman behind a large table. The white man's squarish jaw exuded authority. Chitaranjan introduced his friend, Monindra to Mr. John Davidson.

Davidson, impressed by Monindra's intelligence, considered him a strong candidate for a tea estate job.

Monindra returned to Comilla and eagerly awaited the offer.

One evening, upon returning home from work, Monindra found a long envelope in his mailbox, the long-awaited appointment letter from Mr Simpson, the proprietor of the Shan Tea Gardens in Burma. He was offered the role of assistant manager.

Unable to contain his excitement, he went to his father, who was happy for him. But his wife, Ratnaprobha, said, "I'm happy for you, but I'd like to stay in Comilla with your parents."

Monindra was relieved at Ratna's reaction. He didn't want to travel to a foreign land with his family. He promised his wife that at the first opportunity, he would come and fetch her and their two boys, Amalendra and Debendra. At last, Monindra felt a sense of adventure. The unknown beckoned.

5

The Land of Golden Pagodas

In the summer of 1888, Monindra began his journey to Burma, then known as "Suvarṇabhūmi" or the "Golden Land". He travelled by Eastern Bengal Railways from Chittagong to Calcutta, then took a ferry across the Hooghly River to Outram Ghat. From there, he boarded a British India Steam Navigation Company steamer.

Four days at sea brought him to Rangoon. There, he transferred to the RV Pandaw of the renowned Irrawaddy Flotilla Company, which had its operational headquarters in Rangoon and took him onward to Mandalay.

Upon disembarking, a red-headed Englishman named John Baker, the welfare manager of the Shan Tea Estate, greeted him.

After a few stilted pleasantries, he abruptly said, "Well then, Dasgupta, your escort will take you from here. I have work to attend to in Mandalay."

Baker turned, and a pale-yellow face emerged from behind him. The man was short, with a round, unremarkable face and mild, grey eyes. He bowed, seemingly eager to be included in the interaction. Baker pointed at him and said, "Dasgupta, Maung will take you to the Shan Tea Estate." Monindra smiled and nodded gracefully as they shook hands.

"Have a safe trip up the hills, Dasgupta. It can be rough at times," Baker said abruptly, walking towards a waiting carriage.

Monindra quickly mumbled a "thank you". He then turned to his escort, a Burmese man who introduced himself as Maung Saw Tin.

"Sir, you can call me Maung," he said.

Monindra was pleased with the simplified name.

He extended his hand. "I'm Dasgupta. Pleased to meet you, Maung."

Monindra and Maung boarded a four-wheeled wooden carriage. As they rode, Monindra observed the vibrant marketplace and Burmese women in traditional attire, singing and chatting. He thought: *How different from my land, where women mostly stay indoors.*

Maung interrupted his thoughts. "Sir, we're headed to the hill town of Kalaw, in the north-west corner of the Shan hills. The journey will take five days, with overnight stops."

Monindra nodded, understanding, and admired the changing landscape. Eventually, they arrived at a shop run by a Burmese woman. Monindra was struck by her dress and confident demeanour. He thought: *Back home, you wouldn't find women running their own restaurants.*

The pungent, fishy aroma that greeted Monindra upon entering made him hesitant about the cuisine. They sat on bamboo mats and were served steaming bowls of soup and appetisers. Monindra examined the dishes with curiosity. Maung explained that the soup, hin gyo, was served with fish fritters and dried tofu crackers. Famished from the journey, Monindra eagerly devoured the soup. Just as he briefly thought of his wife's delicious fish curry and rice, a steaming bowl of rice, fish curry, and a small plate of fried vegetables with salad were placed on the table.

Maung pointed at the steamed rice and said, "This is the main dish, and the accompanying dishes are known as 'hin' in Burmese." Then, picking up the salad, he continued, "This is a tart salad known as laphet thohk, a green tea salad made from pickled tea leaves."

The tart salad looked strange to Monindra. So, he remarked, "Back home, we don't eat tea leaves, Maung. We only drink tea by brewing them."

Maung laughed. "I know, sir. Here too, we drink tea by brewing the leaves." He paused. "These aren't ordinary tea leaves; they're fermented or pickled, eaten on their own. And the salad, sir, is a national dish of Burma, packed with nutrients."

Monindra quickly developed a taste for the unique mix of the salad's crunchy, crispy, and saucy texture. He also enjoyed the Burmese lunch. Following the sumptuous lunch, Monindra mused, "I think I will develop a taste for Burmese cuisine."

Resuming their journey, the carriage halted for the night around 5 p.m.

As they dismounted, Maung stretched. "What is this place?" Monindra asked.

"Kyaukse."

Monindra and Maung spent the night at a bamboo inn. The next morning, the toothy inn-keeper offered tea, and as they departed, Monindra's eyes met the powerful stallions outside. He absently began stroking their manes. Around midday, they stopped at a small village for a simple Shan-style fish-and-rice meal. Monindra noticed the yellow rice, reminiscent of his wife's pulao.

They continued their journey, stopping for the night in Suu Lay Kon, still within the Mandalay division.

The following day, they reached Myogyi, finally entering the Shan State, much to Monindra's relief. After another day of travel, they arrived at the hill village of Pindaya.

Maung excitedly explained that Pindaya is famous for its 200-million-year-old limestone caves, which house thousands of consecrated Buddha images and have been a place of worship for centuries.

Monindra was visibly impressed. Maung continued to inform Monindra that Pindaya was also known for its Shan paper and umbrellas made from mulberry trees. Monindra expressed interest in visiting the caves someday.

The next day, their carriage navigated a winding, misty path, arriving in Ywangan by 5 p.m., a southern Shan state known for poppy farming. Monindra found himself growing fond of Maung's enthusiasm.

The following day, on the final, steep leg of their journey, Monindra was excited to hear they were nearing Yatsagi village and his tea garden in Kalaw. The mountain air invigorated him. As they approached, Monindra was captivated by the stunning beauty of Shan state, passing a waterfall and a creek. Awe-struck, he met Maung's gaze. "This scenery… it's absolutely breathtaking, straight from a storybook."

Maung, proudly declared, "Sir, you are in the golden land of pagodas," pointing to the shimmering gold structures.

By 7 p.m., they arrived in Yatsagi. A quaint wooden cottage greeted Monindra, bathed in the mystical silence of gentle moonbeams. He gazed up, mesmerised.

The next morning, they had mohinga, a traditional Burmese breakfast of rice noodles in fish broth. After breakfast, they began their uphill hike to Kalaw through a thick fog, with a porter carrying their luggage.

During the climb, Maung shared insights about Shan, explaining it was once a princely state and highlighting its local industries like cheroot and bamboo weaving.

Monindra took in the fresh air, his eyes wide with wonder. *It's like something out of a dream. Could this really be my new home?*

He shot a glance at Maung, his eyes wide with amazement. "I've never seen anything so beautiful. It's like we're in a painting."

Maung smiled.

Then, as they reached the final stretch, Maung pointed to the tea plantation and wooden bungalows, announcing, "Welcome to your new home, sir."

6

The Telegram

Monindra felt dwarfed by the sheer magnificence of his surroundings. He saw charming wooden bungalows with smoking chimneys, nestled at the base of the Shan hills, surrounded by vibrant gardens and evergreen pines. Maung explained they were the assistant managers' bungalows. As they approached, a line of servants stood in the portico, ready to greet their new *sahib.* Maung introduced them to Monindra.

Just as Monindra was about to sit, he noticed a benign-looking gentleman in a hat ambling up the driveway towards the bungalow.

Maung flashed a hurried look at Monindra and said, "That is our Burra Sahib."

He then ran down the driveway, nodding vivaciously. Monindra was left in suspense. As Maung and the Englishman approached, Monindra met them halfway up the drive.

The Englishman said, "I was just passing by and thought I'd check if you'd arrived, Mr Dasgupta."

He extended his hand and said, "I am John Gordon, the manager of this garden."

Monindra blurted, "Honoured to meet you, sir."

John Gordon then invited Monindra to his bungalow for dinner, which Monindra graciously accepted.

Maung explained that the tea estate managers lived in the *burra* bungalow, the big bungalow, while the assistant managers' quarters were the *chhota* bungalows, the small ones.

He added, "Sir, these bungalows are more than homes; they are status symbols for the tea garden managers."

Monindra, impressed by the explanation, nodded.

Then, pointing at the waiting servants, Maung said, "One of them will escort you there."

He gave the servants some instructions and, turning to Monindra, said, "Now you relax, sir. I'll see you tomorrow." With that, he abruptly left.

Monindra returned to the porch, where servants awaited with trays laden with snacks and a decorative teapot filled with black tea. They delicately poured the tea into ornate cups, offering milk and sugar from separate, elegant pots. Monindra, fascinated, observed the scene. A sense of pure delight washed over him as he sat on the veranda, taking in the riot of colourful blossoms and the towering pines reaching towards the sky, all while enjoying the elaborate tea-pouring ceremony.

That evening, Monindra went to the burra bungalow. After the gateman let him in, a young lad ran down the driveway and escorted him into a large drawing room.

Inside, Mr Gordon was packing tobacco into his pipe while talking with two other men. One was English, and the other appeared to be Bengali. Both were smoking cheroots. Mr Gordon introduced the Bengali gentleman as Mr Arindam Ghosh and the Englishman as Mr Robert Walsh, the manager of a neighbouring tea garden. After a round of shaking hands, they all settled down into the large elegantly furnished drawing room.

Mr Gordon looked at Monindra with a humourless smile. "Dasgupta, I hope that a Bengali friend for company will keep you from being homesick."

Monindra nodded his head graciously.

After dinner, Monindra and Mr. Ghosh walked beneath the pines. Monindra drifted to sleep, filled with a sense of adventure and captivated by Burma's culture and grandeur. He was struck by the freedom of Burmese women. They were uncovered, spoke freely, and laughed openly, a stark contrast to the societal constraints he knew. He secretly envied their liberation, pondering that his own country needed such freedom to prosper.

Years passed, marked by brief postcards as his only family connection. Despite his happiness at work, a persistent loneliness gnawed at him. A few months later, his wife informed him of his father's illness, prompting a short leave. He returned home, found his father suffering from pneumonia, and stayed until he recovered. Later, a letter brought joyful news: Ratnaprobha had given birth to their third son, Satyendra. Monindra was overjoyed but couldn't visit immediately, finally meeting his four-year-old son during a month-long visit before returning to the tea estate.

Monindra dedicated himself to work, content that Ratnaprobha capably raised their three sons while he sent money home, free from daily parenting burdens thanks to the joint family system. As time blurred, Monindra became deeply immersed in Burma, captivated by its free-spirited women and the absence of rigid social constraints. He often contemplated that this freedom was precisely what his own nation needed, a thought accompanied by longing and guilt.

Then came his father's letter: Ratnaprobha was ill. A flicker of guilt arose, but the familiar routine of the tea estate quickly extinguished it. He rationalised, believing it was a minor illness his father could manage, and the urgency to return home waned.

*

The telegram arrived on a sweltering afternoon, the paper limp in his hand. "Ratnaprobha Debi passed away." The words blurred, and the room spun. Monindra felt a coldness seeping into his bones, a chilling realisation of his years of absence. He broke down. *I am to blame, I took it lightly, I should have gone.*

Monindra returned to Comilla, and the silence in the house was a chilling testament to Ratnaprobha's absence. She had succumbed to malaria and passed away. The familiar rooms felt alien. He moved through them like a ghost, the weight of his years of neglect pressing down on him.

His sons, Amalendra, Debendra, and Satyendra, regarded him with wary eyes, their grief a silent accusation. He felt the burden of his absence physically. They had grown up under the care of his wife and parents, with him a distant figure.

Overwhelmed and confused, Monindra was unsure how to raise his three sons—Amalendra, fourteen; Debendra, eleven; and Satyendra, seven. After much contemplation and consultation with his parents, he decided to send Amal, the eldest, to his affluent maternal grandparents' home in Calcutta. Ratnaprobha's father was a zamindar, a feudal landlord from the British era. Monindra knew Amal would receive the best educational opportunities in Calcutta.

As Monindra prepared for his journey, a glimmer of light pierced his dark world. Calcutta, the capital of British India, the Raj era's premier city, beckoned. Fourteen-year-old Amal, gaunt and weary, his face etched with grief, walked beside his Baba, shoulders hunched under his books and a tin trunk. They boarded the Eastern Bengal Railways train. The train rattled a mournful rhythm echoing Monindra's despair, and after a thirty-four-hour journey they reached Howrah station.

From Howrah Ghat, they took a ferry to Outram Ghat in Calcutta. Monindra hailed a phaeton, and they sped through Calcutta's vibrant streets, a cornerstone of the Raj.

Amal was captivated by the *Rajbaris*, or houses of kings, and the Roman, Gothic, and Mughal-inspired architecture. Calcutta, then, had earned the sobriquet "City of Palaces".

After disembarking at the Chowringhee tram stop, they boarded a horse-drawn tramcar. Amal was enraptured by the novel experience as the horses galloped along the tracks.

They arrived at the Ballygunge tram terminus in southern Calcutta, an area known for its large garden houses. Developed around an 18th century Bali Bazaar, or sand market, the locality became a hub for the educated Bengali middle class alongside Europeans. George Mandeville, a notable European resident, even lent his name to Mandeville Gardens. Highlighting its reputation as an intellectually affluent locality in India, Emily Eden, the author and sister of Lord Auckland, who toured India in 1840, likened Ballygunge to Eltham or Lewisham, London villages.

After another tonga ride, Monindra and Amal arrived at Ratnaprobha's childhood home. Amal's grandparents, Jatindra Mohan Roychowdhury and Monibala Roychowdhury, joyfully embraced him. Monindra, however, was visibly nervous. He humbly explained to his father-in-law, Jatindra, that he had brought Amal so he could receive a good education.

Jatindra, wiping his eyes, graciously accepted, stating it would be their pleasure to raise their eldest grandson and firmly declined Monindra's offer to send money for expenses.

A profound sense of liberation washed over Monindra.

*

Amalendra began his education at Hindu School in Calcutta, where he quickly excelled, passing his matriculation with distinction and earning a scholarship. This led him to Hindu College, later renamed Presidency College where he again graduated at the top of his class with another scholarship.

His final scholarship allowed him to study civil engineering at Calcutta Civil Engineering College in Howrah, the city's sole engineering college, later known as Bengal Engineering College, Shibpur. Amalendra graduated at the top of his class in 1905 with a civil engineering degree. Meanwhile, his brothers, Debendra and Satyendra, raised by their paternal grandparents in Comilla, also thrived academically.

Years later, at his father's last rites, Monindra was pleased to see Amalendra as an engineer, Debendra pursuing a master's in chemistry at the University of Calcutta, and Satyendra in tenth grade.

With Debendra in Calcutta and Amalendra working for the railways, Satyendra was left in Comilla without a proper guardian, his ailing grandmother his only companion at home.

PART III
1906–1959
Comilla, Paksey, Calcutta

7

The Ancient Chains

Under the blazing Bengal sun, the Padma River twisted through a wild, overgrown region. The British, with their relentless ambition, were carving a settlement out of this wilderness, aiming to build a bridge across the meandering, sun-glinting Padma River.

Amalendra, a young railway engineer, arrived at this new site. Mosquitoes, thick as a shroud, buzzed around his ears, their bites raising angry welts on his exposed skin. The air, heavy and humid, carried the cloying scent of decaying vegetation, a stark contrast to his familiar native town in Comilla. The village, if it could be called that, was a mere clearing.

Each morning, Amalendra watched as native labourers, their faces etched with weariness, approached their English supervisors.

"*Sahab amra pak saf korte jaitesee,*" they'd say, their voices a weary chant: "Sir, we are going to clean the pak." These labourers could hardly distinguish between a "pak" or a "park" They only understood that the masters gave orders to clean the large grounds, which they referred to as parks; while the British masters heard the same phrase, "pak-saf, pak-saf" repeated day in and day out, they gradually interpreted 'pak-saf' as the name of the place, which later softened to "Paksey".

In 1905, the British Indian government divided Bengal into east and west, primarily along religious lines. Amalendra had grown up on the eastern side, a predominantly Muslim region where people lived harmoniously alongside their Hindu neighbours. In contrast, the western side of Bengal was predominantly Hindu, with a Muslim minority. Despite these demographic differences, Bengalis across the region shared a common identity. However, this partition ignited widespread unrest, with Bengalis from both east and west vehemently opposing the division. Faced with these growing protests, the Raj government ultimately decided to reunite Bengal in 1911, six years after the division, and it remained united until the partition of the Indian subcontinent in 1947.

During this period of significant activity and change in Bengal, there began the monumental task of erecting the Hardinge Bridge across the Padma, employing 24,000 labourers in a round-the-clock effort. Amalendra was immersed in his drawing board, elaborating the details of each span of the bridge. He was so engrossed in his job that he often worked after office hours. He was dedicated to his work. Each day brought new experiences and knowledge.

The steel railway bridge, crossing the Padma River between the towns of Paksey and Bheramara, was 1.8 kilometres long. It was finally completed in 1912 and named after the Viceroy, Lord Hardinge. Admiring the state-of-the-art structure, Amalendra quietly thought: *The bridge is surely a symbol of unity between East and West Bengal.*

Following the completion of the bridge, a sudden lull occurred due to an outbreak of cholera amongst the workers, and Amalendra received a transfer that sent him back to Comilla, a town within East Bengal's Chittagong division. He was overjoyed to be posted back to his native place, his *adibari*, where his forefathers once lived.

Amalendra acted swiftly. He purchased land and constructed a large, two-storeyed house, complete with a rose garden, a pond, and expansive acres of agricultural land. A long driveway, bordered by eucalyptus trees, led to the residence he envisioned as his retirement home. However, to his dismay, a couple of years later, in 1915, Amalendra was summoned back to Paksey for the formal inauguration of Hardinge Bridge.

As he stepped off the train at the Paksey railway station, he was awestruck. The station was perched atop a mound and looked like a picture postcard. From there as he looked down, his heart skipped a beat. He couldn't believe what he saw.

What a transformation, he mused. The mosquito-infested swampy grounds had undergone a complete facelift. Paksey seemed to have grown into a charming British hamlet, rising from a jungle. Amalendra thought: *It was indeed a testament to the relentless hard work of the British.*

Amalendra noticed that the British had gradually colonised much of the forest land beside the Padma River, transforming it into a picturesque settlement which they named "Paksey". This newly established settlement became the headquarters of the Eastern Indian Railways, and he was awestruck by its metamorphosis. Paksey had transformed into a well-ordered railway town with manicured gardens and structured streets. Observing this, he began to contemplate making it his retirement home, envisioning a life of peace in contrast to Comilla, which had become a bustling cantonment town.

*

The year was 1922, and Amalendra resided in the railway quarters in Paksey. Sundays in Paksey were often dedicated to *shikaar*, the hunt. Amalendra, like many of the affluent, found a thrill in the chase, the sharp report of his rifle echoing through the dense foliage. Sunday mornings were typically reserved for this favourite weekend sport.

The shooting party would venture into the woods, armed with rifles and a .22-calibre shotgun, in pursuit of small game and birds. But one Sunday, the wilderness presented a different tableau. The air hung heavy with the smell of damp earth and decaying leaves. The forest pulsed with the drone of insects and the rustle of unseen life. Amalendra, rifle slung over his shoulder, pushed through the dense undergrowth, his men close behind.

Ahead, a clearing unfolded, revealing a scene that made his stomach churn. A putrid stench, thick and cloying, assaulted his nostrils, a stark contrast to the earthy scent of the forest. Then, the sharp, frenzied barks of dogs, a cacophony of fear, ripped through the usual quiet of the woods.

He pushed through the last of the undergrowth, and the sight before him stopped him cold. The casual brutality, the sheer, senseless violence, sent a wave of nausea through Amalendra. He retreated; the image seared into his mind with a terrible foreboding that it was going to be worse. It was a glimpse into a darkness he had not known existed.

He returned home, his usual swagger gone, his face pale. "I'm done with hunting," Amalendra told his wife, Swarnaprobha, his voice tight.

She stared at him, bewildered. "What happened?" she asked. "You live for Sundays."

He shook his head, unable to articulate the horror he had witnessed. "What I saw today . . . it changed everything."

Swarnaprobha, sensing his agitation, didn't press him. But she noticed the change.

The guns remained untouched, cleaned only by his men, a silent testament to his unspoken trauma. The jungle, with its dark, hidden truths, had cast a long shadow, its unsettling memory now warring with the natural beauty of the place and the lingering smell of putrefied flesh.

In the aftermath of the jungle incident, Amalendra, once indifferent to the town's children, now watched them with a strange, unsettling intensity. Their innocent games, their petty fights, their carefree screams, each triggered a visceral reaction within him. He would observe them wrestling in the dust, their small fists flying, and the raw, unbridled violence of the jungle scene would flash before his eyes. He would shout at them, shooing them away like stray dogs.

"*Ayee ki korcho tomra ar kono kaj neyee naki?*" he'd bellow, "Hey, what are you doing? Don't you have any other work?"

They would immediately scatter, their voices echoing. "*Na chacha amader ar kono kaj neyee, raastaye khela chara!*" they would shout back. "No, Uncle, we do not have any work other than playing on the roads!"

Amalendra was lost in thought, grappling with the co-existence of the refined and the uneducated. He felt torn between the orderly present and the savage jungle scene, uncertain which would ultimately claim him.

8

The Seeds of Change

The jungle's image, a raw tableau of violence, clung to Amalendra like a second skin. The thrill of the hunt, once his Sunday ritual, now tasted like ash.

Swarnaprobha, observing his haunted silences and the untouched rifles, finally broke through his wall of silence. "What troubles you?" she asked, her eyes searching his. "You've forsaken your Sundays, and a shadow has fallen over you."

Amalendra's reply was a raw confession. "How can I bear to watch the children of this town . . . slay each other?"

There was a hitch in Swarnaprobha's breath when she spoke. "Is that . . . what you saw in the jungle?" He nodded, the memory a fresh wound. He recounted the horrifying scene from his hunting trip: children, their faces contorted in violence, mimicking a twisted version of the hunt. They were slaying each other and some were hanging from the trees, their small bodies swaying in the breeze. This disturbing image had lodged in his mind, transforming the familiar into something grotesque. The casual brutality he witnessed that day, combined with the rough behaviour he observed in town, haunted him, leading to sleepless nights and a pervasive sense of dread.

Swarnaprobha, seeing his distress, spoke with quiet urgency. "They need an outlet, a way to channel that energy. Something constructive."

Her words struck him like a bolt of lightning. Suddenly, he understood his purpose.

Amalendra had always home-tutored his children before sending them to boarding schools across East and West Bengal. This experience highlighted a stark truth: he had the privilege of providing his children with an education while less fortunate families in Paksey watched their children grow up without any access to schooling. He saw first-hand how this lack of opportunity and guidance was creating a different kind of wilderness within those young lives. Initially, British schools were set up in India for the children of British soldiers and Anglo-Indians. Over time, this expanded to include children from the Indian elite and upper classes, but the vast majority of native Indian children remained uneducated by the British system.

*

Amalendra's grand retirement home, for which he had already secured land, suddenly felt insignificant compared to the pressing need before him. He shifted his focus, purchasing the neighbouring plot and setting his retirement dreams aside. Construction began in 1923, and by 1924, thatched-roof classrooms dotted the landscape as the Paksey English Medium Junior School welcomed its first, solitary student. Undeterred, Amalendra became a tireless advocate of education, personally visiting families and persuading them to enrol their children. The school's enrolment increased significantly when one of his own sons became a student, creating a ripple effect that drew children from the surrounding villages.

Following this, he established a clubroom for the youth of Paksey, offering indoor and outdoor games like carrom, table tennis, football, and cricket, with the aim of fostering productive engagement. Recognising the importance of reading, Amalendra initiated a public library by donating books from his own collection. He then expanded the clubroom to incorporate a well-stocked library, gathering books for all ages. This endeavour began to transform the idle minds of Paksey's children, drawing even rebellious youths into constructive pursuits.

More than just providing education, Amalendra sought to offer them a brighter future, and his dedication profoundly impacted the community. The once-idle minds, prone to mischief, found purpose in learning and play, while rebellious energies discovered constructive outlets. Amalendra, evolving from a figure of authority, became a respected leader and a beacon of progress for Paksey.

He would brood: *I am educating all my own children. Then why should the native children be deprived?*

Amalendra's eyes had been opened by his experience with his eldest daughter, Charulata, revealing the detrimental consequences of early marriage and insufficient education. This realisation prompted a significant shift in his approach to his other daughters. He ensured they received a proper education before marriage became a consideration. Thus, when his second daughter, Sarojubala, completed her Intermediate of Arts (IA), he made a point of marrying her to a learned professor of mathematics. Amalendra was immensely proud of all his daughters, whose academic successes made them his prized jewels.

*

Amalendra's frequent travels between Calcutta and Paksey allowed him to acquire books from College Street and visit his father-in-law's Kakulia Road house in south Calcutta. Witnessing the decay of his father-in-law's estate, which was just a shadow of its former glory, he decided to renovate it. He also bought the neighbouring land, adding rooms for a few of his children who were by then pursuing their education in Calcutta.

With the school thriving, Amalendra finally turned his attention to his long-delayed retirement home, as his love for Paksey by then had grown immensely. So, he embarked on his next project and started building his retirement home in his much-loved picturesque village.

His stately home was ready by 1930, and he named it "Arohi Bhawan", after his youngest daughter, Arohi, a toddler at that time. A few years before his retirement, Amalendra shifted from his railway quarters to his newly built home. It was a sprawling estate, a testament to his success, but also a reflection of his values. Amalendra envisioned and built a sprawling, harmonious estate. The main residence, centred around a tranquil courtyard and boasting numerous bedrooms, was thoughtfully designed with distinct spaces: a separate drawing room for receiving guests, a traditional baithak khana for formal gatherings, and a dedicated marble temple honouring Goddess Kali.

His deep appreciation for nature was evident in the meticulously landscaped gardens and productive orchards, which provided generously for his family and the wider community. The walled property, accessed through a grand entrance known as the "Shingha Dwarja", or "Lion Gate", also included comfortable quarters for the family priest and staff, cultivating an atmosphere of idyllic serenity and understated aristocracy.

Amalendra's nurturing spirit extended to his beloved pets, who he ensured were fed before he himself partook of meals.

The Paksey English Medium Junior School, a vibrant testament to Amalendra's vision, flourished, casting a bright light across the quaint railway town of Paksey. Yet, as the school thrived, its inhabitants remained unaware of the shadow that lengthened with each passing day—a light that would soon be dimmed by the advent of an impending, darkness.

9

The Inferno

Amalendra's vision flourished in the thriving Paksey Junior School. Situated just a short distance from Arohi Bhawan, its classrooms buzzed with the enthusiastic voices of the children. Overseeing its daily operations, Amalendra felt a deep sense of fulfilment.

However, Amalendra's focus began to shift. While the school continued to thrive, his thoughts were increasingly occupied by the growing unrest in the country and the whispers of political change that reached even the quiet corners of Paksey.

The year was 1932. Amalendra was in the midst of a meeting at the Calcutta Railway Board when the peon boy walked in and said in Bengali, "*Sir, ekta telegram esheche Paksey theke*; Sir, a telegram has come for you from Paksey."

One glance, and Amalendra froze, abruptly standing up, his middle-aged countenance taking on a deathly pallor. Thrusting his lean visage forward, he joined his palms together in a namaskar, "I'm sorry, gentlemen, it's an emergency; I have to rush back."

Heads turned and conversations stopped as they stared at his retreating back. Amalendra had no time to think; he just wanted to be on the train that would take him home.

The train journey to Paksey was a blur, the crumpled telegram's stark message burning in his mind: "Paksey School set on fire, come at once."

A chilling dread settled over him, a pervading horror that seeped into his bones as the train crossed the Hardinge Bridge and pulled into Ishwardi station.

A sombre crowd awaited his arrival. As the coach halted, they jostled forward. Amalendra, gaunt and hollow-eyed, stepped off, the weight of their silent condolences mirroring the devastation he felt. His face, etched with lines of exhaustion, bore the look of a man who had lost someone dear. Raising his drooping head, Amalendra sensed the collective sorrow of the people gathered to console their beloved benefactor and teacher. Then, amidst the crowd, he spotted a fourteen-year-old lad. The boy came forward and said, "We are with you; we can rebuild your school, sir." Amalendra was struggling internally to cope with the agonising defeat. He just nodded his head and embraced him.

The school grounds were a scene of ruin. Smoldering ashes lay where his dream had stood, and a raw, gaping wound opened in his heart. As he stood amidst the wreckage, a silent question echoed in his soul: could any man truly master his fate?

The subsequent inquiry yielded nothing, only the bitter knowledge that the blazing fire had consumed the school before help could arrive. The following months were a descent into an emotional abyss. The jungle scene, a twisted tableau of violence, replayed in his mind, a constant, mocking echo. *We are back to square one*, he thought, the words a bitter taste on his tongue.

*

The thought of defeat was an unbearable weight, made even heavier by his impending retirement from the railways. The burden felt crushing, demanding immediate action. He called repeated meetings with the school committee, but funds remained stubbornly scarce. Driven by desperation, he proposed a profound sacrifice. He would pledge his entire provident fund to the school's reconstruction if they renamed it Ratnaprobha Vidyapitha, in memory of his late mother, Ratnaprobha Debi.

The board members, recognising the gravity of the situation and the generosity of his offer, had no choice but to agree. With all the necessary documents secured, the reconstruction of the school commenced.

Amalendra, leveraging his railway connections, enlisted his brother Satyen to procure steel scraps. This time, the school would rise from concrete, a fortress against future attacks. Slowly, his provident fund dwindled as the school took shape. It was a tribute, not just to education, but to his mother, Ratnaprobha Debi, whom he had lost at the young age of fourteen.

By 1934, Ratnaprobha Vidyapitha stood anew, its concrete walls a testament to Amalendra's resilience. Students returned, their laughter a fragile counterpoint to the lingering smoke. Amalendra, with his retirement nearing, began planning his future in Paksey, unaware of the looming political storm that would soon engulf Bengal.

He stood, a man who had faced the inferno and rebuilt from the ashes, but the shadows of the fire and the jungle still danced in his eyes.

10

The Revolution

Satyendra developed a strong sense of patriotism during high school, participating in rallies with his classmates. He used his singing talent to express this patriotism, often finding himself in trouble. As a juvenile, however, he typically received only warnings or minor punishments. He sang songs composed by renowned poets like Rabindranath Tagore and Nazrul Islam, who were creating patriotic works to support the nationalist cause. This movement in Bengal began to significantly impact the nation's literature and culture.

Upon entering college, Satyen initially maintained a low profile. However, by his second year, he had settled into a routine with friends, often gathering beneath their usual neem tree to enjoy tea from clay cups. One afternoon, their peaceful gathering was interrupted when Satyen noticed a senior boy approaching them with determined strides. The senior, of medium height and athletic build, had sweat glistening on his face in the late afternoon sun.

He stopped in front of the boys and said, "I am Krishnakanta. Is anyone interested in joining the national movement?"

Satyen, then twenty, immediately agreed. His friends nodded in assent.

"Then follow me, boys," Krishnakanta said.

They meekly followed the senior off the college campus. Satyen, tall and lanky, had a tanned complexion and a narrow, moustached face that betrayed no emotion. As they walked, they passed a series of secluded houses, and the sounds of the city began to fade. The senior led them into a nondescript house and then vanished. Immediately, the three friends felt a wave of tension, exchanging uneasy looks. A faint light, rising from a crack in the floor, caught their attention. Satyen carefully lifted a floorboard, revealing Krishnakanta holding a lamp at the bottom of a spiralling descent. "Come down," he whispered.

"Who will close the trap door?" Satyen, the outspoken one, asked.

"Don't worry about it. Just come down," came the brusque reply.

At the bottom of the stairs, they found a dingy room. Several men sat on the floor, examining a map. Krishnakanta introduced them to the group's leader, a man in his forties wearing gold-rimmed glasses. In Bengal, 'Dada', which is often shortened to 'Da', is a term of reverence shown to an older man. In accordance, Krishnakanta said, "Dada, these boys are from my college. They are interested in joining our party."

The leader gestured for them to sit.

"Does the group have a name, Dada?" Satyen asked.

"We are part of the 'Dacca Anushilan Samiti'. This is its Comilla branch," the bearded gentleman replied.

Satyen, already aware of covert groups seeking independence through revolution, chose to join the Samiti. He and his friends began attending weekly meetings. After each meeting, Satyen felt a surge of zeal, envisioning a free nation liberated from British rule. He graduated with a degree in physics, chemistry, and mathematics. Then he followed in his father's footsteps and secured a job at the Bank of Bengal in Chittagong, a bank thriving under the Bengal Presidency.

Despite the demands of his banking career, Satyen devoted his weekends to the Anushilan Samiti, moving through the city to collect funds, the weight of the revolution heavy in his satchel. His brother, Debendra, a lecturer in Calcutta, moved in similar circles, aiding the Jugantar party, a related revolutionary front. The brothers, though separated by distance and varying levels of involvement, were united by a shared passion for freedom.

The exploitative British Raj became their enemy, a force to be resisted. Thus, Satyen's desire to liberate his country grew daily. As the British exploited the nation's resources, causing economic hardship and industrial decline, Satyen and his friends became increasingly involved, progressing from peaceful protests to violent resistance. The movement's ideology of "Atma Shakti" empowered them to challenge authority, leading the British to label their actions "revolutionary terrorism".

The 1905 partition of Bengal, intended to weaken nationalism, had the opposite effect, igniting the Swadeshi movement. Satyen embraced this movement, which involved boycotts and protests. It gained support from wealthy Bengali aristocrats who had previously avoided political involvement. Bengalis, both Hindus and Muslims, were united by a shared sense of nationalism, fostered by the Bengali intelligentsia. Realising this, the British annulled the partition in 1911 and moved their capital from Calcutta to Delhi, attempting to distance themselves from the revolutionary Bengalis.

After the construction of the Hardinge Bridge, when Amalendra returned to Comilla, Satyen became a frequent visitor to his *Barda*, his elder brother's home.

One day, he said, "Barda, our group needs your help."

Amalendra, surprised, asked, "What assistance do you require, and which group are you a part of, Satyen?"

Satyen explained that he was a fundraiser for the Dacca Anushilan Samiti, Comilla branch, and that they needed money to buy weapons and ammunition to fight against British rule.

"Barda, it is crucial that wealthy households like yours assist us if we are to achieve liberation from these oppressors," he emphasised.

Amalendra pledged financial support but cautioned Satyen against active involvement. Satyen merely nodded, already deeply committed to the Samiti.

Satyen visited Amalendra every month to collect funds. It was a complex mix of emotions for the brothers, with Satyen feeling excited and Amalendra gratified to contribute to the freedom movement.

In 1914, the audacious Rodda Arms Heist in Calcutta sent shockwaves through the British administration. Revolutionaries stole a large shipment of pistols and bullets from Rodda & Company, a British arms store. They then spirited the stolen weapons away by the least suspicious mode of transport, a bullock cart, and distributed them among their ranks.

A year later, in 1915, Satyen was at the Calcutta Anushilan Samiti, where comrades were receiving assignments and weapons.

Picking up a gun, Satyen asked, "Dada, are these pistols from the Rodda & Company heist?"

The leader confirmed it, adding that the weapons had been given to freedom fighters like Chandrashekhar Azad and Bhagat Singh. Satyen's chest swelled with pride.

"In a few days, you will begin your arms training. Are you ready?" the leader asked.

"I am looking forward to it, Dada," Satyen replied enthusiastically.

Upon returning to Comilla, Satyen dedicated himself to weapons training and participating in conspiracies. After months of planning, he and three others prepared to rob the Darjeeling Mail, which transported British funds.

On the night of the heist, they hid in thick shrubbery near the train tracks. At Satyen's signal, they boarded the guard's cabin, overpowered him, and searched for the money bags. The plan failed as the British had been tipped off. A scuffle ensued, and Satyen seized the guard's pistol, issuing an order before jumping off the train. His comrades followed, having tied and gagged the guard.

In 1925, Satyen was involved in the Kakori Train Conspiracy. They looted three bags containing a hundred thousand rupees, which were being transferred to the British treasury.

By 1930, Satyen was preparing for the Chittagong Armory Raid, a significant event led by Surjo Sen, known as Master da. Master da, a mathematics teacher, was a renowned revolutionary, and his meticulous planning impressed Satyen. Although the raid's objectives weren't fully achieved, Master da became a symbol of patriotism and rebellion in Bengal.

After the incident, the district town of Comilla was set ablaze in a vengeful manner, indicating that the civil disobedience movement and the battle for independence were on the rise. The revolution's dangerous allure had seized Satyen, forcing him to navigate a treacherous path between his public life as a banker and his secret life as a revolutionary, the constant reminder of the rebellion echoing in his mind.

11

Ye Mothers'

The stark headline in the local newspaper jolted Amalendra. Beneath it, two smiling faces: Srimoyee Chowdhury, his cousin's daughter, and her friend, Srilata Ghosh.

The December 14, 1931 edition of *The Statesman* screamed:

'Schoolgirls Assassinate District Magistrate in Comilla.'

Steve Robinson, the DM, lay dead in his office, felled by the bullets of the two teenagers. They acted, it was said, to avenge the rampant abuse of power by Robinson and to restore the violated dignity of local women.

The two girls, who were fifteen and sixteen years old, had become members of the Comilla branch of the Jugantar party. Initially relegated to carrying messages and weapons, Srimoyee and Srilata yearned for a more active role. They aspired to match the boys in their responsibilities. "What use is our practice stick-and-dagger play if we flinch from real action?" Srimoyee had once declared, her youthful eyes burning with conviction.

Their passion for justice, their unwavering clarity of purpose, drove them to volunteer for a deadly mission. They trained relentlessly, mastering the use of firearms with chilling precision.

The sun peered through a break in the clouds as the girls, with an air of innocence, made their way to the District Magistrate's office. They kept up a light, casual chatter as they were ushered into a waiting room. Clad in their beige and brown saris, with a deep brown shawl wrapped around each of them, they were beyond suspicion. Their young faces did not show traces of nervousness as they giggled and settled into their seats.

After about ten minutes, a dapper man walked towards them. For a split second, the girls were taken aback by his rich, blondish-brown hair and strong, rather forbidding, jawline. They staggered slightly and rose to their feet.

The gentleman asked, "What can I do for you, young ladies?"

Srimoyee stepped forward and handed over the petition they were carrying. The Magistrate frowned. "What is it?"

Srilata promptly replied, "Sir, we need your permission to hold a swimming competition in the pond near our school."

Mr Robinson nodded. As soon as his back was turned, the girls exchanged meaningful glances. The air in the waiting room, thick with anticipation, shifted as Robinson returned with the signed petition in his hand. For a heartbeat, the girls were struck by his imposing presence, the sheer weight of the authority he represented. Then, steeling their resolve, they moved forward.

Yanking the concealed pistols from under their shawls, they fired at him from point-blank range. Robinson's hand flew to his chest, and he stood frozen in the doorway, the signed petition smeared in blood. For a fleeting moment, he stared at the girls in disbelief before his body doubled over and he collapsed to the ground.

Their defiant cries of 'Vande Mataram!', 'Hail the motherland!' echoed through the office, a stark challenge to the Raj. They had struck a blow, a defiant act that would resonate far beyond the walls of that office. The guards soon moved in to overpower the shooters, but the girls put up fierce resistance, even injuring one of the policemen. Even in handcuffs, their faces radiated victory as they said to each other, "*Amra perechee*; We made it!"

As the girls awaited their trial and sentence in the Hijli Detention Camp, they stood their ground with fierce determination. In an interview, they were reported to have stated, "It is better to die than to live in a horse's stable."

Srimoyee was the captain at the Annual Conference of Chhatri Sangha, which was graced by the Indian nationalist leader, Netaji Subhas Chandra Bose. At the end of the conference, Netaji gave the girls his autograph with a message that said, "To preserve your honour, take up arms yourselves, ye mothers'."

News of their courage reached Netaji, who, deeply moved, established bravery awards in their names within his Rani Jhansi women's regiment, enshrining their act in the annals of the freedom struggle.

The nieces and nephews of the Dasgupta family heard from their aunts, how their cousin and her friend were sentenced as third-class prisoners in Hijli Detention Camp and they served seven years of their ten-year terms until they were released in 1939, after the amnesty negotiations between Mahatma Gandhi and the British Indian government.

Though condemned to years of harsh imprisonment, Srimoyee and Srilata emerged with their spirits unbroken. Their lives, after their release, became a testament to resilience, Srimoyee as a doctor and Srilata as a legislator. Their story, passed down through generations, served as a potent reminder of the extraordinary courage that fuelled the fight for freedom.

12

The Secret Mission

Satyendra, consumed by revolutionary fervour, chose a solitary path, abandoning his stable life and respectable job. He embraced the British label "revolutionary terrorist", channelling his fury into fiery articles in local newspapers. To his brothers, Amalendra and Debendra, he appeared merely an enthusiastic supporter of the movement. In reality, he was deeply involved in multiple successful conspiracies against foreign rule.

Meanwhile, in Burma, their father, Monindra, found his tranquil existence shattered by the growing unrest. Drawn into the struggle, he risked everything, secretly transporting arms to freedom fighters in India.

As the summer of 1932 yielded to a crisp autumn, Satyen and his comrades gathered at Chittagong port, a bustling trading hub in British India. The humid, acrid air clung to Satyen as he surveyed the scene. The stifling atmosphere agitated his thoughts as he watched the ship move stealthily through the dark, damp night. He paced restlessly, trying to organise his plans.

The air was raw as eighteen individuals prepared for the perilous mission. Three were teenage girls disguised as boys, while the other fifteen were men and boys, all in their respective boats. Two dinghies and three fishing boats each carried two men and one teenage boy, while the girls signalled from the shore. The air thrummed with nervous energy, the silence broken only by the gentle lapping of waves against the boats. Satyen's heart pounded, each beat a drum against the silence, as the girls signalled the moment to move.

The sea caressed the boats like a large feline, and the tall coconut trees appeared pale in the light of the new moon. The boats approached silently, and then a boy from each jumped into the water, leaving two men behind. Satyen and the other two boys remained in their boat. The night was tranquil, the only sound the splashing of waves as the five cautiously swam to the ship and climbed aboard. After once again receiving the green signal from the girls, they began transferring the weapons in an assembly-line manner, loading them into the boats. Just as they neared completion, red lights flashed from ashore.

"Police!" Satyen's voice cut through the night, a harsh, urgent command. "Move!" Gunfire erupted, shattering the stillness. "*Tomra shabai palao!*" he roared. "We will hold them back!"

"*Na*, Satyenda!" they cried, their voices raw with fear and loyalty. "We die together!"

Satyen, his face contorted with desperation, barked back, "If we all die, the weapons are lost! Go!"

The boats, laden with stolen weapons, slipped away into the encroaching darkness, leaving Satyen and his two companions to weather a storm of lead. Gunfire illuminated the night in stark, bright flashes. Satyen instinctively took point, leaning into the mast, using a metal sheet as a makeshift barrier to protect himself and his comrades as they fought to control the vessel, weaving through the deadly shots that pierced the gloom. A brutal wave of governmental suppression ensued. Then, a sudden, searing pain ripped through his shoulder.

"Satyen da, duck!" his men shouted.

Satyen swung around, and for a fleeting moment, he saw the contorted faces of his comrades, etched with fear and grief, before the next bullet pierced his chest. Two staggering steps forward, Satyen heard a cacophony of voices as his body hit the water. His head bobbed up and down. With his last breath, he raised his gun, firing a final, defiant shot into the night, his cry of "Vande Mataram!" echoing his sacrifice.

*

Dawn broke, painting the sky a cruel, beautiful orange, as Debendra arrived in Paksey. The horse-drawn tonga stopped at the Shingha Darja of Arohi Bhawan. Debendra's eyes widened in surprise as he surveyed the throng of people gathered within the grounds. As he walked up the driveway, he felt every eye upon him as his feet crunched on the gravel. He soon noticed the baithak khana filled with people. As he entered the large drawing room, they parted, making way for Debendra. What he saw was beyond his wildest imaginings: his younger brother, Satyen lay before him, swathed in white linen and adorned with garlands and flowers, his countenance serene.

Amalendra, his face a mask of grief, seemed to have aged years in a single night. Debendra looked around and saw everyone's eyes misted with shock. He felt hot tears slide down his cheeks as he embraced Amalendra. Both wept, overwhelmed by the despair that had descended upon their family.

The Dasgupta family, unaware of Satyen's clandestine life, was shattered by his violent death. In the gunfight, five British troops and three revolutionaries, including Satyen, were killed. The arms operation was a success, as the police were unable to trace the four boats that had fled with the ammunition.

The week ended with a final blow. News of Monindra's death, a telegram as cold and brief as a tombstone. He did not leave Shan Tea Estate until the end. The telegram gave no further details.

After these events, the brothers became aware of the colonial forces' watchful eyes and knew their lives would never be the same. They decided to be cautious about providing financial aid to the Anushilan Samiti.

*

Amalendra, his voice heavy with grief and resolve, entered Debendra's hostel room. He smelled coffee and saw that Debendra had just finished reviewing the final-year students' answer sheets.

Debendra looked up, "Hello Barda, what brings you here?"

Amalendra shuffled into the nearby wicker chair and cleared his throat. "I heard you are getting involved with the Jugantar party. I couldn't bear to lose you too, so I got you a ticket. Your ship leaves in two weeks. You will go to Germany and pursue your doctorate," he declared, the words leaving no room for argument. "Your talent will not be wasted here."

Debendra, stunned, tried to protest, but Amalendra's eyes, filled with the weight of loss, silenced him. The door closed, a final, irrevocable act.

Everything went as Amalendra had envisioned for his family until July 1945.

13

Ruminating Through Time

She rubbed her eyes, seeking consolation. The rasp of Amalendra's final words, "Swarna, do not worry. . ." hung in the sterile hospital air, a cruel mockery of comfort. Swarna pressed her fingers to his lips, a futile attempt to silence the inevitable. Tears blurred her vision, each drop a tiny hammer against her heart.

A couple of years before India's partition, Amalendra lay in a Calcutta hospital bed, his breaths shallow and laboured. In his waning moments, he uttered in a deep, throaty voice, "Swarna, do not worry, all that I am leaving behind will see you through your life."

Swarnaprobha touched his lips, her eyes brimming with tears, and quietly said, "Please don't speak. You are a fighter; you will soon get better."

His words came slowly, punctuated by quick, wheezing breaths. He attempted to clear his throat and spoke in a calming tone, "You can spend the rest of your life in our beloved Paksey. We have educated our children well; they will take care of you." His voice quivered. "Maa Kali is with you."

Swarna bit her lip, stifling an instinctive sigh. She knew, deep within, that these were hollow consolations.

For a fleeting moment, Swarna's mind drifted. She was back in Paksey. The afternoon lull, a gentle, familiar weight, signalled it was time for her siesta. After the midday meal, a lull descended, and she would retreat to the cool shade of her room, the soft rustle of her cotton sari a comforting sound. She would drift, not quite asleep, but suspended in a tranquil space, until the familiar rhythm of Amalendra's footsteps announced his return.

Then, the veranda transformed. The air, still warm from the day, began to cool, carrying the sweet scent of tea brewing in the kitchen. Amalendra, his brow creased from the day's burdens, would settle into his favourite wicker chair, its slight creak a familiar melody. Swarna, perched beside him on the low jute *mora*, felt the rough weave beneath her, a grounding sensation. The ritual began: the delicate clink of porcelain, the warmth of the tea cupped in her hands, the shared stories of the day. As she served homemade snacks, the familiar flavours a testament to their shared life, they discussed the day's tasks, the household rhythms flowing as smoothly as the tea poured into their cups. It was a time of quiet intimacy, a shared space carved out of the day.

As the last rays of the setting sun painted the sky in hues of orange and gold, a different kind of quiet settled. Swarna, with a silent nod, would leave the veranda, the unspoken agreement hanging in the air. The family knew this was her time.

She would retreat to her corner, the scent of incense lingering, the soft glow of the lamp illuminating the small shrine dedicated to Goddess Kali. Seated cross-legged, the cool floor beneath her, she immersed herself in meditation. The world outside faded, replaced by the rhythmic chanting, the quiet hum of her own breath. This was her sanctuary, a space where she could gather her strength, a time to reconnect with the divine, and herself. It was a cherished moment of solitude, a balm for her soul, a necessary pause in the rhythm of their shared life.

The comforting warmth of those memories dissolved, replaced by the sterile chill of the hospital air as Swarnaprobha saw the placid doctor raise an eyebrow, standing near Amalendra's bedside, giving instructions to the nurse on duty. As he looked at his patient, he gave a reassuring nod, as if some invisible message had passed between them.

Amalendra's vision began to swim. His weathered hand, once strong, now frail, grasped hers. "Look after my Ratnaprobha Vidyapitha," he whispered, his voice a fading echo.

Then, a sudden stillness, a slackening of his jaw, a thin line of saliva escaping his lips. "Vande Mataram!" he breathed, "Mother, I bow to thee," and was gone.

"All is well," said that sleeping face. He had finally stepped beyond the boundaries of his lush life. Tears rolled down Swarnaprobha's cheeks, distorting the scene into a hazy blur.

Why him? Why now? Sixty-three, and gone. He'd always been so strong . . . If only he'd taken better care of himself. And now, this talk of partition . . . a cruel, looming shadow, threatening to take everything, she brooded. *The world outside, already fractured by his death, is now threatened by the looming partition, a cruel division.* The pain echoed, tearing through her heart.

The 1905 partition, a wound briefly healed in 1911, reopened in 1947. The division of India in 1947 brought immense suffering, irrevocably changing the fate of countless people. Bengali Hindus in the East were compelled to abandon their homes and heritage, seeking refuge in West Bengal. Simultaneously, Bengali Muslims in the West, motivated by their own hopes and fears, undertook a parallel, painful journey towards East Pakistan, highlighting the shared tragedy of partition.

The Dasgupta family, too, faced the harsh reality of their location in East Bengal. The impending partition forced them to relinquish their deeply familiar world—

their land, their history, their homes. The weight of this loss was immense, turning them into unwilling exiles. With profound sorrow, they chose to leave their established lives and seek refuge in Calcutta.

Yet, even in the familiar surroundings of Calcutta, their hearts remained tied to their lost homeland, each new experience a painful reminder of what they had left behind.

Swarnaprobha would tell her children, "Your Baba spoke of our future in Paksey, a future that would never be. Perhaps it was a mercy that he did not have to watch everything he built be taken away."

14

The Partition Saga

The silence Amalendra left behind was a heavy shroud, suffocating Swarnaprobha. Migraines hammered at her temples, and a constant ache settled in her bones, a physical manifestation of her grief. Her children watched, their hearts heavy, as their mother, once a pillar of strength, became increasingly frail, her spirit dimmed by sorrow.

So, after their father's unexpected passing in late 1945, the siblings made the difficult decision to relocate their Maa to her maternal home on Kakulia Road in Calcutta, where then lived her brother and his family. They hoped the change and better medical care would offer some relief. Arohi and Sushil accompanied her, while the other siblings remained in Paksey, their lives still tethered to their ancestral home. But the religious division that was ripping India apart made the Dasgupta siblings' continued presence there untenable. As Hindus, they were unsure whether they could survive in a Muslim-dominated country.

A large Hindu population, including the Dasgupta family, had lived and grown up in East Bengal. Paksey, their ancestral home, the very ground that held their memories, was now a foreign land. A year before the dissolution of Crown rule, the few Dasgupta siblings still living in Paksey decided to move bag and baggage from their much-loved home. They feared that, after the partition, Paksey would fall under the new Muslim-dominated country of East Pakistan, where their safety could be at stake.

But the thought of leaving was a deep, visceral wound. Forced to confront this painful reality, they felt their will to fight ebbing away, leaving them vulnerable to the currents of fate. Thus, in the midst of the ongoing turmoil, the siblings left behind everything that their father had acquired in his lifetime and boarded the train to Calcutta.

It was a cold January morning in 1946. Arohi opened the door to find four of her siblings, their faces etched with exhaustion, their belongings piled behind them. They had departed from Paksey under duress, their hearts heavy with the weight of displacement.

Swarnaprobha's tears flowed freely, a mixture of grief and relief, as she saw her sons dragging the luggage into the house. She reminisced about the time before the partition when Hindus and Muslims coexisted harmoniously in East Bengal. In spite of all the losses, Swarnaprobha's sons, Sudhir and Sushil, attempted to comfort their mother. "Ma, the education our father provided us cannot be seized like our belongings."

Swarnaprobha mournfully concurred, understanding that they could endure the challenges that lay ahead despite losing everything. She quietly thanked her husband, who had extended and renovated her parental house.

The Dasgupta siblings, scattered by circumstance, began to converge on Calcutta, each carrying their own burden of loss.

The threads of Amalendra's large family had spread far and wide. His two eldest daughters, Charulata and Sarojubala, had already established their own households in Calcutta and Comilla, respectively. Following them, Basanta secured a position as a warden, teaching mathematics and physics at a boarding school in Cooch Bihar, while Mihir became an English teacher in Calcutta.

Among the brothers, the eldest, Abhinandan, worked for a British firm. Tathagata served in the defence services, stationed in Kanpur, and Biswaroop, an engineer, pursued opportunities in Bombay. The younger generation was still in their studies: Kalyanbrata was nearing his engineering graduation, living the transient life of a hostel resident, and Malati was immersed in the vibrant, artistic world of Shantiniketan.

Finally, Swarnaprobha, Mihir, Abhinandan, along with Arohi and Sushil who attended college, began living at their maternal home.

As all the siblings were settling down, one day Swarnaprobha, with a deep sigh, asked Arohi, "The aftermath of the partition of the Indian subcontinent must have resulted in the displacement of around 10–12 million people based on religious grounds?"

Arohi nodded gravely. "Yes, Ma, maybe more."

A couple of years had passed by when a letter arrived from Arif Mohammad, a former colleague of Amalendra who worked in the railways. He had arrived in Paksey due to an official transfer from Lahore which after the partition became west Pakistan. On seeing Arohi Bhawan lying vacant, he had decided to make an offer to the Dasgupta siblings for an exchange of a house which he had in West Bengal. The siblings had no choice but to ultimately agree to the exchange deal of their beloved Paksey home, as their attempts to sell their homes after the partition seemed like a herculean task. They had no other alternative but to let go of their Paksey home, a place brimming with their past, for a house in Dum Dum, north Calcutta. The irony was bitter. Abhinandan and his siblings had no option but to accept his offer.

Following the exchange for the Dum Dum house, they tried to sell their property in Comilla but to no avail. So as the property remained unsold with no claimants, eventually it was taken over by the government.

*

Despite being immigrants, the Dasgupta family found great comfort in their Kakulia Road house. They lived there harmoniously with their maternal relatives for a decade. However, an argument was sparked when Sarojubala, the second eldest among the siblings, visited her family at their Kakulia Road house. Her husband, Moni Mohan Deb, was a distinguished professor at Comilla College, a brilliant scholar recognised as an "Ishan scholar" by Calcutta University, an honour bestowed upon top-performing students across all disciplines. He was a gold medallist in both his undergraduate and postgraduate studies in the 1920s, excelling in mathematics and Sanskrit.

Sarojubala, a woman of strong will and immense pride in her father's accomplishments, took on her maternal uncle. She fiercely argued for her siblings' claim to the family property, citing her father's extensive renovations, buying the adjacent land, and extending the house as justification for their share. Upon her return to Comilla, her daring confrontation had utterly destroyed the home's former tranquility. Mihir couldn't take it any more. So, one day, she said, "I can't bear another night of this, Barokhoka," her voice quiet but firm. The name, a gentle Bengali endearment for the eldest son, felt heavy with her frustration.

"I know, Rangadi. It's been... unbearable," said Abhinandan.

"You think we haven't sacrificed enough? After all we've done?" their aunt's voice floated out from the adjacent room.

"We're not ungrateful, Mamima. But. . ." Mihir trailed off.

Then they heard their Mama say, "But what? You think you own the place? Just because your father, I mean Amalendra. . ."

Their uncle was interrupted by Abhinandan, his voice calm but firm. "It's not about owning anything, Uncle. It's about respect."

Mihir looked at her brother, her voice tight. "Barokhoka, let it go." She paused. "We were grateful for this refuge, Mama. But now I think it's time we found our own place," she said firmly.

Abhinandan nodded.

They stood in silence for a moment, the tension in the room palpable. Swarnaprobha watched them, her face a mask of sorrow.

Abhinandan and Mihir, driven by a need to protect their mother's honour, decided to find a new home. They immediately thought of their Dum Dum house. But to their utter dismay, the house, which lay vacant for years, was brimming with strangers. The locks were broken, and it had been encroached upon and occupied by homeless refugees.

But they found a large, villa-style house on Lansdowne Terrace in south Calcutta, which was perfect for their large family. It was a two-storeyed house boasting a wide front garden and a sprawling backyard. The house exhibited a unique architectural style with both European and Bengal influences, featuring a veranda that offered respite from the Calcutta summers. Its Corinthian-style columns and slatted Venetian or French-style windows were painted green, a feature Bengalis referred to as "Khar Khari". The balcony showcased latticed arches of lace-like cast iron filigree, while the door arches incorporated coloured glass pieces to reduce the glare of sunlight entering the home. These houses also typically included an open roof terrace adorned with intricately detailed cornices and patterned railings crafted from cast iron.

*

Abhinandan's steady employment at a British firm in Calcutta provided a measure of stability. His sisters, Mihir Kumari and Basanti Kumari, both teachers, had established their lives in West Bengal. Basanta, a warden at a Cooch Behar boarding school, returned home during breaks. The house also served as home to the three youngest Dasgupta siblings—Arohi, who had completed her postgraduate-studies and was a college lecturer; Sudhir, who had joined an engineering firm; and Sushil, an apprentice at a pharmaceutical company.

Sarojubala's son, Ranju, an engineering student in Jadavpur, frequently visited during university breaks. These visits often coincided with those of Reena and young Anu, fostering a close bond between Ranju and his cousins. One day, Ranju overheard his uncle and aunt talk about the fate of their Dum Dum property. He immediately chipped in and asked why they were still holding on to that property.

He said to Abhinandan, "Baromama, it's already a decade since you got the house exchanged with grandfather's Paksey house." He stopped to look at the reactions of his maternal uncle and continued, "Do tell me if I can be of any help."

"I think Ranju is right. It's time we sold it off," said Mihir in a grave tone.

So, after several years of contemplation, the Dasgupta siblings decided to sell off their Dum Dum property. Unable to move the illegal occupants, they ultimately sold the house, along with the occupants, for a pittance. It felt as if they had to throw the baby out with the bathwater.

The loss of the Comilla property, on top of the disastrous Dum Dum exchange, left the Dasgupta siblings reeling. A sense of utter helplessness settled over them, a feeling that fate had dealt them a merciless blow.

PART IV
1960s
Calcutta

15

The Time Machine

Anu was blessed with a large family. From a young age, she learnt that in Bengali culture, it was respectful and loving to address elders with specific prefixes rather than their given names. As she grew, she also learnt that the term for blood relatives, *attiyo*, was derived from the Sanskrit word *atma*, meaning "soul".

Anu's beloved aunt, Rangapishi, was Mihir Kumari Dasgupta, also known as Chapa. She was her father's elder sister, his Rangadi. Mihir had studied English at the prestigious Scottish Church College in Calcutta. When Anu was three, she enjoyed spending vacations with her mother at her grandparents' home, where she admired her Rangapishi getting ready for school every morning. Mihir was an English teacher at Kamala Girls' High School in south Calcutta.

Every school day, Mihir, armed with a yellow duster cloth, would wipe each piece of furniture in her room, removing every speck of dust that dulled its shine. Anu would also get a handkerchief and emulate her aunt. After her bath, Mihir would emerge from behind a heavy curtain, her demeanour regal, and walk towards the mahogany dresser with its large oval mirror. Her cheeks would flush pink, and her damp black hair would frame her oval face. She always wore a radiant white sari, adorned with a striking gold and silken embroidered border, draped to accentuate her elegance.

Anu, in open admiration, would ask, "Rangapishi, why do you always wear a white sari? You should wear nice colours; you would look even more beautiful."

Mihir would smile indulgently and say, "Anu, my days of wearing coloured saris are over."

Anu would look puzzled.

Mihir would laugh and say, "I am ageing, dear Anu, and at my age, we don't wear colourful saris any more."

Anu would nod, then say, "But you are so pretty, Rangapishi. White also suits you."

Mihir would bend down and ruffle Anu's hair, saying, "You are my very sweet niece."

Anu would beam and do a little jig.

Mihir would apply minimal makeup, only a compact on her cheeks and Vaseline on her thin pink lips. Anu would watch as Mihir styled her hair in a bun, discreetly covering grey strands with hair dye. With her sari neatly pleated at the shoulders, she would first organise her room, maintaining it in perfect order, before leaving the place.

Anu would wait, and when Mihir gathered her purse, she would run to fetch the notebooks of Mihir's students, which she had brought home for checking. Then, Mihir would head to the oval veranda, with Anu trailing behind. Putting on her Bata sandals, she would adjust the pleats of her sari, radiating a sense of readiness.

Anu, her young companion, would follow her to the stairs. Mihir would hug her niece, promise Cadbury's Gems, and say a warm goodbye. As she walked down the steps, Anu would rush to the lattice cast iron grill that adorned the long veranda and watch her Rangapishi until she reached the wicker gate of the compound.

Then there was Anu's uncle, Subimal, three years younger than Tathagata and very fond of Anu. After his bath, he would style his hair, tying a scarf tightly around his head.

Anu would watch him intently and later try to tie a handkerchief around her own hair.

Subimal, Anu's Kakamoni, would, once ready for work, walk towards the stairs, with little Anu following. Then with a sweeping bow and a mischievous grin, say, "Babumoshai, Babumoshai, may I take my leave now?"

This was a bit of fun between the uncle and niece.

Anu would ask her Mamoni, "Mamoni, why does Kakamoni call me 'babumoshai'?"

Sheela would laugh and say, "He's playfully calling you that because he is respecting you as a babumoshai, a respectful little man."

Anu beamed and nodded.

As the sun climbed towards its zenith, Anu eagerly anticipated Mihir's return from school, looking forward to cuddling up to her aunt and listening to stories.

Mihir's room exuded a cosy, classic charm. A single bed stood in one corner, its counterpart neatly stored away. A side table and a comfortable easy chair flanked the bed. Against the opposite wall, a writing bureau displayed carved figurines, family photographs, and a gold-rimmed table clock. Beside it stood a bookcase filled with books and intriguing antiques. A magnificent mahogany lacquered chest, with a large oval mirror, completed the elegant setting. More than just furniture, these pieces were her silent companions, each object holding a whisper of the past, linking her to a world that existed only in memory.

One day, Mihir told Anu that most of the exquisite period furniture in her room had to be altered to fit the smaller rooms of their Lansdowne Terrace house. Anu couldn't quite grasp what was amiss with the furniture in Rangapishi's room but nodded in agreement.

Mihir would often say, "These inanimate objects help me glimpse the past. They are the only link to my parents and the bygone years I left behind in our beloved East Bengal. This furniture has travelled through time, much more than any of us." Her voice, when she spoke of these things, carried a different weight, a deep, almost reverent sadness for a home and a life irrevocably lost.

On Sunday mornings, Mihir had extra cleaning to do. She would carefully dust the vintage oak bookshelf tucked away behind the door, treating each book as if it were a precious artefact. These were not merely books; they were a tangible connection to her father, a library that held not just stories but the very essence of their family's intellectual legacy from a different land.

These little things stayed with Anu as she grew up.

One day, pointing at the row of thick books, Mihir asked Anu, "Can you tell me what these books have in common?"

Anu noticed the letters ACDG engraved in gold on the black leather spines. Instantly, her face lit up, and she said, "Yes, of course! All the books are very thick and have brown leather covers." She paused and then added, "And they all have the letters ACDG engraved on them."

Mihir nodded. "Yes, the books are all leather bound with black spines."

Anu's ears perked up. "Why do these books have leather covers, Rangapishi; all my story books have paper covers?"

Mihir smiled. "Your Thakurda was a man of high tastes, so he would get leather-bound books and get his name, too, embossed on it."

Anu smiled and nodded.

Mihir continued, "So Anu, now can you tell me what the letters ACDG represent?"

"Amalendra Chandra Dasgupta?" Anu clapped her hands, realising she had answered the quiz correctly.

Mihir smiled fondly. "That's right, Anu. Those are your grandfather's initials. Can you guess what they are engraved with?"

Anu thought for a moment and quipped, "*Shona*, gold."

"Yes, Anu dear, you're right. It's pure gold," Mihir replied.

With childish enthusiasm, Anu blurted out, "Oh, the books are wearing gold ornaments?"

Mihir smiled and said, "In a way, yes, Anu. In that era, books, too, were adorned with gold."

Anu looked amused and then, with a serious expression, said, "But isn't gold a very costly item, Rangapishi?"

"Yes, it is, dear Anu. Some people in those days adorned rare books with gold lettering."

Anu looked visibly impressed.

But Mihir looked at them with a forlorn expression. These books, standing in grave silence, tucked away in a corner of their own solitary world, evoked troubling memories for the Dasgupta family. In Mihir's gaze, Anu could sense not just nostalgia, but the quiet burden of carrying these memories, of being the living link to a family history etched in every cherished object and whispered tale.

16

A Fog of Nostalgia

Swarnaprobha Debi's face, a delicate map of time etched in countless wrinkles, lay before her first granddaughter. Yet, when she gazed at Anu, a spark of vibrant life flickered in her eyes, a stark contrast to the frail body that confined her. Wisps of white hair framed her aged visage, and four-year-old Anu, perched on a little cane chair, watched, mesmerised.

Despite Swarnaprobha's physical state, her face would break into a smile, revealing cracked teeth and ruined gums, whenever she looked at her granddaughter. She endearingly referred to her as "Lokkhi", the Bengali term for the Hindu Goddess Lakshmi.

Little Anu found her Thakurma, her paternal grandmother, perpetually supine in bed. So, she would sit beside her Thakurma, while she regaled her with tales of their lives in the charming railway town, Paksey.

Swarnaprobha told Anu that her Thakurda had built a grand house in Paksey, which had large rooms, unlike the ones they had in Calcutta.

When Anu asked if it was like their house in Khamaria, Swarnaprobha would nod and say, "Your Papa stays in his office quarters, while the Paksey house was our own house, built by your Thakurda."

Anu didn't understand the concept of "our own house", so she would just nod in agreement.

"Lokkhi, you've never seen a house like that. They don't make them any more."

"What type of house was it, Thakurma?" She scratched her head. "Papa says our house in Khamaria is a bungalow."

"Yes, Lokkhi, the bungalows were built by the English people. It's different. We, too, stayed in bungalows before your Thakurda retired. They were our railway quarters, just like your Papa's quarters."

Anu tried to wrap her head around the difference, looking confused. But she understood that her Thakurda's house was much bigger than their Khamaria house, and that her Thakurma was so happy there.

So, she mused, *Maybe shifting to a smaller house had made her fall sick and take to her bed.*

Then one day, as Anu sat beside her Thakurma for story time, Swarnaprobha said, "Today, I am going to tell you a secret."

Anu was all ears and placed her hands beneath her chin, her anticipation building.

Swarnaprobha continued, "Every morning, before anyone woke up, I would visit the cemented bathing pond; a *pukur* that your Thakurda had built for me. It featured steps that led down to the water."

"*Ami jani,*" Anu, who had never encountered a pond before, exclaimed, "Oh, I know! In our garden too we have a *chowbaccha.*"

"No, my dear Lokkhi, a pukur is a pond. It is a large body of water, while a chowbaccha is a small cement tank for storing water," Swarnaprobha replied gently.

Anu, seemingly satisfied but with her curiosity still piqued, then asked, "But Thakurma, didn't you have a bathroom?"

Swarnaprobha smiled. "The bathroom was for the other members of the house; I preferred the pond. I loved the sound of the water and the sweet scent of the surrounding garden. After my bath, I always collected flowers from the garden and went to our temple to offer them to our Maa Kali."

"Did you swim in the pond?"

"Yes, I did. I enjoyed the water; it was always so cool and refreshing."

"You were so lucky, Thakurma."

Anu tried to visualise her Thakurma splashing in the water, just as she herself would splash in the small cemented tank they had in their garden back in Khamaria. Then, with a twinkle in her eyes, she asked, "Thakurma, where is your Maa Kali now? Did you leave your God behind in Paksey, just like you left your house and pond?"

Swarnaprobha, quite taken aback, responded with an indulgent smile, "We could not do that, as she was the protector of our family. Anu, our deity is very *jagrota*!"

"What is jagrota, Thakurma?"

"Jagrota means she is an awakened one. She has the power to fulfil the wishes of her devotees. One day, your Rangapishi will take you to see our Maa Kali."

Her explanation satisfied Anu, so she secretly thought that when she went to the temple of their Goddess Kali, she would ask for a wish.

Swarnaprobha recounted how her husband would spend the weekends taking his sons and the neighbourhood boys to their fishing pond, where he would also teach them mathematics while they waited for the day's catch. Then she told Anu how their house was surrounded by a variety of fruit trees, and how her Papa and her uncles would return home from school and gorge on the fruit by climbing the trees.

Anu promptly replied, "Oh really? I climb our fruit trees in Khamaria too."

Swarnaprobha, with an indulgent smile, said, "Then you are a tomboy."

She affectionately squeezed her granddaughter's cheeks and kissed her forehead, calling her "my Lokkhi shona".

As Swarnaprobha recounted these stories, she would glow with an indescribable light, as if the past was a worn-out book whose warmth and words she could seek, even though her fingers could just brush the tips of the pages. While her little Lokkhi listened with a mesmerised visage, her tiny brain absorbed it all like a sponge. Swarnaprobha's voice would soften, weaving tales of Paksey, and Anu felt transported. The stories were like shimmering threads, pulling her into a world of grand houses and hidden ponds, a world that felt like it was straight out of her fairy-tale books.

*

It was the month of October, and little Anu experienced her first Durga Puja in Calcutta. Sarojubala's son, Ranju, was home for his puja break. Anu stood in front of a gorgeous Durga puja pandal, or pavilion, holding onto Ranju, her dada. Then, as they went inside the pandal, Ranju told Anu the story behind the homecoming of Mother Durga. He pointed at the idols positioned on both sides of Goddess Durga and explained that they were her sons and daughters, elaborating that Goddess Durga, after vanquishing a demon, had come to Earth from her husband's home at Kailash Parvat in the Himalayas to visit her father's home.

Anu listened, captivated.

Ranju gestured towards an idol and said it was of Goddess Lokkhi, the daughter of Mother Durga. Anu's ears perked up at hearing the nickname her Thakurma had given her.

Upon returning home, Anu rushed to her Thakurma and asked why her Ranju dada had said that Lokkhi was Goddess Durga's daughter, when her Maa was Reena.

Swarnaprobha smiled and tousled Anu's hair, saying, "You are my Lokkhi shona, my precious little one." She continued, "Because you are a good girl, you are also my Lokkhi Thakur, my Goddess Lokkhi, as you have brought good fortune into our family."

Anu, in her innocent way, felt a special warmth in that name. She nodded her head joyfully and wondered whether she was a Goddess too! Then a happy glow illuminated her countenance, and she thought perhaps she too must be awakened and have the power to grant wishes.

Anu looked at her grandmother with a smug feeling.

Swarnaprobha passed away when Anu was just five years old. However, her aunts, Rangapishi and Sejopishi, conti nued to share stories, keeping her Thakurma's memory alive and instilling within Anu a deep love for the family's history and a longing for a past she never knew. Those stories, like seeds planted in fertile ground, blossomed within Anu, shaping her understanding of family and the power of memory.

17

The White Elephant

After Swarnaprobha passed away, and with most of the Dasgupta siblings moving out, Mihir, Basanta, and their brother Abhinandan were compelled to relocate from their spacious Lansdowne Terrace house to a smaller residence. The new dwelling, with its rooms arranged like train compartments leading off a long veranda, presented a challenging adjustment. Initially, they missed the expanse of their former home.

This change, however, brought a welcome lightness, especially after Anu discovered Priya, the landlord's daughter, who was her age, making holidays at Rangapishi's truly delightful.

Basanta Kumari's sun-ripened pickles, left to mature on the windowsill, became the target. The fate of those jars was in the hands of the two young raiders, Anu and Priya. When the household was deep in their post-lunch siesta, these two girls would stealthily sneak into Sejopishi's room, and by the end of the week, the jars would be half empty. Rangapishi's larder, too, was no match for their appetites. Spoons laden with pickles and pockets brimming with treats, they would climb the stairs to the terrace, devouring their stolen bounty on the attic steps. The two girls frequently indulged in mischief, exploring storerooms and rummaging through old trunks. Their shared love for dress-up led to impromptu performances, filled with singing, dancing, and dramatised fairy tales, providing endless entertainment for their family. They truly enjoyed a joyful childhood.

Being an educationist, Mihir used her school breaks to take Anu and Priya on fun and educational trips, allowing them to explore places such as the Calcutta Museum, the Birla Planetarium, the Zoological Garden, and the Nehru Science Museum. These trips sparked their curiosity, leading to engaging science projects upon their return. Thus, throughout Anu's Calcutta days, a deep bond formed between her and Priya, their journey blossoming from childhood playmates to steadfast friends.

Anu looked forward to the afternoons, when she nestled beside Rangapishi, listening as Mihir painted vivid pictures of their past in East Pakistan. Mihir's tales, rich with the melodies of the wind and the sway of the paddy fields, were fragments of a lost world, captivating Anu's imagination. Basanta, too, wove her own youthful memories, each sister adding intricate details that brought the past vividly to life. These stories, tinged with nostalgia, left a lasting impression, stirring Anu's mind.

*

The secret hidden on the staircase to the terrace was a wooden almirah, off-limits and rumoured to be Anu's Thakurda's *bonduk* almirah, his gun cabinet. One vacation, as Anu bounded up the stairs, she was shocked to find the almirah doors wide open.

Her Rangapishi stood beside it, holding what appeared to Anu to be a *bonduk*, or a gun. Thunderstruck, Anu hid behind a pillar, watching as Mihir handed the menacing weapon to a hirsute man who resembled a monstrous gorilla. Later, Mihir explained that the cabinet belonged to their Thakurda, filled with his shotguns and rifles. With an indulgent smile, she added, "Anu, your Papa was the only one who took after our father. He loved the sport too."

"I have vague memories of Papa bringing home a deer once in Khamaria. I must have been three," Anu replied.

"Yes, perhaps," Mihir said. "The sport was popular then, but with the clearing of jungles, its popularity has declined. It's slowly dying out."

In a way, Anu felt relieved.

*

One Christmas holiday, Anu met the past. After a delightful breakfast of Christmas cake and other treats, Mihir Kumari took her by the hand, and they walked down a dim corridor. Anu chatted cheerfully until they reached a door at the far end of the hallway. Mihir unlocked it, and Anu peered in, astounded by the small, airless room filled with cobwebs and dust.

"Anu, I brought you here to see the ancient relics." Mihir said. "I don't know how long we can hold on to these white elephants."

Anu wrinkled her nose. "Where are the white elephants, Rangapishi?"

Mihir smiled. "There aren't real white elephants, Anu. It's what we call costly, useless things we still keep."

"Have you ever seen a white elephant, Rangapishi?"

"No, they're rare, and need great care. They're albinos."

Anu, curious, peered into the musty room, now home to cockroaches and mice. She gaped at the cobwebs hanging from the ceiling like muslin drapes and listened as Mihir explained how spiders create these intricate webs which look like netted curtains. In the centre of the room stood an oval table cluttered with chandeliers and lanterns of different shapes and sizes covered in a mist of web, illuminated by fat bars of sunlight from a solitary ventilation window.

Mihir silently pointed to the relics. Her past, like a fog, was closing in. A couch and carved chairs, swathed in polythene, stood in a far corner. Dismantled four-poster beds, table lamps, and stands stood in mute agony. A rolled Persian carpet, worn rugs, and faded draperies occupied another corner. Framed portraits, leaning against each other, seemed to stare at Mihir with grave melancholy, like expressions of human souls. In stark contrast, her dark eyes gleamed with life as she pointed to the echoes of the past. Pieces of furniture and curious, whispered stories of a glorious past. Mihir, her eyes crinkled in contemplation, pointed to a tall, cobweb-hidden clock.

"Anu, that's a grandfather clock. It's lost all track of time."

Anu's eyes widened. "Oh, it was my grandfather's clock?"

"Yes, your grandfather's, but that's what these tall clocks are called."

Anu nodded, picturing herself in Paksey, surrounded by grandfather clocks and white elephants.

Mihir shut the door. Walking back through the dim corridor with the eight-year-old clinging to her, fearing the creepy crawlies, Mihir's mind was filled with painful memories.

"Anu, our Paksey house was filled with these things," she said, her voice resonant. "We don't have the space or need for them now."

With a sad, wry smile, she added, "One day, they'll all go to auction."

At that tender age, the antiques meant little to Anu, but the attention made her feel important, like a character in a fairy tale, with Rangapishi as her fairy godmother. As years passed, these moments, like pages from her childhood pop-up books, became etched in her memory, while Mihir lived with her ruined dreams.

PART V
1956–1974
Jabalpur, Ambernath, Calcutta, Munich

18

The Voyage

Tathagata, a civil engineer and gazetted officer with the Indian Ordnance Factory Services (IOFS) in Jabalpur, was astounded at his selection for a year-long assignment in Munich, Germany. He immediately sent a telegram to his elder sister, Mihir with whom he shared a close bond.

On hearing the news, his mother, Swarnaprobha, was reminded of her husband sending his brother, Debendra, to Germany for his PhD to escape the rising revolution that had gripped the nation. Now, the same land beckoned her son.

Tathagata was to sail from the Port of Bombay. He packed his suitcase, kit bag, and attaché, and boarded the train. Tathagata's excitement was sharp and bright, yet beneath it, a quiet anxiety stirred. Leaving India, his home, his family, for a whole year, was a daunting prospect.

Upon arriving at Bombay Central Station, he changed trains, intending to spend the night at his colleague Biswajit's place in Ambernath. The Ambernath Ordnance Factory was situated on the outskirts of Bombay. After an hour-long train ride, the train reached Ambernath Terminal. Tathagata stepped forward to the carriage door and spotted Biswajit, who promptly reached for the luggage. Biswajit lived within the ordnance factory campus in Ambernath West. They took a taxi to his bungalow. Upon their arrival, a young servant warmly greeted them and took Tathagata's luggage to the guest room.

Fatigued, Tathagata sat down in a chair while Biswajit poured drinks. They spent the evening chatting and enjoying each other's company. The chef, his *bawarchi*, prepared a delicious meal for them before they turned in for the night.

The next morning, Tathagata discovered a rodent had chewed his brand new attaché case. Biswajit calmly took him to Ambernath East, where much to his relief, Tathagata found an identical replacement. After lunch, the servant loaded Tathagata's luggage into a rental car.

Tathagata sauntered out, cigarette glowing between his fingers. He stifled a smile as he found a battery of joyous manservants gathered to bid him farewell. He gave the head cook all the Indian coins from his wallet to distribute amongst them.

Tathagata and Biswajit both got into the waiting yellow Ambassador taxi and settled in, Tathagata securing his brand-new attaché case between his legs. Upon arriving at the port of Bombay, they were awestruck by the spectacular ocean liner RMS *Strathnaver*, a silver giant looming against the vibrant blue of the harbour. The vessel was one of the five ships which were referred to as "The White Sister" due to their white hull and buff funnels.

The air thrummed with the sound of the ship's powerful engines, and the salty tang of the sea filled Tathagata's nostrils. He felt a thrill, a sense of stepping into a world far removed from the familiar streets of Jabalpur.

Biswajit exclaimed in admiration, "What a magnificent ship!"

Still in a trance, Tathagata responded, "Indeed, very impressive."

He then expressed his gratitude to Biswajit for his warm hospitality, shook hands, and took his leave.

*

Tathagata boarded the magnificent RMS *Strathnaver*, captivated by the vibrant crowd on deck. He navigated through the throng to his cabin. After giving a generous tip to the porter, he felt he was finally in his own space. He slumped into a chair and took out his cigarette tin.

He surveyed his new, well-equipped space. On the notepad atop the table, he spotted the name of his ship: RMS *Strathnaver*. He stowed away his ticket in the drawer. His destination was marked as the seaport of Bremerhaven, 7,677 nautical miles away, with an estimated journey time of twenty to twenty-five days.

The next morning, Tathagata explored the magnificent RMS *Strathnaver*, a Royal Mail ship noting its various decks housing cabins, amenities, and recreational areas like the promenade, children's playground, hospital, dancing space, dining hall, and reading rooms.

Adrift at sea, he spent his mornings on deck, lounging with a book and his Capstan Navy Cut cigarettes. He would be mesmerised by the vast blue ocean and the graceful albatrosses in zig-zagging arcs, a sight he had only read about in books. He felt the gentle ocean breeze ruffle his hair as he rested the novel over his eyes, allowing the words to press against his eyelids. His cigarette smoke wafted away towards the horizon.

He was blissfully unaware of the enraptured gaze of Neela, a fellow passenger.

Neela was filled with melancholy as she gazed at the sunset, which painted the sky with stunning shades of orange and purple, and it was thus that her eyes fell on Tathagata—his sun-kissed, golden skin, and sleek black hair, perfectly framed by his sharp jaw and angular cheekbones. With his legs casually crossed, he seemed to be either reading or simply soaking in the tranquillity of the moment.

Neela was drawn to this young man, who seemed content to spend his time with his books and his cigarettes.

She mused, *one full month at sea without a friend, I think I am going to lose my mind. I need a friend on board.*

Wondering how to approach the stranger, she shuffled closer to him.

Tathagata was engrossed in his own world until he heard the rustle of a sari. Looking up from his book, he noticed an Indian woman smiling shyly. He jumped up and blurted out, "Oh, I'm sorry. Are you looking for a seat?"

Neela smiled and said, "No, no, please be seated. I just thought I'd introduce myself as I am also going to Germany." Neela stopped. "One full month confined to a ship could be a challenge, in fact, boring."

Tathagata, quite taken aback by this sudden intrusion, mumbled, "Yes, of course."

Neela noticed the depth of his eyes and the gentle expression of his voice, and then she introduced herself, "I'm Neela Bhandarkar from Bombay. I'm going to stay in Heidelberg, and you?"

Tathagata gave an appreciative nod. "I'm Tathagata Dasgupta; I am going on a year-long deputation-cum-training programme to Germany." He paused. "I'll be primarily based in Munich."

Neela nodded and replied, "I will also be in Germany for a year. I am pursuing a PhD and will be staying on the Heidelberg University campus."

Tathagata observed that Neela Bhandarkar was a tall, slender, and charming lady.

He asked, "So, you hail from which part of India?"

"I live in Bombay with my parents. I am a Maharashtrian." Neela paused. "I have a sister elder to me who is married, and I have two younger brothers. And you?"

"I am a Bengali, and right now I am posted in Kanpur."

"Pleasure to meet you, Mr Dasgupta. I must go now," she said, hurriedly walking away, her saree pallu fluttering in the breeze.

Tathagata nodded and stared at her retreating figure. Then he smiled. *The lady is quite smart. I wouldn't have been able to approach a stranger here.* An introvert by nature, Tathagata admitted he was pleased to have met a fellow passenger. He leaned on the balustrade, watching the breeze weave its poetry on the water.

Later in the day, Tathagata, in a tailored suit with a tie, a pocket square tucked into his breast pocket, was sipping lemonade in the dining lounge. He noticed a man walking towards him with a pleasant grin. The man was tall and heavy-set with a stubble.

He greeted Tathagata by joining his palms together, saying, "Namaskar," a typical Indian style of greeting.

Tathagata rose from his chair with a curious smile playing on his thin lips; he folded his palms and replied, "Namaskar, are you a Bengali?"

The gentleman nodded and replied in a mixed dialect, "Yes, *ami Bangali.* I am Bijoy Roy, a Bengali; I am from the Ordnance Factory Kanpur and going to Germany for work."

Tathagata was pleased to find a colleague on board the ship. "Do you mind if I join you?" he asked.

"Sure, why not?"

Bijoy Roy sat down; he had recognised his own kind. As they chatted, Tathagata noticed Neela walking in and waved to her. She came over and introduced herself to Bijoy. Gradually, Tathagata, Bijoy, and Neela formed an inseparable bond, fusing together like birds of the same flock. Neela spent a lot of time with Tathagata, discussing politics, her research, and whatever else they found to talk about.

*

On a rain-soaked afternoon, Neela extended her arm, letting the raindrops splash on her fingers. The crisp, clean air carried a delightful aroma, like the smell of a new book. She noticed Tathagata emerge with his faithful cigarette tin and a book, but remained unobtrusive. Neela was enamoured by the tall, attractive, well-attired man whose aristocracy and polished etiquette had bewitched her. The windy day brought a mysterious atmosphere, as if it were blowing away the mind's cobwebs. Tathagata went and settled himself in his favourite deck chair. He took a deep breath and drifted into a peaceful reverie, blowing smoke rings in the cool air. He, too, was gradually drawn to Neela, whom he would watch while feigning sleep on the deck. The sails flapping in the breeze and warm sunshine created a delightful ambicnce.

Neela woke up dreaming of Tathagata and blushed. She was drawn to this smart gentleman, but she also had her fears. *Tathagata is a Bengali,* she would think, *and Bengalis can be rigid when it comes to cross-cultural marriages,* a shadow of doubt crossing her mind.

On their final night at sea, they were seated in the grand dining hall, with silver candelabras burning brightly. Tathagata and Bijoy had ordered beer, as they had learnt from German co-passengers that, in Germany, water was not a common drink. They would have to get used to the alcoholic drink.

That day, the silence in the dining hall was heavy, a tangible thing. It was the silence of unspoken goodbyes, of a shared experience coming to an end. The flickering candlelight cast long shadows, mirroring the uncertainty in their hearts. After supper, they went up on deck, basking in the peaceful stillness of the star-studded sky.

They didn't know how long they had been sitting there. After a while, Neela murmured, "The days of being in motion beneath the sailing clouds are about to end."

"It was just the other day we boarded the ship," Tathagata mumbled.

"Yes, I didn't realise we have been here for about three weeks now," Bijoy muttered dreamily.

They yawned and bid a fond goodnight as they retreated for the night.

*

The trio sat on the edge of their seats, filled with curiosity and excitement as the *Strathnaver* anchored in the port of Bremerhaven. For them, it was like a baby's first encounter with a dog. They felt raw and inexperienced, realising they had only lived half a life, and the other half was still fresh, waiting to be explored. The sun shone brightly, and the cheerful colours of spring were like a pick-me-up.

They stood on the pier, bidding their goodbyes, and then set off with their suitcases. Tathagata went to Munich, Neela to her university campus in Heidelberg, while Bijoy went to Stuttgart. All three entered a strange new world with no idea of what the future held.

In the new country, Tathagata rapidly adjusted to the local culture, the language, and even the unfamiliar weather. He even switched to beer from non-alcoholic drinks. The locals' generosity impressed him.

After a month into his European stay, he had nearly forgotten his uncle Deben until he found his mother's letter. Debendra, a scientist in a Munich's quantum chemistry lab, had married Margaret, a German lady. Eager to meet him and fulfil his mother's wish, Tathagata, with his landlady's help, spent hours combing through *Das Telefonbuch* and knocking on doors every weekend. Quite exasperated, he thought: *This quest is like searching for a needle in a haystack.*

After his demanding search, Tathagata cherished the solace and friendship in their monthly gatherings with Bijoy and Neela, rotating between Munich, Heidelberg, and Stuttgart. Even when Tathagata's work took him to Zurich for a month, he looked forward to their reunions, which felt like a lifeline, offering a sense of home.

During breaks, Neela often visited her aunt in Munich, allowing her and Tathagata more time together. A strong, comforting bond developed between them; Neela felt a deep connection with him. Tathagata was equally drawn to her, feeling a sense of completion. However, he kept his feelings hidden, fearing their bond might not endure beyond their time abroad.

Now, amidst this growing friendship, their shared meals presented a minor difference. They would sit down to eat, but Neela would adhere to her vegetarian dishes, while Tathagata enjoyed non-vegetarian cuisine.

Bijoy would jokingly tell Tathagata, "Dasgupta, don't get too involved with Neela." Then, with a broad grin, "*Shabdhan, o apnake shakahari baniye debe*; be careful, she will turn you into a vegetarian."

Tathagata would smile. "When, and if at all, it happens, we'll see."

19

The Suitcase with the Name Tag

The bungalow, tucked away in Ambernath's Ordnance Factory Estate, hummed with a warm, chaotic energy as Biswajit's mother, Tarala Debi, and his sister, Leena, arrived with her four children—the eldest having already married. A crisp winter sun, low in the sky, painted the porch in a honeyed light, warming the cool stone beneath their feet. The air, sharp and clean, carried the scent of damp earth and the subtle, resinous fragrance of the tall, glistening trees that ringed the property. The rhythmic thump of a football against worn leather echoed across the lawn, punctuated by the high-pitched squeals of boys in playful pursuit. Nearby, the metallic clink of badminton poles being assembled mingled with the rustle of the net as the girls stretched it taut.

Weekends transformed into miniature expeditions. The dusty scent of the jeep's interior, mixed with the sweet, lingering aroma of packed lunches, filled their senses as Biswajit chauffeured his nieces and nephews. One day, it would be Kala Talao; the next, a trek up the rocky, uneven path of Malanggad, warmed by the midday sun. The ancient stones of the Ambreshwar Shiva Temple resonated with a quiet, solemn energy, the air thick with the lingering scent of incense.

With the children enjoying a final afternoon of football before their departure, the house fell unusually quiet. It was during this lull that Biswajit's sister, Leena, while tidying the storeroom, stumbled upon an old attaché case labelled "Mr T. Dasgupta". The surname "Dasgupta" piqued Leena's interest.

Excited, she spoke aloud, imagining possibilities. "Dasgupta! This appears like our caste, the Vaidya clan. I should ask Biswajit about this T. Dasgupta. Reena is now of marriageable age."

Among Bengalis, unions within the same caste were deemed the most favourable. So, when her brother returned, Leena asked, "Biswajit, who is this T. Dasgupta whose attaché is in your storeroom?"

Biswajit said, "Tathagata Dasgupta is my colleague. He is on his way to Germany now. What about him?"

Leena was truly excited and said, "I think I'll look into this Dasgupta family." She realised Tathagata could be a suitable match for Reena, who was in the final year of her master's programme.

*

The taxi, a battered Ambassador, sagged under the weight of brightly wrapped gifts and clay figurines, a testament to two weeks of Ambernath's warmth. Biswajit touched the feet of his mother and sister, Leena in reverence, a *pronam.*

"Come again," he said, peering into the taxi. He waved as the taxi lurched forward, trailing a plume of dust.

Upon returning home, Leena discussed the situation with her husband. Reena's father, Prafullo Ratan Gupta, a railway officer in Assam, returned home from office the next day, quite excited.

"I was talking to Mr Chatterjee today. Remember him, the one from my office?" said Prafullo.

"Yes, the one with the booming laugh," Leena replied. "What about him?"

"He mentioned a colleague, a Mr S.R. Dasgupta," Prafullo continued, his eyebrows raised. "Apparently, he's Tathagata's uncle."

Leena's eyes widened. "Tathagata? Our Tathagata?"

Prafullo smiled. "Leena, he is not *our* Tathagata yet." He took a sniff from his favourite snuff box. "And that's not all. Mr S.R. Dasgupta's wife is your teacher friend, Shakuntala Dasgupta."

"Shakuntala?" Leena echoed, a spark of hope igniting in her voice. "That's incredible! It feels like a sign."

Prafullo agreed, a smile spreading across his face. "Maybe this connection will give us a way to approach the Dasguptas, a way to build a bridge."

Leena clasped her hands together, a sudden surge of optimism filling her. "We need to talk to Biswajit. He'll know how to proceed. This could be exactly what we needed."

*

After a year in Germany, Tathagata returned home with mixed emotions and fond memories, a medley of experiences and insights. He attempted a smiling facade, but beneath it lay a muted, unnamed melancholy. He had formed deep friendships in Germany, which invigorated him, but anxiety about his mother's reaction to Neela weighed heavily on his mind.

Arriving in Mumbai, he immediately boarded a train for Calcutta, where his family joyfully welcomed him, marvelling at the transformation they saw in him. He had arrived like a benevolent Santa, bearing gifts for all. After a brief period of rest, he found himself grappling with a blend of nerves and eagerness, knowing he needed to confide in his sister, Rangadi, about his feelings for Neela.

One day, he braced himself. "Rangadi, I met a girl on my way to Germany," he said, watching his sister's reaction. "I quite like her."

"Okay, I hope she's Bengali," said Mihir.

Tathagata knew he had lost before he began, but tried, knowing his family valued education. In a sheepish tone, he said, "No, she's Maharashtrian, and a PhD scholar."

Despite Mihir's initial shock, Kanu was her favourite brother. She didn't dismiss him but promised to discuss it with their mother.

Swarnaprobha, raised in a different era, struggled to accept a non-Bengali bride from another state. She vehemently protested, "Has Kanu lost his mind after staying in a foreign land?"

The matter ended there.

*

The Guptas were travelling from Pandu, a small port town in Guwahati, Assam, to Calcutta. The breeze caressed Reena's face, tossing her hair, as the train chugged along until it reached Howrah Station.

At a distance, Reena spotted the Howrah bridge. She immediately crossed her fingers and murmured to herself, "I hope this deal with the Dasgupta family doesn't work out."

The printed cotton saree felt like a cage against her skin, each rustle a tiny, mocking applause. Reena stared out the taxi window, the passing scenery blurring into a hazy, unwelcome backdrop to her inner turmoil.

A display mission, she thought, the phrase a bitter taste on her tongue.

It wasn't marriage she objected to, not entirely. It was the process, this ritualistic parading of her virtues as if she were a prize-winning item at an exhibition. A sigh escaped her lips, a wisp of rebellion against the suffocating expectations. She had dreamt of romance, of a whirlwind courtship. The novels she read were filled with passionate declarations and stolen glances, her heart yearning for a connection that transcended the practicalities of arranged unions.

Then, she considered the age difference. Eleven years . . . thirty-two. The number felt heavy and daunting. *Is he already set in his ways? Has his romantic fire long extinguished? Would he see me as a child, a mere extension of his established life?*

Thoughts swirled through Reena's mind as she arrived at Pandu Railway Station, accompanied by her father, Prafullo; her mother, Leena; and her younger sister, Juthika. Settling on a platform bench, she clutched her book like a security blanket, a distraction she'd grabbed from her nightstand. She idly flipped through the pages, which fluttered like pigeon wings in the wind, but her interest quickly waned.

A loud clang of wheels announced the arrival of the rickety train. She boarded and occupied a window seat with the magazine her Baba had bought at the bookstall. She read until her eyes grew heavy, then ate the sandwich and boiled egg she had brought for a snack.

*

Mihir and Basanta, having received a marriage proposal from the Gupta family, were interested in furthering the alliance, as both families belonged to the same Vaidya Brahmin clan. After Tathagata was well rested, his sisters expressed their eagerness to meet a prospective match.

Tathagata dolefully nodded his head.

On a sweltering summer evening, Tathagata, accompanied by his sisters Mihir and Basanta, strolled down the street, feeling the tropical, sticky air. They arrived at the radio shop of Kaya's husband Dhurjuti, where they were warmly greeted. Entering the dingy store, they settled on a threadbare couch. Tathagata struggled to reconcile with the unexpected turn his life had taken. On the one hand, he had Neela and Munich; on the other, an arranged marriage to a stranger.

After pleasantries, Mr Dhurjuti Sen led them inside, up a dimly lit staircase. Approaching a door with a curtain billowing in the breeze, they ducked their heads and entered. Inside was a large four-poster bed and a mismatched sofa set. Tathagata felt a mix of emotions. He sat beside his shy siblings, dressed in a crisp cotton striped shirt, grey pleated baggy pants, and polished black Bata shoes.

Reena and her parents had already arrived at Reena's aunt Kaya Mashi's small two-room apartment on Gariahat Road in south Calcutta. Reena, defiantly dressed in a typical university girl's cotton sari, made no effort to impress.

Tathagata's gaze swept over Reena, taking in her small frame perched on the edge of the four-poster bed. Her feet, in simple sandals, barely touched the floor, and a flicker of amusement, quickly suppressed, crossed his face. *Puppet,* he mused. He noted her dark, intelligent eyes, sharp nose, and cascade of black hair against her fair skin, begrudgingly admitting she was attractive. Yet, a sense of detachment settled over him. *Too small,* his mind whispered, latching onto the detail. It was a flimsy excuse, but a reason to justify his growing unease. Tathagata's mind reeled, contemplating the decade-old age gap. *She's only 21, a decade younger than me!* Deep in thought, searching for excuses to avoid the wedding, Tathagata was jolted by Mihir's nudge, urging him to talk to Reena.

Reluctantly, he asked, "So, what are you studying?"

"A master's, final year, political science and philosophy," Reena replied.

"Ah! Any plans to finish your studies?"

"Yes, I do," Reena said.

Tathagata felt a wave of relief; here was another chance to stall. He found it unbelievable that he was expected to marry someone a foot shorter than himself. On his journey home, he tried to convince his sisters to abandon the match, using her unfinished degree as his main argument.

But Mihir, impressed with Reena, simply replied, "She can always return to Guwahati for her exams."

Desperate, Tathagata played his trump card. "But Rangadi, isn't she too short for my height?"

Mihir stared, confused. "Kanu, you can't dismiss a girl for her height. What's gotten into you?" She continued, "It's the person that matters. She's intelligent, pretty, talented, and well-educated. We're not judging a decorative item; we must respect her and her family."

Tathagata turned cold, his manner stiff. He visualised his dreams fading as he gave a faint, bitter nod.

*

Prafullo and Leena eagerly awaited news from the Dasgupta family, despite Reena's objections to the age gap. Her family, impressed by Tathagata, shared stories of successful marriages with similar age differences, but Reena remained unconvinced, secretly hoping he would decline.

After a week, Mihir called, saying Tathagata needed more time. Reena was relieved; her family, disappointed.

A few months had passed when Tathagata received a letter from his Rangadi persuading him to accept the alliance. Conforming to his upbringing and wanting to please his family, Tathagata finally agreed. Subsequently, Mihir called the Gupta household with the good news. She said they would accept the alliance, but with one condition: "Reena needs to finish her post-graduation."

Prafullo gladly agreed. Reena's parents were overjoyed; they were already impressed by the aristocratic family and rich lineage. Mr Gupta was ecstatic, as Reena was his favourite daughter.

One day, returning from the university, Reena informed her Baba that the support staff strike had indefinitely postponed their exams. Her parents were devastated, while Reena was secretly pleased, hoping to avoid the wedding. But that was not to be, as Prafullo requested Mihir to proceed with the wedding, guaranteeing Reena would take her exams when they were rescheduled.

Reena closed her eyes, the image of her Prince Charming fading, replaced by an unknown face, a face that held the potential for disappointment or unexpected happiness.

Maybe, she thought, a fragile hope reaching out, *maybe he'll surprise me. Maybe he'll see beyond the "display" and find the woman beneath.*

But the "maybe" hung in the air, fragile and uncertain, easily shattered by tradition and the looming, unknown Tathagata.

20

The Lion Gate

On a lazy Sunday afternoon in Jabalpur, the oppressive heat, broken only by the occasional crow's caw, mirrored the heaviness in Tathagata's heart and amplified his solitude. With a sense of weary resignation, he was compelled to pen down his thoughts about his shattered dreams to Neela, a desperate attempt to hold on to the past and seek a connection across the distance that now separated them.

"Dear Neela,

I remember your words, 'I wish we could always sail together,' and I wish that too. It's proving harder than I anticipated to move on from our shared moments, but we will. Life goes on, and we will evolve, holding on to the positive memories. It was a pleasure knowing you. They say 'time heals all wounds,' and I hope that's true. Wishing you a happy future.

Take care,

Tathagata."

Despite his efforts, his sisters' decision was final. It was as if he was the unfortunate hero of a doomed love story. A tiny rodent had sealed his fate by gnawing his attaché case.

Tathagata mused. *I barely know Reena, my intended bride, but her education gives me hope.*

Despite his reservations, a sense of inevitability settled over him; he knew that in the end, he had to resign himself to this path.

However, when Tathagata met Reena a second time to formalise their nuptials, he couldn't deny her intelligence and attractiveness. Further, he was impressed to learn that she was an AIR artist in Guwahati.

The marriage ceremony, a sombre affair on a rain-soaked August evening, felt more like a logical step than an emotional one. Before Tathagata could even begin to know his new bride, duty called him back to work, leaving Reena alone with his family. Thus, both the bride and groom barely had time to get to know each other.

Reena, alone in a new home, found herself drawn to a framed black-and-white photograph. A woman, surrounded by eleven children, radiated an old-fashioned elegance, her gaze warm and loving.

She turned around and looked questioningly at her shashurima.

Swarnaprobha smiled. "*Haen Bouma, dekho bhalo kore*; yes, Bouma, it's me with my children. Your husband, Kanu, is there too. Can you find him?"

Reena, pointing at a young lad, said, "Is this the one?"

Swarnaprobha raised her head and nodded. "*Thik dhorecho*; Bouma, you got it right."

Swarnaprobha, confined to her bed after her husband's death, became Reena's window into the past. In the month following the wedding, Reena listened to tales of a life in East Bengal, a life of aristocratic grandeur now dimmed by age and loss.

Swarnaprobha Debi was once a woman of strength, hailing from a landed aristocratic family, but now, beaten down by old age, was trapped in her bed.

"Bouma, the partition was a devastating blow," Swarnaprobha said, her voice strained. "We lost all your *shashurmoshai*, your father-in-law's, property."

Her solemn dark eyes staring back at Reena. "He was an engineer, but looking at his lifestyle, people thought he was a wealthy landowner." She paused for a fleeting moment. "He had great taste and was a spiritual man."

Reena was totally enthralled.

On some days, Swarnaprobha would talk about her husband's fervour with a faraway look in her eyes: his love of nature, and his passion for his flowers, especially his rose garden and vegetable gardens, and his bucolic farmland.

Reena pondered: *My father-in-law must have been a man of great taste.*

She was captivated, picturing a life of abundance and pride in the fertile lands of East Bengal. Swarnaprobha, fearing her legacy would be lost with her, filled Reena with stories of their family's involvement in the freedom struggle and her husband's philanthropic endeavours. Reena, wide-eyed, was transported to a world she never knew.

One day, Swarnaprobha, her frail hand gesturing with surprising firmness, directed Reena to a grey album on the bookshelf. As Reena carefully lifted the album, its aged paper emitting a faint, musty scent, she sat beside Swarnaprobha and began to flip through the delicate pages. Swarnaprobha watched with a mix of pride and curiosity, her eyes crinkling at the corners. They were photos of Tathagata in Germany and Switzerland, the black-and-white images holding a silent echo of a distant past.

Reena began to sway in a mix of joy and intimidation as she saw photos of her husband in a foreign land, surrounded by smiling German men and women. Swarnaprobha recounted, her voice a soft murmur, the story of the Swiss watches her son Kanu had bought for each of his siblings, her words carrying the subtle click of memory. Saying that, she proudly asserted that Tathagata had inherited his father's refined taste.

Reena recognised that her spouse was a "foreign-returned gentleman", which back then held a status of high regard. She felt a mix of pride and apprehension, wondering if she could meet the expectations of this sophisticated family.

The day Reena visited their family's Kali Temple on Kakulia Road, she heard a fascinating story about her father-in-law's vision. They said he had been travelling in a railway saloon car when he received a divine order to build a *Nat Mandir*, a temple of Goddess Kali. He sketched the temple and built a marble structure with a magnificent Singha Dwarja or Lion Gate. Two lion sculptures perched atop the pillars of the gate. A lion-guarded gate was a symbol of aristocratic grandeur.

Swarnaprobha spoke of the temple's inauguration, where 108 pundits from Bhatpara, a centre of traditional Sanskrit learning, were invited. The Kali idol, crafted from granite, was modelled after the Dakshineshwar Kali Temple in Calcutta, built by a queen, Rani Rashmoni, a woman of lower caste who had risen to royalty.

Reena listened, mesmerised.

*

A few months prior to the partition of the country, with Swarnaprobha barely mobile, the family had faced a difficult choice: either immerse the idol in the Padma River, or risk moving it to India. Tathagata supported *visharjan*, the immersion of the deity in the Padma River, as he feared that in Calcutta their deity might not receive proper honours, as it was the idol of their father's dream and he was no more. However, the vote went in favour of the women in the family.

Transporting a Hindu idol amidst the riots was no easy task. Then began the planning. Under the cover of a new moon night, the brothers, Sudhir and Sushil, along with the family priest, the gardener, and the farmer, dug up the idol, their fear palpable in the eerie silence. They loaded the idol into a specially made crate and onto the waiting van.

The van crept out of the Singha Dwarja and crawled along a lonely, wind-raked road. The wild, gloomy countryside swept ceaselessly by. They reached the Paksey Railway Station, which sat at the crest of a hill, with the railroad tracks built on the Hardinge Bridge threading through the base of the hill. The lantern-lit, picturesque station was glittering and toy-like.

As they all got out of the van, they noticed human shadows standing in silence against the waiting train. The brothers exchanged shocked and fearful glances until one of the boys spoke, "As-salaam Alaikum, sir."

For a brief moment, they were startled when they once more heard the standard salutation of the Muslims, but this time in a hushed unison: "As-salaam Alaikum, sir; Peace be unto you, sir."

Hearts pounding, the brothers glanced through the shadows and identified a few boys. They were students of Ratnaprobha Vidyapitha. They stepped forward and assisted in loading the wooden crate into the train compartment. Maa Kali travelled to Calcutta, accompanied by the family priest.

As the train started to leave, the boys said a heartfelt goodbye to their benefactor, the Dasgupta family, and looked on with tears in their eyes.

The idol, accompanied by the priest, arrived safely in Calcutta. Swarnaprobha told Reena that her eldest son, Abhinandan, had purchased a piece of land and built a modest temple on Kakulia Road, near her maternal home.

After hearing the story, Reena, though not much of a worshipper, muttered, "At least Maa Kali was able to come to a safe haven in Calcutta."

Swarnaprobha had said with a morose face, "Bouma, I could not imagine leaving my deity behind in Paksey after the Partition."

"*Bhabo ki hoto?* Imagine the plight it would have gone through, left unattended in East Pakistan?"

Reena nodded. "Very true, Shashurima; this partition, in a way, killed us alive."

*

Every year, as the date for the magnificent Abhishek Puja at the Kakulia Road Maa Kali temple drew near, a thrill of anticipation would flutter in the chests of the Dasgupta family, a spectacle Reena had come to cherish. The first time she witnessed it, a wave of awe washed over her. The Goddess! Adorned in shimmering gold, her iconic protruding golden tongue seemed to wink with ancient secrets. Reena looked on, breathless.

Maa Kali, the Divine Mother, was revered as the Adi Shakti, or ultimate power. This tradition of Kali Puja, initiated by Rajas in the 18th century, had gradually spread to wealthy landowners in the 19th and then to individual families in the 20th century, becoming an integral part of their annual gatherings. But amidst this vibrant tradition, a small, persistent shadow would always arouse Reena's curiosity. On the very day of the Abhishek ceremony, as joyous hymns filled the air, Reena would invariably spot Tathagata standing near the temple entrance, a solitary figure with a cigarette held between his fingers. A quiet defiance emanated from him, a silent refusal to participate in the jubilant proceedings. When she would tentatively enquire, Tathagata would simply offer a shrug or a dismissive wave, his eyes holding a depth she couldn't quite fathom.

The pieces of the puzzle finally clicked into place one quiet afternoon when Swarnaprobha, her voice laced with a mother's understanding, confided in Reena.

She said, "Bouma, Kanu held a deep reverence for the deity and vehemently opposed any suggestion of transporting her to Calcutta." She paused. "With his fierce protectiveness, he feared that away from their ancestral home, the family might fail to bestow upon the goddess the honours and devotion she so richly deserved." She looked at Reena and said, "*Ekhon bujhte perecho rahossho ta*; Now I hope you understand the mystery behind his actions."

That day Reena understood that Tathagata's quiet vigil by the entrance was his own subtle, poignant form of protest, a silent stand for tradition and respect.

As the years gently unfolded, weaving their tapestry of shared moments and whispered stories, Reena began to truly grasp the weight and beauty of the heritage she had married into. Each anecdote, each unspoken gesture, like Tathagata's silent dissent, painted a vivid picture of a family bound by deep-rooted beliefs and a profound connection to their past. She found herself utterly captivated, drawn into the rich narrative of their lives, her heart swelling with a newfound understanding and a quiet sense of belonging.

Reena would feel a deep admiration for her in-laws and could hardly believe that she belonged to such a wonderful legacy.

21

The Bungalow

After a month-long stay at her in-laws' place, Reena was finally joining her husband. As she stepped out of the first-class carriage with her brother-in-law, Sushil, her gaze immediately landed on a tall figure waiting on the bustling platform. A wave of timidity swept over her, a familiar feeling she hadn't anticipated. It was Tathagata, and seeing him again after so long brought a mix of relief and nervousness.

After a year in Europe, he must have changed so much, she mused, *I just hope I measure up to his new standards.*

While Tathagata was astounded by her innocence and beauty, he also noticed Reena had put on a pair of high heels to match his height. A smile touched his lips. *I hope my bungalow will meet the expectations of my bride,* he mused, a touch of weariness in his thought. *The last month was really hectic.*

As their eyes met, Reena quivered with a mix of fear and excitement at the intensity of his gaze. For a moment, she felt like a young schoolgirl.

"Oh no, Tunu's here too? Of all the people to tag along!" he muttered under his breath.

Tunu was Tathagata's younger brother, Sushil, who had accompanied Reena. Thus, the warm welcome which

Tathagata had planned for his bride vanished in a flash. The carefully chosen words, the gentle hand-holding, a warm hug—he could do none of it, knowing his brother was conservative and wouldn't look at that appreciatively.

Tathagata grunted. *Tunu would probably clear his throat loudly and give us that disapproving frown he reserves for anything remotely affectionate in public. Better not risk the awkwardness.*

Then the three of them walked out of the railway station, where they saw Tathagata had arranged a taxi. Tathagata looked at his brother and decided to sit beside the driver, while Reena happily sat beside her brother-in-law. As they drove past the Cantonment area, one of the main arteries of the town, and entered Khamaria, Reena was captivated by the tree-lined streets of the Ordnance Factory residential area.

When the taxi stopped in front of the cottage, Reena was in awe as she saw the charming bungalow with the slanting roof and a veranda lined with wooden pillars. Two large trees stood in the two corners of the boundary wall of a small but well-manicured lawn.

Lallu, the lanky servant boy, rushed out to open the creaky wooden gate, followed by Marium, a large-built woman, who came out to greet their master's new bride.

Reena looked at Marium and saw a warm, smiling face greeting her. "Namaste," she said. "Welcome to your new home."

Meanwhile, Lallu offloaded the suitcases and carried them in.

Reena was taken in by the elegant décor of the bungalow. The white lace tablecloth on the dining table, paired with the neatly arranged hot pad, table mats, and serviettes, sparked a warm flicker of nostalgia. It reminded her of childhood visits with her mother to the homes of the English ladies in their town, a world of refined manners and delicate beauty. A thrill of pride and exhilaration coursed through her—

this was her home now. She ran a tentative finger over the smooth, starched linen, a small smile playing on her lips.

While Reena stood there, lost in her own thoughts, Sushil was already on a quiet inspection tour of the room. "Tunu," Tathagata said with a smile, using his younger brother's familiar nickname. "You haven't changed a bit." Sushil smiled back, feeling the familiar weight of his older brother's presence, then turned his attention back to the decor.

"Mejda," he exclaimed, "your bungalow is full of furniture that doesn't look very Indian to me."

Tathagata's smile widened. "A good eye, Tunu." He paused before continuing, "I bought the sofa set, the dining table, and those brass planters from a German delegate at the Ordnance Factory. Mr. Leon Werner was returning home and was selling most of the household items he had brought with him from Germany."

Tathagata paused. "The furniture is a bit bulky for this cottage, but the gentleman was selling such good stuff at a throwaway price, I couldn't resist." He smiled. "I know I won't be in this cottage for long. My next promotion will get me a bigger bungalow."

Tunu nodded. "Good decision, Mejda."

Tunu knew that among all his brothers, Mejda had developed the finest tastes, just like their father.

Meanwhile, Reena had strolled into the drawing-room and was admiring the wall-to-wall carpet. Seeing his wife's admiration, Tathagata said, "I bought this carpet from the German gentleman too. But those gorgeous bedside carpets you see, I got from a Kashmiri seller."

Tunu paused, admiring the two beautiful Holland palms that graced the brass planters in opposite corners of the drawing-room.

Reena moved through the house, a quiet sense of unease creeping beneath her excitement. On a sideboard, a gleaming chrome contraption, a coffee percolator she vaguely recognised from magazine illustrations, seemed to hum with an alien energy. Beside it sat a sleek electric kettle and a toaster with flaps on both sides.

Her inner voice, cautious and familiar, whispered a warning: *Best not to touch those. You wouldn't want to cause trouble.* She instinctively kept a respectful distance, her fingers itching with curiosity but held back by a deep-seated unfamiliarity. The bachelors she had known were so disorganized, but here, everything was immaculate. *Tunu will leave in a couple of days,* she thought, *then I'll explore.*

This new life, she sensed, held a certain beauty but was also filled with bewildering complexities she hadn't yet begun to understand.

*

Reena was gradually acclimating to her new life, surprised by how quietly and unobtrusively Tathagata had come into it. She had been raised in a large extended family, often taking on leadership roles among her cousins, organising cultural events and activities. She was a patriotic and idealistic young woman, one who was captivated by the writings of Rabindranath Tagore. His portrayal of female characters inspired her to challenge traditional gender roles and societal expectations.

The woman who had a wide range of hobbies and a flair for writing poetry and short stories was now trying to fit into a new world. She started to change her wardrobe, opting for chiffons and elevated platform sandals. However, despite all that added height, she could barely reach his shoulder.

One month gently slipped by, and Reena was beginning to find a rhythm in her new home, a quiet confidence blooming within her. She found comfort in the routines of domestic life, but her old passions still lingered. One day, while cleaning the bookshelf and arranging the books she had brought with her, she was diverted as she held Rabindranath

Tagore's *Gitanjali* and *Gitabitan*, which her friends had gifted her. She began humming a famous Rabindra Sangeet, the one that had been her last performance aired on All India Radio.

One afternoon, a gentle hum of boredom settled over the bungalow. A quiet impulse, a desire to surprise Tathagata with the comforting aroma of home-cooked chicken curry, began to take hold. It was a dish she had often seen prepared in her mother's kitchen, and she decided to try her hand at it. Little did she know that invisible lines, unspoken rules, governed the very space she was about to enter.

Drawn by the rhythmic thwack of a cleaver against a wooden board and the savory, burgeoning fragrance of onions and spices sautéing in ghee, Reena approached the kitchen door. She pushed it open, a hopeful smile on her lips, ready to help.

The scene that greeted her was anything but welcoming. The cook, a tall, thin man with a sharp nose and a neatly trimmed beard, stood frozen mid-chop. A raw chicken was clutched precariously on the block, and the cleaver slipped from his grasp, clattering loudly onto the stone floor. The chicken fell with a soft, unsettling thud beside it.

Without a single word, the cook stared at her, his face a mask of disbelief. He then turned abruptly, the clatter of his wooden sandals echoing sharply on the kitchen tiles as he strode toward the back door. It slammed shut behind him with a resounding bang.

Reena felt shocked and deeply insulted. *How could he just walk out on the mistress of the house?* she thought. A prickle of shame quickly followed her confusion. *What had she done?* She hadn't expected to cause such a reaction.

Everything in her new house felt foreign. It was only later, through a hushed and embarrassed explanation from another member of the household staff, that Reena understood. The cook, a devout Muslim *khanshama*, considered the kitchen his private domain, a workspace where women, according to his beliefs, did not belong.

That evening, a distraught Reena sat in the drawing room, her eyes red, waiting for Tathagata to return. Her voice trembled as she recounted the cook's abrupt departure. "My innocent attempt to make chicken curry led to him walking out," she explained, her voice thick with emotion. Reena was left to manage the kitchen on her own, a constant reminder of her own limited cooking skills and a longing for the old *khanshama's* expertise. The subsequent days were a struggle, each meal highlighting her inexperience.

22

The Cadbury Book

As Abhinandan, the oldest son, had chosen to remain unmarried, Anu was the first grandchild of the Dasgupta family and a truly cherished infant. Since her birth by C-section, a less common procedure at the time, her mother, Reena, had spent the first six months recuperating at her parents' home. Once Reena felt strong enough to manage the baby, she and Anu moved to her in-laws' residence on Lansdowne Terrace. For three months, Anu was instantly embraced by her paternal aunts, uncles, and her bedridden grandmother, her Thakurma, who doted on her like a precious gift.

When Anu was nine months old, her father, Tathagata, was ready for his wife and daughter to join him in Jabalpur. Reena's own father, P. R. Gupta, a well-regarded official with the Indian Railways during British rule, arranged for his personal aide, Ahal Singh, to escort them. As the train pulled away from the platform, a pang of uncertainty hit Reena. This was her baby's first train ride, and she couldn't help but feel a little anxious about caring for Anu all on her own.

At the Jabalpur Railway Station, Tathagata and his friends were waiting to welcome them. While Reena was excited to be reunited with her husband, she was also worried about managing her new life. Little did she know the delightful surprises that awaited her.

As their car approached the wicker gate of the bungalow, the September blossoms lining the street offered a cheerful welcome. Tathagata had prepared for their arrival with a keen eye for detail. The servant boy, Lallu, and the cocker spaniels, Puppy and Guppy, bounded across the driveway to greet them.

Reena, not confident around dogs, was startled by their enthusiastic greeting and almost dropped Anu. Tathagata immediately instructed the servants to restrain them. At that moment, Marium, the ayah, stepped forward and gently took Anu from Reena, allowing her to relax after the long journey.

The bungalow seemed to sparkle with anticipation for Anu's arrival. The doors and windows were spotless, and the wicker garden chairs on the veranda sported a fresh coat of paint. A pretty tablecloth adorned the oval glass-topped wicker table, making the space feel warm and welcoming for the newest member of the family.

Reena stepped inside, and Tathagata guided her to the room next to their bedroom—a space he had deftly transformed into a nursery for his infant daughter. Mickey Mouse curtains hung at the windows, and nursery rhyme charts decorated the walls. A baby cot sat in one corner, a perambulator tucked away in another. Reena's admiration grew with each new discovery. When she learned he had bought the baby cot at an auction to stay within his budget, she was filled with an even deeper appreciation, thinking, *I truly have a husband with fine taste.*

*

Reena had taught her little girl to address her as 'Mamoni.' She often recalled the elaborate birthday celebrations Tathagata would plan for Anu in Jabalpur. He would take the day off from work, decorating the dining room with balloons and streamers and even creating a whimsical makeshift fireplace using cellophane and an orange bulb. The highlight of each birthday was always the cake.

Reena especially loved to tell the story of Anu's second birthday, which was near Christmas. "You woke up to a Cadbury 'book' beside your pillow, a gift from your Papa," she would say to her. "But you were too young then. You barely had a few squares." Reena would smile at the memory. "Your Papa, who loved chocolates, devoured most of it. I must have gotten a few pieces."

Later, when Anu was older, Reena showed her the empty chocolate box she had preserved as a memento, pointing out how it resembled a book. Reena would then tell her, "Your Papa would often bring home small Cadbury bars from work, a habit that resulted in chocolate stains dotting all your woolen frocks." Anu would always grin and say, "Papa truly spoiled me." The memories of those small moments were a comfort, but the present was just as joyous.

It was Anu's third birthday, and she was happily rocking back and forth on her brand-new rocking horse. She was clad in a stunning blue coat dress that her maternal grandmother, her Didibhai, had knitted. The intricate stitches shone like jewels in the light. Anu's Didibhai and the rest of her maternal family, including her aunt Juthika, had traveled from Calcutta to join the December celebrations.

Despite the chill in the air, a festive spirit warmed everyone. The party began with an elaborate snowman cake, ordered by Tathagata from the Cantonment, complete with a fondant carrot nose and Belgian chocolate eyes. After the children blew out the candles, they dashed around the garden, their faces smeared with cream.

Later, after the parents had taken their children home, they returned to the bungalow for dinner. That evening, Juthika entertained the guests with old melodies played on her Hawaiian guitar. Juthi was one of the many relatives who had travelled from Calcutta for the celebration, and even then, Anu admired her immensely.

Anu's admiration for her talented aunt would grow over the years. When Tathagata was posted in Nagpur, the family often sought respite from the scorching heat by travelling to Poona, where Juthi lived with her husband, Srinjoy Sen, an army major and doctor. It was during these visits that a young Anu, now with her younger sister Jay, would spend time with her aunt's two young daughters, Mitu and Piu. She would fondly recall learning to operate a sewing machine under her patient guidance, and watching as Juthi excelled at machine embroidery and created stunning canvas paintings that garnered considerable attention.

*

Determined to cultivate elegance and poise in his daughter, Tathagata engaged an Anglo-Indian tutor for two-and-a-half-year-old Anu. Miss Mathews instructed her in English nursery rhymes, the alphabet, numbers, and the fundamentals of feminine etiquette.

However, every morning, as Miss Mathews hobbled up the gravel path to the veranda, Anu would promptly hide, not being particularly fond of the strict disciplinarian. Lallu would then have the task of coaxing the reluctant student from her hiding place. Despite her initial resistance to formal lessons, by the age of three, Anu began to show a keen interest in singing, dancing, and drawing.

After Anu's third birthday, Tathagata's long-desired promotion, led the family to a picturesque colonial-style officers' bungalow. The new home, with its vibrant front lawn and large vegetable backyard, was the perfect place for them. Tathagata's German furniture fit perfectly within its spacious rooms. The front garden teemed with the quiet rustling of leaves and the bustling of small creatures. Rabbits frolicked among the bushes, and grapevines with their spiraling tendrils coiled around the wooden pillars of the long, red-roofed veranda. Plucking the mouth-watering clusters became one of Anu's favorite pastimes. Each morning, Mali, the gardener, would cut fresh flowers and place them in metal-engraved vases, which Reena arranged throughout the house.

As the mild days of autumn began to cool, the evenings in Jabalpur held a mysterious charm. After their tea on the lawn, Reena and Tathagata would watch Anu play with her cocker spaniel, Puppy. Their games were illuminated by the soft glow of glow-worms that dotted the grass. Anu, fascinated by these nocturnal creatures, would capture them in a transparent box, only to find them lifeless the next morning.

Anu spent her mornings chasing rabbits and butterflies across the front lawn, her hands often dusty with the powder from butterfly wings or the pollen from flowers. Later in the day, while Reena enjoyed her afternoon siesta, Anu would sneak out to climb her favourite trees, intently observing crows feasting on ripe mangoes and fruit flies buzzing around cracked jackfruit. During the season, the backyard became lush with jamun berries, which Anu loved to collect in her basket, savouring their juicy sweetness as she ran around, her purple-stained hands flapping with delight.

By the time she turned four, she amazed Reena by her attempts to learn knitting. Reena recognised Anu's creative spirit, observing her daughter's enjoyment in clay modelling and the innovative structures she created.

One afternoon, Anu was watching Lallu, the servant boy, when he pointed out a beehive nestled in one of the mango trees. Fascinated, Anu watched from the window, her nose pressed against the glass, as Lallu and Mali climbed the tree with a smoky flame to gently drive away the bees. She observed them carefully removing the honeycomb pieces, straining the rich syrup, and bottling it in large jars. The experience provided her with a glimpse into traditional beekeeping practices in India, sparking a curiosity about nature that would stay with her as she grew older.

While her curiosity about nature was growing, the most cherished part of her day was the morning routine she shared with her father. Each morning, Anu would diligently mimic Tathagata's movements during their special father-daughter exercise ritual.

After dressing for work, Tathagata would step onto the veranda to retrieve his shoes from the rack. Anu, in turn, would swiftly grab his hat and trouser clips, rushing to his side. Tathagata would then roll up his trouser legs, securing them high at the ankles with the clips to prevent them from billowing. Meanwhile, Lallu waited attentively with Tathagata's bicycle, a beautifully restored piece he had acquired as junk from a German gentleman.

With a final touch, Tathagata would place a cigar between his lips, secure his hat under his chin, and ride off. Reena would watch him with a quiet admiration. His departing figure, with his hat and cigar, reminded her of a hero straight out of an old Hollywood film.

23

The Wood Sniffers

Every prosaic afternoon, Reena would dress her three-year-old Anu in frilly frocks and send her to baby Sai's house. Saisri, or Sai, Mrs Mazumdar's ten-month-old, would erupt in delightful giggles when tossed in the air. Anu would watch, a quiet yearning in her eyes, wondering if her own Mamoni would ever hold her with such carefree joy.

But these outings became a subtle torment for Anu. Lallu, her escort, revelled in his temporary authority. As twilight fell, he would spin terrifying tales of *lakarsungas*—men who snatched children into gunny sacks. Anu, her young mind easily captivated, pictured them as shadowy figures, unaware they were just woodcutters. Her heart hammered as she tried to keep pace with Lallu, who cruelly darted ahead, whispering, "Anu baby, *bhago bhago*, lakarsungas are behind us!" His words and pounding sandals amplified her terror.

Terrified of the imagined lakarsungas, Anu would sprint and fall, her cries and scraped knees met with Lallu's mocking laughter. These outings morphed into a cruel, recurring nightmare.

Reena rarely noticed Anu's distress, dismissing it as playtime. When injuries were undeniable, Lallu gave glib excuses: "Baby runs and falls." Reena, often preoccupied, would believe him.

Lallu like a cunning chess player, manipulated Anu, threatening her with "lakarsungas" if she revealed his torment. Sworn to secrecy by fear, three-year-old Anu endured a silent, unending nightmare, while Reena remained blissfully unaware, believing her child was under an artist's care.

Sai's mother, Mrs Mazumdar, an artist, had adorned her daughter's nursery walls with vibrant rhymes. Anu would wander among the life-size Jack and Jill, the twinkling stars, and the woolly black sheep. Reena saw this artistic environment as a sign that her little one was in good hands, a stark contrast to her own often-absent presence, engrossed in books or directing cultural programmes.

Anu longed for the playful attention her mother reserved for dresses and ribbons. A naturally curious and talkative child, Anu would chatter incessantly about her day, desperate for a genuine connection. Reena, however, would listen for a while before turning back to her own world. She was content that Anu could entertain herself by building imaginary worlds, providing Reena the quiet time she needed to finish her novels. This was her me-time.

*

Jabalpur's extreme weather created distinct rituals for Anu's family. In the cool evenings, Anu enjoyed the familiar act of setting up cots outdoors with Marium and Lallu, a stark contrast to the harsh but cozy indoor winters.

The family's routines changed when her father, Tathagata, received an award for the Best Engineer of the Year. He immediately traded his bicycle for a scooter. This new luxury made Sundays special, as they would take trips to the nursery for new treasures. A man of strict principles, Tathagata showed his love through thoughtful gestures: chocolate, elaborate birthday celebrations, and these special scooter rides. He also taught Anu practical lessons, from proper etiquette like scooping soft-boiled eggs to working in his garage.

Anu found a unique bond with her father in that garage, becoming his little assistant. She learned the names and uses of various tools—spanners, screwdrivers, and more—which became as familiar to her as the names of fruits and vegetables. Recognising her aptitude, Tathagata fostered her interest with model-building toys and taught her basic household repairs, seeing a reflection of himself in his daughter. To ensure she had a well-rounded childhood, he also fostered her love for nature, gifting her a gardening set and her own patch of earth for her fourth birthday.

*

Reena was pregnant with Jay. After a recent cold spell had lifted, Tathagata's friend, Uttam, suggested a picnic to Pariyar Tank. The sky was a dynamic mosaic of clouds, hinting at recent rain.

"Uttam, I'm not sure about the scooter tires on these swampy roads," Tathagata said, voicing his concern.

Uttam, ever the adventurer, dismissed his worries with a wave of his hand. "Dasgupta, don't be so cynical. It's just a passing cloud."

Reluctantly, Tathagata agreed. Anu stood securely between her father's legs on the scooter. The trip was uneventful until they neared their destination. Puddles dotted the road, and when a hidden pothole gave way, Tathagata lost control. The scooter careened into a boulder. He instinctively shielded Anu as Uttam was thrown, the sickening snap of his arm echoing through the trees.

A sharp pain shot through Tathagata's jaw, but he straightened the still-purring scooter, blood trickling from his mouth. Holding tightly to Anu, he drove straight for the hospital. Uttam, groaning in pain, clung to his shattered arm behind them. Miraculously, Anu was unharmed, but her father's jaw was broken.

Confined to home for a month, Anu found a strange fascination in watching her Papa drink through a straw.

She even tried it herself, and Reena was pleased when her daughter began to enjoy milk this way. Though Tathagata recovered, the accident left a lasting, unseen impact on his health, which would manifest in a big way and deeply unsettle Anu's teenage years.

24

Clive House and the Seven Tanks

Anu's studies at St. Mary's Convent were put on hold when her mother, Reena, had to travel to Calcutta for a C-section. After the birth, doctors advised Reena to recover at her parents' home, and she couldn't leave little Anu behind.

Months later, when it was finally time for Anu's new baby sister, Jayina, to make her journey home to Khamaria, their father, Tathagata, had a special surprise. He had just purchased a cherished second-hand black Fiat. "I bought the car to bring my princess home," he proudly declared. True to his word, Jayina's first-ever trip was in her father's newly polished car.

Tathagata would proudly drive his little princess around Jabalpur, but this cherished experience was short-lived. His work required another relocation, this time to the Dum Dum Gun and Shell Factory in Calcutta. The family's assigned quarters, a grand mansion once Lord Clive's, were conveniently near his workplace. Reena was delighted by the move, anticipating life in a mid-18th-century heritage building and being close to her parents. Anu, too, was excited. She ran around, watching men paste "Handle With Care" stickers on large crates and boxes and observing her father's careful supervision of the bulky German sofa set.

After a twenty-hour train ride, they finally arrived at Howrah. Reena was awestruck as their taxi pulled into Lord

Clive's House, a rumoured summer residence. Its grandeur was immediately apparent, situated on a hillock with a vast football field and a tree-lined driveway. The first floor, a half of which was allocated to Tathagata, was equally spectacular. The winding wooden steps led to a drawing room as large as a badminton court, with tall French windows and a door that opened to the Gari Baranda, a large sit-out where Anu and her sister played with their cocker spaniel. Tathagata would often park his car under this large porch, and a little away from the mansion was a row of garages with adjoining quarters for the domestic help.

Six-year-old Anu found joy in the aftermath of the Kal Baishakhi, the Nor'wester winds. She would dart around to gather the tamarind pods scattered beneath the trees, cuddling them in her frilly frock before dashing up the spiralling black wooden stairs. Once in the kitchen, she would let them tumble onto the floor. While the cook made pickles, Anu would savour the ripe tamarind.

Their stay in the mansion was brief but it left an indelible mark on Anu, as Tathagata's work soon moved them from Clive House to the Cossipore Gun and Shell Factory. Upon their arrival, they discovered their new home was in the historic Seven Tanks Estate, a beautiful bungalow with a lawn of seasonal flower beds, a majestic peepal tree housing monkeys, and a large backyard with a vegetable garden and fruit trees. Behind it were the outhouses.

As Anu explored the rooms of the bungalow, the beautiful pencil sketches of English men and women in the bathrooms caught her eye. Admiring them, she heard footsteps behind her and turned to see her Papa.

Tathagata, too, was admiring them and said, "Anu, this shows that the previous occupant was an Englishman." He paused. "And he must have been an artist."

Anu happily nodded and said, "Papa, I think we should let them be on the wall. They are very nice."

"Yes, let them be there. They are decorating the bathroom wall so beautifully."

This concept of displaying artwork on the walls of the bathroom made a significant mark on the creative mind of the eight-year-old. It remained with her throughout her mature years. Eventually, she enjoyed decorating bathroom walls with paintings and wall hangings.

The picturesque Seven Tanks Estate, with its employee quarters, also had the legendary sports club, the Cossipore Club. The club, built during the Raj era, had a grand pediment held aloft by seven fluted columns with Corinthian capitals. The club overlooked one of the tanks, creating a magical atmosphere. Anu and Jay would stand in front of the tank, mesmerised by the wavering reflection of the majestic clubhouse, and feel dwarfed by its immense volume.

The Ordnance Factory Club celebrated Christmas with immense enthusiasm, featuring a unique entrance for Santa Claus who would emerge from a tank, his sack miraculously dry and full of presents for the children. The youngsters, of course, never questioned how his sack remained unsullied.

Anu and Jay thrived for three years on the lively campus, enjoying its sports club, tennis courts, and swimming pool. The club offered various indoor games and had separate hours for children and adults. Tathagata reluctantly coached Reena in the pool during adult hours, and both Anu and Jay had their first swimming lessons there.

Anu loved swimming, badminton, and table tennis. Tathagata played lawn tennis, golf, and billiards, while Reena played badminton. The club's bar, open to children until 5 p.m., was a favourite hangout for Anu and Jay. They would sit on barstools, often sharing a 25-paise bottle of Vimto. With 40 paise, they splurged on pineapple juice, and with an extra 10 paise, they'd indulge in *chanachur*.

As the girls grew up, Reena found comfort in the estate's tall perimeter walls and secured entry, a welcome sense of safety.

One day, Tathagata brought home a dilapidated bicycle. When Anu saw the junk, she was intrigued by what her father was up to and asked, "Papa, where did you dig this up?"

Tathagata smiled. "This, my dear Anu, belonged to the ten-year-old son of a German gentleman. But don't judge a book by its cover!"

"Then why did you bring it home?"

"Anu, don't fret. Your Papa is going to do some magic, wait and see."

True to his word, over the next month, Anu would see her Papa bringing in small gadgets and parts from the office and, over the course of a month, transform the junk into a grand, gleaming bike.

"Papa this is truly magical!" Anu exclaimed, her eyes wide with wonder, and for the next few days, she couldn't take her eyes off the magnificent creation. Then she asked, "Papa, can we keep it?"

Tathagata, true to his word, let Anu ride the sparkling refurbished bike before it left their house. Afterward, Anu pestered her father until she received her own red bicycle after her fourth-grade exams. She and Jay would then spin around the estate, with Jay as a pillion rider. Anu was always eager to run errands for her father, especially when it involved getting extra treats from the club canteen. She would sneak in through the back stairs to pick up the snacks of the day.

All was going well for the family, until one day, Tathagata returned home without his black Fiat Bug. His girls were surprised to see their Papa get out of a taxi.

Tathagata, in a serious tone, began, "Girls, our beloved Blacky has been hit by a truck and needs to be taken to the hospital."

Anu and Jay promptly asked with great concern in their voices, "Papa, is our Blacky badly hurt?"

Tathagata nodded, "Yes, our Blacky needs a makeover. Its body is bashed up."

The girls nodded.

A paper game with his daughters chose powder blue for its new colour, and the car returned sparkling. Tathagata's passion for his car was evident as he continued to bring home packages with new parts for it. Handles, bumpers, and wheel plates all arrived in sparkling condition after being dipped in electrolytic solutions.

Every weekend, this obsession intruded on family time. His daughters danced around the garage, begging for an outing, while Reena grumbled that Blue Bug had become her husband's first love, consuming their family time. Tathagata was indeed obsessed with his mechanical tools and his Fiat Bug.

25
Boundaries of Life

After spending five years in Calcutta, in late 1969, Tathagata was transferred to the Ambajhari Defence Project, a ground campus of the Ordnance factory located outside the city limits of Nagpur. The landscape of the wild campus was barren, dotted with scattered shrubs that seemed indifferent to the changing seasons.

Tathagata's passion for driving transformed the long road journey into an adventure. Upon arrival, a peculiar scene greeted the family—donkeys grazed freely in the open fields. As their car honked its way onto the campus, the jack donkeys responded with a chorus of raucous hee-haws. Anu and Jay, initially startled by the unexpected sounds, soon erupted in laughter, a sound so novel it felt preposterous.

Ambajhari was a nascent defence project, its grounds laid out with identical two-storeyed houses. Housing, ranging from Type A to Type D, was allotted based on the personnel's designation. Tathagata found his assigned flat in the officers' colony noticeably smaller than the sprawling, British-built bungalows of his previous postings in Jabalpur and Calcutta. A sense of resignation settled over him as he accepted it; there was no alternative.

Located outside the city's bustle, Ambajhari offered a practical solution for the children's commute to school—a defence project school bus that navigated Nagpur each morning and afternoon. This meant Anu and Jay spent their after-school hours in the company of friends. The bus journeys became an extension of their school day as the vehicle wound through the city, picking up children from various institutes. This often led to the children arriving home quite late.

*

The evening air hung heavy and sweltering as Tathagata drove home, the heat radiating through the steering wheel, stinging his fingers. Inside their flat, Anu and Jay would recognise the familiar groan of the garage shutters rolling down.

A mischievous glint would ignite in their eyes; a quick, surreptitious glance at their untouched homework, and then they would bound down the stairs, eager to greet their father. The car would finally sigh to a halt, the engine clicking off into silence. The heavy thud of the garage door closing echoed in the stillness before Tathagata turned to find Jay, his little whirlwind, already racing towards him; Anu, a smiling shadow, just behind. Jay would tangle herself in his legs, her small hands gripping his trousers. All the way to their flat, the girls would tumble over each other, narrating the highlights of their day to their Papa, their voices a cheerful stream. By the time the trio reached the landing, beads of sweat glistened on Tathagata's honey-coloured forehead.

Tathagata observed with quiet satisfaction how quickly his daughters were settling into their new school. Intent on providing them with a well-rounded education and a broader perspective than their previous convent schools in Calcutta offered, Tathagata had enrolled them in Bishop Cotton School, a co-educational Protestant institution.

This new environment fostered Anu and Jay's confidence through interactions and competitions with boys. Tathagata also approved of the school's emphasis on morals. Anu excelled in extracurriculars; becoming class monitor and later house captain marked the early blossoming of her leadership potential and self-confidence.

Sunday mornings were sacrosanct, dedicated to Tathagata's beloved Fiat, his Blue Baby. Anu, his willing assistant, would prepare the "royal bath" for the car, often peppering her father with arithmetic problems. One Sunday, she noticed a change; instead of his usual Capstan Navy Cut tin, he pulled a cigarette from a packet of Wills.

"Papa," she enquired, "where is your Capstan tin?"

Tathagata grinned, a playful light in his eyes. "I'm on a cigarette diet, so I've downsized my intake."

Anu found his explanation amusing, yet a part of her missed the familiar sight of the tin in his hands. She had, in fact, grown up with a curious fondness for the smoky, herbaceous, woody scent that always accompanied her father. "But Papa," she said, "you look good with the cigarette tin."

Tathagata's face broke into a wide grin, and patting his daughter on the back, he began to narrate the history of the cigarette brand. That day, Anu learned that Capstan was a foreign brand, crafted by the renowned British company W.D. & H.O. Wills in Bristol. She gazed at the packet, a sudden pang of regret that she hadn't kept one of the tins.

As if reading her thoughts, Tathagata said gently, "Yes, Anu, if you had kept one of those tins, many years from now, it could have become a valuable collector's item."

A wave of disappointment washed over Anu. This made her think of other lost treasures. "I can't find the box where I used to keep my coins! I think it got lost during the move."

One day, as Tathagata watched the tendrils of smoke curl from his lit cigarette, he turned to Anu, his voice taking on a thoughtful depth. "Anu, here in Nagpur, you're experiencing the best of both worlds, aren't you? The culture of Bengal blending with the influences of other places."

A flicker of surprise crossed Anu's face, her eyes silently questioning her Papa about what he was leading up to.

Tathagata continued, "Anu, living here in Maharashtra, you and your sister are being raised as *probashi Bangali*—expatriates—because our roots lie in Bengal. My job, you see, takes me across India, wherever there's an ordnance base." He paused, then picked up his cigarette, its glowing tip a tiny firefly in the afternoon light. "But there's a wonderful aspect to this kind of life, Anu. It gives us the chance to learn about and connect with the diverse cultures of India."

Anu nodded, understanding dawning in her eyes. "Papa, my classmates come from all over India. We get along really well, even though we all speak only in English."

"Yes," Tathagata affirmed, "English medium schools often discourage the use of other languages." A sense of quiet satisfaction settled over him; another small lesson imparted.

Conversations about her identity and belonging often led Tathagata to share anecdotes from his own formative years as an engineering student at Jadavpur University. He recounted how their grandfather had bought a car for his elder brother, Barda Abhinandan, and how they had shared a rented flat instead of living in the university hostel. A mischievous smile would play on his lips as he described their weekend escapades, driving friends around town. Whenever these stories unfolded, a certain pride would illuminate his eyes.

Anu would often interject with a playful question. "So, Papa, you behaved like rich kids?" Tathagata would laugh, a hearty sound. "But we were never spoiled, mind you."

In her childhood, Anu found joy in the tangible connection to the world scanning through the *Junior Statesman* and making pen pals across the globe. These early experiences, including navigating different cultures and collecting first-day covers, coins, and stamps from distant lands, forged an unseen bond across the globe. These early fascinations perhaps subtly shaped her future ability to connect with people during her travels abroad. However, it wasn't until much later, during her travels with Mrinal, that the true depth of her father's earlier conversations truly resonated with her.

*

Every evening, as dusk settled, Reena joined Tathagata on the veranda. He would relax in his recliner, a cigarette in hand, feet propped up, while the maid quietly served tea and snacks, before retreating behind the sliding glass door.

As the moonlight bathed the landscape, the couple would sit in comfortable silence, sipping tea and observing the tranquil scene. Reena looked forward to these precious moments of quietude when she would share the happenings of her Ladies Club with her husband, while Tathagata recounted office anecdotes. Their conversation often drifted to nation's political currents. Reena's keen interest in political science sparked engaging discussions.

After a while, she would excuse herself to help her daughters with their homework, leaving Tathagata to immerse himself in his suspense thrillers.

On that fateful day, Tathagata returned from the office in unusually good spirits. Reena found him already settled with his evening tea, an unlit cigarette resting in the ashtray beside him. Suddenly, the sharp ring of the doorbell sliced through the quiet.

"*Sahab, postman aahe*; Sir, it's the postman," the maid announced, her Hindi and Marathi a charming blend.

A ripple of excitement ran through the girls. "Papa, it's the postman with the evening post!" Anu and Jay exclaimed in unison, already racing towards the door, eager for the interruption.

A knot of unease tightened in Tathagata's stomach as he took the telegram from the postman's hand. His fingers trembled slightly as he hesitantly unfolded the crisp paper. The contents struck him with the force of a physical blow. He recoiled, a strangled sound escaping his lips, as the unexpected news of his elder brother seared through him. It was a bolt from the blue.

His eyes momentarily fell on the unread newspaper beside him, the printed words swimming and blurring before his eyes, the familiar script now alien.

The stark words of the wire seemed to leap off the page: "BAROKHOKA PASSED AWAY DUE TO HEART ATTACK AT JAMMU STATION. STOP."

26
The Kashmir Sojourn

Abhinandan, Anu's paternal uncle, possessed a quiet, almost regal presence. Anu cherished her memories of her jethamoni, a man whose introverted nature belied a quiet dignity. Every evening, he would call her to his room, offering two crunchy, berry-like Cadbury Nutties. Sundays were a quiet ritual; Anu would carefully pluck silver strands from his rich dark hair, earning a paisa for every five. This small reward often funded her candy treats. During vacations, the simple act transformed into a shared game for the cousins, a gentle scramble for stray silver amongst the aunts and uncles as they relaxed with their books, each child hoping to earn their daily paisa or two.

He was a chartered accountant for the well-known British firm, Price Waterhouse & Chartered Accountants, in Calcutta. Though his once-dashing physique had softened with time, he appreciated the finer things. A hushed rumor from his youth, a bout with tuberculosis and the lingering social stigma attached to the disease, was often whispered as the reason behind his lifelong bachelorhood.

Each summer, Abhinandan, with his sister Mihir, his Rangadi, and their cousin Bhulu embarked on adventures. The summer of 1972 found them drawn to the allure of Jammu and Kashmir. After a long train journey from Calcutta to Jammu, they hired a taxi, their itinerary encompassing the famed valleys of Kashmir, Gulmarg, Sonmarg, Srinagar, and finally, the ascent to Pahalgam. The high altitude of Pahalgam, 7,200 feet, immediately seemed to weigh on Abhinandan, prompting him to retire to his room upon arrival while Mihir and Bhulu ventured out.

The sheer scale of the mountains, verdant lower slopes giving way to icy peaks, stole Bhulu's breath. He nudged Mihir, a wide grin on his face. "Imagine, Chapa, this very view has graced countless Bollywood films!"

Mihir nodded, equally captivated. "No wonder they call it 'Mini Switzerland'."

Once he was feeling much better the next day, Abhinandan accompanied them to the "Valley of Shepherds", where the Lidder River met the serene Sheshnag Lake, a valley that unfolded before them—a tapestry of dense pine forests against the majestic Himalayas.

The following day, after a seemingly peaceful night, Abhinandan was dressed and waiting in the lobby. Mihir noted with relief that he showed no signs of discomfort, though a certain quietness still clung to him.

She remarked, "Barokhoka looks better today." Bhulu nodded as the porter assisted them with their luggage while they prepared for the journey back. Abhinandan was Barokhoka to the family.

Confined to the back seat with Mihir while Bhulu chatted with the driver, Abhinandan found the winding roads exacerbating his returning unease. He squeezed his eyes shut, each dip and curve of the desolate terrain causing a fresh wave of discomfort. True to his nature, he suffered in silence, loathing any fuss. Mihir, however, was lost in the sensory experience of the journey, the wind whipping through the open windows completely masking her brother's quiet distress.

When they finally arrived at Jammu Tawi Station, a swarm of coolies flocked to the car, shouting, "Babu, do you want a coolie?" Abhinandan frowned, overwhelmed by the sensory assault, while Mihir found the scene almost comical, like fruit flies buzzing around ripe mangoes.

Bhulu spotted a shy young coolie observing the bustling crowd. He quickly negotiated with the boy and returned with a satisfied smile.

As their bags were unloaded, Abhinandan stood beside Rangadi, his face now flushed and his breath shallow from the disembarking chaos.

Bhulu returned, the young coolie trailing, boasting about his ten-rupee negotiation. Mihir, frayed by the station's intensity, sharply interjected, "That's enough, Bhulu. Barokhoka can't handle this chaos any longer."

The young coolie fashioned a cushion from his red *gamcha*. With Bhulu's help balancing suitcases on his head and kit bags on his shoulders, he led the small group through the station.

Slowly, a deathly palour began to creep across Abhinandan's features, a stark warning sign that tragically went unseen as Mihir tried not to lose track of her cousin Bhulu and the coolie.

Abhinandan, his breath coming in shallow gasps, dragged himself.

Mihir looked at Abhinandan and could feel the distress and asked. "Are you all right, Barokhoka?"

Abhinandan his voice strained and hoarse, replied, "Yes, you go ahead, I'll cach up."

Abhinandan, leaning against a pillar, struggled to steady himself, his breathing shallow and rapid. His ingrained stoicism kept his suffering internal. Reaching the carriage, he stretched out for the door handle, but his strength failed him.

Inside, amidst the usual task of arranging their bags, a sudden unease flickered within Mihir. *Where is Barokhoka?*

She turned to the door, and her breath hitched. Abhinandan stood frozen on the platform, his face utterly drained of colour, eerily still, like a wax effigy. Disbelief drained the colour from Mihir's face as she whispered, "Bhulu, Barokhoka is not moving." Passengers continued to stream onto the train, oblivious.

Then, abruptly, the commotion ceased, a hush falling as if someone had lifted the needle from a spinning record. The sharp tug of the emergency chain confirmed it. But it was too late. By the time help arrived, Abhinandan had already succumbed.

There, at Jammu Tawi Station, reaching for the train, he had suffered a fatal heart attack. Abhinandan had faced death in his own quiet way.

27

The Cubicle of Time

As Tathagata and his family settled in Nagpur, the Naxalbari movement was at its peak. It was the early 1970's and radio broadcasts painted a grim picture of their beloved city, leaving it, in Anu's young imagination, a distant war zone. The air in their Nagpur home remained still, a world away from the tremor that had gripped Calcutta, yet the news of the unrest seeped into the Dasgupta family through hushed conversations, newspapers, and the radio.

One afternoon, Anu overheard her parents discussing the latest reports. She tugged at her mother's sari, her voice small. "Mamoni, we are so lucky we don't live in Calcutta. We don't have to face those scary Naxalites that are terrorizing the city."

Initially, Reena would simply nod. But as the movements continued, she began to sense her daughter was developing a negative view of Bengal. Reena decided to tell Anu the tale of Naxalbari, determined to ensure her children would be proud of their birthplace.

Reena tried to brighten the image of her beloved city and its people and said, "Anu, there was a time when people all over India looked to Bengal for new ideas."

"What sort of ideas, Mamoni?"

"Phrases like, 'What Bengal thinks today, the rest of India thinks tomorrow,' which was coined by the social reformer and freedom fighter Gopal Krishna Gokhale, were used with immense pride all over the country."

"Oh really, so Bengalis truly had brains those days."

Reena laughed. "They still do, Anu. It's just that there is a political upheaval in Calcutta now." She carried on, her voice filled with melancholy. "Anu, Calcutta used to be a great city, a source of pride for India. During our childhood days, we would go to Calcutta; it was such a modern and vibrant city. It was the second city after London, all built by the British. Calcutta was our pride."

She paused. "But after the partition in 1947, it went through some bad times as a huge number of people from East Pakistan had crossed the border, and India wasn't ready to handle such a massive influx of refugees. Neither was the government of West Bengal capable of feeding the extra mouths that had come in, nor did they have proper resources to settle them."

Anu was quite intrigued as she listened to her Mamoni.

She suddenly remembered the stories that she had been reading in her English history book about the colonial era, when Calcutta held significant geopolitical importance as India's first metropolitan city, and that the city was originally established by the British East India Company and later governed by the British Crown. She had learnt that Calcutta experienced rapid growth throughout the 19th century, becoming the empire's second-largest city.

All excited, she said, "Mamoni, my history book tells me that Calcutta was modelled after London. Then the expansion gave rise to a distinct cultural blend of European influences and Indian customs."

"Yes, Anu, Calcutta evolved from a colonial port to a bustling metropolis."

"Then why are the Bengalis spoiling and ruining our beautiful city?"

"It is because the homeless refugees who came to West Bengal created groups to fight for their rights. This led to a series of movements."

Anu nodded solemnly and thought of her Rangapishi's stories, and how they had to leave their homes and property in East Bengal.

Reena carried on, "Now, the peasants of Naxalbari revolted and raised their bows and arrows against the feudal landowners. Ever since then, the city has been burning. This defiance had risen because of the enormous discrimination between the landless peasants and the landlords, resulting in the current Naxalite movement which is taking over Calcutta."

Anu nodded her head gravely; it made sense to her. But with the Naxal movement all over the news, Anu's history teacher would joke and say that when she closed her eyes, she would see Bengal like a flickering candle.

So, a scared Anu asked Reena, "Are the Bengalis an aggressive lot?"

Reena calmly reassured her daughter, "Anu, Bengalis hold a significant position in the country's history due to their intelligence, culture, and intellect. They are considered a progressive group of individuals, although they tend to have strong political leanings. Therefore, if provoked, they are known to respond in a forceful manner." She paused and said, "Bengali is also one of the most melodious languages in the world, with a rich literary history rooted in Aryan culture."

Anu smiled smugly.

Then one day, unexpectedly, her history teacher praised her for being Bengali. A warm feeling swept over her, and she felt a surge of pride in hailing from Bengal.

*

The year 1971 crackled with the news of the Bangladesh Liberation War, the radio a constant source of updates.

When the telephone rang, Tathagata answered, his response terse, "Yes, just heard it in the news." He hung up, turning to Reena with a grave expression. "It was Rangadi. They're devastated."

"What news?" Reena asked, a knot forming in her stomach.

"The Hardinge Bridge, Reena. Spanning the Padma River. Heavily bombed."

Shock registered on Reena's face. "What! They even bombed the Hardinge Bridge?"

The news struck the Dasgupta family like a personal blow. Anu often witnessed her father's worried discussions with friends, conversations that stirred half-formed memories of her Thakurda's connection to that very bridge.

A few years prior, Mihir lost her favourite brother. As she recuperated from this loss, news of the Hardinge Bridge bombing hit, making her feel as though all their connections and memories were slipping away. Tathagata, equally devastated, suggested that his favourite sister come stay with them in Nagpur. However, Mihir, preferring to cling to the memories in the house where Abhinandan's presence still lingered, chose not to move.

Then, cutting through the static of the radio, Sheikh Mujibur Rahman's fiery voice resonated, each impassioned word a pulse of desperate yearning for freedom that seemed to amplify the hushed tension in her parents' exchanges. Though the distant upheaval in East Bengal was beyond her full comprehension, Anu felt a strange stirring within, a deep resonance with the struggle. When Rahman's resonant baritone declared, "*Amader dabaye rakhte parba na*! You cannot suppress us!" a shiver traced its way down her spine.

It was more than just a string of words; it was a raw, collective cry for liberation that transcended geographical lines. Along with that, Reena's soft sighs and her wistful recollections of their ancestral home in East Bengal, combined with the familiar comfort of their shared dialect, painted a vivid picture in Anu's mind. It felt as if a cherished part of their family history was fighting for its own birth, a painful yet hopeful emergence of a new nation.

*

Tathagata was reluctantly preparing for the inevitable, knowing his time in Nagpur was drawing to a close, and he had to once again think of packing.

Reena opened the door. Her husband stood there with a bemused expression. She asked, "Why are you home so early?"

Tathagata showed her the transfer order. Reena was overjoyed. "That is good news; we can once again go back to our beloved Calcutta."

Tathagata was less enthusiastic, as organising the move left him feeling exhausted. Hearing the news, Anu was in two minds. Facing the challenges of her teenage years, with boys in her class annoying her, she was open to the idea of change despite the unknowns of moving to a new city.

Lost in thought about the logistics, Tathagata didn't notice Anu standing in the doorway until her small voice broke through his calculations.

"Papa, please, why can't we keep the dining table? Jay and I have such wonderful memories with it. We are really going to miss it."

"Packing these bulky pieces is not easy, Anu. I too like it, but. . ." Tathagata's voice trailed off.

Reena, too, was not pleased with this decision, but as packing was Tathagata's department, she had no say in the matter. The relocation order had put Tathagata in a tough spot; he had to choose between selling off his furniture or going through the rigmarole of packing it into huge crates.

Ultimately, he chose to sell the large German pieces, such as the black lacquered couch, sofa set, glass-topped coffee table with its Gabriola legs, the grand dining table and chairs, and the sideboard. He intended to replace them with lighter cane furniture.

As the clock ticked, Anu was apprehensive, hoping her father would reconsider, especially regarding the dining table, which held too many fond memories. But she knew that her Papa's decision was final in these matters. The day came when the movers silently hauled each item out of their flat.

Anu felt they were all bidding a reluctant goodbye to her. Tears rolled down her face as she imagined them in the homes of strangers.

*

Anurima was in the middle of her high school year when her parents, Tathagata and Reena, decided that the smoothest way for her to adjust to her new school would be to initially stay with Reena's parents in Calcutta. This would give Tathagata the time he needed to pack and finalize their affairs in Nagpur before the family relocated.

During her stay, Anu learned about the progressive beliefs of her maternal grandmother, Leena Gupta. A forward-thinking woman for her time, Leena prioritized her children's education while encouraging their personal interests. Anu would hear stories of her grandma's younger days, and at times, Leena would express her regret at not being able to break free from societal norms to pursue her own education.

In her childhood, while still in Nagpur, Anu would often ask her didibhai, grandmother to write to her in English. Anu noticed the address was always written in neat English handwriting, and she would say, "Didibhai, your English handwriting is so beautiful."

Leena would reply, "I cannot compose a letter in English, Anu. I write to you in Bengali. But whatever little English I learned was from your dadu, your grandfather. I can read a little and write the address only."

Despite her limited resources, Leena had a knack for quality, enjoying the fragrances and soaps her brother brought from Germany. She always dressed impeccably in a starched sari and a hand-embroidered blouse. The memory of her elegant didibhai and her quiet regrets stayed with Anu. During her college days, Anu often borrowed her mohair wool shawls and flaunted them at college events.

PART VI
1975–1984
Calcutta

28

The Mystic City

After his six-year sojourn in Nagpur, Tathagata was once again back in Calcutta, residing within the stunning Seven Tanks Estate on the Ordnance Factory Cossipore Club campus. However, the Naxalite movement had left the city wounded, with much of its old-world charm lost. Nevertheless, the Victorian architecture, a testament to its enduring spirit, stood firm against the turmoil in India's first city.

The clamour of Calcutta pressed in on Anu, its processions, traffic jams and clanging trams a stark contrast to the quieter rhythms of Nagpur. Everything in Calcutta felt unfamiliar to her, from the cacophony of street vendors to the nuances of its culture and the layout of her new school. In Nagpur, she had felt confident, but Calcutta seemed to have upended her sense of normalcy. Once the 'City of Palaces', it now felt more like a city of challenges. Even the way she addressed her mother shifted; 'Ma' replaced the affectionate 'Mamoni', echoing the way her classmates spoke.

Calcutta saw Tathagata enrol Anurima in class nine at the prestigious Methodist school, Calcutta Girls' High School, while Jay began class five at Auxilium Convent.

A sense of not belonging washed over Anu when she started high school. The other girls, she observed, appeared more mature and self-assured. In contrast, she was a petite fifteen-year-old with wavy black hair neatly styled in two plaits. This feeling of inadequacy deepened as she witnessed her peers skipping school for clandestine meetings with boyfriends. Having attended a co-ed school where competition with both genders was the norm, Anu found this intense focus on the opposite sex perplexing. This unfamiliar desire left her feeling inexperienced and vulnerable. Yet, not all her classmates were the same; a few appreciated her straightforward and uncomplicated nature.

Anu had inherited most of her father's features, but her height, at five feet three inches, didn't match his stature. Her complexion was dusky, and a pair of expressive almond-shaped eyes, the colour of a dark, stormy sea, shone beneath her faintly etched brows. Jay, on the other hand, had their mother's lighter skin tone and large eyes. Taller than Anu, she often appeared older.

At school, Anurima's English teacher, Miss Sen, offered consistent encouragement and support. In Calcutta, it was customary for students to address all their female teachers as 'Miss', a tradition Anu quickly adopted. "Anurima," Miss Sen would often say, "you have a lot of potential; simply be yourself, and you will soon find your own path."

The Nagpur days had forged Anu's personality, and she sensed a distinct advantage over her new friends. Her co-educational background meant she never hesitated when interacting with the opposite sex. However, her first real challenge in Calcutta arose from starting school mid-term; all the school bus seats were taken. Initially, her father provided transportation, but eventually, her mother arranged for Ramu, a sweetmeat seller, to escort Anu to school on public transport.

Ramu readily agreed to this arrangement. For him it presented an opportunity, selling his sweets outside Anurima's school offered a chance to earn extra income. Each day, a tin box brimming with sweetmeats rested on his shoulders, his primary motivation for accompanying her.

Anurima was still navigating this new routine when, one sweltering day at the bus stop, buses crammed with waving, shouting people zoomed past. Then, a roaring, overflowing bus lumbered into view.

Stunned, Anu watched as the passengers barely managed to secure a foothold on the footboard, one hand a lifeline gripping the handle. Their other limbs flailed in the air. Like precarious monkeys, they dangled as the bus swished past. Anu was staggered; such a sight was alien to her Nagpur experience. The lopsided weight of the vehicle seemed to defy gravity.

Ramu, the more seasoned traveller, suggested they walk to the next stop. As they began to walk, Anu saw buses moving at a snail's pace, trailing a large procession. Intimidation washed over her as she watched hundreds marching with banners and slogans. Never before had she witnessed a *michil*, a procession. Then, without warning, a shove propelled Anu onto the footboard of a passing bus. She immediately felt the steadying arm of the bus conductor preventing her from falling. Then, as she got inside, she found herself wedged within the sweltering mass of bodies; she felt utterly trapped, and moments later, panic struck. Her school bag, containing her coin purse, was still with Ramu, who she then spotted struggling to keep up with the bus.

Relief flooded Anu as she yelled, "Ramu dada, *amar bag ta diye dao*; Ramu dada, pass me my bag!"

Deftly, Ramu shoved the bag through the window. The bus, however, remained too crowded for him to board.

An abyss of uncertainty opened before Anu as she managed to get off at the correct bus stop, eventually making her way home.

Later that evening, a knock echoed at the door, and before she could answer, Reena was already there.

Then, Ramu Dada's slurring voice reached them, "Hope your daughter made it home. . ." His voice trailed off as he saw Anu.

Seeing Ramu dada, Anu heaved a sigh of relief and asked, "*Ramu dada, eto deri holo je;* Ramu dada, what took you so long?"

The words tumbled out, and she looked at the man in the doorway. An intense, haggard look marked his face, as though a cyclone had just passed. Slobber glistened on his lower lip, and his mouth was set in a strained line.

Ramu responded stiffly, "*Amar paisar bag keu uthiye niyechilo amar pocket theke, tai hat te holo;* My wallet was pickpocketed in the crowd, so I had to walk all the way."

As Anu listened to his story, her gaze fell to his feet, noticing his torn slippers. Quickly, she grabbed the pair of extra Bata Hawaii sandals from the shoe rack and offered them to him. Ramu thanked her, but he refused to take Anu to school after that incident.

*

Anu sensed that she would have to take the bull by the horns if she wanted to survive in this city. She explored different bus routes, sometimes losing her way but always eventually finding the way home. Through these solo journeys, she familiarised herself with the streets and their names.

She also began to absorb Bengali culture; their spontaneous political gatherings, the ubiquitous banners and slogans, the frequent parades, and their rapid responses to events. New Bengali words and expressions entered her vocabulary as she listened to conversations among bus passengers discussing the fish market and the day's prices.

One day, Anu made a very amusing discovery when her classmate asked her whether she was a *ghoti* or a *bangal.* These terms were new to Anu; she had never encountered them in Nagpur, and the question left her utterly bewildered. Her curiosity, however, quickly prompted her to ask Reena.

Reena explained, "In Calcutta, people from East Bengal were referred to as 'Bangal' and showed a preference for 'ilish' or hilsa fish, while those from West Bengal, known as 'Ghotis', favoured 'galda chingri' or lobster."

"Anu," she elaborated, "after the partition of British India, these two social groups began to coexist in West Bengal. Over time, the distinction became more of a playful activity for Bengalis rather than holding significant geographical weight."

Anu would not stop at her discoveries of Calcutta. She would be intrigued by the ubiquitous sweet shops that dotted every corner of the city. "Ma," she would often joke, "Calcutta now looks like a 'city of sweets'." Reena would reply jovially that the Bengalis' deep love for sweets had even permeated their language, lending it a sweet and lush richness.

Now, Anu and Jay lacked knowledge of their mother tongue, Bengali, so Reena took it upon herself to teach them during school breaks. She felt it was vital for her daughters to understand and appreciate Bengali culture, the home of Nobel Laureate Rabindranath Tagore and his profound legacy.

As Anu began reading Bengali novels, she was particularly struck by Tagore's portrayal of women as individuals with their own voices, capable of positively influencing society.

Reena, a proud Bengali, held the state's history in high esteem. Consequently, she educated her daughters about Bengal's notable figures; its Nobel Laureates, scientists, revolutionaries, politicians, cinema directors, superstars, writers, poets, philosophers, musicians, and artists.

"You name it," she would proudly declare, "we have

them all." She also emphasised the significant influence of the Bengal Renaissance, led by Raja Ram Mohan Roy, on Indian society. Anu and Jay would listen intently.

Suddenly Anu asked, "Ma, other than Tagore, do we have any other Nobel Laureate hailing from Calcutta?"

"Yes, of course, scientist C.V. Raman got the Nobel in 1930 while working at the Indian Association for the Cultivation of Science in Calcutta."

"But he is not a Bengali, Ma?"

"That really doesn't matter, as his early life and research everything was based in Calcutta, Anu."

"Okay, if that is so. . ." said Anu, scratching her head.

Reena deeply admired Swami Vivekananda, the Hindu monk who captivated the 1893 Parliament of Religions in Chicago, earning the title "Cyclonic Monk from India". Her accounts of his impact on the West, particularly the US and England, inspired Anu to be courageous and explore the wider world.

Reena's passion for poetry was boundless. She loved reciting Tagore's poems from his anthology *Chaitali* to her daughters. She was especially fond of "Bongo Mata", which concluded with the poignant line: "*Rekhecho Bangali kore manush koroni;* You have kept them restricted to a Bengali identity, not permitting them to explore the greater potential of humanity."

This line often bemused Anu, leading her to ponder, *Was Tagore urging Bengali mothers to grant their children the freedom to explore the world?*

"Tagore," Reena would explain, "being an avid traveller himself, wanted Bengalis to break through their preconceived notions and view the world through a different lens."

She would often encourage her daughters to step outside their comfort zone, saying, "Never be a frog in a well."

Reena's teachings remained with Anu and Jay. So, whenever Reena opened her 'bong coffer' of cultural knowledge, her daughters were always dazzled by the hidden gems of Bengal.

29

The City Speaks

Calcutta unfurled itself before Anurima, a scroll of novel and captivating experiences. She quickly observed a prevalent belief in Bengal that men possessed an inherent intelligence. The educated Bengalis she encountered seemed like living encyclopaedias, their enthusiasm for reading sparking a wide array of interests, from the weighty tomes of classic literature to the abstract realms of philosophy and the tangible world of science.

As she mingled within this community, Anu keenly sensed the profound significance of the word "Bengal," a resonant symbol of their rich cultural heritage, passed down through generations of captivating storytelling. However, she also noticed that this intellectual demographic was markedly opinionated, a trait that initially frustrated her. Adding to her growing list of observations, she perceived a rather languid pace of life.

This slow rhythm was most apparent on her way back from school, when Anu would often find shops shuttered, their owners lost in their afternoon naps. Her own mother, Reena, also enjoyed this customary post-lunch slumber, referred to in Bengal as *bhat ghum*, a customary sleep after a heavy lunch. Over time, Anurima came to view this clan as a unique collective that prized books, engaged passionately in politics and culture, and indulged in their afternoon naps.

Reena would frequently share with her daughters how Bengalis were early adopters of Western education, a direct consequence of Calcutta's pivotal role as the erstwhile British capital. She spoke with reverence of the Bengal Renaissance, a transformative period spearheaded by educated Hindus who steered Indian society towards modernity, boldly challenging entrenched traditions like the rigid caste system, the oppressive practice of dowry, and the horrific ritual of Sati.

"What exactly was this Bengal Renaissance movement, Mamoni?" Anu asked one day, her curiosity piqued by the very sound of it.

"Ah! That movement prompted a significant socio-religious reform, the 'Brahmo Samaj'," Reena explained, her voice taking on a more serious tone. Anu pondered this new information, a fresh perspective on her heritage beginning to take shape.

"So, Ma, the past wasn't always as . . . progressive as things seem now?"

Reena nodded slowly. "Indeed, Anu. The social life of Bengalis then differed quite significantly from European societies; our gatherings mostly centered around vibrant festivals and joyous weddings. But gradually, the *bhadrolok*, the educated Bengali gentleman, began to emerge as a prominent and influential figure."

"The concept of this *bhadrolok* thing sounds interesting, Ma."

"Now, Anu," Reena continued, "this period also ushered in the idea of *adda*. In Bengal, it began as a vital forum for intellectual discussions and spirited brainstorming, mainly held in the convivial atmosphere of clubs or bustling coffee houses, where current ideas and prevailing beliefs were keenly deliberated."

"So back then," Anu enquired, "were women allowed to partake in those so-called *adda*?"

"Anu, during those times, women were not permitted to sit with men freely. We are talking of the 19th century, my girl, a different era altogether. However, a select few educated women, respectfully referred to as *bhadra mahila* or genteel ladies, were occasionally allowed to join these sessions. But yes, by the 20th century, the concept of *adda* blossomed into a common and cherished practice among the general population."

Anu felt a newfound wisdom settle upon her. As she acclimated into her new surroundings, she began to absorb the nuances of the tradition of *adda*, recognising its profound significance in Bengali culture. She noticed how the word rolled off people's tongues, each utterance imbued with a particular warmth and deep fondness. The city, Anu mused, seemed to thrive on these spontaneous get-togethers, a vibrant and intricate tapestry woven into the very fabric of its streets. Even elderly retirees had their own cherished circles, where discussions frequently revolved around lofty idealism and the ever-present, often heated, topic of politics, revealing just how crucial these exchanges were to the very essence of the Bengali way of life.

*

It was Durga Puja, and a palpable wave of excitement surged through the air as Anu, Jay, Sri, Mili, and Doli, a vibrant constellation of cousins adorned in their new festive clothes, gathered at the welcoming home of their aunt, Mihir, and uncle, Basanta. They were all eagerly anticipating their traditional *pandal-hopping* adventure.

Stepping out into the bustling streets, the city vibrated with the deep, rhythmic beats of the *dhak*—drums—and the cheerful melodies of devotional music. The sweet, musky scent of incense mingled enticingly with the tempting, spicy aromas from street food vendors. Each pandal, a temporary yet often elaborately decorated pavilion, showcased unique interpretations of temples and monuments, transforming the city into a vibrant five-day carnival.

The air hummed with the animated chatter and joyful laughter of the throng of people, their faces bright with festive cheer as they moved from one pandal to the next. The rich textures of silk saris, crisp cotton kurtas, and the smooth, cool clay of the meticulously crafted idols added another sensory dimension to the immersive experience. Indeed, the entire city was a veritable feast of sights, sounds, and smells. Bengalis admired the exquisite decorations and the masterful artistry of each unique pandal, with the government of West Bengal even organising a prestigious competition to recognize the most outstanding artwork.

The cousins enjoyed a fun-filled day together, their adventure made easy by Anu's kind uncle, Moni, who had thoughtfully provided a car and a patient driver. They began with a morning of admiring impressive pandals, then caught an afternoon movie show. Afterwards, they savored phuchkas, those small, crispy, tangy street food delights from roadside vendors.

By 6 p.m., the girls were happily satiated. They had capped off their outing with a satisfying meal at a bustling Chinese restaurant and, of course, a sampling of various *mishtis*, the sweets of Bengal, like roshogolla and sandesh. They returned to the comforting familiarity of their aunt's house, where they relaxed in their favourite room while the adults engaged in their own lively socialising. The girls would spend the quiet hours immersed in their respective storybooks.

Mili looked up from her well-worn Mills and Boon novel and offered Anu a warm smile. "I sincerely hope your father doesn't have to move away from Calcutta. You'd miss out on all the incredible excitement of Durga Puja!"

Jay chimed in with a touch of nostalgia, "In Nagpur, we used to have such a swell time during Durga Puja. Maa would direct elaborate Tagore dance dramas, with rehearsals that stretched for a full month! It was like the grand pre-party to the main event! But yes, even I have to admit, Calcutta possesses a truly special energy when it comes to Durga Puja."

Anu nodded in agreement. "Yes, Nagpur was certainly fun and had a homelier feel for me. Here, it feels a bit too formal, somehow."

Jay, ever curious, interrupted, "Can somebody tell me more about the Durga Puja festival itself?"

"It's all about venerating the powerful goddess Durga, celebrating her victory over the demon Mahishasura. They say Maa Durga returns with her children to visit her natal home during this auspicious time." With a slight pause, Sri continued, "This deeply rooted tradition has been observed since the 16th century and gained significant popularity among the aristocrats in the 17th and 18th centuries. Bengalis wholeheartedly participate in the vibrant festivities of the last five days of the major Hindu festival, Navratri."

"It symbolises the triumph of good over evil," Sri said, her tone thoughtful and serious. "Following the grand celebration, on the fifth day, the Goddess makes her return, a departure expressed through her ritual immersion."

Then Mili added with a playful smirk, "And you know, wherever you find even just ten Bengali families clustered together, you can be absolutely certain to find the joyous celebration of the Durga Puja festival, be it in the icy Arctic or in remote Antarctica!" Mili paused. "You should see these ladies dressed up in their traditional silk saris!"

"It has truly blossomed into a worldwide phenomenon now," said Jay, frowning.

Everybody nodded their heads in amused agreement.

Doli suddenly exclaimed, her eyes sparkling with anticipation, "Shopping for fashionable new clothes is undeniably the ultimate highlight of Durga Puja!"

"Absolutely!" Anu wholeheartedly agreed.

Then, a mischievous chuckle escaped her lips as she peered up at the grand portrait of Amalendra, their grandfather, elegantly framed in rich mahogany with delicate gold trimming.

She remarked with a twinkle in her eye, "You know, I've somehow always thought Thakurda's face bore a rather uncanny resemblance to an Easter egg!"

"Anu didi, you truly possess such a wonderfully active imagination!" Mili giggled.

"Once, Thakurma affectionately said my face resembled his, and all I could think was what a pity he was stuck forever in a frame!" Anu added shyly, glancing up at the portrait again. Anu then shifted her gaze upwards and pointed to the smaller frame nestled just above their grandfather's imposing portrait. "Look," she said, "that is our great-grandmother, Ratnaprobha Debi, the very person in whose name Grandpa so generously rebuilt the school."

"Our grandfather was a shining example of true selflessness, something so rarely encountered in the often-self-centred modern world," Doli said gravely, her tone filled with respect.

"Mamoni used to narrate a poignant story about how, after her father finally retired, he had absolutely no money left in his provident fund," Sri added, her voice soft with emotion.

Everybody solemnly nodded their heads in quiet understanding. After a satisfying dinner, they all made their way back to their own homes, the echoes of the festive day lingering in the air.

30

The Melody of Belonging

In Calcutta, Reena steadily rose to a position of prominence within the Women's Welfare Association or WWA, an organization affiliated with the Ordnance Factory. As its dedicated president, she spearheaded the establishment of a nurturing school called Shishu Vihar for the young children residing within the Cossipore Club, Seven Tanks Estate campus. She also initiated the thoughtful creation of an annual WWA souvenir, a cherished collection of articles and heart-warming stories.

With her passion for Tagore's profound works, Reena enthusiastically organised captivating performances at the Cossipore Club auditorium, skillfully directing plays and enchanting ballets that featured the soul-stirring melodies of Tagore songs or Rabindra Sangeet. She always involved her talented daughters, Anurima and Jayina, and the eager children of the Ordnance Factory employees in the graceful Rabindra Nritya Natya, or dance dramas.

Reena had diligently trained her daughters in the intricate art of Bharatnatyam, a classical and highly expressive traditional dance form from Tamil Nadu. Anurima, with her natural elegance and poise, was invariably the lead dancer, while young Jayina participated in group dances, often charmingly dressed as a boy.

Reena also enjoyed coordinating a variety of engaging events, such as the lively *Anandamela*, a vibrant food fair, and meaningful charity events to support various worthy causes. During the challenging wartime period, Reena and the other dedicated members of the WWA could often be seen diligently knitting warm sweaters for the brave soldiers.

Even though both Anurima and Jayina had good singing voices, Reena deliberately emphasized their dancing abilities to the family. At gatherings, Anurima was frequently asked to dance. Feeling awkward without a proper stage, she would politely decline and instead sing one of the Tagore songs she had learned just by listening to her mother.

Reena herself was a good singer, but she lacked the resources to provide her daughters with any formal musical training. Still, Reena's relatives expected Anurima, as the eldest, to be a talented singer, given their mother's history as a respected radio artist. This expectation was rooted in the pervasive Bengali cultural belief that girls should be inherently skilled in Rabindra Sangeet.

Thus, Anu would often find herself reflecting, *Back in Nagpur, my musical talent was genuinely recognised and appreciated by my school.*

In Nagpur, both Anu and Jay were integral members of the school choir, their voices blending harmoniously in hymns and Western songs at various school events. However, upon moving to Calcutta, the overwhelming preference for Tagore songs in social settings made Anu feel like an outsider, overwhelmed by the local preference for Tagore songs.

The once confident girl from Nagpur felt her self-assurance begin to waver. *I need to integrate into this rich local culture*, Anu thought, feeling a strong pull to seek formal training in the intricacies of Rabindra Sangeet.

To her surprise, her new classmates in Calcutta repeatedly asked her to sing Tagore songs during music class. Despite her limited exposure to the extensive repertoire, her friend Juni became a dedicated fan, complimenting Anu's voice and suggesting it was uniquely suited to the genre—a compliment that took Anu completely aback.

Subsequently, Juni suggested a reputable music school that specialized in the nuanced art of Tagore songs. Anu was excited but also hesitant to ask her parents. With encouragement from her classmates, she eventually convinced her parents to consider her request.

Finally gaining admission to the prestigious Rabindra Sangeet music school "Gitabitan" filled Anu with an overwhelming sense of elation and accomplishment. After a year, this joy gave way to a profound anticipation, mixed with a healthy dose of nerves, as she stood nervously in the wings for the highly anticipated Annual Day at the esteemed Rabindra Sadan auditorium.

When her name echoed through the hushed hall, a powerful wave of pure accomplishment washed over Anu as she took her first confident steps forward on the stage. Holding the award in her hands, a quiet thrill coursed through her veins, and she thought with a newfound certainty, "This is it. Now, I can truly sing Rabindra Sangeet with confidence and joy in any gathering."

The award wasn't merely a tangible recognition of her efforts; it was a profound validation of her dedication and a powerful affirmation of her burgeoning talent, marking a significant step on a path she had longingly dreamed of.

Her parents, Tathagata and Reena, watched from the audience with immense pride as she achieved the commendable second position in her batch. Tathagata turned to Reena, a warm smile gracing his lips, and remarked, "Anu has come such a long way in her very first year in Calcutta, hasn't she?" Then, he lowered his voice slightly and added, "Reena, you never really encouraged your girls' singing. You always primarily portrayed them as dancers."

Reena, however, was not particularly pleased with her husband's pointed observation and replied with a hint of defensiveness, "Yes, but these things need to come from within. In Nagpur, the girls hardly had any free time; their schedules were completely packed with school and all the various extra-curricular activities they were exposed to."

Tathagata wisely decided that it was best to remain silent on the matter.

Anu had successfully crossed another significant milestone in her ongoing journey through the vibrant landscape of Bengal, but she could intuitively sense that more challenges and unexpected turns likely lay ahead, so she was covertly bracing herself for whatever might come.

Every day felt a bit like a game of snakes and ladders; one moment she would find herself on top of the world, filled with optimism, and then, seemingly out of nowhere, a new stumbling block would roll in, catching Anu completely off guard. It took Anu a considerable amount of time to truly blend in with the unique rhythm and nuances of Calcuttan life, but eventually, the captivating city began to weave its subtle magic, and she found herself increasingly drawn to its distinct charm.

31

The Shifting Tides

Reena, a contemporary woman, wouldn't compromise on her daughters' education. Haunted by her own post-graduate studies stalled by university strikes, she was determined her girls would achieve their academic aspirations. She drilled into Anu the importance of academics for success, a mantra that echoed through Anu's school years.

While she prioritised academics, Reena also recognised and encouraged her daughters' artistic flair. Anu excelled in ikebana, painting, interior design, and furniture sketching. Jay, meanwhile, showed a natural talent for imaginative face-sketching and was a gifted young poet. Anu, like her father, enjoyed tinkering but also possessed grace, a contrast to her tomboyish enjoyment of playing and competing with boys.

As the girls grew, Tathagata beamed with pride at their blossoming talents. Teenage Anu became a perfectionist, excelling in extracurricular activities like essay-writing, elocution, and debate, earning praise for her varied skills. High school sparked a love for biology, physics, and chemistry, leading to long hours of meticulous lab work. Observing Anu's meticulous frog dissections, Reena often mused that she'd make a great surgeon. Yet, Anu's love for fixing things around the house with tools made her future path unclear, as her interests were so varied—except for mathematics, which was definitely not a favourite.

Jay's intelligence, however, was a different kind. A quick and gifted learner, she was also easily bored, flitting from one activity to the next. During holidays, Reena had to find ways to keep her engaged, like typing or shorthand classes. Books, however, could hold Jay's attention for hours; she would devour them and store the knowledge in her remarkable memory, earning her the nickname "bookworm."

Around the age of seven or eight, Jay sneaked Pearl S. Buck's *Good Earth* from Anu's shelf and devoured it quickly. Later, sitting on her Papa's lap, she proudly narrated the story. Early in life, Reena had instilled a love of books in both her daughters, encouraging them to become members of several libraries in Calcutta.

Jay's innate talent for language blossomed early; by the age of three, she was already composing short English poems. This precocious ability solidified Reena's conviction about her daughter's path, leading her to remark, "As the morning shows the day, childhood shows the man." Thus, when Jay arrived in college, her decision was unwavering, for she pursued her passion and majored in English.

Despite a somewhat unfocused start in the initial two years, she eventually topped the university. Jay always needed a push and encouragement from her Didi, Anu, to get her back on track. Anu was proud of her kid sister's impressive memory, so whenever Jay would falter, Anu was right there beside her.

*

Reena and Tathagata would often note their daughters' contrasting yet complementary strengths. Anu excelled in analysis and logic, while Jay favored theoretical ideas. Their differing talents seemed to perfectly balance one another.

While Anu was drawn to science and planned to pursue it in college, she needed direction on a specific subject. What she didn't expect, however, was her mother's sudden shift in focus from Anu's academics during her high school years. As Anu depended on her mother for these matters, Reena's distraction and her own secret plans, where academics were not the priority, left Anu unsure of what was expected of her. This created a dilemma regarding her academic future.

The unusual life of Calcutta pressed in on Anurima, each day a new hurdle. As she progressed through high school, a deeper unease was brewing at home. Her father, Tathagata, the family's sturdy anchor, was losing his moorings. A tremor flickered in his hands, the once-decisive movements now slow and uncertain; his health began to deteriorate, and his motor skills were declining, making it hazardous for him to drive, even the simple act of turning the ignition key a fraught affair. He was diagnosed with Parkinson's disease and advised to retire early from his job.

This news weighed heavy on Reena. She was in a dilemma as to how she would manage two young daughters and a retired husband. The insistent voices of her parents and cousins, sharp and well-meaning, chipped away at her resolve, their reminders of her 'duty' to secure Anu's future echoing in her ears.

Though the idea initially felt like a betrayal of Reena's own aspirations for Anu, the image of the Sunday newspaper, its thin pages rustling with the promise of suitable matches, attracted Reena. While her family meant well, each scanned column added another layer to Reena's growing anxiety, each listed detail a potential turning point in Anu's young life.

32

The Marriage Bazaar

The most challenging part of Anurima's journey began when, at family gatherings, she started noticing the subtle but unmistakable weight of their gazes on her darker complexion. Her maternal aunts and uncles would exchange worried glances, their hushed tones carrying anxieties about Anu's marriage prospects. Their comments chipped away at her self-esteem and fostered a growing sense of being an ugly duckling, a stark contrast to the acceptance she had felt in Nagpur.

Anurima keenly felt the disparity in attention, compared to her lighter-skinned female second cousins. This observation was compounded by the senior women in her maternal family, who seemed to value fair skin above education, a bias that deeply resonated with Anu's growing insecurity. *Why is it suddenly different here?* she wondered. *Am I not good enough because of my skin?*

The constant compliments showered upon her cousins, in stark contrast to the subtle disregard she felt, highlighted the unspoken hierarchy where a fair face appeared to outweigh intellectual merit. *So, being fair is all that matters? What about what's inside?* thought Anu.

At times, an older relative might offer a fleeting compliment on Anu's long, dark, wavy hair, but their words never lingered on her essay prizes or her other aptitudes, leaving Anu with the deflating feeling that her hair was her sole offering in this strange new world. *They don't see anything else about me. Just my hair. My own people are so strange,* mused Anu.

A cold surprise washed over her when she discerned that her own mother, the champion of education, seemed to have unwittingly joined the "fair skin" bandwagon. In those moments, Anurima felt a profound sense of inadequacy, the unwelcome label of the ugly duckling settling upon her. *Even Ma? She believes this too.* The bitter irony was not lost on her; given that Reena's own siblings were a diverse palette of warm and light skin and an undeniably educated group. It was a bitter pill Anu swallowed in silence.

These were the times when Anu would ruminate, *In Nagpur, I was in awe of my classmate, Kasturi, who was a stunning dark beauty with such poise and charm.*

So back then in Nagpur, Anurima Dasgupta was a vibrant girl with a glowing complexion, at ease with her brown skin. Alongside, in Calcutta her maternal first cousins Binu and Kinu appreciated Anu's carefree, smart, and energetic personality. In their presence, Anu felt she was appreciated for more than just her complexion. Then there was Bapi, the son of Anu's paternal aunt Sarojubala's eldest son Jhulan. He was technically her nephew, but they were close in age and great childhood buddies. They were all birds of the same feather who flocked together.

Anurima's paternal family was extremely supportive and valued intelligence over physical appearance. Mihir and Basanta made sure Anu was respected as the eldest cousin in the Dasgupta family. One day, Basanta surprised Anu by announcing that she would be given the family's prized heirloom necklace, a decision that was supported by all her cousins. This act deeply moved Anu and reinforced the significance of her paternal family in providing emotional support and boosting her self-esteem. Thus, Anu, at times, would be perplexed by the conflicting beauty standards of her maternal and paternal kith and kin.

As Anu geared up for her high school board exams, Reena, facing family pressure, busied herself with finding a potential husband for her elder one. She would browse the matrimonial columns in the newspaper to identify suitable suitors, using a standard template to send letters, merely changing the names before mailing them.

Consequently, Anu struggled to juggle things: her focus on her exams, college entrance, medical entrance preparations, and the marriage market's emphasis on her looks over her intellect. As the eldest, she bore the brunt of these conflicting pressures.

During meetings with potential suitors, their gazes lingering over her demeanour, they would ask Anu to sing or answer trivial questions about her hobbies, making her feel like a mannequin on display under their scrutinising eyes. Secretly she would muse, *How contradictory it is that the Bengalis, known for their culture, literature, art, and progressive views, still seem to hold such superficial values.*

Despite navigating these wildly different pressures, Anu excelled in her exams, qualifying her to apply to Calcutta's top three colleges, where first-division marks were the entry ticket. However, the night before her entrance exam for her top choice, Presidency College, her father fell ill, preventing her from taking the exam. Though disappointed, she accepted this twist of fate. Her spirits lifted when she was accepted without a hitch into her second choice, Bethune College, Calcutta's historic first women's college.

To Anu's amazement, her first year of college went without much interruption. However, her relatives were quietly persistent, constantly emphasising that marrying young would be advantageous for Anu due to her complexion being considered less desirable in the marriage market, a concern amplified by her father's declining health.

In her second year, the pressure to find a suitable match intensified, with her mother Reena painting an idealistic picture of married life. This would initially spark a flicker of excitement in Anu. She would muse, *Perhaps this proposal will be the one.* She would dream a little: about companionship, a new home, a different chapter in her life.

However, these nascent hopes were often brutally crushed when proposals fell through. The reasons could be anything—a mismatch in family expectations, her complexion, or astrological incompatibilities. The abrupt shift from hopeful anticipation to crushing disappointment left Anu emotionally drained.

But ironically, each failed proposal made her confidence soar higher. But the most jarring aspect of Anu's experience was the constant flip-flopping of priorities by her mother. One moment, Reena would be actively pushing Anu towards marriage, emphasising its importance and painting a rosy picture. The next, upon a proposal falling through, she would abruptly pivot, urging Anu to focus solely on her studies. This inconsistency created a significant emotional and mental strain on Anu. It was as if her life was a pendulum swinging between two vastly different expectations. It made it difficult for her to fully invest in either her studies or the prospect of marriage, leaving her feeling perpetually off-balance.

But interestingly, the repeated experiences of rejection, while initially painful, had an unexpected, positive outcome. Anu started to detach emotionally from the process, recognising its inherent flaws and the limited control she had over it. This detachment, coupled with her continued focus on her studies and her own intellectual capabilities, gradually seemed to empower her, fostering a sense of self-reliance and a stronger belief in her own potential beyond the confines of marriage.

Now in college, Anu began picking up new slang words like "Atel" or "Atellectual", which she soon realised was a popular satirical term for pseudo-intellectualism among the students.

Then on her twentieth birthday, Anu confronted Reena. She said, "Ma, why would boys be interested in girls with limited education like myself?"

"Well, some boys like young girls."

"But Ma, education gives women the ability to navigate life."

Reena hesitated, but knew Anu was right. She mused, *In our society, if girls are less educated, men can dominate their wives.* Then a thought crossed her mind, and she realised how times were changing and how girls should be financially independent. A moment of quiet acknowledgment passed as she finally conceded Anu's point.

For the next few months, marriage was a taboo topic. Yet, the arrival of each new proposal would trigger Reena's old stance, peppered with stories of her cousins who had married without degrees and completed their education later. For Anu, it felt like an uphill battle against Reena's entrenched perspective.

The progressive ideals Anu so admired in her intelligent mother seemed to vanish whenever marriage proposals arose, leaving Anu in a state of bewildered disbelief. She couldn't reconcile Reena's current views with the stories of Thakurda, who, decades earlier, had championed his daughters' education, enabling them to become teachers. *Why this stark contrast for me, knowing our family's history of female enlightenment?* This question would loop in Anu's mind, a constant reminder of the chasm between the mother she knew and the one navigating her marriage prospects.

Tathagata, despite his physical limitations, would remain neutral, but he made efforts to keep Anu focused on her studies. He secretly hoped that the marriage plans would not succeed. He would say, "Anu, marriage is not child's play. It takes time; let your mother handle it." His words had a calming effect on Anu, as she knew she could bank on her Papa for this.

Anu had read about the traditional practice in the nineteenth century where Indian parents would marry off their daughters as soon as they reached puberty but thought such practices were fading away. Hence, Anu was surprised that her own family still held on to these conservative customs in the late 20th century. However, she took comfort in the fact that her dusky complexion reduced her chances of getting hooked at such an early age.

But there were times when she would cross the "dusky barrier", and Reena would get a positive response from a suitor. Anu promptly resorted to tactics like pretending to have a squint or telling a white lie. To the utter dismay of Reena and her maternal aunts, these strategies would salvage her. Anu was gradually learning how to outsmart her overly concerned maternal relatives.

33

A Dense Tangle of Choices

As her family became preoccupied with finding her a husband, Anu's academic passions were sidelined. She entered college in a daze, initially awestruck to be at India's oldest and most prestigious women's college, a place that promised an escape from early marriage. Yet, her awe quickly turned to disappointment when she discovered her chosen major was all about rote memorization, a skill she had never enjoyed. Though she felt trapped and her true interests lay dormant, she clung to the small comfort of having avoided the fate her relatives had planned for her.

While on the home front, Reena continued to organise Tagore dance ballets, with Anu often taking the lead. During a college break, Anu proudly shared photographs from a Tagore dance drama in which she had performed, staged at their Cossipore Club Auditorium.

In an instant, her friend Sudeshna playfully swiped a striking solo shot, and it quickly spread through the classroom.

"Look at those eyes," someone murmured, the photo passing from hand to hand. "Any guy would fall for them." A flush crept up Anu's neck. "That's enough," she mumbled, trying to take the picture back. "You're embarrassing me!"

Jayanti leaned closer. "They're so expressive, Anu. Haven't you ever heard that before?"

Anu frowned, a flicker of a forgotten memory surfacing. "Not really . . . you're all making a big deal out of nothing."

She vaguely recalled the senior girls in school, their excited chatter as they adorned her for a dance, their compliments about her eyes. But she'd been too shy to truly register their words. Then, a less pleasant memory surfaced: the giggling girls in the physics lab, their cruel jokes about her cornea.

"My relatives," she murmured quietly, looking away, "only ever mention my hair. Everything else . . . it's just behind my brown skin."

From behind, Sumana's voice, usually gentle, held a sharper edge. "It speaks volumes about their limited perspective, Anurima. Some people are so consumed by their own reflections that they are blind to the light in others."

Juni snorted. "Constipated outlook, indeed!" Then, with a mischievous glint in her eyes, she nudged Anu. "Whoever does your wedding makeup is going to have a field day with those peepers!"

"Juni, stop it!" Anu's face burned. "You're all taking this too far." She waved a dismissive hand. "Honestly, it's just a feature of my face. Nothing special."

Despite the awkward encounter, a subtle shift began within Anu. Perhaps it was the unexpected attention, or the realisation that she possessed a quality others admired. Anu had by then graduated to her third year. Gradually, she found herself drawn into the intellectual currents of college life. The debates sparked in her mind, the complex theories intrigued her, and for the first time, her college major which initially was rote learning felt like an exploration rather than a chore.

When the college centenary approached, Anu, to her own surprise, eagerly volunteered, her organisational skills and artistic talents blossoming as she choreographed dances and even found her voice as the lead singer in the Tagore dance drama.

*

When Professor Madhuri Chatterjee requested Anu's presence in her office, where the members of the centenary committee were gathered, a sense of significance settled over Anu. The committee's proposal, to have a student represent their college in All India Radio's "Yuva Vani," resonated with a mixture of excitement and trepidation.

Selected among a handful of students, the immediate task was daunting. It involved articulating a scientific concept in a written paragraph and then voicing it aloud within an hour.

Overwhelmed yet strangely exhilarated by her selection, Anu felt a knot of worry tighten in her stomach. *Could I truly embody the spirit of my college on such a platform?*

To her astonishment, Anu's elocution and debating skills in school came in handy. This marked the beginning of a remarkable journey, as she continued to engage with audiences on AIR with powerful talks and insightful debates throughout her academic career and beyond.

A new chapter had begun, and with her growing confidence and powerful voice, Bengal was taking notice. The expectations that once felt like a burden now fuelled her, and a sense of optimism bloomed in the bustling cityscape. A quiet confidence settled upon her. She carried herself with a newfound grace, her conversations deepened, and a subtle elegance marked her style.

Immersed in the vibrant intellectual atmosphere of Calcutta, she began to truly understand the Bengali reverence for books—a cultural cornerstone, a shared obsession that transcended material wealth. She observed with fascination the almost sacred act of book hoarding, a testament to the value placed on knowledge within this culture.

Anu's initial venture into the affectionately named "Boi Para" or College Street revealed a true booklover's haven, a sensory experience marked by the buzz of bartering, the rustle of pages, and the mingled scents of old books and street food. Navigating the bustling, narrow lanes, a literary maze of towering stacks, Anu observed Bengalis with gleaming intellectual curiosity searching for elusive first editions, those literary treasures.

Exploring these tightly packed streets with her friends further immersed Anu in this world, where stories seemed to whisper from every corner. Then, one day, she noticed a group of young men engaged in animated conversation on a *rowak* outside a nearby, age-worn house. The familiar scent of chai and cigarette smoke drifted towards her, and she smiled. *This is it*, she thought, *the quintessential Bengali adda.* It wasn't just about the chai and the cigarettes; it was the camaraderie, the easy flow of conversation, and sometimes, the fervent intensity of their discussions.

Anu smiled, recalling her childhood in Calcutta and those distinctive outdoor cemented platforms, the rowaks, extending from the buildings, tucked under a window or beside the entrance stairs. More than just places to sit, she thought, they were vital communal spaces, a lifeline of connection and debate.

Another day, as she was walking with Urmila and Shanti through the narrow lanes of Boi Para, a sudden curiosity pulled Anu towards a building with a modest sign: Indian Coffee House. She remembered snippets of conversations, her friends referring to it as a haven for Calcutta's literati. Stepping inside, Anu's gaze swept across the room, her eyes wide with a searching intensity, as if trying to conjure the ghosts of conversations past.

"Anu," Shanti said, a knowing smile playing on her lips, "we practically grew up on stories about this place."

Anu's breath hitched. "They say this was the very heart of the literary and cultural movements, wasn't it? More like an intellectual battleground," Anu added, a spark of excitement in her eyes.

As Shanti nodded, the rich, roasted aroma of freshly brewed coffee filled the air, a comforting and stimulating scent that seemed woven into the very fabric of the place. The gentle clatter of cups and saucers, punctuated by the low hum of countless conversations, a vibrant tapestry of voices rising and falling, created a unique ambience. It wasn't a boisterous noise, but rather a continuous murmur of intellectual exchange and friendly banter.

"Shanti," Anu said thoughtfully, her gaze drifting around the room, "I am aware, once upon a time, this place had renowned patrons . . . artists, singers, film directors, writers. All the illustrious people of Bengal."

"Yes," Shanti chimed in, her voice a little hushed with reverence, "they say Rabindranath Tagore, national leader Netaji Subhash Chandra Bose, filmmaker Satyajit Ray, actor and director Aparna Sen during her Presidency college days, and noted authors, poets, singers, have all had their adda sessions here, from where great ideas sprung up."

Urmila, having ordered their coffee and shingara, a savoury snack, continued in a near whisper, "Since the pre-independence days, this coffee house was a favourite hangout for freedom fighters and revolutionaries, serving as a hot spot for radical discussions over contemporary topics of that era." She took a breath and then looked at Anu, a smile playing on her lips. "So you are in exalted company, Miss Anurima Dasgupta."

A twinkle lit up Anu's eyes as she absorbed the atmosphere, the weight of history palpable in the air.

"Hey," she said softly, "this place reminds me of the Café de Flore. . ."

"Where is that? Sounds French," chirped Shanti.

"Yes, I have read it's one of the oldest coffee houses in Paris, once famous for its high-profile writer and philosopher clientele," beamed Anu from ear to ear.

As her eyes moved around the room, Anu felt shivers run down her spine. She tried imagining the great figures sitting there amidst the chatting crowd, suddenly feeling as though she was rubbing shoulders with the literary giants of that bygone era.

Then the girls explained that the coffee house had been Albert Hall before being renamed Indian Coffee House after independence. Anu could see that structurally it still retained its old-world charm with high ceilings and modest tables and chairs.

Later, while walking with Shanti through the bustling streets, Anu commented, "You know, I get this feeling about the people here. It's like they have multiple heads on their shoulders, all trying to talk at once."

Urmila, raised an eyebrow. "Multiple heads?"

Anu elaborated, "Yes! One minute they're intensely focused on their work, the next they're swept away by the beauty of a song or the emotion of a family gathering. It's like each person has so many strong passions and interests pulling them in different directions."

"Yes, good observation, Anurima," smiled Shanti.

Anu reflected on the many ways Bengalis blurred the lines between personal and professional life. She recalled her normally stern cytogenetics professor interrupting a complex explanation to passionately describe Durga Puja decorations and invite students to his family's pandal. This sudden, passionate shift in his demeanour highlighted how deeply their personal sentiments were integrated into every part of their lives.

Anu continued to be surprised by the cultural nuances she observed. She noticed that middle-class Bengalis often prioritized their emotions in areas like food, romance, and finance over pure business pursuits, favouring nine-to-five jobs and evening adda sessions on their favourite benches, or rowaks. One crisp afternoon, while discussing the Krebs cycle with a classmate outside a scholar's unassuming home, she overheard his mother's concerned voice drift through the window, saying, "Don't stay out too long, you'll catch a cold!" The scholar, a young man deeply immersed in molecular biology, actually blushed and assured his mother he was fine. Anu exchanged an amused glance with her friend.

Later, while recounting the incident to her mother, Reena chuckled. *"Thanda lege jabe,"* or "you will catch a cold," is practically a Bengali mantra. Bengalis instil the fear of a chill from the cradle. With a broad smile, she added, "Bengali mothers like to keep their boys close." This observation rang true as the onset of winter arrived and Anu would be amused to see Bengali men wearing their monkey caps, or *mankicaps*, all through the month of December. Reena would grin and say, "Once the temperature dips to twenty-five degrees Celsius, Bengali mothers immediately bundle their boys up with caps and scarves." Anu would laugh. "Bong moms can be really silly."

Anu's exploration of Bengali culture continued to yield surprises. One day she met a little girl named Buri. Anu frowned, as *buri* in Bengali meant "old lady," and this was a little girl. To her utter amazement, she found that Bengalis gave funny, affectionate pet names to their little ones. The newborn, besides a formal name, was given a pet name, or *daak naam*, full of love and originality. This naming process would at times include calling a young girl, lovingly, Buri; a boy Bhuto, meaning "ghost"; or, if fate would have it, the son of the house might share a name with their neighbours' four-legged family member, their beloved pooch.

*

When Anu graduated, a wave of disbelief and triumph washed over her. Professor Tapati had just announced her name as the university topper in practical exams. Rote learning was never her strength, but her hands-on work—the tangible application of knowledge—had proven her capabilities. A quiet sense of gratitude settled within her, a feeling of being ready to step beyond the familiar college walls. Looking back, she saw how every experience had shaped her, adding layers of wisdom and maturity.

Her success wasn't just academic. Anu had also managed to outwit the persistent marriage proposals that had come her way, and she could feel that both her aunts, Rangapishi and Sejopishi, were her silent supporters. They cheered her on to keep studying and would laugh when Anu shared her creative tactics for avoiding suitors.

"Anu, what do you do to scare them off?" Rangapishi would ask with a warm smile.

Anu would grin. "I'd sport a squint, or ask if they own a car and then tell them I love driving, makes them take a step back."

"Really!" Rangapishi would say, looking stunned before a proud smile spread across her face. "Anu, I'm so proud of you!"

Sejopishi, listening quietly, would then say with a playful grin, "Anu, you're too smart for those boys!"

34

The Proposal

The challenges of her undergraduate years had forged a new resilience in Anu. As she began her post-graduate studies at Ballygunge Science College, she felt a quiet shift in power, a burgeoning confidence rooted in a growing sense of self-worth. She was evolving into an assertive young woman, and this transformation was accelerated by her fiercely feminist friends—Sumana, Debi, Jayati, and Runa. Surrounded by their conviction in the power of women's education and inner strength, Anu's views on a woman's role were solidified through spirited debates in the college canteen.

It was also common then for students to marry their contemporaries, so Anu and her friends had plenty of suitors vying for their attention. Anu and Sumana, in particular, formed a strong bond through their shared academics and the challenges of fending off persistent marriage proposals.

That year, the Science College reunion was just around the corner, and the ongoing batch traditionally organised the event. Anu and Sumana, sharing a passion for music, were excited to perform as lead singers in a staged Tagore dance drama. Much to Anu's surprise, her songs echoed in the corridors of Science College long after the event had concluded. She couldn't believe her ears; it was a moment of pure magic.

Following the reunion, the annual departmental picnic was a much-anticipated event, bringing together post-graduate students and department scholars. There, a senior, clearly impressed by Anu's performance, asked her to sing.

"Sing, really?" Anu exclaimed, taken aback.

"Anurima, no excuses please," the senior replied with a smile. "We all heard you at the reunion."

Anu blushed. "Okay, but just one Rabindra Sangeet."

"We'll see about that! Go on, Anu!" everyone chimed in.

Anu, who had by then quite mastered Tagore's songs, performed several of them, her lively personality and beautiful voice quickly making her a popular figure in the department. Immersed in the captivating intricacies of genetics and biochemistry, she found an intellectual haven within her studies. Her engagement extended far beyond mere absorption of information; she was now an active and assertive voice in every discussion.

This intellectual sanctuary offered a stark contrast to the persistent societal pressure of marriage, a shadow that often loomed over her academic aspirations. This pressure solidified into a tangible proposition in her third semester, when Reena's cousin, Moni Mashi, a well-intentioned but traditional aunt, envisioned a potential alliance for her.

One day, as Anu returned from college, Reena nervously broached the topic. "There's this young man, Mrinal Sensharma, who after his training in the Sunderbans is passing through Calcutta on his way to Pune. Your aunt Monimashi wants you to meet him tomorrow," Reena said.

Anu learned he was a top student who had graduated from the prestigious Indian Institute of Technology, Kharagpur. Despite not having marriage on her mind, she thought to herself, *No harm in meeting him. An IIT topper, now that's impressive.* She warned Reena that she wouldn't look her best, having practical classes that day. Reena, just pleased that Anu had agreed to meet Mrinal, nodded in understanding.

Growing up with cousins Binu and Kinu and nephew Bapi, who all attended IIT Kharagpur, Anu was well aware of the institution's prestige. She knew it was India's first and one of its most celebrated engineering colleges. This, along with her mother's urging, was enough to pique her curiosity and convince her to meet Mrinal.

Much to Moni Mashi's displeasure, Anu arrived at her home disheveled, only to be promptly dressed in a silk sari. While marriage wasn't her priority—she was determined to complete her master's degree first—she had agreed to check out the guy at her mother's request.

Once the introductions were complete, both families showcased their profiles. Reena proudly highlighted Anu's singing talent, and Anu, in turn, sang her favorite Tagore number, "*Din guli mor shonar khachaye roilo na roilo na, sheyee je amar nana ronger din guli...*; My days in a golden cage could prosper no more, those days of mine with such hue and colour..."

Visibly impressed, Mrinal asked, "Can I talk to Anurima separately, please?"

"By all means," Reena immediately replied. "Both of you go to the veranda."

Anu led the way, and they stood in a corner of the large sit-out. Their initial conversation touched on various topics, including Pune, where Mrinal was working, before he abruptly turned the conversation to Calcutta and began comparing the two cities.

The room hummed with the impressed murmurs of the relatives, but the air suddenly felt cold to Anu. Mrinal's criticism of Calcutta was not just a casual observation; it landed like a physical blow, instantly dimming the hopeful glow that had surrounded her. A wave of dismay washed over her, as his words felt like a personal affront to the city that had so thoroughly captured her heart.

Anu quickly changed the subject, stating that she was in her final year and too preoccupied to consider marriage. But Mrinal was clearly impressed and reluctant to let her go that easily. He suggested she could continue her studies even if she were to get married.

Anu gave him a pointed look. "There are many girls out there who are ready to get married right away," she said coolly.

Mrinal simply nodded and followed her back into the living room. Anu was disappointed. She could already sense their incompatibility, and a future with him seemed impossible. Yet, as she looked at her parents, she saw a different story. Tathagata and Reena looked thoroughly pleased, their smiles a clear reflection of the young man's impressive credentials and the fact that he had shown interest in their daughter.

After leaving Moni's, Reena, eager to share the news, drove straight to her parents' house. As soon as they arrived, she began to recount the evening's events with palpable excitement. The entire family, hearing about the young man's impressive credentials, couldn't hide their delight.

Uninterested, Anu looked around the drawing-room and quietly slipped away, climbing the stairs to the terrace. A sound from the terrace room drew her attention, and she peered inside to find her cousin Kinu, on vacation, relaxing with a magazine. This room was a favourite hangout for all the cousins.

"Hey Anu," he said, looking up. "Heard an IIT guy came to meet you. He seems like a good catch. Go for it!"

"He may be a top student from your great institute," Anu snapped, "but that doesn't mean I have to wear his gold medal around my neck, too. There's more to marriage than a husband's academics, Kinu." She shook her head in finality. "I've already refused."

"You must be crazy!" Kinu blurted out, disbelief thick in his voice. He paused, shaking his head. "The best of the best wants you, and you turned him down. I just don't get it."

Anu met his gaze, her chin held high. "And you have a problem with that?"

Kinu let out a short, amused chuckle. "Your parents seem pretty excited about him."

"So, I'm supposed to be excited by default?" Anu shot back.

"Hey, the guy's a topper! He must have a great IQ," Kinu countered, as if that settled the matter.

Anu simply sighed. Back then, it was all about who had the highest IQ. But Anu knew in that moment that a sharp mind wasn't enough. The things that truly mattered, the kind of intelligence you couldn't measure on a test, were the things Mrinal was missing.

"So, you think this IIT guy has a good IQ?" Anu said, her voice laced with sarcasm. She paused, a flicker of irritation in her eyes. "Well, I felt his social graces were lacking."

"Kinu, grades don't show how smart someone truly is," she continued, her frustration growing. "To a large extent, they portray one's ability to just memorize information and get it out on the answer sheets." She shook her head. "It's quite misleading to measure someone's personality, let alone their intelligence, based on that."

"You seem to be acting like a pro," Kinu said with a smile, chewing on his gum. "Give it a thought; don't make a hasty decision."

"Kinu, at times, human psychology intrigues me," Anu retorted. "But for now, I just don't feel good around Mrinal. He seems to lack emotion, and he's too bossy."

Kinu laughed. "You and your romantic ideas! Anu, you can't judge a guy that quickly."

Anu shrugged. "We just didn't click. He seemed too domineering, the 'my way or the highway' type. This whole marriage market is getting on my nerves, Kinu." With that, she stalked off.

Kinu just chuckled to himself. For Anu, her cousins were more than just family; they were her best friends. They gave her the strength and confidence she needed during difficult times. She could be herself around them, knowing they respected each other's inner qualities over outward appearances.

Upon returning home, Anu wasted no time telling her family how disappointed she was with Mrinal. This initially upset Reena, but Mihir quickly came to Anu's defense, reminding his wife that their daughter needed to complete her master's. Tathagata's gentle reminder that Anu was old enough to make her own choices seemed to finally resonate with Reena.

The next day, as anticipated, Mrinal's parents called, eager to proceed. While Reena's initial excitement resurfaced, Anu's resolve remained unshaken; her master's degree came first. After a day of quiet contemplation, a shift occurred within Reena, a gradual acceptance of her daughter's independent spirit. With a sigh that held both resignation and a newfound respect, she penned a letter to Mrinal's parents explaining Anu's decision. A wave of profound relief and joy washed over Anu; her mother had finally honoured her wishes.

35

The Big, Fat Envelope

Anu, well advanced in her post-graduate studies, had developed a keen sense of intellectual discernment. She could now easily distinguish between superficial engagement and genuine intelligence, a quality she prioritized in her interactions. The years had also solidified her understanding that a person's true worth had nothing to do with their complexion. With Anu immersed in her master's program, the persistent anxiety that had shadowed Reena began to dissipate. The matrimonial columns lay untouched, replaced by a more accepting, go-with-the-flow attitude.

During this time, Anu found herself drawn to a classmate, Udeep Sengupta. Their budding attraction felt like a natural part of her young adulthood. Despite their connection, a pragmatic understanding soon settled between them—their paths were likely to remain a close friendship.

While Anu understood her parents' desire for her to marry an established man, her friend Sumana was secretly smitten with a research scholar, Arunava Banerjee. Too shy to confess her feelings, Sumana leaned on Anu to help her navigate the budding romance.

Then one day, returning home from college, Anu's attention was caught by a letter on her father's writing desk. The handwriting was strikingly elegant. Seeing her interest, Reena explained, "It's from the IIT guy we met a few months ago, Mrinal Sensharma. He's asking your father's permission to correspond with you."

Anu's immediate reaction was a firm "no way".

But Reena, seeing a chance, suggested, "Anu, you could always stop replying if he doesn't interest you."

Intrigued by the distinctive script and a flicker of curiosity, Anu found herself considering it. A different kind of mind might lie behind that elegant hand. She decided to humour her mother and agreed. A silent exchange of cautious hope passed between mother and daughter as Reena's face lit up with quiet pleasure.

The exchange of letters began, with a crisp envelope arriving on Anu's desk every fortnight. Reena initially shared the pleasure of reading them, but she soon noticed a subtle shift in her daughter. A blush would steal across Anu's cheeks, and she would retreat with the letters, a private smile playing on her lips. Reena, in turn, felt a genuine glimmer of hope. Anu, meanwhile, began sharing the contents of Mrinal's letters with her close friend, Sumana, as they relaxed in the college canteen.

One afternoon, Anu returned home to find a familiar thick envelope. She tore it open, her eyes scanning the page, until a particular sentence caused a surge of unexpected joy, prompting her to do a little jig. Mrinal had unequivocally stated his disbelief in the dowry system. "My principles will not allow me to marry a woman whose family feels obligated to provide material wealth," he had written. "I will accept only my bride."

Reading these words, a significant barrier in Anu's mind crumbled. Mrinal's stance on dowry wasn't just a principled statement; it was a profound rejection of the very pressures she and her family had faced. She found herself unable to dismiss this man who held such admirable convictions.

Tathagata and Reena, upon learning of Mrinal's stance, felt a wave of relief and gratitude. Even among the educated, parents typically still went out of their way to provide for their daughter, but Mrinal's words had removed any sense of obligation. They considered themselves fortunate to have found such a principled potential son-in-law.

Sumana, reading the letter over Anu's shoulder, couldn't hide her excitement. "Anu," she exclaimed, her eyes wide. "Considering everything you've been through, your background, your upbringing, this guy seems like a truly good match."

Anu nodded gravely. "You think so too?"

A shy smile touched Sumana's lips as she confided that Arunava was also ready to get married. Anu was genuinely thrilled for her friend, knowing she had played a part in their connection. As their time at university wound down, marriage was a popular subject of conversation among Anu's friends, but Anu was beginning to feel that her own path might be unfolding in a way she never expected.

Gradually, as Mrinal's presence in her life grew through his thoughtful letters, Anu found herself increasingly drawn to him. He offered glimpses of a world beyond the familiar confines of Bengal, subtly awakening a realization within her that she might have outgrown her current environment. She would ponder, *Perhaps I should take this leap with Mrinal. Otherwise, as Ma says, I might become trapped, like a frog in a well, even succumbing to Bengal's stifling "crab-bucket" mentality.*

Then, a letter arrived, announcing Mrinal's trip to Calcutta. A nervous anticipation settled over Tathagata and Reena, who were unsure of Anu's true feelings about meeting him again. But when Anu confided in her friend, Sumana urged her to say yes if he proposed. By then, Anu's affection for the writer of those captivating letters had grown, and she eagerly awaited their meeting.

When Mrinal finally arrived, Anu felt a flutter of excitement mixed with nervousness. For their first date, Mrinal chose a sophisticated restaurant on Park Street. As they finished the main course, dessert was served. Anu was delicately navigating her tiramisu when her spoon slipped and clattered to the floor. Mortified, she glanced around.

Mrinal was plucking the long-stemmed rose from the elegant vase on their table, and she could sense a tremor of nervousness in him as he seemed to gather his courage.

Anu's eyes sparkled in the soft candlelight. Aware of the charged atmosphere, she quickly bent under the table to retrieve her fallen spoon.

"Leave it," she heard Mrinal say gently, "they'll bring you another." Then, with a sheepish yet endearing smile, he asked, "So, what do you think, will you marry me, Anurima Dasgupta?"

A blush bloomed on Anu's cheeks. With a mischievous glint in her eyes, she playfully teased him for a moment before finally accepting the offered rose stem with a puckish grin. Mrinal visibly relaxed, a wave of relief washing over him. He wiped his brow with a handkerchief and joked, "I was about to have a heart attack, ma'am, but I'm feeling a lot better now."

Anu placed the rose stem back into the vase, and Mrinal offered an apologetic smile. "I'm sorry I couldn't be your Prince Charming," he said, his eyes filled with a nervous sincerity. "But you'll get your engagement ring, I promise."

A warmth spread through Anu as she felt a sense of relief at his earnestness. "It's okay," she said softly. "I'm excited, and I owe you one too." Taking a deep breath, she looked at him with a directness that matched his own. "But before I officially agree, I need to adjust the timeline a bit. I need to postpone the wedding by eight months so I can finish my master's."

Mrinal's response was immediate and without hesitation. "Of course, you should complete your studies, Anurima. That should be your first priority. Education is really important to me."

Anu's smile widened. After taking a bite of her tiramisu, she continued, "There's one more thing I need to make clear, just so there won't be any misunderstandings later."

Mrinal's eyebrows shot up. "What is it?"

"After marriage, I plan to pursue a Ph.D. If that doesn't work out immediately, I'll take up a job. I intend to work after marriage."

Mrinal nodded thoughtfully. "Of course, whatever you want. I wouldn't want you to be just a homemaker." His gaze met hers. "That's one of the things I look for in a partner. Education should never be wasted."

A wave of genuine pleasure washed over Anu. "Thanks," she said, her voice warm. "That's exactly what I expected from you."

Anu returned home feeling a smug sense of happiness. Her first date had exceeded her expectations, and she felt like she was walking on air. Back at home, Tathagata and Reena were a bundle of nerves. When Anu walked in, their anxious faces were etched with unspoken questions.

Anu had initially planned to tease them, but seeing their worried expressions, she softened. With a playful smile, she announced, "Ma, don't worry. I've taken myself off your hands. I accepted Mrinal's proposal."

Reena promptly replied, a hint of lingering concern in her voice, "Anu, it's not about that. We just want to make sure you have a good life."

Anu often pondered the enduring prevalence of arranged marriages in their culture, even in the 20th century. She had overcome so many academic challenges and societal pressures, and now, despite the traditional context, she felt a profound sense of relief at not having to marry a stranger. She was content with her decision to marry Mrinal, a man she had grown to admire and even love through his eloquent letters. His attractive appearance, academic achievements as a gold medalist, and his career in the defense services further solidified her contentment.

Meanwhile, Tathagata's long-held wish for his daughter to marry a Bengali expatriate, a *probashi Bangali*, was also fulfilled. Mrinal had spent his formative years outside

Bengal, much like Anu, who had been brought up mostly outside Bengal due to Tathagata's transferable job. This suggested a potentially similar lifestyle for her, making the match all the more perfect.

*

When Anu confided in Sumana about her engagement, Sumana's excitement bubbled over. "Why don't we get married around the same time?" she suggested eagerly.

Anu smiled warmly. "But let there be a gap in between, so that we can both attend each other's wedding."

"Yes! That sounds like a perfect plan," Sumana agreed.

With the wedding date set and Anu's graduation just a few months away, a new kind of countdown began. Preparations too were already in full swing, with invitations being sent out. However, a month before the wedding, Mrinal had to undertake an unexpected business trip to the US, causing a fresh wave of concern for Tatagatha and Reena, who worried about a possible postponement.

Amidst the flurry of preparations, Mihir, Basant, and Arohi were brimming with excitement for their favourite niece's wedding. The wedding felt like a much-needed breath of fresh air; annual vacations had been a distant memory since her beloved brother, Abhinandan, had passed away. Anu insisted on having her Rangapishi by her side for all the shopping. Mihir, though it stretched her budget, joyfully bought Anu an exquisite wedding saree of her choice. Their shopping spree continued as Mihir took Anu to Calcutta's renowned jewellers, placing orders for magnificent gold ornaments, delighting Anu beyond measure.

Meanwhile, Anu also received her final exam results and had excelled in her last semester. As her friends began submitting applications for doctoral programs, a common aspiration among her peers, a part of her longed to do the same. She knew her parents were eagerly anticipating the wedding, but a flicker of hope for a postponement took hold. That flicker was extinguished, however, when she received news that Mrinal would indeed be back in time for the ceremony. Anu felt a complex mix of emotions, torn between her own academic ambitions and her desire not to cause further stress for her parents.

The day before the wedding, Mrinal flew in from the US. Anu's wedding trousseau was a lavish display, boasting an array of branded French perfumes and lingerie alongside heavy, shimmering silk sarees, leaving relatives and friends in awe. The young women at the ceremony looked on in envy. Anu herself looked breathtakingly beautiful in her traditional Banarasi sari and the exquisite gold jewellery, some of which were treasured family heirlooms.

Jay's friends arrived with a huge, vibrant bouquet. Some of them were meeting Anurima for the first time and exclaimed in genuine awe, "Wow, Jayina, your sister is truly attractive, in fact, quite hot! She has it all."

Jay, ever the protective younger sibling, retorted playfully, "Hey, she's my elder sister, my didi!"

Anu was flattered by the unexpected compliment, having never received such direct admiration before. She smiled warmly at Jay, her heart swelling with affection for her little sister. Her attention then shifted to the wedding pavilion as the groom arrived.

Mrinal looked every bit the traditional Bengali groom in his *dhuti-panjabi* and emerged from the flower-bedecked car with a brand-new SLR camera, loaded with slide films, slung casually around his neck. It was a rare and impressive sight in those days, and he promptly handed it over to his friend, Tuhin. The guests were captivated as Tuhin moved around the *biyer mandap*, the wedding pavilion, expertly capturing the unfolding moments.

To Reena, the wedding felt like a triumphant victory. Her dusky-skinned daughter had secured a partner who was not only accomplished but also a gold medallist from the prestigious Indian Institute of Technology. As she floated among the guests, her pride was palpable and she appeared utterly content.

As the wedding ceremony progressed, Anurima's dark eyes sparkled with joy as she watched her US-returned groom, handsome in his traditional attire, chanting the ancient wedding mantras while surprisingly chewing a stick of Wrigley's spearmint gum.

This unique atmosphere was further enriched by the priest, a distinguished Sanskrit professor, who translated the sacred Sanskrit verses into both Bengali and English. This thoughtful gesture allowed all the guests to fully connect with the profound meaning of the ceremony and participate in the ancient wedding rituals.

PART VII
1984–1997
Pune, Nainital, Calcutta, Tezpur, USA, Bangalore

36

A New Home, A Hidden World

Anu stepped into her new home, a small apartment in Pune, the charming hill town also known as the Queen of the Deccan Plateau. Her husband, Mrinal, worked as a scientist at the Defence Research and Development (DRDO), and this new city, previously known as Poona, was a far cry from the bustling chaos of Calcutta.

Her initial impression of Mrinal's apartment, which he shared with his friend and colleague Gaurav, was of a typical bachelor's den. But moving around, to her surprise, she saw that Mrinal possessed a number of modern appliances. A refrigerator hummed quietly in the corner, a gas oven stood gleaming, and a cassette player rested beside an SLR camera and a slide projector. Other than these electronic goods, the rooms sported an untidy look.

Anu mused, impressed by his unexpectedly sophisticated taste. *He certainly was an enthusiast of electronic goods.* Her thoughts drifted back to her mother, Reena, and the stories she often recounted of her own arrival as a bride in her father's sprawling Jabalpur bungalow—a far cry, Reena would say, from a bachelor's cottage, complete with a territorial cook who had nearly marched out upon seeing the new lady of the house in his domain. Anu chuckled at the memory.

Anu and Mrinal plunged into an exciting honeymoon, their days a whirl of movie premieres, theatre performances, and bustling restaurants. For many of their outings, they were joined by Gaurav, a witty friend and colleague of Mrinal's from their trainee days at DRDO. His jokes and remarks invariably added to the laughter.

On other occasions, Mrinal's bachelor friend Abhijeet would also join them, turning their evenings into lively gatherings. In these animated discussions about books, characters, films and actors, Anu was often at the heart of the banter, her laughter ringing out. In contrast, Mrinal's quieter presence, punctuated by occasional interruptions, sometimes faded into the background of the vibrant scene. But Mrinal made a conscious effort to impress his new bride by introducing her to all his vibrant friends and colleagues.

Anu appreciated Mrinal's generosity and his love for the finer things in life. As they moved to the DRDO quarters, Anu embraced her new role as a wife and began to conform to traditional expectations, feeling proud of her husband.

Around the same time, Mrinal's friend Tushar also shifted to the DRDO quarters with his newlywed wife, Boni, and Anu found a companion in her. Then, after a few months, Gaurav wed Archana. The three couples then bonded very well with weekend get-togethers and parties.

Anu was settling into her new life as a married woman. Settling in as a pure homemaker was not her forté, yet she decided to enjoy this new phase. Marriage brought new experiences for Anu, as Mrinal was an introvert who enjoyed spending time in the kitchen trying out new recipes. Anu, on the other hand, was more outgoing.

While Anu admired Mrinal's cooking skills, she often noticed that whenever she tried sharing her day's experiences with Mrinal, he would steer the conversation towards the menu of the day. She realised Mrinal struggled to participate in normal conversation.

When Anu confided in her mother about her experiences, Reena would say, "Anu, the way to a man's heart is through his stomach."

"But Ma," Anu would reply, "I hardly know how to cook."

Homesick and keenly aware of her lack of culinary skills, Anu eagerly awaited her mother's letters, which now included handwritten recipes. Reena's letters would read: "Dear Anu, fish curry . . . vegetable pulao . . . and so forth," ending with, "Take Care. Yours, Maa."

Anu quickly picked up the skills and developed a passion for cooking, much like her enjoyment of chemistry practicals. As she settled into her new life, she began to notice other, more subtle aspects of Mrinal's personality. One Sunday, emerging from a bath, she heard someone singing on their balcony. She rushed out and found Mrinal quietly smoking.

"Were you singing?" she asked.

He gravely shook his head.

Her curiosity piqued, she then overheard Mrinal singing in the bath, which delighted her as she secretly hoped for a husband with a good singing voice. When he returned home from work that evening, Anu, her heart full of hope, asked him to sing for her.

"Who told you I can sing?" Mrinal asked, his voice full of feigned surprise.

"Come on, I heard you in the bath," Anu insisted with a laugh.

He then shyly turned on the tape recorder, and a pleasant, mature voice filled the room. Anu looked at Mrinal, her expression questioning. He nodded shyly, admitting, "It's me, the bathroom singer."

The warmth of his recorded voice revealed a hidden facet of his personality, one that belied his usual shyness and reticence. While this discovery was a pleasant surprise, it also led Anu to a new realisation: Mrinal thrived in his own private world. She came to understand that engaging in conversation, especially in social settings, was not one of his strengths.

Anurima slowly began to adjust to the reality of her partner's nature. She sensed that Mrinal enjoyed solitary activities, such as watching television, going to the movies, and dining out. These activities excited Anu too, so they did have some common ground. He was also surprisingly innovative in the area of intimacy, and this was something they both enjoyed. One day, he even surprised her with Dr. David Reuben's bestseller, *Everything You Always Wanted to Know about Sex*, since Anu was quite inexperienced in this field.

Anu gradually adjusted to the new relationship with Mrinal, who was significantly older and had more experience in life. She often found herself yielding to his expertise, feeling like a student on a learning curve.

One day, Anu found Mrinal looking through his collection of souvenirs. He pulled out an embossing label maker, a type of hard plastic tape with a colourful hue Anu had not seen before. To her astonishment, he began embossing her name on the tape and sticking it on all of his electronic devices.

Fascinated, Anu asked in a playful tone, "Why are you putting my name on all your electronic stuff?"

Mrinal gave a bashful nod. "Well, I'm not very good at dealing with people, especially when they ask me for things," he explained. "I once lent my SLR camera to a friend, and when he returned it, the case was all bashed up. He claimed he accidentally dropped it in a body of running water. So now, I'm putting your name on all my humble belongings. From now on, if anyone wants to borrow something, I'll tell them they need to get your permission." Mrinal grinned.

Anu was amused, nodding with a satisfied smirk. "So you're making me the bad guy!" she laughed aloud.

Over time, Anu began to notice other quirks. While Mrinal was a reservoir of knowledge with a truly photographic memory, he often stayed quiet in group situations, a silent observer until directly addressed. When prompted, however, he would often deliver a surprisingly insightful or witty remark that would momentarily stun everyone into impressed silence. Anu found this entertaining, a sign of his hidden intelligence.

This quiet brilliance also appeared during open-house quiz competitions, which Anu was always eager to attend with him. She looked forward to the numerous prizes they would win, but was often confused to notice that Mrinal never raised his hand to respond to questions, merely mumbling the answers under his breath. Nevertheless, they would consistently win a substantial number of prizes. Anu later learned that during his college years, Mrinal had been a quiz enthusiast.

At dinner parties, Anu noticed a distinct pattern in Mrinal's behaviour. For most of the evening, he would sit quietly, offering only nods and smiles. However, whenever the conversation snagged on a complex technical issue, someone would inevitably turn to him: "Mrinal, you've been quiet. Any thoughts?" Without hesitation, he would provide a concise and brilliant solution that garnered immediate agreement. Anu was always initially impressed.

She came to realise that Mrinal appeared at ease only when his friends and colleagues discussed general politics or work-related technical subjects. The moment their partners joined in, shifting the mood to a more personal and lively exchange, he would withdraw to the sidelines. Anu recognized this stark contrast: his sharp intellect shone brightly in a specific context, only to dim considerably in casual social interactions. She understood it wasn't just shyness; Mrinal genuinely struggled with the fluid, often unspoken rules of social engagement.

In contrast, Anu thrived in such engaging conversations, and her vibrant energy positively affected those nearby. She gradually recognized the extent to which Mrinal's social skills were lacking. Yet, she also observed curious contradictions. During their visits to Calcutta, her mother, Reena, was often taken aback by her son-in-law's demeanour. With his school and college friends, Mrinal would converse loudly and clearly, even cracking jokes—a sharp contrast to his usual reserved nature. With the passage of time, Anu also observed that despite possessing an impressive recall, Mrinal seemed strangely disconnected from any drive or ambition, portraying a remarkably laid-back approach to life.

*

The pleasant buzz of their evening with friends slowly faded as they walked back home under the starlit Pune sky. They discussed Dominique Lapierre's recent novel, *City of Joy*, and how Calcutta was gaining its new nickname. As they were about to reach home, the comfortable silence, however, was soon broken by Mrinal's familiar tone of mild disapproval.

"Anurima," he began, his voice carrying a hint of a sigh, "did you really have to bring up that anecdote about my disastrous attempt at repairing the hair dryer?"

Anu frowned, the warmth of the evening beginning to dissipate. "But it was a funny story, Mrinal! Even you were laughing about it at the time."

"Yes, but these are personal things, not to be discussed in public, especially in front of friends."

"What is so personal about it?" Anu echoed, a sharper edge creeping into her voice. "They're our friends, Mrinal! We share stories, we laugh together. It's part of what makes our bond with them strong."

"There's a difference between sharing and oversharing, Anurima," Mrinal retorted, his tone becoming slightly more pointed.

Anu stopped walking, her hands clenching slightly at her sides. "Oversharing? What is that supposed to mean?"

Mrinal stopped as well, turning to face her under the soft glow of a nearby streetlamp. "It simply means you talk too much, Anu."

"In a social gathering with friends, everybody talks and shares things; that's how people bond," Anu spat back. "Unlike you, keeping mum like a dumbo."

"I don't blab unnecessarily like you," Mrinal said with a dismissive wave of his hand. "And honestly, sometimes the things you say . . . like that comment about Gaurav's new haircut? It wasn't particularly flattering."

"I was just teasing him!" Anu protested. "He knows I didn't mean anything by it. We have that kind of relationship."

"But do we need to dissect everyone's appearance and life choices quite so openly?"

Anu stared at him, a wave of frustration washing over her. "So, now I'm not only talkative but also tactless? I was simply trying to be friendly and engaging. It feels like no matter what I say or do, you always find fault with it."

The joy of the evening had completely evaporated, replaced by a familiar ache of being constantly judged and found wanting. As days turned into weeks and weeks into months, the initial harmony between Anurima and Mrinal began to fray. Their perspectives diverged on a growing number of issues, leading to frequent and impassioned debates.

Anu observed a curious dichotomy in Mrinal; despite his vast reservoir of knowledge, he often struggled to translate his sharp analytical and logical reasoning into practical application. In contrast, Anu possessed an innate and readily deployable analytical intellect, capable of dissecting situations with clarity and logic. Beyond this intellectual divergence, Mrinal's social interactions were noticeably stilted, so he mostly enjoyed a non-verbal presence. Anu also came to realise Mrinal's deep-seated reluctance to share anything personal, be it his inner thoughts or details about his work, preferring to keep his world tightly sealed within himself.

She would, however, observe that his true interests lay in the kitchen. There, he would sing his favorite Bollywood numbers, or perhaps a Sachin Dev Burman or Rabindra Sangeet, as he transformed even leftovers into delicious meals. This led Anu to sometimes think, *Perhaps he would have thrived in the hospitality business.*

A year had gone by, and one day Mrinal, looking both upbeat and perplexed, approached Anu. "Anu," he said with a frown, "why do we have so many disagreements and struggle to see eye to eye?"

Anu was surprised and took a moment to think before responding. "I believe it's because we both hold strong opinions," she said. At that age, she believed their differences stemmed from immaturity and ego. She had been raised to be a fighter with a positive outlook, while Mrinal seemed weighed down by negativity. Deep down, she began to acknowledge that she would have to be the one to make concessions and adjust to her partner.

37

The Lake District of India

After a brief stint in Pune, Mrinal relocated to Haldwani in the Nainital district of Uttaranchal, the Gateway of Kumaon. But the bustling commercial town didn't suit them, and the couple soon desired a quieter life. They found it in Nainital, a picturesque Himalayan Lake town located at an altitude of approximately 7,000 feet above sea level. Anu was excited to learn that their new home was known as the "Lake District of India". The town was nestled in a valley with an eye-shaped lake surrounded by seven hills, and they soon heard the local legend that its name was derived from its resemblance to an eye—"Nain" for eyes and "Tal" for lake.

As Anu began decorating her quaint cottage, her attention was drawn to the empty bookcase. She started to fill it with books of various genres, a task that made her recall Mrinal's modest apartment in Pune, where his bookcase had looked bare with only a few journals and some books huddled like aged crones. She had even thought of her own collection of storybooks gathering dust in Calcutta, but then Mrinal had surprised her with a catalogue from the Standard Literature Publication. Much to Anu's delight, books on various subjects had been delivered periodically ever since, and now she had a beautiful collection to fill her new shelves.

Mrinal enjoyed his daily commute to work, navigating the winding pathways that led him on unexpected adventures through the charming hill town, with its colonial-era architecture, brightly coloured villas, bungalows, rickshaws, and trotting ponies. One day, as Anu and Mrinal were strolling, they came across a breathtaking building.

They stared in awe at the majestic gothic structure, which evoked the elegance of the past. It was the Governor House, once the summer capital of the English Governors. The locals told them that after British rule ended, it was renamed "Raj Bhawan" and was often compared to a Scottish castle or even Buckingham Palace in London.

Now, Raj Bhawan served as a summer retreat for the Governor of the state, particularly during the National Golf Tournament. It spanned 200 acres, complete with a swimming pool, lush gardens, the golf course, and verdant expanses of deodar and oak trees.

As they attempted to enter the premises, the guards informed them that the area was off-limits to the public, but they would be allowed entry if they became members of the golf club. Mrinal decided to become a member, granting them access to the vast green grounds of the golf course. They marvelled at its magnificence and learned that it was India's oldest golf course, founded in 1936 on forty-five acres of rolling terrain.

*

During the summer months, the picturesque hill town would be bustling with both Indian and foreign tourists, creating a vibrant atmosphere. Anu often saw them at the Mall Road Bazaar, engaging in the usual bargaining while shopping for local handicrafts and woollen clothing. The road, dotted with shops and cafés, vied for the visitors' attention.

In the evening, as the sun set behind the mountains, the hill station transformed into a captivating fairyland. Anu enjoyed strolling down the Mall Road, which ran through the heart of the town parallel to the lake, a vestige well-preserved from the colonial era.

After settling into this new rhythm of life, Anu began to consider pursuing a doctorate degree and started exploring options at the university. While Mrinal had no qualms about it, limited funds in the hill town restricted her options. At the suggestion of her aunt, Pinku Mashi, a high school biology teacher at St. Mary's Convent, Anu applied for and secured a job as a middle school science teacher at the same school.

A year later, realising the importance of further education for her career growth, Anu enrolled in a Bachelor of Education program. Upon completion, she began teaching chemistry and biology to high school students, finding a new sense of purpose in her career.

A few months later, Anu and Mrinal were visiting Julie Mashi, a colleague of Mrinal's from DRDO, and her husband, Sisir. They had a son named Neil. During their conversation, Julie sprang a surprise on Anu. She showed her a newspaper with a half-page advertisement from the DRDO for the post of a biochemist at their Haldwani laboratory. It read: "Candidates with a master's in biochemistry or botany with plant physiology or any biochemical background may apply."

Reading the advertisement, Anu could not contain her excitement, as it was a perfect fit for her. Her eyes lit up with enthusiasm as she considered the possibility of later pursuing her doctorate within the same organisation.

Aunt Julie encouraged Anu to seriously consider the job opportunity, her gaze shifting pointedly to Mrinal, a subtle challenge in her expression.

"Women deserve the autonomy of a career, and a dual income would undoubtedly enhance a family's security," Julie argued, handing Anu the newspaper, the crisp paper a tangible symbol of a potential new path.

On their way home, the silence in the car was thick with unspoken thoughts. Finally, Anu broached the subject, asking Mrinal for his opinion. Instead of the enthusiastic support she had hoped for, a furrow creased his brow.

"You know," Mrinal began, a thoughtful expression on his face, "if you were to work in the same organization as me, wouldn't that create potential professional competition . . . within our own household?" He paused, a subtle note of unease in his voice, murmuring, "And what if you were to . . . surpass me in our shared field?" He then cleared his throat and continued, "There's also the practical side of things. Once we start a family, how will we both manage demanding full-time careers? It feels like it could become a logistical nightmare, with our attention constantly divided."

Anu listened, a knot tightening in her stomach. She wasn't entirely convinced by his reasoning, sensing a deeper, perhaps unspoken, discomfort beneath his practical concerns. Yet, a familiar pattern of prioritising his preferences, ingrained over their time together, began to assert itself.

A quiet ache of unfulfilled academic dreams resurfaced as Anu considered her latent wish to pursue her doctorate. She sensed that Mrinal, secure in his own professional standing, would be more content if she remained within the familiar realm of academia, perhaps viewing the corporate sphere as too competitive or assertive for his liking.

Later, when Anu tentatively confided in Reena about the DRDO opportunity and Mrinal's reservations, her mother, with her characteristic pragmatism, advised her to side with husband.

"He is older, Anu," Reena had said, her voice carrying the weight of tradition. "He has more life experience and he graduated from a leading institute in the nation. You should respect his judgment."

Anu, though a flicker of rebellion stirred within her, did not argue. The familiar deference to her husband's seniority and societal expectations held her back. Yet, a quiet sense of being stifled, of her own ambitions being subtly curtailed, lingered. Each opportunity that arose fell victim to Mrinal's job relocations, and Anu, by then, had resigned herself to her fate.

Another US trip followed soon after, and Mrinal returned with suitcases full of thoughtful gifts. While these were a tangible reminder of his affection, they were also a subtle reinforcement of their established dynamic.

As time went by, Anu found herself increasingly enchanted by the serene charm of Nainital, its emerald mountain lake, the majestic towering oak trees, and the playful sight of vibrant sailboats dotting the water.

She was gradually falling for this picturesque life, a life that was beautiful, but also held the quiet echo of her deferred dreams.

38

The Echo of Loss

Anurima looked lovingly at her six-month-old daughter, Aisha, or Aish, sleeping peacefully in her crib. This pregnancy had been particularly special to Anu, as it had come three years after a devastating miscarriage. To exercise caution, she had left her job and traveled to her parents' home in Calcutta during her sixth month of pregnancy, a common practice among upper middle-class Bengali families. Her husband, Mrinal, remained in Nainital while she spent three months before and after the delivery with her mother.

Raised with a familiarity for astrology and numerology, Anu readily believed in their insights. As her June 25 due date approached, her paternal aunts, who followed Pythagorean numerology, held a particular hope that the baby would arrive on June 28, a date they considered auspicious because its digits added up to the lucky root number 1.

The summer heat intensified, and Anu passed her due date. On the morning of June 27, she felt the first light contractions and silently encouraged her baby to wait just a little longer. By June 28, however, her labour began in earnest, and her mother took her to Woodlands Nursing Home, an elite facility in Calcutta. By noon, her amniotic fluid had started to leak, but the baby remained unconcerned.

Around noon, her gynecologist, Dr. Purabi Mukherjee, walked in to check on her. The doctor's grave expression immediately put Anu on edge.

"Mrs. Anurima Sensharma, I think we have to go in for a cesarean section," she said. "The baby is in distress."

Anu nodded, her gaze sweeping the room for Mrinal. She also needed her mother, Reena, to sign some papers, but neither was in sight. A wave of helplessness washed over her as she closed her eyes, the clinking of surgical instruments echoing nearby and the sharp scent of antiseptic drifting from the adjacent operation theater. Just then, a hand touched her forehead. Her eyes fluttered open to see her mother standing beside her, with Mrinal grinning sheepishly at her side.

Anu, still in the Intensive Care Unit, groggy from the anaesthesia, opened her eyes. She saw her aunts Mihir, Basanta, Arohi, and Uncle Bhulu, standing beside her bed. They had come to bestow their blessings on the newborn. They were overjoyed to welcome the latest family member, a wonderful gift from their beloved niece. Born on June 28th, the baby was a root number one according to numerology, bringing extra joy to the family.

Despite her beliefs in numerology, Anu was aware of the influence of genes on human traits. Still, she mused, *At least my baby was born on June 28, which made my Rangapishi and all my paternal aunts happy.*

The following day, when the nurse brought in the little pink bundle, Anu gasped in amazement. "Are you really my baby?" she cooed. "You are too cute to be true!"

During her pregnancy, Anu had been inundated with fear and skepticism; her only wish was for a healthy baby, regardless of the sex. For the first few days, it was hard for her to believe that this perfect little bundle was truly her own. As she drank in the moment in utter relief and began to fuss over her baby, she was reminded of her childhood doll, Jill, which she had bought with the savings from her piggy bank. Each day deepened her adoration for this tiny joy, and she made an unspoken promise to nurture her with all her strength and protect her from every hardship until her dying breath.

After a period of post-natal care with her mother, Anu returned to Nainital with her three-month-old daughter, Aisha, an adorable baby full of gurgles and smiles. As they absorbed themselves completely in parenthood, the earlier differences that had strained their relationship began to fade. Anu even chose to take a break from work, dedicating herself fully to this new, joyful chapter.

*

Weekend parties were a custom in Nainital, and it was Anurima and Mrinal's turn to host their regular shindig. Anu had worked hard to ensure the perfect evening, meticulously planning a lavish meal of chicken soup, mutton biryani, raita, fish fingers, baked chicken drumsticks, and canapés and olives with a mint dip.

By evening, she had laid out the crockery and cutlery. As the sun dipped behind the horizon, sharpening the air and making it quite cold and unsympathetic, friends began to arrive.

Anu answered the doorbell. Usually a cheerful chime, it sounded apathetic that day as she welcomed her guests. The party began with men and women chatting over canapés and wine, creating a congenial atmosphere. But Anu sensed a faint whiff of something troublesome lingering as she floated around with the appetisers, a plastic smile pasted on her once so buoyant countenance. Each time she made eye contact, her smile faltered like a flickering bulb.

"Anu, I hope everything is okay," Aparna inquired. "You don't look like your usual self."

"Something uncanny happened this morning," Anu replied, her smile faltering completely. "I'll tell you about it later." As she moved away, she tried to shake off her unease, but her mind couldn't help but drift to the familiar dynamics of her social circle.

Mrinal and Gaurav's lives mirrored each other in many ways. They had married around the same time, were often relocated to the same places, and once returned from a US training program having spontaneously bought their wives identical sets of crockery, cutlery, and gadgets. Their synchronicity was so ingrained that Gaurav often relied on Mrinal's discerning taste, which frequently led to the humorous, yet sometimes unsettling, acquisition of identical items.

It was no surprise then that when both couples were transferred to Haldwani, they naturally decided to settle near each other in the charming hill town of Nainital. For the first ten years of their marriage, they were practically inseparable, their bond so strong that they even acquired adjacent plots in Nainital and built their homes side-by-side.

Aparna, with her calm demeanour as an ophthalmologist, had formed a particularly close bond with Anurima. They subsequently met Jishnu and Abhiroop, who were single and worked at the Haldwani lab. Later, their friends from Pune, Tushar and Boni, along with Proshun and Shobha, also became part of their circle.

Ultimately, Jishnu wed Suma, and Abhiroop tied the knot with Banto. The group was finally complete, and they enjoyed exploring Nainital and going on picnics together. Anurima was happy to see that Mrinal had such great friends and looked forward to a life filled with fun.

Now, at their own home, the party was in full swing. Anu headed to the buffet table and announced dinner, then poured herself a glass of sparkling rosé wine and settled in a corner of the room. Aparna offered her some biryani and raita, but Anu had no appetite.

All of a sudden, the doorbell rang, its croaky sound cutting through the vibrant atmosphere. Anu glanced up at Mrinal, who seemed to read the exhaustion on her face, and he got up to answer the door. When he returned, he wore a mysterious expression that Anu could not decipher.

She looked up at him, an inquiry in her eyes. "Was it the watchman?"

Mrinal simply shrugged, leaving Anu with the feeling of trying to catch a balloon that had just escaped her reach. She usually enjoyed these weekend parties, but this one felt different. When the last guest, Jishnu, left at 11:30 p.m., Anu felt an unfamiliar wave of relief. She entered the kitchen, where the loaded sink and the heaped garbage seemed to cast a dirty look at her. She couldn't care less. She switched off the light and began picking up the ashtrays, paper napkins, and scattered books in the living room. Her eyes fell upon the bronze and brass figurine of Nataraja, and childhood memories flooded her mind. She realized her past was not a fading journey but a vast spring meadow where no winter could ever descend.

After cleaning up all remnants of the party, Anu sat in a wrought iron chair on the veranda, deep in thought. Unbeknownst to her, Mrinal was watching her through his dark-framed glasses, a cigarette hanging between his fingers. Anu looked at him and raised her eyebrows.

"Let's go inside, Anu," he said. "I have something to tell you."

Anu's heart dropped as she remembered the doorbell and Mrinal's odd behaviour. He led her back to the living room, and she plopped into a chair, feeling as heavy as a pile of wet cement. Mrinal pulled up a seat and took out a folded piece of paper. "This came in the late evening post while the party was at its peak," he said. "I didn't want to ruin the evening with the news, so I decided to wait until later."

Anu's eyes widened as she saw the telegram in his hand. Her heart racing, she reached for it. One look, and her mind froze. Tears welled up as she read the stark, terrible words: "YOUR RANGAPISHI PASSED AWAY IN HER SLEEP ON 13 FEBRUARY AT 4 A.M. STOP."

39

An Ocean Apart

Mrinal was relocated to Tezpur, a city in the state of Assam. Given the volatile situation in Assam due to the ULFA movement, his priority was the safety of Anu and Aish. Consequently, he decided it was best to move them to the relative calm of Calcutta.

A year later, Mrinal arrived in Calcutta, his eyes sparkling with excitement! "Guess what?" he announced, a wide grin spreading across his face. "I've got a business trip . . . to Houston, Texas!" He could barely contain his enthusiasm as he explained to Anu that he would be working at NASA's Johnson Space Centre. With a spring in his step, he shared that he had already found a lovely condominium on Westheimer Road and was leaving in a couple of days. He paused. "And the good news is, this time I am allowed to take my family with me."

Anu couldn't believe her ears and embraced Mrinal. "Wow, I still can't believe it."

After landing in Houston, Mrinal eagerly anticipated Anu and Aish joining him soon. His joy was palpable, radiating with the thrill of this new adventure and the prospect of having the family together again. Anu was just as excited, but they soon faced a significant challenge. The US Embassy required proof of their return to India, and as a young couple, they struggled to provide sufficient evidence. After long hours of deliberation, they made the toughest decision of their lives and chose to leave their five-year-old daughter in the care of Anu's mother.

Once the decision was made, Anu approached the US Embassy, the weight of her choice evident in her demeanour. When she explained to the consular officer that she was leaving her young daughter in India with her mother and her nanny, the officer smiled. "Good decision, madam. Your daughter could always go to the US when she is old enough to enjoy the country." Her casual remark completely missed the emotional complexity of Anu's mental state.

Anu and Mrinal then organised a small vacation for Aisha and her caregivers. Aisha was accompanied by her grandmother, her nanny, and Rinki, Anu's cousin who had a special fondness for her. Anu ensured her daughter was surrounded by familiar faces. After Aisha's school let out, the group headed to Jay's home in the scenic hill town of Binsar, where Jay lived with her husband, Abhishek, and their daughter, Mia, who was three years younger than Aisha.

With the comforting presence of her nanny, Asha, the picturesque train ride to Binsar became a source of happy memories for Aisha. The crisp mountain air offered a refreshing change from Calcutta's heat upon their arrival. Meeting her cousin Mia sparked immediate joy; their giggles and playful tumbles on the grass were a testament to their instant connection. Aisha's aunt Jay, her Mumu, further brightened her arrival with a warm hug and a bag of goodies.

During the initial days, when Anu and Mrinal would call weekly, Aisha would tell them to return soon. But as Binsar filled with picnics, stories, games, and fancy-dress parties, her longing lessened. Anu felt a wave of relief as her daughter slowly but surely settled into her new surroundings. Anu mused that at least this trip to Binsar had given the two cousins an opportunity to bond.

Aisha also quickly grew comfortable with the affectionate interactions with her Moshai, Abhishek. While Aisha was a baby, his playful swings sometimes worried Anu, but his pediatrician's touch reassured her, and his loving ways clearly made Aisha feel at ease. This bond with her Moshai, which would prove to be a recurring source of support during transitions, was beginning to form. Later, as Aisha grew up, her aunt Mumu became her fun-filled companion.

*

Anu had opted for the "Visit USA: VUSA", a discounted airfare program that, back then, allowed extensive travel within the US for international visitors. For Anu, this VUSA pass wasn't merely a trip; it was an odyssey to bridge distances, connecting with relatives and friends scattered across a vast continent.

Houston became her first sanctuary. Her days melted into hours at the Johnson Space Centre Museum, which she often visited with Mrinal. Anu found herself swallowed by awe—the towering presence of the Saturn V boosters, the reverent silence of the control centre replica, the almost sacred sensation of touching a moon rock.

But it was the smaller, more intimate relics that truly captivated Anu. A worn spacesuit glove, a scuffed helmet, a handwritten checklist—these whispered stories of human striving and unimaginable dedication. On their way back home, Mrinal answered Anu's endless stream of questions. With each answer, the museum transformed from an exhibit hall into a portal to extraordinary possibilities, leaving her with a renewed, almost childish wonder.

After a month in Houston, Anu launched into her month-long VUSA tour. She was brimming with anticipation for the wonders she had only heard whispers of. Her first stop was El Paso, Texas, where her cousin Mili and husband Andy were waiting for her at the airport. On the way back to their home, Mili, with an impish smile on her face, asked, "How was your experience with our Continental Airlines?"

"It was okay, but they just served peanuts."

"Ah! So you got an experience of our famous 'peanut flight'?" Mili asked with a hearty laugh, and Andy joined in.

"Seriously, Mili, are they nicknamed 'peanut flights'?" Anu asked, laughing along.

Mili and Andy took her around El Paso, and one day, they took her camping to Cimarron Canyon State Park in northern New Mexico. She enjoyed the tranquility of the Cimarron River as it flowed through the forested canyon. Lying inside the tent, Anu experienced a bear's low growl and a sky ablaze with stars. The raw, untamed beauty of that night left an indelible mark, a visceral reminder of nature's power.

After seven fun-filled days with her cousin, Anu wanted to see the mountains of the United States, so she flew to Denver. Mrinal's friend Buta lived there with his wife Susmita and their two children. Anu had met Buta once in India when he was a bachelor, so an invite from him excited Anu, as she wanted a glimpse of the majestic peaks of Colorado and to meet his family. Susmita and Anu became friends, and Susmita would often take Anu shopping. One weekend, Buta took Anu on a trip to Vail. There, amidst America's largest ski resort, Anu saw the Colorado Rockies, their silent, ancient grandeur humbling her. The quaint charm of Vail village, with its cobbled streets and chalet-style buildings, offered a cozy counterpoint to the mountains' immensity. *What a heavenly place,* Anu mused, *I wish I could stay here.*

40

The Wonderland

It was October, the month of Durga Puja, and Anu decided to visit her uncle's family in Baltimore, Maryland, for the festival. Upon landing, she was embraced by the warmth of family and Bengali culture. She was greeted by her uncle, Shubhendu, aunt, Ruma, and cousin, Riju.

As a passionate Rabindra Sangeet singer, Anu eagerly participated in various functions with her Tagore-enthusiast uncle while devouring Aunt Ruma's delicious cuisine. In the US, the Durga festival is celebrated on weekends, so Anu and her aunt, decked in gorgeous sarees, visited celebrations in Washington D.C. and the Kali Temple in Virginia. As they walked into the pavilion, the air vibrated with the scent of incense, the sound of conch shells, and the rhythm of drums.

"I'm truly impressed," Anu said to her aunt and uncle, "how the Bengalis have maintained their vibrant culture and heritage so far from home."

Her uncle, Shubhendu, a Rabindra Sangeet aficionado, grinned. "You've only seen the puja. There's more to it," he said. "Hold on and buckle your seat belts, Anu, until you see our evening functions."

Anu was charmed. Every moment felt precious, filled with outings and late-night cultural programmes. She was so impressed that she resolved to visit them on future trips, especially during Durga Puja.

Anu's other maternal uncle, Krishna, and his wife, Kanta, lived in Atlanta, Georgia, so she decided to visit them next. Her time there was a delightful blend of urban vibrancy and serene nature. Krishna and Kanta took Anu on city tours that offered glimpses into Atlanta's rich history. One day, her uncle suggested a hike up to the summit of Stone Mountain

Anu was initially reluctant. "Krishna mama, may be next time. It could be a tiring climb."

Krishna immediately retorted, "Anu, don't be lazy. I can tell you it will be a rewarding experience."

On reaching the top, Anu was taken aback by the sweeping panorama of the Atlanta skyline. The view of the distant rolling hills offered a moment of profound clarity, a sense of belonging in this diverse tapestry. Atlanta left an indelible mark on Anu's journey.

On her way back, Krishna mama suggested Anu go to Boston to visit his daughter, Anu's cousin, Minku. Minku was excited to hear Anu was visiting. She lived with her Danish husband, Victor, and their two children. Victor's easy-going warmth instantly put Anu at ease.

Both Minku and Victor drove Anu around Boston. It was a revelation to watch Minku, petite yet commandingly driving a large SUV, expertly navigating Boston's historic streets. Their tour led them to Howard University, a place radiating with Black excellence and student pride, and then to MIT, whose modern architecture and intellectual gravitas left Anu not just awestruck, but deeply humbled. Each new encounter and landscape was quietly reshaping Anu, expanding her understanding of the world, and subtly revealing more about herself.

*

Anu was swept away by her whirlwind tour of the US. It was a dream come true, and her heart was full. Back in Houston, she made the most of her time, enrolling in a two-month crash course in business communication. After a busy week, Anu and Mrinal would spend their weekends either exploring the city or socialising with his friends and colleagues. Thanks to Mrinal's strong ties to his alma mater, Anu quickly enjoyed his Houston social circle.

She also found a strong support system in other friends and acquaintances. Before Mrinal's departure from India, his DRDO friend, Prashun Bhowmick, had thoughtfully connected him with his sister, Joyee, a doctor's wife in Houston. Joyee became a great source of comfort for Anu, often taking her shopping. When Mrinal would return home from work and find shopping bags all around, he'd ask with a mischievous grin, "So, what were you up to today?"

Anu would simply reply, "Today, Joyee took me shopping at Galleria mall."

Another of Mrinal's former DRDO colleagues in Houston, Rajendra Singh, and his wife, Sarojini, also extended warm hospitality. Sarojini, who hailed from a small Indian town, particularly impressed Anu with her kindness. Over the weekend, Sarojini would often take Anu on casual city tours, which typically ended with the cheerful suggestion, "Let's take you shopping to a few malls; there is always a sale out there. You can buy stuff for your little one."

Sarojini's generosity continued with thoughtful gifts from her work at Walmart, which deeply touched Anu. "Your friends, especially Sarojini, have been so incredibly welcoming," she remarked to Mrinal. "They've made us feel right at home."

Mrinal simply smiled, acknowledging their warmth.

The USA in the 90s was a shopper's paradise, and with friends like Sarojini, Anu and Mrinal took full advantage. They frequented places like Toys 'R' Us and Radio Shack, spending hours browsing and buying. Anu focused on dresses, toys, and gadgets for their child, while Mrinal's generosity ensured Anu had a fantastic time. Even years later, Anu's eyes would sparkle as she recounted their shopping sprees.

*

Anu cherished her US trip, grateful for the valuable life lessons and the quality time she spent with Mrinal. As the trip drew to a close, she packed three large suitcases, a stroller, and a Casio keyboard for her return. Anu departed while Mrinal stayed on for two more months. When Mrinal eventually packed, he discovered his belongings exceeded the airline limit and required shipping.

Anu arrived back in India, touching down at Netaji Subhash Chandra Bose International Airport in Calcutta, excited to reunite with Aisha. But when Aisha saw her, she dragged her chair to the room's farthest corner, looking glum. It took a suitcase full of treasures, including two life-size dolls and a stroller, to finally entice Aisha. She giggled, her eyes sparkled, and she dashed into her mamma's arms.

41

The Weeping Sister

The old family photo album lay open on the table at Mihir's house, its yellowed pages whispering tales of years gone by. A comfortable murmur filled the room as the cousins, a familiar constellation gathered once more, relived cherished memories. Their annual trip to Calcutta, a tradition echoing their childhood vacations, had brought them together again. Babul, Polly, and Shanu had also joined this year's gathering.

Casually, Babul turned a page. "Hey, look at our Rangapishi, quite the beauty!" An impish smile played on his lips. "Remember their Comilla pride?" He nudged Shanu. "Didn't you tease her about it?"

"Just a bit of fun," Shanu replied quickly.

Anu chuckled. "And Rangapishi, never one to back down, gave him the full Dasgupta history lesson, Comilla being our ancestral home."

Shanu grinned. "I was just wondering, why that pride in our native place?"

"Come on, Shanu," Sri said gently, smiling. "She reminded us it was a revolutionary hub during the British Raj, a place where a lot happened."

The cousins settled back with their lemonades and colas. All eyes turned to Sri, who was gazing at a photo with a shy smile.

"What's got you grinning?" Anu asked.

"Look, it's Mamni's photo from her college days."

A poignant silence fell as they all leaned in to see. They remembered Arohi, who had succumbed to cancer the previous year. Her husband, Monigopal, Anu's pishe, was also frail. The cousins began to reflect on how few remained from that older generation.

"Actually," Sri began, her smile widening, "I suddenly remembered a funny story Aunt Mihir told me about Mamni during her university years." Doli and Mili exchanged amused glances and nodded in anticipation.

"Yeah, our Mamni was truly unique," Mili added.

Intrigued, everyone looked at Sri.

"Well," Sri continued, "when Mamni's post-graduate exam results were due, she practically barricaded herself in her room. She was so anxious, convinced she had failed, that she cried and refused to go to the university to get her results."

"Rangamashi," she glanced at Anu, Jay, and the others, "your Rangapishi, apparently found Mamni huddled in a corner, her usually neat hair disheveled, a picture of utter despair and certainty of failure."

Jay, with a puzzled expression, interjected, "Ma said she had dropped a year as she couldn't imagine being anything but the best. But that year, she had topped!"

"Yes, that's correct," Sri affirmed with a smile. "She had dropped, as she felt she was not well prepared."

Sri then looked at Anu and Jay. "The story goes that your father, our Mejomama, finally managed to coax his distraught younger sister out of her room. He took her to the university office and waited outside. Mamoni reluctantly went in, returning with a nonplussed expression that made your father assume the worst. But in reality, she had topped the entire university!"

"Yes, she was the postgraduate topper in History at Calcutta University that year," Jay added excitedly.

The three sisters nodded gently, a shared memory passing between them. They remembered Arohi as a thoughtful soul who found immense joy in books, and whose career had begun as a college lecturer.

Anu smiled softly. "And Pipi, your mother, had a way of making me feel so special. The most beautiful dresses for my birthdays and Durga Puja always came from her." A warmth entered her voice as she continued, "Being the first granddaughter, I think I held a special place in her heart. She truly spoiled me. I remember stories of being a little girl, dressed in frilly frocks and ribbons, and Pipi taking me to her college." She paused, turning to Sri. "And you too, Sri, when you were a little older, maybe around three, Pipi would often take us both. My memories of those times are a bit hazy." Anu paused again, a fond look on her face. "Even during my college days, the most exquisite saris would come from Pipi."

"The undeniably pampered grandchild of the Dasgupta family," Mili chimed in, a smile in her voice.

Anu's smile softened, and a pensive mood settled over her. "Now," she said, her voice trailing off as she gazed out the window at the setting sun, "there's no one left to truly take us back to that era. Only their memories and their words echo in our ears."

Just then, the door creaked open, and Shanu strolled in, the tail end of a cigarette between his fingers.

"Look at Shanu! Went up to the terrace for a smoke and has the audacity to come back with a lit cigarette!" Doli said sarcastically.

Shanu laughed, taking a seat and stubbing out the cigarette on an empty plate.

"Just showing off his smoking prowess!" Mili teased, wrinkling her nose.

Laughter rippled through the room.

Shanu adopted a serious expression. "You know, on my way to the attic, past the staircase landing, I remembered our Thakurda's gun cabinet that used to be there. It brought back a slightly scary memory." All the cousins turned to him; amusement mixed with curiosity. "I was maybe seven or eight. It was one of those languid weekend afternoons we Bengalis cherish, the world seemingly asleep."

A chorus of agreement and laughter followed. "Very true."

Shanu continued, "The afternoon was still and quiet. Sunlight striped the floor where Ma slept beside me. The grandfather clock ticked softly, and the combined snores of Sejopishi and Rangapishi drifted from their rooms as I sneaked onto the veranda, ready for a grand adventure."

He paused, taking a savoury from the plate and munching thoughtfully, enjoying their rapt attention. "Remember Rakhal, the rather hairy cook? I wasn't very comfortable around him back then."

Anu smiled. "Neither was I."

"More like a man with a beer belly and a fur coat!" Mili added, bursting into laughter.

"Ah yes, the unforgettable Rakhal," the cousins said in unison, chuckling. Shanu then revealed how he had tiptoed past the slumbering giant on the staircase landing and ventured into the forbidden attic. He'd opened the mysterious cabinet, and the sight inside had made his breath catch.

In a fright, he slammed the door shut, tripped over the sleeping Rakhal, and tumbled headfirst onto his mother.

"Oh my God! Not surprised at all. Shanu was always getting into mischief," Doli exclaimed.

Shanu grinned, pleased with the effect of his story. "No more suspense, Shanu, carry on," Mili urged.

Clearing his throat, Shanu continued with a solemn face, "I had come face to face with our Thakurda's gun cabinet!"

"Oh wow," Jay breathed.

"That childish memory has lingered with me for years, like the ghostly branches of a dead tree." He chuckled, his characteristic sound. Mili's eyes lit up as she exchanged a look with her older sister, remembering their mother's tales of their grandfather's hunting passion.

Then Anu spoke, "When I was little, the gun cabinet was on the landing. I once saw Rangapishi holding a rifle, talking to someone mysterious. I think she was selling one of Thakurda's shotguns." She paused. "I also have faint memories of Papa bringing home a deer to their house in Lansdowne, and once in Khamaria too."

Babul stood up with a flourish. "Ladies and gentlemen," he announced with a bow, "after these fascinating stories of our esteemed ancestors, can't you just feel our aristocratic lineage?" With another sweeping bow, he sat down.

"Hold on, Babul, let me finish the 'gun cabinet' saga," Anu interjected, smiling. "That ancestral relic now resides at my mother's place."

"Yes, a constant reminder of the early to mid-20th century, when hunting was a popular sport among the affluent," Jay added.

"This cupboard," Anu began playfully, a hint of amusement in her voice, "is actually a little piece of our history, a tangible link to our family's past. Perhaps one day I'll even embark on a hunt . . . but with a bit of a different spin!"

"And pray tell, what kind of a spin?" Mili asked, biting her nails with anticipation.

"It will be a hunt in search of my roots," Anu replied with a mysterious smile.

"So, about actual hunting," Shanu began, a knowing look in his eye, "it's been a part of Indian culture for centuries, right? From the epics to the Mughals, the British Raj, even Anglo-Indian traditions." He fiddled with his cigarette packet. "But then it was banned in '72 by the Wildlife Protection Act, which saved a lot of species," Jay chimed in.

Mili rolled her eyes playfully, a wide grin on her face. "But Shanu dear, Anu didi was talking about a different sort of hunting."

"Come on, I know that, Mili didi," Shanu frowned. "I was only trying to educate you guys." With an impish smile, he lit another cigarette.

42

Married His Letters

Mrinal returned from the US, and the family relocated to Bengaluru, a city in the south-western Indian state of Karnataka. Aisha pranced alongside her parents, excited about her school admission test.

They were flying out from Tezpur, which had a basic airport. It featured a single terminal with a modest capacity for passengers, offering only essential amenities like drinking water and washrooms. As the terminal gate opened for passengers to board the airside transfer bus, Aisha was nowhere to be found.

While Mrinal and Anu were busy handling their hand luggage, Aisha had darted off. She ran onto the wide-open space, which appeared too tempting a game, leading Mrinal and the airport staff on a brief chase before they found her twirling on the runway. Upon reaching the school, the playground beckoned, and she took off again, requiring Mrinal to retrieve a giggling Aisha. Finally, settled and energized by her adventures, Aisha playfully completed her test and secured a place at St. Paul's English School.

With Aisha happily occupied, Anu turned her attention to settling into their new home. As she opened a carton, her eyes sparkled as she recounted their shopping sprees in the US. Rummaging through Aisha's toys, she found the radio with its karaoke mic, the life-size dolls, the perambulator, and the soft toys.

"Oh, Mrinal," she giggled, nudging him playfully. "Remember the mountain of toys we bought from Toys 'R' Us? We made it up to Aish. She was so happy!"

Mrinal nodded, rummaging through his things and finding the Walkman, the CD player, the cassette player, and a digital clock. Anu leaned in, a fond smile on her face.

"You would spend hours poring over things at Radio Shack, wouldn't you? You were like a kid in a candy store! Honestly, sometimes I thought your gadgets were your first love!" The warmth in her voice made it clear it was a teasing remark, born of happy memories.

By the time Anu was fully settled and all the boxes were unpacked, she discovered that all the teaching positions for the year were filled. Consequently, for most of the year, Anu was primarily a homemaker. During this time, a subtle shift crept into Mrinal. His initial comments were light jabs disguised as banter. "Enjoying the extended holiday?" he would say with a wry smile. "Plenty of time for hobbies now that you're not correcting and grading copies, isn't it?"

Anu, still adjusting and hopeful, initially laughed them off, but as the missed teaching session sank in, his teasing became pointed, a subtle criticism pricking her optimism.

"I thought you had ambition," he would remark, "but you're just sitting at home waiting for the next season?"

"But you wanted me to stay in teaching, away from the corporate world," Anu retorted, a hint of frustration in her voice.

"Yes, before the US," he continued. "Sticking to high school teaching will get you nowhere. You'll be stuck. Unless you get a PhD for college teaching."

Anu stared at him, a whirlwind of emotions churning within her. Just a year ago, he had pushed her towards teaching, even encouraging her to pursue the B.Ed. course. His encouraging words now felt like a cruel trick. Beneath her confusion, a deep hurt simmered, intensified by a surfacing anger. His dismissive tone and the implication that her profession was beneath him stung deeply, a betrayal of his past support. Her thoughts disjointed, she thought, *How dare he dictate her ambition after guiding her here?* His smug pronouncements about her needing a Ph.D. felt belittling, leaving her bewildered, wounded, and resentful.

Anu mused, a knot tightening in her stomach, *that life here might be a constant uphill battle.*

*

With the academic year yet to begin, Anu found herself weighing the possibilities of school life against other career paths.

Then, one day, Mrinal cut through her indecision. "Anurima," he stated, exhaling a plume of smoke, "you're letting precious time slip away. Start exploring opportunities beyond academia." A dry cough punctuated his next thought, "Why let that business communication expertise you gained in the States go to waste?"

Anu's eyebrows rose, a hint of surprise on her face. "Okay," she said, her voice a little softer, "if that's what would make you happy."

With a renewed sense of purpose, Anu began to search for a new career, diligently scanning the daily newspapers. It wasn't long before an advertisement for a Business Communication coach at 'The Learning Systems' caught her eye. Her US certification, along with a natural talent for teaching and training, proved to be a valuable asset. The job involved training engineering students in soft skills like communication, personality development, and stress management.

A year later, an unexpected opportunity arose. During a class visit, a software company's HR Manager was so impressed that he extended an offer for the position of in-house communication consultant. The proposed salary was staggering—four times her current earnings. Astonished by the sudden and lucrative offer, Anu didn't hesitate to accept.

It was the era of the "brain-drain" in India, and Bangalore had become a hub for mainframe computers. US-based software companies were keen to export their most promising engineers, but there was a major hurdle: the communication skills of these brilliant young men were often appalling. When asked a simple question, they would just shake their heads like bobble-heads, making it impossible for Americans to tell if the answer was "yes" or "no." This bizarre behaviour earned them the nickname 'head-shakers'.

Anu's new professional journey began at Infotech Computer Consultants. Her role was to recruit and equip engineering students from local colleges with essential communication skills, and this work brought a renewed focus and a noticeable lightness to her home life. She later uncovered the intriguing truth behind her unexpected job offer: the very students she had been meticulously coaching were, in fact, the software company's own trainees who had successfully secured positions in the US.

After a year, the company encouraged Anu to pursue a management degree to facilitate a more structured corporate progression. She resigned to pursue an advanced marketing management diploma, much to Mrinal's unmistakable delight.

"Why is Mrinal so happy when I study? Does he secretly want me to be a lifelong student?" Anu often wondered.

Anu cherished her time at home with Aisha. During her study breaks, Aisha would playfully tease, "Mamma, you are also a student like me, so we are equal!"

These moments allowed Anu to devote more time to her daughter, following her more closely and feeling a swell of pride as she watched her princess blossom in her new school.

Upon completing her management course, Anu was offered the position of Assistant Manager in HR at her former workplace. A mix of excitement and nerves washed over her. *Assistant Manager!* she thought. *My corporate career begins.* The news felt even sweeter as Aisha's beaming smile caught her eye. Anu realised her daughter looked so proud, and that having a working mom meant something to her.

Alongside this newfound happiness, Anu began to observe a troubling pattern with Mrinal. While he would dedicate quality time to Aisha, often taking her for long drives on weekends, he never seemed proud of her successes. Aisha was growing up among the children of Mrinal's friends, all of whom were excelling and making their parents proud. While his friends would flaunt their children's accomplishments, Mrinal rarely spoke of Aisha's. Worse, back at home, he would immediately begin comparing Aisha to the other children. Each comparison chipped away at their daughter's spirit, causing a hurt and angry Aisha to retreat into herself.

These painful father-daughter interactions frustrated Anu deeply. Instinctively, she would try to boost Aisha's confidence, determined that her daughter wouldn't be defined by her father's undermining words. Anu remained a steadfast presence, always there to encourage Aisha to shine.

Anu often reflected on Mrinal's behaviour. Instead of cherishing his little princess, he would compare her to others and diminish her achievements. His persistent focus on her faults and his blindness to her accomplishments, even as trophies filled the house, a testament to her talent, baffled her.

Anu observed Mrinal's ingrained habit of criticism, a pessimistic lens that seemed to obscure his appreciation for his family. She often mused, "It's surprising that someone who was raised well and graduated from a premier institute in India holds such perspectives."

*

Anu was getting recognition in her workplace, but slowly the atmosphere at home once again began to take an ugly turn. Mrinal was constantly irritable, always finding something to criticise. Their differing views often led to arguments, fueled by his evident ego. Anu sought to understand him, but his silence about his work environment left her with little insight. She could only assume he was weathering a professional storm and had made her the target of his frustrations.

Anu sought solace with her mother and friends, but their suggestions of compromise felt like a dull ache. A battle raged inside, leaving her adrift. Her own upbringing, once a source of strength, now seemed distant and unfamiliar. The air felt alien. Anxiety tightened as she watched Aisha in their unspoken conflict.

Mrinal seemed to treat marriage as a game, his family as possessions. Over time, Anu felt like a puppet. Then she would ponder, *Why is he so intimidating despite having the best of everything?*

Just for Aisha's sake, Anu began to navigate the situation carefully. Hoping to bridge the divide, she suggested shared activities, which they enjoyed together but everything proved futile. Mrinal's pessimism was steadily eroding Anu's own resilience.

When all efforts failed, Anu remembered her mother's wisdom about the potent effect of silence. She created emotional distance from Mrinal, a decision that transformed their shared home into a space where they coexisted as strangers.

Her childhood was full of encouragement, she thought, a wry smile touching her lips. It was a bitter acknowledgment of the strange twist of fate that had bound her to Mrinal. She pictured his letters, those carefully crafted words that had painted a vibrant image—a stark contrast to the man she had barely noticed at their first meeting. *It wasn't him I fell for, she realized with a pang, but the romantic illusion he created through his letters.*

As Aisha entered middle school, Anu again prioritized her child, taking a career break. But idleness wasn't for her. She enrolled in a postgraduate diploma in HRM, which later led to an HR Manager role at Vetro Software Consultants.

After several years, the demands of her job became overwhelming. Drawing on her previous experience coaching engineering students in life skills and business communication, she became her own boss, transitioning to a freelance life coach and establishing her own Coaching Institute. During this phase, Anu began studying different personality types, which led her to human psychology and emotional intelligence.

*

Anu leaned back, sunlight streaming across her desk. She was engrossed in Daniel Goleman's *Emotional Intelligence: Why It Can Matter More Than IQ*, a book that had just revolutionised the market with its groundbreaking concept. IQ, EQ, spirituality . . . for so long, they had seemed separate.

Clarity dawned after weeks of study. Anu realised how the intelligent quotient (IQ) measured intellect, while the emotional quotient (EQ) applied to social dynamics. Inner peace, which is spirituality, grounded both. *They're not just concepts,* she mused, *but the very fabric of who we are. The way these interact . . . it must be rooted in our unique neurological architecture.* The deep insight from her studies provided a new framework for understanding herself and the people around her.

Around this time, her mother Reena, who had been observing Anu's personal journey, once again advised her to pursue a doctorate. It would provide a distraction and enrich her life, she said. The idea resonated with Anu. Her mind, now buzzing with new ideas, began to connect the dots. *Why not a PhD in IQ, EQ, spirituality?* she wondered. *It could be intriguing research!*

PART VIII
1998–2004
Kolkata, Bangalore, Europe

43

The Cursed House

Mili had travelled from the United States for her yearly trip to India, and Doli had come from Delhi. Reena invited the three sisters, Sri, Mili, and Doli, for a lunch gathering because Anu and Jay were also in town.

"Now girls, let's reminisce about the days of your grandfather," Reena said, a warm smile on her face. "We've gathered here for a reason. You have all grown up hearing tales about the heroic deeds and philanthropic activities of your grandfather and his family."

Mili grinned mischievously. "So I bet all of us have a wee bit of that streak running through our veins, Mejomamima."

Reena smiled back. "We have a surprise for you all."

Jay's gaze flitted around the room, a nervous yet excited energy about her. She leaned forward, as if on the verge of sharing something significant. "You won't believe what I did," she began, a playful glint in her eyes. Unable to hold back any longer, she revealed, "While I was in Bangladesh, I had some spare time, so I decided to visit Paksey."

Reena chimed in, "That is the surprise item of today's lunch get-together."

Everyone looked at Jay. "Ah! You visited Paksey. Then you are the lucky girl," Doli said.

Jay beamed. "So, I am one up on you guys."

It was the late 20th century, and Jayina had become a frequent visitor to Bangladesh. During one of her work trips, she visited their grandfather's property in Paksey, which was in the Rajshahi district. She began telling them that, on reaching the place, she had experienced a sense of profound unease.

She began, "I reached Paksey when the shadows were yawning and stretching at twilight, so I could hardly fathom the vastness of our grandfather's property. I found out that the owner of the house was Arif Mohammad, who was locally known as Arif Punjabi, as he hailed from Punjab."

She paused. "I stood in our Thakurda's land and vented out my emotions, hugging onto a large mango tree, the girth of which spoke of its age."

Jay looked at the reaction of her audience and carried on, "Then I saw a gentleman watering the vegetable garden with a hose pipe. I later found out that he was Raheem, the eldest son of Arif Mohammad. This gentleman wanted me to spend the night in the house built by our grandfather."

Jay paused. "In the beginning, I had shown reluctance to spend the night in that mysterious house with a bunch of strangers. But later, after I talked to the female members of the family, they convinced me that I must experience my grandfather's house."

Jay stopped, looked at the eager faces, and continued. "So, after a nice meal, I ultimately gave in and spent the night in our legendary ancestral house, about which we had heard so much."

"What did you feel, Jay? Did you feel transported to that era?" asked Mili.

"I felt a wee bit strange, all right, with an unknown family all around me, but I slept well." Jay paused, a distant look in her eyes. "The next day at breakfast, I noticed

Raheem Chacha had a faraway look. Then he said something very strange."

Doli leaned forward, her voice low. "What was that? You're making it sound so mysterious."

"It is," Jay said, her eyes wide. "I was terrified."

Raheem Chacha's words, spoken slowly in Bengali, echoed in her memory: *"Eta abhishopto bari, Jayina;* It is a cursed house, Jayina."

Doli gasped, her brow furrowed in confusion. "Oh my God, he said?"

"Why should it be a cursed house?" Sri asked meekly. "It was once our grandfather's vibrant household."

"Yes, I wasn't prepared for that kind of comment," Jay admitted. "I looked at him, and I could feel him trying to shake a dull ache from his head." Jay cringed slightly at the memory. "He narrated how their father, Arif Mohammad, was stabbed to death by the locals right in the living room during the Bangladesh liberation war."

"Raheem Chacha said they hailed from Lahore, which was then in West Pakistan."

"God, how gory! It sounds like a movie plot," Doli said, a hand pressed to her chest.

Jay nodded grimly. "Yes. I had never heard anything like that. As I listened, my conscience began to unravel. I felt a dizzying spin."

Everyone was listening with rapt attention. Jay suddenly stood up, grabbed the bottle from the table, and took a long swig. "Hang on, girls," she said, her voice a little shaky. "There is more.

"Later, as I followed Raheem Chacha on a tour of the property, I saw acres of land full of vegetables, grains, flowers, and fruit trees. He pointed at them and said it all still belonged to the Dasgupta family."

"Really?" Doli said, her voice laced with disbelief.

"Yes. I was too shocked to even respond. I had to cut the tour short because I had a flight back to India later that day."

Jay continued, her brow furrowed in thought. "Raheem Chacha had mentioned that our Thakurda's eldest son, Abhinandan, had exchanged his Paksey house with his father's Dum Dum house. But his father couldn't afford to buy the land surrounding the house, so our uncle kept it in their care."

"He couldn't have," Mili said, looking at Jay. "That was a huge amount of agricultural land, surely beyond him."

Reena, who had been listening quietly, interrupted. "Yes, after the partition, the fear of being killed prevented your uncles and aunts from venturing into the new country, East Pakistan. So, the land technically still belongs to the Dasgupta family."

Jay nodded. "Everything felt so alien yet so dear. I was too confused to say anything." She took a deep breath, a relieved expression on her face. "That was quite an experience indeed."

"But what about our grandfather's school, Ratnaprobha Vidyapitha?" Anu asked, completely absorbed by the story. "Did you see it?"

Jay shook her head. "None of them spoke about it, so I didn't ask. They did, however, show me the remains of the Maa Kali Temple."

The others looked at her, and a playful light entered their eyes. "We should rub against you, Jay," someone joked. "You're the only one who's actually been there."

"It's true," Anu chimed in. "What we have left are just stories. We've never experienced any of it with our own eyes."

Mili bit her nail, her gaze serious. "So true, Anu didi, but no one can take away our pride or our bloodline."

A distant look crossed Anu's face. "Our family is full of heroic deeds," she murmured. "Remember our aunt, Srimoyee?"

"Yes, she and her friend Srilata spent seven years in the Hijli detention camp," Sri said.

"Exactly," Anu replied. "I was telling Mrinal about how Srimoyee pishi and her friend fired point-blank at the District Magistrate of Comilla. When he heard the story, he told me something astounding. He said the old Hijli detention camp had been converted into the Indian Institute of Technology, Kharagpur—India's first technical institute after independence."

"Really?" everyone said in unison, their faces still showing shock.

As they processed the last story, Reena got up. She returned from the next room, holding a small packet tied with a red ribbon. "After everything Jay has told us," she said, her voice soft, "I feel like I have the perfect coda for this story."

Mili and Doli exchanged glances. "More surprises, Mejomamima? We're still trying to digest Jay's story."

Reena smiled as she untied the ribbon. "This is for all of you. It's a collection of short stories, and the main character in the first one is Jay, inspired by her experiences in Paksey." She presented a copy of the book to each of them.

The three sisters held the books, their expressions a mix of awe and wonder. "We can't wait to read it," they said. "Our rich heritage... we're a part of it, too, aren't we?"

Anu ran her hand over the cover, a wave of feeling washing over her. She knew, with an undeniable certainty, that she was being pulled toward her ancestral land.

44

The Solitary Postcard

The years had blurred, the pages of the calendar turning into memories. Most of Anu's paternal aunts were now just figures in memory, their voices echoes in the familiar room. The cousins had reconvened once again, a familiar constellation in the room that held the ghosts of their childhood. The sun shone through the drapes with a distant, uncaring serenity, and the familiar scent of old wood and the faded patterns on the drapes echoed gatherings from years ago. Looking around, they felt as if time itself had stood still.

"Can you believe we're almost in the 21st century?" Mili said, her voice carrying a hint of the fast-paced life she led as an economist in the United States.

"I just heard our good old 'Calcutta' is officially going to become 'Kolkata' this year," Anu replied.

Jay, who worked for an NGO in Uttarakhand, nodded. "It's a move to shed its colonial identity and embrace its original name."

"The Bengali pronunciation is the same, so the change has had little impact on the local populace," Sri added, her academic tone reflecting her career as a geography lecturer in Kolkata. Her gaze drifted to the wall where the solemn portraits of their ancestors hung like silent witnesses.

"Remember the days," she began, her voice soft with nostalgia, "when we would all gather in this room, chatting and listening to stories from our aunts?"

A wistful sigh escaped Anu. "Those were the golden days," she murmured. "Rangapishi's passing was such a loss. She was so well-known for her distinctively generous personality. Many even compared her to a father figure in the Dasgupta household." Anu smiled faintly. "Her faith in people was so unwavering. I remember one time, we all tried to dissuade her from giving our temple priest, Kanchon, a box of priceless ornaments for the deity. But she just said, 'I am doing my duty. I do not doubt people, so my conscience remains clear. If they misuse it, the guilt will prick them, not me.' That was just who she was."

A silence settled in the room as the cousins reflected on Rangapishi. Then, Sri turned to Anu, a somber note in her voice. "Speaking of uncanny things... do you remember that postcard you wrote to her?"

"Oh! Yes," Anu said, her eyes widening. "You're talking about the one I wrote after that strange dream... the one where she came to bid me goodbye. I'm still in awe when I think about it. How could such a thing have happened?"

Sri nodded, her expression mirroring Anu's awe. "I remember that day so clearly. We were all stunned, beyond words. It was the eleventh day after Rangapishi's passing." She paused, her gaze softening. "The shraddha ceremony, the last rites. The obituaries had been in all the leading newspapers, and the hall was full to the brim. Her students, friends, and relatives came from every corner of Calcutta to pay their respects to their beloved teacher, their friend, their aunt. Rangapishi was known to everyone as Mihir, or Mihir-di."

Tears welled up in Anu's eyes. She recalled the dreadful dream where Rangapishi caressed her forehead before melting away. In the dream, her Jethamoni, Abhinandan, had seemed to be floating in mid-air.

Sri continued, her voice dropping to a near whisper. "The ceremony had started, but a puja ingredient was missing. Our uncle Bhulu went to fetch it from the house. When he entered, he noticed a solitary postcard peeking from behind the glass of the letterbox. He froze in shock when he saw the handwriting."

Sri stared at Anu. "It was your letter," she said softly. "Dated February 15, 1991—the very day she had passed away in her sleep."

Bhulu returned to the prayer hall, waving the postcard. He handed it to Basanta, a science postgraduate who was usually a beacon of logic. She was left speechless. She cleared her throat and read the words aloud, her voice trembling slightly:

"Nainital District, UP Feb. 15, 1991

Dear Rangapishi,

I hope this letter finds you in good health. Today, at the close of dawn, around 4 A.M., you visited me in my dream. I woke with a start. It was so real, yet so distant, and it filled me with a sense of uneasiness. I am confused and bewildered by what I saw. Ma says you haven't been keeping well, so I must confess you have been in my thoughts these past few days. I am truly worried. Please take care of yourself. Looking forward to hearing from you. See you soon.

With prayers, wishes, and warm regards,

Yours, Anu."

A stupefied silence fell over the guests. No one could reconcile the event with any scientific principle.

Jay screwed up her eyes. "Really? That sounds like a freaky coincidence." Doli nodded. "But it did happen, Jay. It was the talk of the family for years."

For the rest of her life, that uncanny encounter with Rangapishi was Anu's keepsake, worn like an amulet.

*

Anu's home life felt like a relentless cycle. A month of quiet peace would pass before Mrinal's familiar criticisms and sarcastic comments would send her spiraling back into a familiar, suffocating pain. She cursed her life, desperate for a way to vent the frustration that no amount of confiding in friends or family could ease. She felt morally crushed, suffocated, and unable to focus on her work, finding her only solace in returning home to cuddle up with her daughter.

She knew she was at a breaking point. Escaping this fragile state would demand a lion's heart, a bold decision she was terrified to make. The weight of her suppressed feelings had become too heavy to ignore, pushing her toward a precipice where breaking free felt like a terrifying free fall. Yet, as she looked ahead, the suppressed feelings, and the stories of her family's resilience, urged her forward, leaving her to consider what it meant to have a lion's heart.

45

The Shadow of Unknowing

The year 2000 was etched in Anurima's memory, a year that began with a tumultuous internal struggle. Her emotions were a live wire, untouchable, like trying to defuse a bomb. A tempestuous storm brewed within, threatening to shatter her carefully constructed life, her mind a whirlwind of fragmented thoughts. The pain felt raw, as if her skin had been stripped away and exposed to a bleeding wind.

Trips to medical centers offered no relief; specialists couldn't diagnose her ailment. Anu would wake to an agonizing ache that immobilised her back, each movement a jarring scrape. Some mornings, it felt as if a heavy stone had been inexplicably placed on her lower back, making rising from bed a monumental effort. Even painkillers brought no ease.

She developed an unhealthy palour, her skin losing its natural warmth and taking on a sallow, almost greyish undertone, as if her vitality had been drained. A slumped, listless posture became her norm. At work, she couldn't concentrate and would return home with a splitting headache, a pain pills offered only temporary relief from. Each day was a nightmare, and as the intensifying pain fuelled her doubt, deepening despair numbed her to her stagnant life. A psychological wreck, she listlessly dragged through her days, her dull eyes mirroring only inner sadness.

The doctor's gaze had already drifted to the next file as he said, "It's probably just stress. Try to relax more, get some rest." Anu clutched the crumpled list of her symptoms, each one dismissed with a casual wave. Outside, the bright sunlight felt like a cruel mockery of the darkness closing in, a stark reminder of her isolation in this baffling illness.

The weight of her undiagnosed ailment bore down on her, leaving her too fragile to save her coaching centre. She fought to keep it afloat, but the struggle was a losing battle, and she eventually had to shut it down.

Now, her days were spent in the quiet solace of her well-stocked library. Sunlight filtered through the dusty windows, illuminating the worn spines of her cherished books. One day, she pulled out a Mills & Boon novel she had once doted on, its pages filled with pictures of a love that felt foreign to her. As she read, a tear escaped, tracing a lonely path down her pale cheek. She sipped her green tea, its warmth offering only a fleeting lift from her oppressive sorrow.

A brief respite from her solitude arrived with Aish's return from school. Anu cherished these moments with her lively daughter, who would burst in from evening games, toss her toys aside, and leap onto her lap, asking to play Ludo or Chinese checkers. Knowing her mother's love for movies, Aish would sometimes suggest, "Mamma, I'll finish my homework in a jiffy, then let's watch a movie."

These interactions with her daughter reminded Anu that she needed to bounce back for Aish's sake. Lost in thought, she would muse: *If my body is sound, why am I at a crossroads? Where am I going wrong? What are these puzzling pains? Or are these necessary, painful lessons to grow up in life?*

Driven by a desperate need for answers, Anu decided on a full health check. As she lay in the hospital bed, connected to an IV drip, she closed her eyes and breathed in rhythm with the beeping monitor. A chilling numbness crept through her legs, and in her heightened anxiety, she braced for the worst. *Am I prey to a carcinogen?* she brooded. Aish couldn't fathom what was wrong with her mom, looking at her with fear-filled eyes, unable to grasp the cause of Anu's failing health.

The hospital room offered no comfort; her hope was as barren as the walls. The lone green curtain felt like a flimsy shield against the unknown, and each cough from behind it amplified her own precarious fragility. The crisp, starched sheets beneath her felt shockingly cold against her feverish skin. Even the distant sunlight seemed clinical, devoid of the life-giving energy she desperately craved. Lying there, Anu finally understood why people brought flowers to loved ones in hospitals; she desperately needed a bunch to lift her spirits. Weeping had always been a healthy release, and as the "blue feeling" washed over her like an unwanted wave, her sandcastles were knocked flat as tears rolled down, creating wet splotches on the silvery white sheets.

The two days in Arcott Hospital were an unforgettable ordeal. Nurses, appearing at odd hours with stacks of reports, would summon a petrified Anu away, leaving her to dread their contents. Even the fluorescent corridor lights seemed menacing whenever a nurse, face tight with detachment, appeared abruptly at her bedside.

"Another test," the nurse stated curtly, snatching Anu's chart. Her heart hammering, Anu was bundled through a labyrinth of rooms and intimidating machines, her senses numb. A masked, impersonal technician gestured for her to lie down. Cold plates pressed on her skin as a mechanical voice droned incomprehensible instructions. Trapped under the machinery, Anu felt like a specimen under a microscope. Each passing day intensified her feeling of being a victim of a mysterious malady.

46

The Path to Light

Mrinal opened the door and let out a visible sigh of relief when he saw Sumana. "Thank goodness you're here. I don't know what's happening to your friend," he blurted out, his brow furrowed with concern.

Sumana, who had been confused by Anu's letter and had journeyed to Bangalore to check on her, replied calmly, "I have a feeling it's nothing too serious; she just needs a change of scenery." She quietly followed Mrinal into the guestroom. On the way to his office, Mrinal dropped Sumana off at Arcott Hospital.

Sumana entered the room and stopped. Lying on the hospital bed was a still form. A worried question escaped her lips, "Hey Anu, what have you done? You look so sunken."

Anu's weary eyes fluttered open, and she offered a weak smile. Sumana's heart ached as she looked at her friend. The once expressive eyes were now hollow and shadowed. Anu had been a force of nature, an inextinguishable fire of positive energy. Their friends used to joke, "Even in darkness, you'd see Anu's inner flame, ready to ignite anew."

Sumana's mind drifted back to their university days, remembering the vivacious Anu who would effortlessly train dancers and lead chorus singers for their reunion's dance drama. Her charismatic presence and lively gestures had always captivated people. Staring at her friend in disbelief, she murmured, "Anurima Dasgupta, your once radiant beauty is now just sorrow."

As Sumana looked out the window, the harsh, bright sky softened into twilight grey. A question settled over her: despite her friend's fairytale wedding, envied by many for Mrinal's brilliance and Anu's US trousseau, had Anu truly found happiness? Sumana sighed, a quiet, internal release.

The next day, standing before her dispirited friend, Sumana felt a sense of unfamiliarity. Sunlight streamed through the blinds, illuminating the sallow tones of Anu's skin. Soon after, Anu requested a discharge, but the nurse on duty told her to return, as the final test was still pending.

Their heels clicked through the hospital corridor as the two friends left Arcott and journeyed toward Anu's home. Anu looked forward to finally confiding in her best friend and catching up on gossip about their classmates in Kolkata. As they chatted and laughed, navigating Bangalore's busy streets, the familiar rhythm of their friendship felt like a much-needed balm.

On reaching Anu's place, Sumana used the spare key Mrinal had given her before he headed to work.

*

The living room was dark and stale as the friends stepped into the hallway. The gladioli in the flower vase had withered, exuding a heavy, stale aroma. Sumana and Anu worked together, sorting laundry, cleaning the house, and preparing lunch before Aish returned from school.

As the afternoon progressed, Anu took off the mask she wore for others. With her best friend by her side, she wanted to be her normal self again. She spoke her heart out, and Sumana listened patiently. Sumana recalled how for years, Anurima had hoodwinked their friends with a cheerful facade, hiding the pain behind her smile at every Science College reunion.

A call from her daughter, Tushai, meant Sumana had to return to Kolkata. Her daughter was the same age as Anu's, a detail that had always bonded the two friends. After Sumana left, Mrinal received a call from Arcott Hospital, informing him that Anu still had a pending test. He accompanied her to the hospital, where they sat together in the waiting lounge.

Anu's feelings smouldered like embers beneath the surface. Mrinal looked at her, seeing a deep darkness in her familiar eyes, but he couldn't reach the bottom of it. Her gaze held a silent fear, a profound suffering, and a deep loneliness that went unnoticed by him. Feeling unable to comfort her, he stepped out for a smoke. As he stood outside, he secretly admired her strength and courage, a silent observer to her private battle.

The day arrived that Anu had endured countless restless nights for. She reached Arcott Hospital, clutching Aish's hand as she gathered her reports from every department, her heart pounding like a racehorse. To her surprise, she received a clean bill of health. She couldn't trust her eyes.

A sigh of immense relief escaped her lips. *It's all in the mind,* she murmured. *The problem was psychological. I need to bury these pain-filled memories and emerge afresh.*

She knew her mind was in need of repair, and she held up a hand to her unnerving thoughts, as if stopping a runaway train. She pictured every joyous memory, every happy moment, and built a mental fortress to combat the upsetting events of her life, which she knew her brain might replay without warning. This time, she was prepared to fight back.

Anu wondered, *Our brains must be hard-wired from the times of the cave dweller to remember the nasty stuff along with the good!* She then told herself, *No more self-pity. I need to bounce back, for the sake of my little girl.* The next morning, as Anu leapt out of the covers, a seed of hope sprang into the ground. She clung to that bright star in her dusky universe, feeling its brightness fill her inner self through light-years of distance.

The fighter in her stirred. *"You are going to win this match,"* it said. *"Get up, Anu, take a nine-count if you must, but be ready to stand and throw down the gauntlet."*

Anu confronted her situation by parking herself in front of her computer. Her mind was a vortex, and she murmured under her breath, *"My software is corrupted, time to clean."* Breathing shallowly, her fingers hovered over the 'delete' button, a subconscious act of trying to erase her pain. As she looked at the screen, a wave of calm washed over her, the panic receding. The digital chaos before her, though meaningless, offered a strange flicker of renewal. It was a forced attempt at positivity, a mental decluttering.

*

A month later, Anu's phone rang. It was Runa, another old friend, who said she had work in Bangalore and was planning a trip. Anu's spirits lifted immediately. She desperately needed a distraction, and nothing could be better than time with a college friend. During the call, Anu asked, "Are you coming all by yourself?"

"No, I am bringing my son, Rupak. He has a midterm break."

Anu felt a jolt of happiness. She had sensed her daughter, Aish, slowly secluding herself, unable to fit in. She hoped that having Rupak, who was the same age, would help Aish feel more engaged.

When they met, Runa was surprised to see her friend. "Anu, I've always known you to be a strong-headed personality," she said. "What is all this?"

Anu grinned sheepishly. "Life has thrown such challenges that I was bowled out."

Runa's two-day visit, packed with laughter and gossip, revitalized Anu. Her natural conscientiousness and self-assurance kicked back in, making her feel strong enough for anything and back in charge.

Meanwhile, Mrinal was relieved to receive the reports from the hospital. The doctor at Arcott had confirmed that Anu had a clean bill of physical health. He had advised Mrinal to visit a psychologist, as he believed the root cause was a mental health issue exacerbated by stress.

When Mrinal met with the psychologist, she began by asking, "How is your married life?" Mrinal couldn't answer and simply lowered his head. The psychologist continued, "Physically, there's nothing wrong with your wife. She needs a change, and she'll bounce back." She then noted the clear discord in their relationship. "I can see that your personalities clash. Mr. Sensharma, marriage isn't a competitive game where one must be 'right' and the other 'wrong.' You need to go hand-in-hand." Pausing, she added, "I request that you both work on this together."

On his way home, the psychologist's words echoed in Mrinal's mind. He thought about how he had always gone against Anu, criticising her and crushing her morale for every little thing. The cold truth of his actions suddenly struck him. *Am I too hard on her?* he mused. *Why am I unable to handle married life? I think I need to change my attitude.*

47

Ray of Sunshine

Anurima had let the silence of her home become a weight. The mundane routine, the same four walls, it all felt like a cage. One morning, with a sharp inhale, she decided she'd had enough. The Anurima who felt stuck was gone. In her place was a woman with a new purpose. She grabbed her laptop, her fingers flying over the keys as she designed a new business card, a tangible promise of a life waiting to be rebuilt.

She not only reopened her Business Communication and Life Skills Coaching Centre but also expanded her reach. She took on external assignments, facilitating workshops in universities and corporate offices, serving as both a life coach and a corporate trainer.

Her flexible schedule gave her back her free time, and she dove headfirst into her creative passions. Singing, her favourite cultural pursuit, was at the top of the list. But her renewed energy didn't stop there. She also began staging ballets and hosting shows, turning her passions into new projects.

The telephone rang one afternoon, pulling Anurima away from her work. It was her friend, Jayati.

"Anu, I'm hoping you're in Bangalore. We're thinking of coming to your place," Jayati's voice buzzed with energy.

"Oh, wow, really?" Anurima's heart lifted at the surprise. "That's wonderful! Just you?"

Jayati didn't let her finish. "The whole family! I have a conference in the city, so we decided to make a trip out of it."

"That's fantastic! You have to come over," Anurima insisted, her mind already buzzing with plans. "This weekend I'm hosting a show, and I think you all would love it."

"A show? Seriously? It sounds like we picked the perfect weekend to visit," Jayati said, a note of genuine delight in her voice.

"I know! It'll be so much fun. Just come over, Jayati. I can't wait."

*

Anu's first gig was to co-host an event with Rahul Mitra, a prosperous businessman. When she arrived at the auditorium, she spotted him instantly. He looked every bit the part of a successful entrepreneur, his well-fitted maroon Nehru jacket a stylish counterpoint to a long Tussar silk kurta. Anu adored Tussar silk, an exquisite "wild silk" she knew came from a yellow-brown moth.

He certainly has good taste, she mused, walking down the aisle toward him.

When she reached him, he greeted her with a warm, traditional namaskar, a flamboyant smile on his face. "I've heard great things about you, Anurima," he said, his eyes twinkling.

Anu laughed. "I hope they were all good." She offered her hand. "At long last, we meet," she said, her charming smile on full display.

"I understand you're a fantastic Rabindra Sangeet singer," he said, looking visibly impressed.

Anurima lowered her eyes, a slight blush on her cheeks. "I just love it. That's all."

Rahul shifted his weight, a sheepish grin replacing his confident one. "I must apologise. I simply couldn't find the time to make it to the rehearsals. But let me glance through the script now."

"No problem at all. You have the main script," Anu said reassuringly. "We can just play it by ear, can't we, Rahul da?" She added the respectful "dada" for "elder brother," a common term of respect in Bengal.

Rahul then introduced her to his family; his wife, Reena, and daughter, Rohini, a young woman with a graceful hourglass figure and striking smoky blue eyes.

"Hi, nice meeting you, Rohini. We should catch up sometime," Anurima said, flashing her radiant smile.

"Sure, we must, Anu di," Rohini replied with a grin, using the respectful "di" for "elder sister."

"Ah, Anurima," Rahul said with visible pride, patting his daughter's shoulder, "my daughter is a very good dancer."

"Wow, then all the more reason we must catch up, Rohini. We'd make a great team," Anurima said, her mind already racing with ideas.

Just then, Rahul looked past her. "Where is your family, Anu?" he asked gently.

Anurima, feeling a little flustered, said, "Oh, they're here too."

She spotted Jayati, Mrinal, and Jayati's husband, Shubham, walking down the aisle, with Aisha and Jayati's daughter, Jamini, right behind them, deep in conversation.

"This is my friend Jayati," Anu said proudly. "She was the topper of our postgraduate class."

Jayati blushed. "Stop it, Anu. We're not here to talk about college."

"Okay, okay," Anurima chuckled.

Mrinal spoke up. "She's a very good friend of Anu's. They've come all the way from Kolkata."

After a round of introductions and polite conversation, Anurima and Rahul excused themselves and moved to the front of the auditorium. They quickly reviewed the script, with Rahul already discussing potential filler material.

When the first bell rang, they walked to the stage, moving the heavy curtain aside. As they took their places at the podium, Rahul turned to her and said, "Hey, let's just keep it casual. What do you think?"

"Sure, sounds good to me," Anu replied.

The two of them immediately clicked, charming the audience with their storytelling styles. Rahul's deep, booming baritone filled the auditorium, complemented by Anu's smooth, husky voice. She spoke with confidence and poise, her tone captivating the crowd.

When the show was finally over, Rahul let out a long sigh of relief. "Phew, what a relief!" he said, a sheen of sweat on his forehead.

Anu nodded, exhaling herself. She smiled at him. "You did great, Rahul da. I think we did a pretty good job, especially considering this was our first time hosting together."

"I hope so. I was really nervous at the beginning," he admitted.

"Me too," she confessed. "Ready to face the crowd and see what they thought?"

Rahul grinned and nodded, eager to see their reaction.

Another round of applause greeted them as they got off the stage. Rahul and Anurima looked at each other, their faces radiating with relief as they saw the crowd cheering them on.

"Hey, you two rocked!" someone shouted from the audience.

Rahul grinned at Anu. "I think we pulled it off."

The program was a clear success, and the director, Mr. Asit Kumar Raha, beamed as he saw Anurima and Rahul walking toward him. Approaching them with a goofy smile, he said, "You both did a great job, even though it was your first time. A few small mistakes can certainly be overlooked."

Rahul nodded, giving Anurima a meaningful glance. Mr. Raha was her former mentor—a polished, witty, and well-read gentleman with an undeniable air of authority. She had immense respect for his ability to think through any problem that arose during his events. To everyone in their circle, he was simply "Raha da."

As Rahul and Anu walked towards the tea area, Rahul suddenly said, "Have you heard of an American business opportunity that is soon coming to India?"

Anu shook her head, as business was something she was least interested in. She soon excused herself as she spotted Jayati trying to catch her attention. Thus, the conversation died instantly.

*

The Bangalore summer arrived in a blaze of bougainvillea, prompting Anu to host a casual get-together, a respite from her busy schedule of workshops and rehearsals. She could never have guessed that amidst the laughter and mango lassi, a quiet conversation in a corner of her large sit-out would sow the seeds of a future she could have never envisioned. Rahul Mitra, a glass of lemonade in hand, gestured her away from the animated chatter.

He began, "Anu, what are you doing these days? I gather you left your job?"

"Yes, Rahul da, I am on my own now." Anu paused. "I have become a facilitator, imparting training to the trainees of software companies."

"That is interesting," he began, his dark eyes serious. "I have something rather unconventional to propose. I think you will enjoy it, though it's a business proposition."

His words hung in the humid air, immediately sparking a sense of unease within Anu.

"A business, Rahul da?"

Anu shook her head, lost in thought. A familiar ghost from her childhood returned, the long-ingrained belief that business was a murky world, best avoided by respectable Bengalis. Better to live a life of modest means than to risk soiling oneself with commerce.

So when Rahul unveiled the business model, which focused on training programs and skill development workshops, a wave of bewilderment washed over her.

Sensing her confusion, Rahul leaned in. "Anu, this business requires someone exactly like you, someone who genuinely enjoys training people," he reassured her. "You would be in a leadership position, responsible for shaping people's lives."

Anu was intrigued. Teaching and training were her passions. Still, she remained torn.

Then, a few days later, the phone rang. "Hello, Sensharma residence," she answered.

"Hello, Rahul Mitra here. Am I speaking to Anurima?" the deep baritone voice asked.

"Hello, Rahul da," Anu said, a smile on her face.

"I just called to remind you about the business proposition we talked about,"" he said.

"Oh yes, Rahul da, I've been thinking about it," Anu blurted out.

"That sounds promising," he replied.

Anxious to learn more about the launch Rahul was so excited about, Anu awkwardly asked, "So, when is the event, Rahul da?"

"It's tomorrow at The Sheraton."

"Okay."

"Could you come to my place at 5 p.m.? The program starts at 6:30, and The Sheraton is right by my house. We can go together," he offered.

"Sure, Rahul da. I'll be there, 5 p.m. sharp," Anu said.

"I'll look forward to it, Anurima," he said, the excitement in his voice clear as he hung up.

Anu took a deep breath. She had been foolish to hesitate. Rahul Mitra was, after all, a successful businessman. She recalled him mentioning that an Englishman he met in London had introduced him to the idea, a concept that originated in the United States.

I definitely need to check this out, she thought, her mind made up.

*

A cool December breeze followed Anu and Rahul Mitra as they approached the five-star hotel. The foyer was a vibrant sea of people in business attire, their energy crackling like a storm. They moved with a swagger that made Anu think of Olympic champions, and she felt a small wave of unease. She kept her eyes on Rahul, navigating carefully through the throng, determined not to get lost.

Meanwhile, Rahul had gone forward, found a seat, and was keeping an eye out for Anu. He spotted her standing in the crowd, looking confused, stood up, and gestured for her to come over. Anu quickly made her way down the aisle and demurely sat beside him. Little did Anu know that she was at a juncture, about to embark on an exhilarating journey, and this was the lead-up.

As the curtain rose, Anurima saw a stage filled with individuals from around the globe. Rahul's enthusiastic voice boomed, explaining that twenty members of the President's Team and Chairman's Club had come to India to launch this new business. The formal attire, company badges, and the slogan "Shaping Up To A Great Lifestyle" created a sophisticated and inspiring atmosphere.

Anu was mesmerised by the success stories and the business and health products they introduced. The air buzzed with an energy that made her feel as if she was on the brink of an incredible journey. Then, a single speech by a Chairman's Club member completely captivated her.

By the end of the five-day event, Anurima Sensharma felt completely transformed. She saw this multi-level marketing concept not as a risky business venture, but as an adventure. It required training new people in soft skills—a challenge she was more than confident she could meet.

The weight she had been carrying for so long finally lifted. She was ready to soar, a new feeling bubbling up inside her. It was a mix of the unknown and something deeply joyful that promised a brighter future.

48

The Strange Caller

On that quiet, sultry afternoon, Anurima's heart fluttered with a new kind of anticipation as she rang the bell at the Mitra residence. Each visit now held the promise of her new venture.

The maid smiled and led her into the elegant living room, where two muted, desert-toned conversational areas invited comfort with their plump sofas and squashy cushions. Across the room, a dry bar stood, and thriving geraniums brightened the windows.

Rahul Mitra arrived, inviting Anu to make herself comfortable. He assured her he'd be right back to discuss her expanding role in the new enterprise. Settling into the rocking chair by the window, a quiet pride blossomed within her, a direct result of her recent success.

Rahul then joined her with a smile, immediately praising Anu's quick grasp of the venture. Their discussion flowed, moving onto new strategies and the upcoming business development speech. Just then, the silent telephone in the far corner shrilled, abruptly interrupting their conversation.

Rahul swiftly answered the call, his voice dropping to a hushed murmur as he spoke. Anu, across the room, couldn't make out a word. After a while, Anu settled back in her rocking chair, the grandfather clock's rhythmic tick-tock her sole companion. She drifted into a happy afternoon siesta, waking abruptly to a rough nudge. Before she could gather her wits, Rahul Mitra thrust the cordless phone into her hands. Then, with a meaningful nod, he commanded, "Go on, talk to him."

Anu, her brow furrowed, asked, "Who is it, Rahul da?"

"Just answer it," he said with a grin, leaving her staring at the phone and his retreating back.

Composing herself, she offered a meek, "Hello, Anurima Sensharma here."

To her utter surprise, an English voice responded. "Hello Anurima, I am Richard Gardner from the UK. Rahul Mitra has just told me about you, and I wanted to congratulate you on your recent success," the voice said, his tone warm and genuine.

Taken completely by surprise, Anu could only manage, a stunned "Thank you so much."

Richard then introduced himself as a member of the President's Team for the business group she had just joined, adding that he lived in Manchester, UK.

The next hour was a monologue, punctuated only by Anu's brief responses. At first, she was guarded, but with each passing minute, her defenses lowered. Richard Gardner's words were almost musical, a captivating stream of encouragement that made her wonder if she had heard him correctly. Overwhelmed by the sudden shift, she could only nod, her nerves buzzing as the reality of speaking with a member of the President's Team sank in.

Hesitant at first, Anu chose her words carefully, but she soon found her confidence. She began to outline the business strategies she planned to implement the following month, the enthusiasm in her voice clear. Despite her mix of intimidation and excitement, she sensed that Richard's mind was already several steps ahead, formulating a sophisticated strategy that was beyond her current understanding. His insightful questions and genuine interest spoke volumes.

This kind of direct motivational talk was a completely new experience for Anu. In India, at that time, such encouragement was uncommon, both within families and in the workplace. Anu felt a surge of exhilaration. *This gentleman is so genuine*, she thought, his sincerity radiating through the phone.

As the hour passed, Richard's words floated like confetti, and Anu became lost in their ephemeral charm. Time slipped away until she suddenly heard,

"Well, I'll let you go for today, Anurima. Oh, and may I call you Anu?"

"Oh, sure."

"I'll call again. Please email me your home number." He paused. "My email ID is with Rahul Mitra, you may take it from him, so we can stay in touch?"

"Certainly, I'll do that." Anu replied.

"I'll look forward to your email then. Take care, Anu. Bye." With that, he hung up.

Anu was dumbfounded. She stared at the receiver, her body frozen, mouth dry. A spark of hope flared in her chest as she sank deeper into the chair, her grip on the phone tight, palms slick. An undeniable sincerity resonated from his voice, a sense of rightness and a comforting familiarity that eased the tension in her body.

For a split second, Anu was lost. This foreign caller, had treated her as an equal, as if she were a precious commodity. The wall clock's hourly chime sliced through the mental haze, jolting Anu out of her daze.

Had the last ninety minutes even happened? She moved slowly, as if testing the ground of this strange new moment.

Across the room, Rahul Mitra's eyes held a knowing glint as he watched her. Coming closer, he noticed a vibrant new fire in her typically gentle gaze.

Lost in the reverberations of Richard Gardner's words, a thrill coursed through Anu, a deep sense of completion unfurling within her. Richard had unveiled a world beyond her wildest dreams. A surprise washed over her, a sudden, overwhelming realisation: the caller was going to be her mentor.

Rahul came forward, his voice full of concern. "Anu, what happened? Are you all right?"

Seeing Rahul standing before her, Anu gulped and regained her composure. She stared at him, momentarily speechless, before softly murmuring, "Rahul da, I still can't believe what our President's team said."

"What did he say?" Rahul's curiosity was palpable.

"He said it's an international business opportunity, one that might take me around the world." Anu paused. "He also told me not to be intimidated, as he would guide me through the concept, step by step."

Her words hung in the air, and a radiant joy bloomed in Anu's eyes, so intense they began to shimmer.

*

The woman who had entered the Mitra residence with hesitant hope now walked with a newfound lightness to her car. Had she heard him correctly? "Arunima, may I call you Anu for short? You have the potential to be a STAR," he had said.

Anu hoped her ears hadn't deceived her. A stranger, a foreigner from a distant land, had actually spoken those words. "Anurima... a STAR." The phrase echoed in her mind, a persistent refrain on her drive home. Night had fallen, blanketing the city in darkness, and the streetlamps cast an artificial glow on the empty sidewalks. As she pulled up under the porch, the engine fell silent, but the words still resonated.

A sudden stillness descended, cutting through her exhilaration. *I need to take control of this*, a small voice reminded her.

She stepped out of the car, the crunch of fallen leaves on the walkway a satisfying sound beneath her feet. The porch's warm, yellow glow greeted her as she walked up the pale concrete steps to the spacious sit-out. Thriving potted plants in artistic blue and earthy orange pots, adorned with pebbles, seemed to reach out in welcome.

As she opened the front door, the potent scent of tuberoses from a vase on the table greeted her. She sank onto her chaise longue to gather herself, just as Aisha rushed toward her, bubbling with tales from her school day. While Aisha's animated voice filled the air, Anu drifted through her living room, a space she had imbued with her own artistic flair with cane and wrought iron pieces. It was this personal touch, the way she transformed mere rooms, that Mrinal so appreciated, often conveying his admiration through quiet, lingering gazes.

Knowing Mrinal would be in the kitchen, his "culinary laboratory," Anu headed there. She found him amidst a flurry of cooking, hands smeared, the kitchen table a war zone. But even the sound of her footsteps made him pause.

He turned around, taken aback by the transformed woman before him. A faint, almost imperceptible smile touched Anu's lips as she met his surprised gaze. *Did I surprise you, Mr. Mrinal Sensharma? I bet I did*, she mused inwardly.

Anu stood there with a newfound confidence, her large, gleaming eyes questioning his stunned expression. The future was unknown, but somewhere deep within, she had been waiting for this moment. An elixir to ignite the fire that had been trapped inside her, a fire now burning bright.

49

Tug of War

Anu felt a sense of relief and liberation, as if a large child had just jumped off her back after an enjoyable piggyback ride. She walked with newfound confidence, her steps lighter and more carefree. Hope seemed to reflect, coating her skin like dew on spring grass. She didn't know whether this was a fleeting feeling or the start of a new chapter, but after yesterday's telephonic conversation with Richard, she felt ready to take on life head-on. Yesterday was history, tomorrow a mystery, and today a gift.

The past held a mix of treasured and despised memories, while the future was uncertain. Life's ups and downs had left her both amazed and intrigued, yet she now faced them with a renewed sense of purpose.

Every Friday, Anu eagerly looked forward to spending quality time with Richard, who would listen patiently as she shared her week's news.

"Anu," he had said with conviction during their last call, "you've got so much potential. Don't be afraid to aim high; the sky's the limit. You have to put yourself out there to achieve your goals."

These conversations often surprised Anu, making her wonder if she had heard him correctly. "I live life on my own terms," Richard would continue. "I try to carve my own destiny."

His words echoed in her mind.

Months into her venture, Anu's training centre had undergone a remarkable transformation. The shelves were now neatly packed with her new line of "Healthy Life" health and nutrition products. This new venture flourished alongside her soft skills coaching centre, which also grew steadily. Anu was running the business in a structured, professional manner, and she had built a large network of distributors to help reach the market. The positive effects of the products weren't just a marketing slogan; they had a tangible impact on her own health, making her feel even more connected to her work.

Anu's business began to flourish, each month's success surpassing the last. Richard was impressed by her rapid growth, and as Anu gained his confidence, the Englishman truly took her under his wing. She found herself enjoying her newfound success, the work no longer feeling like a chore but a reflection of her own potential.

Six months into her venture, as she became deeply immersed in her abilities and the business she had built, it was Friday once again. At the usual time, the phone rang.

"Anu," Richard's voice came through the receiver, laced with an unmistakable excitement.

"What's the matter, Richard? You seem unusually happy," Anu asked.

"Anu, I have some news for you," he announced, his voice warm with excitement.

A mysterious laugh followed, before he slowly revealed, "How about me flying over to India?"

Anu's mind reeled. "You mean to Bangalore, to India? But why?" she blurted out.

"Aren't you happy? You'll be meeting your President's Team!" he exclaimed.

"Yes, of course, but..." Anu fumbled, her thoughts racing.

There was a pause. "I am actually impressed with the way you're handling the business, Madam Anurima Sensharma," he said teasingly. "I'm planning on staying for three weeks to give you the boost you need and to tap into the potential I see in you. Someone needs to ignite that."

Anu felt faint. "Are you serious? I can't believe this is happening!" she asked, her voice filled with disbelief.

"Why are you so surprised? We do that often when we spot a 'star'!" the voice on the other end quipped.

The word hung in the air, bringing back memories of their first call. He had called her a star then, and he had said it again. Anu could hardly believe her ears. Her heart pounded as she finally understood the depth of his confidence in her.

Richard had an ambitious plan to expand his business throughout India, and Anu had to plan a demanding three-week itinerary. Richard arrived in Bangalore, Anurima's home ground. Travelling with him to seven major cities, Anu, managed every detail, from flights and hotel rooms to conference halls, always booking two separate rooms.

Their first stop was Madurai. After their meetings, Anu took Richard to the famous Meenakshi Amman Temple. He was captivated by the ancient architecture and vibrant rituals, returning to the hotel with his forehead smeared with turmeric, vermillion, and sandalwood pastes—a sight that never failed to amuse Anu.

They had landed in Chennai, the next day morning Anu panicked when Richard was nowhere to be found. A quick check of the lobby turned up nothing, and her heart pounded as she imagined the worst. Relief washed over her when she finally spotted him in a separate lounge, deep in conversation, but it was quickly replaced by irritation as she caught his eye. He was fully aware of her frantic search and gave her a knowing, teasing grin. Later, over dinner, the tension melted away. "So, Anu," he light-heartedly quipped, "I got you truly worried."

"Absolutely, you are new to this country and in a way, you are my guest, Richard."

"Okay, my apologies. Happy now?"

Anu wondered at her comfort and ease with this gentleman, contrasting it with her college days when she felt equally at ease with male classmates, a feeling that was absent in her marriage with Mrinal.

*

From Chennai, they flew to Trivandrum. With each passing day, Anu felt a growing freedom of speech, enjoying playful banter with the Englishman. They reached Kolkata, where Anu took Richard to visit her mother.

Reena instantly liked him, impressed by his simple greeting. "Namaste," he had said.

But Reena was in awe of her daughter. "Anu, you seem so at ease with an Englishman," she said, her voice full of wonder. "You've never interacted with one before, have you?"

"True, Ma, but somehow I feel comfortable in his company," Anu paused, a slight frown on her face. "Unlike with some of my own kind."

Reena was taken aback. She changed the subject abruptly. "I hope Aish is okay without you?"

"Ma, her Papa is there, and her ayah too, to take care of her when she returns from school."

Reena gave a satisfied nod. Richard and Anurima were on the penultimate leg of their India tour, waiting at Kolkata Airport for their flight to Mumbai. Upon landing, a chauffeur from the Taj Mahal Palace Hotel awaited them with a placard bearing Richard's name. After two hectic days exploring the bustling city, they traveled to Pune. Anurima had booked a ride on the Deccan Queen Express from the Chhatrapati Shivaji Maharaj Terminus. During the four-hour journey, they laughed and chatted, with Richard occasionally reading while Anu dozed.

During his stay, Anu's self-confidence and meticulous planning had deeply impressed Richard. After each meeting, they would relax with a drink, a simple ritual that she began to anticipate. She realised she had been emotionally undernourished for years and that interacting with Richard was a delightful verbal dance—full of laughter, easy banter, and a stirring of the heart.

Outside, the landscape transformed swiftly from dry plains to vibrant greenery. Lush forests brushed the windows, their earthy scent seeping in. Distant mountains glimmered, occasionally veiled in mist, while waterfalls cascaded like silver threads, their soft rush a counterpoint to the train's rhythm. Picturesque villages dotted the now deep-green valleys as the air cooled, carrying a hint of unseen blossoms.

Anu woke with a jolt as extra engines joined the train for the steep climb into the Ghats. The unfolding panorama resonated with her inner stirring. The train's determined ascent embodied her own tentative steps toward a new self, a journey away from emotional aridity. Each curve and incline echoed the thrilling yet precarious navigation of these unfamiliar feelings.

A comfortable silence settled between Anu and Richard as she watched him read. Sunlight caught the silver in his hair as the train curved, sparking an unexpected warmth in her.

As the train rattled past a waterfall, Richard observed, "Quite a sight, isn't it, Anu?"

Anu nodded, finding his simple acceptance soothing. A fragile connection bloomed in these light moments, akin to the vegetation clinging tenaciously to the hillsides around them. Bliss and uncertainty washed over her, a subtle happiness that was tempered by a pang of doubt.

*

The first day's meeting in Pune concluded successfully, but a different energy filled Richard's candlelit room later that day. His gaze lingered on Anu a fraction too long, a warmth entering his blue eyes that went beyond professional courtesy. A slight softening around his lips, a subtle inclination of his head as he listened to her speak. A subtle smile touched Richard's lips, his voice a low murmur as he sipped his favourite scotch.

Across the table, Anu felt a quiet thrill ripple through her at his focused attention. A flush warmed her neck as their eyes met in the flickering light, and she quickly lowered her gaze, swirling her dessert wine. A newfound warmth bloomed inside her. She felt a subtle power in his captivated gaze, basking in a feeling akin to a delicate flower slowly unfurling in the warmth of unexpected sunlight.

Overwhelmed by her senses, Anu stood up abruptly. "Richard," she said, her voice a little shaky, "I think I should leave now. Tomorrow will be a long day."

Richard rose with a hesitant stride to see her to the door. In the hotel room passageway, they brushed against each other. Anu caught the scent of British Sterling and felt a long-dormant physical response, a thrilling jolt of electricity that promised an adventure.

Richard then cupped her face. Anu felt the heat of her cheeks against his palm, her heart racing as a girlish, tingly feeling engulfed her. They were almost nose to nose when a voice from the hall said, "Room service," followed by a knock.

Anu smiled and wriggled away, picking up her tote. Brushing past Richard, she went to the door, her fingers fumbling as she unlatched it. A nervous cough escaped her.

"Bye, Richard, see you tomorrow. Enjoy your evening," she blurted out, vanishing into the solitude of the long corridor.

She entered the elevator, the doors closing on the moment they had shared, but her heart still beat a wild rhythm against her ribs. She felt as if she had stepped into an unknown world, one where the rules of her life no longer applied.

Her mind immediately went to Richard. What could a man like him, an Englishman, possibly find so captivating about her? Then she remembered his words from an earlier conversation: "The ladies back home would hanker for your type of gorgeous golden looks, Anu."

What a difference, she sighed inwardly.

These were the weak moments when Anu could feel an unknown thread pulling her toward this foreign gentleman. But the moment her daughter's face would surface in her mind, her thoughts would be thrown into a turmoil, pulling her in two different directions.

*

The next day, as Anu walked to the conference hall, she saw Richard already in high spirits, shaking hands and mingling with the crowd. When he caught sight of her, their eyes briefly locked across the room.

Anu exuded beauty in her Maheshwari sari, its rich fabric flowing gracefully around her. A soft, bashful smile touched her lips as she met his gaze, her eyes sparkling with a gentle warmth. Her demeanour was poised, a quiet confidence now infused with a newfound lightness that seemed to emanate from within.

"Good morning, Richard. You seem to be doing well today," she greeted him.

"Morning, Anu. You look so good in this..." he fumbled for words. "What a beautiful sari you're wearing!"

To Anu's utter surprise, the organisers suddenly rushed in, garlanding both of them. A blush rose on Anu's face as she quickly took off her garland, then walked briskly to the podium, motioning for the crowd to settle down. All the while, Richard stood smiling, clearly charmed by the Maharashtrian tradition.

After the grand success of their Pune meeting, they enjoyed a quiet dinner in one of the hotel restaurants before retiring to their rooms for their early morning journey back to Mumbai on the Deccan Queen Express.

*

The return train journey unfolded quietly. Richard, engrossed in his book as usual, created his familiar, comfortable bubble of focus. A sudden chill traced its way through Anu, raising goosebumps on her arms. Almost immediately, Richard, ever observant, gently placed his warm coat around her shoulders. This unexpected gesture, a silent offering of comfort, subtly broke the quiet rhythm of the journey with a tender warmth.

Upon arrival in Mumbai, they hurried to the airport for their 2:30 p.m. flight to Delhi. The final leg of their tour fostered a surprising stillness in the cab, a silence as profound as Mumbai's stop-and-go traffic. The usual banter was absent, replaced by a comfortable, unspoken understanding that spoke volumes about their shared experiences.

As they stepped out into the bustling Delhi airport, a familiar sight greeted them: the Hyatt Regency chauffeur. But this time, the placard read, "Anurima Sensharma." The hotel rooms were booked in her name, a poignant sign that their professional trip was ending and that she would be the last one to check out after seeing Richard off the next day.

Reaching the hotel, they went to their respective rooms to freshen up before meeting at the reception at 7:30 p.m. In her room, Anu lay on the bed, her mind drifting back over the week, a week so perfect it felt straight out of a Mills & Boon novel.

After a quiet dinner, Richard invited Anu to his room for their final evening together. They sat down, attempting to maintain a professional demeanour as they reviewed the past week's events and future plans on a flow chart. The pretense didn't last long, however. A soft conversation began to flow as Richard sipped a Chardonnay and Anu enjoyed a Riesling with crackers and cheese. Outside, the balmy day had given way to a crisp evening, and a full moon peeked through the French windows, a silent witness to their last night.

Richard abruptly walked to the window. "So, it's a full moon night," he turned and looked at Anu.

Anu joined him; the moon's face seemed to hold a sad smile. In the charged silence that followed, unspoken feelings hung heavy; a shared awareness of the magnetic pull between them, a silent acknowledgment of their fleeting intimacy. His gaze held hers a beat longer than necessary.

Anu's heart hammered against her ribs, a stark contrast to her calm façade, and she mumbled, "I think I better leave now, Richard," her voice softer than intended, the professional tone wavering slightly.

"How time flies," Richard murmured, his usual charm tinged with wistfulness.

Anu simply nodded, unable to speak past the lump in her throat. To speak felt dangerous.

He has made such a difference, she thought, finally breaking eye contact, a profound gratitude and a nascent ache of impending absence swirling within her.

Anu picked up her diary, its pages filled with business details that felt a world away from her inner turmoil. Each step toward the door felt heavy, a premonition of the emptiness his departure would leave. The air in the hallway suddenly felt cold, a stark chill after the warmth of his room. Standing in the solitude of the corridor, she knew this goodbye held a weight far beyond a simple farewell.

Back home, Anu found a new vigour in her work. The chance to see Richard again became her unspoken motivation. She poured herself into her business, and the success of her recent tour and the promise of future ones propelled her forward. It wasn't long before her hard work paid off. She earned her first international trip: a convention in Holland. After the two-day event in Amsterdam, she joined her team in visiting The Hague and Eindhoven, her joy a quiet, constant hum beneath the surface.

Anu's business thrived, earning her spots at conventions in England and, finally, the International Summit at the Kodak Theatre in Los Angeles. Standing before the iconic landmark, she felt a profound sense of accomplishment. As she ascended the grand staircase, the plush carpet muffling her footsteps, a wave of exhilaration washed over her.

Walking down the aisle to find her seat, her eyes scanned the distinguished faces in the audience. That's when she saw him. Richard's genuine smile, a silent acknowledgment across the room, made her heart flutter. Their meeting was brief, but she felt his presence throughout the entire event.

During a break, he found her in the crowd, his hand gently on her arm. He led her to a quiet corner, listening intently as she recounted the hectic details of her trip. His questions were not just polite; they were insightful, making her feel truly seen and valued in a way that had nothing to do with business. The feeling was as warm as the California sun streaming through the grand windows of the theatre.

Later, at a gala dinner, he subtly ensured Anu enjoyed herself, suggesting drinks she might sample. Each thoughtful glance and considerate word wove a subtle spell, leaving Anu with a feeling of lightness and warmth.

The president's summit was a luxurious three-day event. Years later, when Anu revisited the Kodak Theatre, she found it had become the Dolby Theatre of Hollywood, the venue for the Academy Awards. Over time, Anu developed a strong emotional bond with Richard. As her business grew, she eagerly anticipated the extravaganza events. She felt as though Richard had cast a spell on her; his thoughtful mannerisms, laced with wit, always swept her off her feet.

Each time Anu returned to India, she felt as though she had surfaced from a vivid dream, the reality around her so starkly different, it felt unbelievable. This jarring contrast ignited a deep yearning within her, almost a primal desire to return to a state of origin and begin anew.

50

The Limousine Ride

Back in Kolkata after a work trip to the UK. Anu bubbled with excitement, recounting her improbable journey from Bangalore to Manchester via Heathrow. She eagerly showed her mother, the souvenirs she had brought back from London as she unpacked. Reena watched, a gentle smile on her face as Anu's enthusiasm filled the room. Her long black hair flowed down her back, a hint of coarseness now in her fair skin as she aged gracefully. Her distinctive Greek nose was striking between her sparkling dark almond eyes.

"Ma, I almost made a complete fool of myself!" Anu burst into laughter. "I was rushing to leave my hotel and somersaulted over my suitcase, landing right at the feet of a bellboy as he stepped out of the elevator!"

Reena's gaze fell on the open, hard-shell American Tourister suitcase lying on the floor. She pointed and began to laugh. "You mean you toppled over *that* piece of luggage?"

Anu nodded, still chuckling at the memory. The day she was flying out of London, Richard had taken her to the Holiday Inn. The next morning, in her rush to catch the airport shuttle, she wheeled her luggage out and left it in front of the elevator. She had turned to pick it up, lost her grip, and tumbled headfirst, her feet flying into the air as her luggage hit the floor. The bellboy watched in disbelief from inside the elevator as Anu's head landed right near his feet.

Anu laughed heartily, remembering the absurdities of her trip to England. "Maa, this American Tourister has a mind of its own!" she said, gesturing toward the case. "Mrinal always has a keen eye for quality, but he had no idea the dead weight would make it so difficult to manage."

She then began to narrate the incident where she had gone up a giant escalator, struggling with both the suitcase and a stroller. "The ride up was smooth, and I successfully hauled both bags off the escalator. But then, to my horror, I saw the Tourister start dancing its way back down!"

Reena stared at Anu, eyes wide with shock. "Then how did you get it back?"

"I'm sure I must have looked like a damsel in distress," Anu said with a giggle. "A young lad coming up the other side looked up at me, smiled, and brought it back."

"Oh, really? The way you tell it, I feel like I was there holding my breath," Reena said, relief in her voice. "You have to tell Mrinal about this."

Anu's gaze then shifted to the American Tourister, with clothes still spilling out. She mimicked a theatrical bow. "Hats off, you honourable luggage carrier!" she said. "In the future, you shall never accompany me."

Reena watched, a bemused expression on her face. She couldn't quite reconcile this vibrant, glowing daughter with the girl she remembered. She looked on eagerly as Anu stood up, clutching some colourful packets, and sat down on the nearby couch.

"Ma, there's more to my UK adventure. Buckle up!"

"Go on," Reena encouraged, "I'm all ears."

Anu leaned in. "While travelling from Heathrow to Manchester, I sat next to an Englishman who was so engrossed in his local newspaper that he started discussing politics with me, something I knew nothing about. He handed me a page, and I just pretended to be interested, asking a random question to keep the conversation going."

As Reena listened, she was amazed, pondering how time had influenced her daughter. A twinge of guilt surfaced for not nurturing Anu's talents earlier, but she took solace in the fact that her husband had provided their daughters with a good education, instilling confidence in them. She thought about how his German experience and aristocratic lineage had influenced their upbringing.

Anu noticed her mother's distraction. "Ma, where are you? The best part is yet to come!"

Reena snapped back to the present. "I'm admiring your courage, Anu, talking to a stranger in a foreign land and participating in a political discussion you knew nothing about. You astound me, my girl."

Anu smiled and continued, "He then asked me where I lived in England."

"I was so taken aback that I wanted to jest and say I lived in Manchester, where I was headed. But I decided to be honest and told him I was from India and had come on work. The gentleman gave me a curious look and said, 'But your accent speaks otherwise.' Ma, I couldn't believe my ears! I thought he was teasing me, but he looked so serious. I was elated, thinking my accent had developed from interacting with the English over the years."

Reena gawked at Anu, listening to her implausible story.

"The stranger then shared stories of Japan, describing the food and culture with great zeal," Anu continued. "As the plane was about to descend, everyone was securing their seatbelts. The gentleman gave me his business card and asked where in Manchester I was heading. I told him I was travelling to Edale and would take the train from the airport."

Anu paused for effect. "Ma, his business card said he was the CEO of a company, and his name was Mike Feldman."

"Anu, you sound very mysterious," Reena said, leaning forward. "What happened after that?"

"It was such an unexpected offer, Ma; my thoughts raced in a million directions. I had to decide quickly; do I go with an unknown Englishman and take a ride in a limousine, or do I try to navigate an unknown land with this bulky suitcase on my own?"

Anu paused, then continued with a sheepish grin, "Mr Feldman sensed my hesitation and said they would reach Edale an hour earlier by car and that he wasn't doing me a favour, as he lived near Edale."

With her curiosity at its peak, Reena was engrossed in the story.

"Then what did you do?" she asked.

"I needed to inform Richard about the change in plan. Mr Feldman immediately offered his cell phone. In that instant, I knew my knight in shining armour was a perfect gentleman, and I had nothing to fear."

Reena had met Richard on one of his business trips to India when he was in Kolkata.

So, she asked, "Didn't Richard object to you taking a ride with a stranger in a limo?"

With a chuckle, Anu said, "Yes, he did. He thought I had lost my mind to trust an absolute stranger and then pile into his limousine."

"But I told him I was going with my gut and felt he was a perfect gentleman. Then, as we came out of the terminal, sure enough, a limousine was waiting outside with a chauffeur standing beside it."

Reena, aware of her eldest's enthusiasm for cars, could only gape. She gave an uncomfortable cough and asked, "So you got inside the limo?"

"Oh yes, I did. It was quite a beautiful ride. This gentleman, Mike Feldman, with his constant chatter, kept me entertained, and in no time, we reached the Edale Railway station where Richard was to pick me up."

Anu looked at her Ma and continued. "As I stepped out of the limo, a chilly wind made me tremble. Mike sensed my discomfort right away. He quickly reached into his boot, grabbed his wife's coat, and offered it to me. 'Miss, please wear this for now,' he said. 'You can return it to me later; I live nearby, and you have my address.'"

"Then what did you do?" asked a visibly stunned Reena.

"I was so embarrassed. I immediately took my own coat out of my suitcase, and Mike stood by like a guardian angel while I put it on. He waited for fifteen minutes in the parking lot, and there was still no sign of Richard. He then offered to drop me off at Richard's place, but I politely declined, saying my host must be on his way."

"Still a bit concerned, Mike reached into his pocket and gave me a few coins, in case I needed to use a phone booth. I was so thankful, since I had none on me. Then he left, a satisfied look on his face, glad he had been able to help a young woman in a foreign land."

Reena was mesmerised by her daughter's experience. Her expression then softened into a pained sadness. "I wish your Papa was here," she said quietly. "He would have been so proud to see how smart both his daughters have turned out."

She sighed, her voice growing softer. "Especially you, Anu. I wasn't fair to you when you were growing up. I didn't let you shine. As your parents, we only saw that you were our eldest and a girl, and we had responsibilities to fulfill."

Anu frowned. "You're remembering all that now, Ma? Let bygones be bygones."

"It was just… my world fell apart when your father got sick and had to take early retirement," Reena explained, her face etched with distress. "I had to rely on my family's advice because I thought they were more experienced than me. I was a homemaker and had no earnings of my own, so I felt so scared and lost, especially with two young daughters to care for."

Anu nodded gravely, remembering the time when endless ordeals had interrupted her teenage years. Her Ma, she recalled, had never truly understood her, always existing in her own world. Anu had to fight her own battles.

And yet, another memory surfaced. Anu remembered her Cossipore club days and smiled. Ma had definitely known her daughter's confidence and talent, especially when she helped her translate her short stories into English for the souvenir. She had even helped her win those drawing, ikebana, and kitchen competitions for her WWA activities.

A wave of confusion washed over Anu. She looked at her mother. "Ma, you were an educated and broad-minded woman. How did you allow yourself to be influenced by family and mess up the best years of your daughter's student life?"

Anu then looked at her mother's remorse-filled face. She reached out and took her hand. "Ma," she said, her voice reassuring. "Everything happens for a reason. Maybe my struggles were meant to be." She paused, her eyes distant. "Sometimes I feel challenged, and it's like I'm Siamese twins with the difficulty, never to part."

Anu laughed and hugged her Ma, seeing her lost in thought, and said, "Maybe the girl that you see in front of you is a byproduct of the challenges she had to go through. It has shaped her!"

The absolution of Reena's guilt poured forth with sudden relief, and she blurted out, "Just as clouds cannot hide the rays of the sun, nobody can hide one's talent. One day it does come out and see the light of day."

Reena looked at Anu with a proud grin. "Despite societal expectations that daughters are burdens, my girls are a source of strength for me."

Anu smiled and stated, "Parents in India should raise their children without gender bias."

*

In India, the common expectation is that sons will shoulder the responsibility of caring for their parents in their old age, while daughters will typically marry and leave the family home.

Against this backdrop, as Anu and Jay matured and began exploring opportunities across the globe, Reena's heart swelled with a particular pride. By then, she had come to clearly recognise the unique strengths that distinguished her daughters.

One day, Anu happened to be nearby when she overheard her mother confiding in a friend. "Anu always excelled in her practical exams at university; she has a scientific mindset, while Jay is more theoretical."

Her friend had then remarked, "That makes sense. Anu approaches life with a practical bent, relying on sound logic, while Jay definitely gravitates more towards theoretical understanding."

Anu's lips would often soften into a smile whenever she heard her mother analyse them this way. It was a recent change, a new way of seeing. Anu knew that her mother had finally come to appreciate her two daughters as her greatest assets, each with her own distinct traits.

Then, many years later, Anu heard her mother say in her poetic style, "*Amar dui meye prithibi kapachhe*; Both my daughters are rocking the world!"

*

That day, Anu had stood for an hour in the bitter cold gust of wind until she finally spotted Richard driving up to the parking lot. Without a word, Anu got inside the warmth of the car. To her surprise, she found Richard sporting a smile wide enough to crack his face.

Then, with an animated expression, he said, "Ah! A limo ride to Edale should have made up for my delay."

Anu replied with a shrug, "A few more minutes, Richard, and you would have found a frozen sculpture of Anurima Sensharma right here in this parking lot!"

He looked at Anu and clicked his tongue. Then, with a straight face, he said, "You are too strong a woman, Anurima! The snow would need guts to freeze you."

This remark was enough to shut Anu up.

PART IX
2005–2016
Nainital, England, Sundarbans, Scandinavia, USA

51

Beyond the Hill Town

Mrinal relocated once again, returning to the familiar embrace of Nainital. For Anu, the return to the hill town that had once captivated her sparked a new kind of anticipation. Finally, they could settle into their own cottage, a welcome change from impersonal DRDO quarters and rented accommodations.

Aisha's love for television was a constant source of friction. Each evening, Mrinal found her glued to the screen, his frustration mounting as her grades plummeted. The frequent clashes became a heavy weight in their home. Recognising the toll it was taking, Anu made the difficult decision to send Aisha to a boarding school. While Aisha initially resented missing her shows, a remarkable transformation occurred: her grades steadily improved, and she often topped her class.

With the newfound quiet, Anu channeled her energy into making their new cottage a home. Her organisational skills, honed from managing logistics during her travels abroad, allowed her to efficiently source furniture and décor. Mrinal, still absorbed in his work, left Anu to create a space that felt truly their own.

Visits with Aisha became occasions for great pride. The headmaster, Larry Sir, and her teachers never failed to sing her praises, particularly her success in the national debate competitions. Aisha, it seemed, was thriving under their watchful and affectionate guidance, a fact that filled her parents with a quiet joy.

It was during this time that Mrinal's pride in his daughter truly blossomed. One afternoon, while on a leisurely drive, Anu turned to him, a mischievous grin playing on her lips. "One good thing has come out of our union," she said playfully. "I got a daughter with one of your good traits—your memory skills."

Mrinal's brow furrowed in mock seriousness. "Is that so? I don't really see it. She gets those grades by sheer fluke," he chuckled. "And of course, you'd say she inherited your intellect, your talents, wouldn't you?" He paused, a mischievous glint in his eye. "I would say she's a lucky girl!"

Anu gasped in feigned astonishment, her hand going to her chest. Mrinal leaned closer, a touch of his usual sarcasm lacing his words. "She simply inherited the best from both of us. So, the credit doesn't go to her at all. The best genes just happened to align in her making."

The humour evaporated from Anu's expression. "I'm glad, Mrinal," she replied, her voice quiet but firm, "that our daughter is developing into a well-rounded individual, not a nerd like you. We should be proud of her and nurture her confidence, not find fault and diminish her spirit."

*

With Anu's business on the ascent and Aisha settled in boarding school, the next couple of years were smooth sailing. But as Aisha entered the crucial years of high school, Anu, driven by an unwavering love, decided to prioritise her daughter's academic needs. Though a quiet ache lingered for her own aspirations, a deeper conviction resonated within her: Aisha's success was paramount. So, she decided to quit her thriving career, which demanded a fair amount of travel.

Much to Mrinal's initial surprise, Anu took a more direct role in Aisha's life, opting to stay home. Aisha was back, and Anu could feel her daughter needed focused guidance.

Eventually, Mrinal, witnessing Anu's capable handling of both household matters and Aisha's academic progress, even joked about being outnumbered by the intelligent women in his family. These were rare glimpses into his usually guarded thoughts.

To her quiet astonishment, Anu gradually found herself becoming Mrinal's pillar of support. She offered guidance, even though his open acknowledgments were infrequent. With her resilient spirit, she focused on what she could influence. Observing his disinclination toward planning and even basic household repairs, Anu instinctively took charge. When travel plans arose, Mrinal became a passive participant, relying entirely on Anu for itineraries and bookings. His negativity often stifled any attempt at collaboration.

But old habits die hard. Time and again, Mrinal would disregard Anu's advice, only to later lament his stubbornness to friends. "I should have listened to my wife," he would confess after facing the consequences of his choices. Slowly, the realization dawned on him that his pride and his reluctance to trust Anu's judgment had often led to missteps.

Anu, for her part, had long understood the importance of focusing on the positive aspects of her life, leveraging her strengths, and allowing Mrinal his own space. She viewed her marriage not as a perfect union, but as a series of challenges to be met head-on. She found that the occasional risks she took in navigating their relationship boosted her self-confidence.

In quiet moments, Anu reflected on how much she had grown. Perhaps, without Mrinal's constant criticism, she might have still remained in her comfort zone, unaware of her own potential and the richness of the world beyond her initial horizons. She attributed this transformation, in large part, to her extensive travels and the mentorship of a remarkable man named Richard Gardner. Meeting him was a rare phenomenon in India in those days, and their connection had fundamentally changed her outlook on life, equipping her with a wealth of experience she now drew upon daily.

*

One weekend, Mrinal invited his old friend Prodosh for dinner. As they lingered after the meal, Prodosh mentioned his volunteer work at the Ramakrishna Ashram and their need for a master of ceremonies for the upcoming 150th birth anniversary of the Holy Mother Sarada Devi.

Anu's ears pricked up, recognizing the significance of the event.

Mid-sip of his coffee, Mrinal looked up, a rare moment of emerging from his usual critical shell. With a mischievous grin, he gestured toward Anu. "She might be able to help you."

Prodosh, clearly surprised, turned to Anu. "Really, Mrs. Sensharma? You anchor programs?"

Mrinal nodded emphatically. "Yes, she has been doing so for years now. Her genuinc curiosity and ability to engage with people make her a natural orator."

Meanwhile, Anu couldn't help but smile, completely unable to believe her ears.

Mrinal paused, a mischievous glint in his eyes. "She also claims she has a spiritual frame of mind."

Anu stared at him, her face a mixture of disbelief and astonishment.

"I knew Mrs. Sensharma was a talented Rabindrasangeet singer and that she directed plays and ballets," Prodosh exclaimed, "but these other talents were unknown to me!"

"At a DRDO event, Anu effortlessly connected with a diverse group, steering the entire program with ease," Mrinal continued, then went on to tell Prodosh about Anu's incredible life exposure. "Her travels have contributed to her immense growth."

Prodosh looked at Mrinal, bewildered. “When did all this happen, Mrinal da? I only ever knew her as a good Rabindrasangeet singer.”

“She has tasted life, Prodosh,” Mrinal replied. “She’s got immense life exposure. You’re meeting her after about twenty years.”

Prodosh nodded slowly, his gaze shifting to Anu with newfound admiration. “Hmm… but every wife doesn’t get all that exposure, Mrinal da.”

Anu reflected on her life. She recalled the life skills training she had received from Jim Rohn, a renowned Fortune 500 trainer and life coach. These lessons, learned in India and abroad, were instrumental in reshaping her personality and enhancing her communication skills.

Just then, she heard Mrinal’s voice, as he continued his praise to their friend. “She’s a management trainer and a life coach,” he was saying. “She used to run her own firm.” He paused, then went on, “Her journeys abroad exposed her to diverse cultures and communication styles, lessons she integrated expertly into her business communication courses.”

For Anu, it was a profound moment. To hear Mrinal, after so many years of criticism, speak with such pride and detail about her achievements made that day a truly red-letter one.

52

The Scottish Castle

The Governor of Uttarakhand was to preside over the Ramakrishna Mission symposium, a prospect that felt particularly daunting to Anu. Despite her past experience anchoring events, she, a civilian, knew little of the protocols for state dignitaries and made a quick attempt to grasp some jargon online.

Standing at the podium, Anu arranged her notes on the lectern, projecting confidence while inwardly bracing for inevitable missteps. As the program neared its end and she gathered her notes to leave the dais, she was surprised to see a handsome man in military uniform approaching her.

"Excuse me, madam, am I speaking to the emcee of the evening?"

Anu looked up. "Yes, you are. I am Anurima Sensharma."

"I have a message from the Governor. He wants to have a word with you. Can you please follow me?"

Anu missed a beat, but with an air of pseudo-confidence, she nodded and mumbled, "Sure!"

Anu followed him and entered the cordoned area. She saw the Governor seated with the bigwigs from the Ramakrishna Mission who had come all the way from Kolkata. They were the governing body of monks, the trustees of Ramakrishna Math.

Anu walked toward the Governor, her body shaking like a leaf. She was certain he had summoned her to point out the mistakes she had made.

Standing before him, she blurted, "Good evening, sir, I mean, Your Excellency. I'm sorry if I made any faux pas."

To her surprise, the Governor smiled. "What made you think that? You did a wonderful job," he said. "Your diction, your confidence, the way you hosted the event—it felt like you were a pro."

Anu's cheeks flushed. She thought, *What am I hearing?* All she could manage was an embarrassed, "Thank you." But the Governor wasn't finished. He offered her a job working for him in Delhi, a suggestion that completely took Anu's breath away. She had never expected such an offer from the head of state of Uttarakhand.

In her confusion, she blurted out, "I'm sorry, sir, but I have a daughter in high school. I need to be around. I can't leave her and move to Delhi, not at this juncture."

The Governor, however, wasn't ready to take no for an answer. He asked Anu to meet him in his office in a couple of months. A nervous flutter stirred in her belly. Anu apologized for any disappointment she might have caused and offered her help in Nainital if he needed it.

The Governor sported an indulgent smile and simply nodded. "Yes, we'll see."

In her continued fluster, Anu fell back on a professional habit. As a corporate trainer and a life coach, she was used to exchanging business cards. She handed him hers and asked, "Sir, can I have your visiting card, please?"

The Governor smiled and gestured to the military man who had escorted her. Anu saw that he was the Governor's aide-de-camp, and she gave her card to him, taking Major Robert's in return. A wave of embarrassment washed over her—she hadn't realized a state's head of state did not carry a business card.

Then the Governor turned back to her. "You'll get the contact number for Raj Bhavan, the Governor's House, on his card."

Tongue-tied and visibly mortified by her recent faux pas, Anu just bowed, mumbled a "thank you," and hurried out of the room. As the door closed behind her, she finally let out a long, shaky sigh of relief.

*

The countdown began: just two months until she was to meet the Governor of the state. As the calendar ticked off the days, Anu began to get cold feet. While the Governor of Uttarakhand typically stayed at Raj Bhavan in Dehradun, his summer retreat was the one in Nainital. It was there that Anu had been asked to meet him.

As July stretched on, Anu's apprehension mounted. A plausible reason for the requested meeting eluded her, solidifying her conviction that the Governor's invitation had faded from his memory. Finally, on the last day of the month, with lingering nerves, she called the ADC's office at Raj Bhavan to set up an appointment.

As she drove up to the majestic Governor's House, the "Scottish Castle of India," Anu couldn't believe her luck. After clearing security, she parked her car. Standing in front of the imposing edifice, she had to convince herself it wasn't a dream; she had only ever strolled the grounds before.

I am about to enter India's Buckingham Palace and meet the head of state in his office, she mused, a mix of disbelief and excitement settling in.

Nainital Raj Bhawan was built by the British in the late 19th century. Its European Gothic architecture, specifically modeled after Buckingham Palace in London, earned it the nickname, "India's Buckingham Palace."

As Anu followed the guard, she heard her heels clicking on the polished wooden floor. The sheer splendor of the interiors took her breath away. The intricate woodwork and rich carvings were a feast for her eyes. When they reached the office, the guard pointed to a chair.

"Please wait here, madam," he said. "The office boy will let you in." He then vanished down the hall.

Anu waited with a thumping heart for what seemed like an eternity. Finally, she heard a bell ring. A young boy in a khaki uniform emerged from the adjacent room.

"Madam, you may go in now," he said.

Anu stepped inside, and the grandeur of the room enveloped her. She saw the little man, the Governor, sitting behind a massive, intricately carved writing table, immersed in a stack of files. He looked up, his smile turning on at half pressure as he gestured for her to take a seat.

Anu sat gingerly on the edge of the high-backed chair, far from comfortable. She had rehearsed her opening lines, but now, as she looked at the man almost hidden behind the files, she could sense a powerful aura around him. Despite his stature, he seemed to stand tall before her. She was immersed in her thoughts when she sensed the Governor was observing her. A genuine smile was on his lips as he pushed the files aside and removed his reading glasses.

Anu, on high alert, straightened her back. She was toying with her handkerchief when she heard him.

"What can I do for you, madam?"

Anu gulped. It was clear the Governor had not the slightest notion who she was. She screwed up her courage and asked, "Your Excellency, do you remember me, sir?"

The Governor's smile widened. With a gentle twinkle in his eyes, he replied, "How could I forget such an event? You did a wonderful job."

Anu couldn't believe her ears. She felt a wave of relief so strong it almost made her sink through the floor. But she braced herself and went on with the speech she had rehearsed so well.

After the meeting, Anu drove home in a state of disbelief. The Governor of Uttarakhand had offered her a job at the Nainital Raj Bhawan. A strange, exhilarating buzz, an odd and heady sensation, overwhelmed her senses. She was to become a public relations officer and spokesperson for the Governor, even travelling to Delhi to meet the crème de la crème of the country.

In her initial days, Anu was truly green and had no clue what she was doing. But she quickly adapted, making frequent trips to Delhi, and in no time, she soared.

As Mrinal watched Anu handle her assignments at the Raj Bhawan, his attitude began to change. The respect that had been lacking for years suddenly appeared. At times, he would even blurt out, "You have become quite wise, working with the Head of State."

Anu would retort, "I was always the wiser one, but your ego was too big to acknowledge it. You're all about reproducing theoretical information, where logic has no part to play."

Mrinal wouldn't argue. Deep within, he knew what she said was the honest truth.

The days at the Governor's House flew by. Then came the news of his impending transfer to another state, casting a bittersweet ache over Anu. Her time within those hallowed walls had been a dizzying ascent, a dream woven with encounters with the nation's most esteemed figures. It was 2007, the year Uttaranchal was renamed Uttarakhand, and Anu knew that 2008 would bring the poignant moment when she'd have to bid farewell to this extraordinary period.

Though a flicker of possibility remained, Anu's decision to seek a reference carried the quiet weight of a closing chapter. She knew that remarkable experience, those moments of soaring high, would forever shimmer in the tapestry of her memories.

53

The Charm of Stone and Whispers

After her tenure at Raj Bhawan, Anu decided to take a break from work. She joined an online creative writing course, while her daughter, Aisha, crossed the threshold of high school and gained admission to one of the country's premier tech institutes. Seeing Aisha embark on this new chapter, Mrinal felt a surge of pride and began contemplating a special gift for his daughter.

Meanwhile, Anu eagerly anticipated the final quarter of her online course, which required a trip to Leicester University. More than the academic pursuit, her thoughts kept drifting to the prospect of meeting Richard again after six long years, stirring a flutter of something akin to excitement.

Mrinal, keen to broaden Aisha's horizons, suggested she join Anu on the trip to England. He even extended their itinerary to include Scotland and parts of Europe, and Aisha, delighted, buzzed with the thrill of her first international adventure. Anu planned to spend three days with Richard and his wife, Carolene, in Edale, a part of the trip Aisha was also eager for, having read so much about British hospitality.

After landing in London, they made a stop in Durham to visit Aisha's cousin Malabika, her husband Anup, and their little son Shanu. After a couple of days, they proceeded to Edinburgh, immersing themselves in the beauty of the

Scottish Highlands for three days before boarding a train. The picturesque countryside unfolded outside the windows as they made their way to Manchester's Piccadilly station. As the coach hissed to a halt, their eyes scanned the platform's crowd, searching for a familiar face. Then they spotted him.

Richard was leaning against a pillar, cross-legged and engrossed in a book. Even after all these years, his silhouette was familiar. After an initial moment of hesitation, Anu and Richard exchanged relieved smiles and a warm hug in the bustling station before settling into his SUV.

As they pulled away, Richard turned slightly to Aisha. "Aish, let me tell you about our village. We're heading to Edale, which is nestled in Hope Valley." He continued, his voice full of warmth, "This village marks the beginning of the famous long-distance walking trail, the Pennine Way, which starts here and ends at Kirk Yetholm."

Aisha nodded, her sense of wonder growing as she peered out the window and imagined the hikers embarking on their adventures.

The familiar forty-five-minute drive ended at Richard's charming cottage, the converted barn Anu remembered so fondly. She noticed its thoughtful expansions and renovations, a testament to the passage of time. Welcoming them were Richard's wife, Carolene, and her mother, Josephine, who lived in the adjoining house.

The next day, Carolene, a polite and reserved English lady with a graceful demeanour, took Aisha on a village tour. Aisha gasped as she took in the stunning views of Kinder Scout, captivated by the pretty stone houses that seemed to blend seamlessly with the landscape. As Aisha absorbed the picturesque scenery, Anu spent the day catching up on her writing assignments.

In the evening, they all visited The Cheshire Cheese Inn, a historic English pub built in the 16th century. The cozy atmosphere, the rich aroma of real ale, the comforting taste of a home-cooked meal, and the unfamiliar twang of

British country music created a sensory tapestry that Aisha savored. She even hummed along, a little self-consciously, as she embraced the new experience. Carolene then shared stories of the pub's long history, further enchanting the young traveller.

The next day, Anu accompanied Richard to a business meeting in Aberdeen, a city in the north-east of Scotland. Aisha stayed back with Carolene. As Richard drove his new Porsche, Anu felt a familiar thrill, a ghost of her past resurfacing. Being driven to a meeting by Richard evoked a sense of nostalgia for a time she now missed; a period of shared ambition and professional kinship. The meeting itself sparked a flicker of interest in returning to that world, but Anu, cautious, decided to let the idea simmer.

*

Carolene and Aisha found an immediate connection, spending their days cycling around the quaint town's narrow lanes.

"Look, Aisha," Carolene would say, pointing to a charming stone cottage draped in climbing roses. "This one's been here for centuries, I reckon. Imagine all the stories these walls could tell!"

Another time, as they navigated a particularly winding lane, Carolene might chuckle, "Mind you, don't go tumbling into the hedgerows, dear! These paths have seen more than a few wobbly wheels in their time."

One day, Carolene suggested, "How about a special trip? We'll head to Grasmere. You know, where those famous poets, Wordsworth and Coleridge, used to live way back in the 18th century."

Aisha's eyes widened. "Really? We can go there?"

As they walked along a path in Grasmere, Carolene shared anecdotes. "Wordsworth, he used to take long walks around this very lake, finding inspiration in the beauty of it all. Can you imagine the poems that were born right here?"

Aisha shivered with excitement. “It feels . . . amazing to be walking where they once walked.”

Later, at a cozy village pub, the aroma of spices filled the air. Carolene placed a warm, golden bun in front of Aisha. “There you go, love. A hot cross bun. A real tradition around here.”

Aisha took a bite, her eyes widening in delight. “Oh, this is wonderful! What are all the spices?”

Carolene smiled. “Ah, that’s a bit of a secret recipe, I’m afraid! But it’s a treat, isn’t it?”

Aisha nodded, a contented sigh escaping her lips. She hummed the nursery rhyme to herself, a soft melody of “Hot cross buns! Hot cross buns! One a penny, two a penny, hot cross buns. . .” and smiled.

*

The three days in Edale vanished in the blink of an eye, and soon it was time for Anu and Aisha to leave. Richard escorted them to the railway station, the familiar weight of Anu’s suitcase in his hand, while Aisha carried her own small bag. Anu walked beside him, her shoulder bag and tote feeling heavier with unspoken emotions. Back at the cottage, Carolene waved goodbye from the window, a wistful smile on her face.

As Anu stepped onto the train and bade farewell to Richard, a cold, hollow echo of unspoken words resonated within her—a quiet melancholy at their parting. Lost in thought as the train began to move, she murmured almost to herself, “I was embers when I met you. You ignited the fire.”

She reflected on how, over the years, Richard had been a constant source of support, enhancing her well-being and offering guidance through life’s complexities. He had, in a way, illuminated a path for her, helping her navigate its inevitable challenges and providing a sense of purpose. In that moment, Anu recognised the depth of their connection: a true friend and mentor in one.

Anu was so engrossed in her reflections that she almost missed Aisha pointing excitedly at the beautiful Sheffield line view.

"Mamma," Aisha said, "I wish we could stay in this idyllic Edale forever."

Anu smiled fondly at her daughter, a warmth spreading through her despite the lingering ache of departure. All of a sudden, she remembered a time when Aisha had been so full of nervous excitement, sending off her university applications to the UK.

She looked at Aisha. "Remember how helpful Carolene was with your Statement of Purpose? She really guided you, and then, that scholarship! From that prestigious Scottish University! We were all over the moon."

Aisha looked surprised. "Mamma, are you reminiscing about the time I got the scholarship letter from Edinburgh?"

"Yes, Aisha, I wish we could send you there. The scholarship wasn't covering a lot of other expenses, so your Papa was contemplating an educational loan. But, Aisha, I must say, it was such a wave of relief when you got accepted into the tech institute in our own country. At that time, I just kept thinking that we could give you more time to grow up, closer to home, before I let you venture out on your own."

Anu remembered her nagging worry; Aisha, still a teenager, trying to make her way in a foreign country, so far from home. It had kept her up at night.

"I know, Mamma, but whenever I think about it, I still feel a bit sad that I could have pursued my undergrad in the UK," Aisha said. "But it's okay, I got into one of India's top institutes, so I'm happy."

"Yes, and that's the reason you are experiencing foreign lands now," Anu said, her voice soft. "This entire trip is a gift from Papa."

"I know, Mamma. But for my post-grad, I'll get a scholarship and go to the U.S.; that will make you happy, too."

Anu gave an indulgent smile and nodded. "That's the plan, Aisha. Your results are how you'll achieve your dream."

"That's for sure," Aisha said with a firm nod.

Once they reached London, Anu unexpectedly received an invitation from a British friend: a coveted pass to the ongoing Wimbledon tournament at the All England Lawn Tennis and Croquet Club. It was a dream come true for both mother and daughter as they sat in the stands, watching the world's most famous players.

*

The threads of their English adventure still lingered when Anu finally completed her creative writing course. But the fragile peace that followed was soon shattered. The unexpected loss of Reena cast a long, dark shadow, plunging Anu into the depths of mourning.

In the raw ache of her grief, a long-forgotten seed began to sprout: her mother's fervent wish for Anu to earn a doctorate, a dream amplified by seeing her friends achieve that very milestone. It was a beacon in the darkness, a new direction to grasp. Seeking solace not just in remembrance but in purpose, Anu resolved to pursue a PhD in management.

The path her friends had chosen, the familiar trajectory from doctorate to lecturer, had once stirred a pang of envy within Anu. She too had envisioned that life. Yet, as she watched the daily pressures and constraints her friends in their academic roles, a quiet contentment settled within her. She recognized the strength in forging her own path and embracing a passion that had unexpectedly broadened her understanding of life.

And so, with renewed focus, the next five years became a testament to Anu's dedication. This journey culminated in the fulfilment of her mother's cherished aspiration and led her to a management institute in Nainital. There, she found purpose in sharing her unique perspective with undergraduate and postgraduate students, guiding young minds in the interwoven realms of "The Importance of Spirituality in Business Management." Reflecting on her own journey, Anu now understood that the very essence of life's excitement lay in its unknowable future, each turn a fresh page.

54
Echoes Across the Ocean

Aisha's academic brilliance had paved a clear path; postgraduate studies in the United States beckoned. For Anu, her daughter's soaring success filled her heart with a mother's profound pride. But a shadow of reservation clouded Mrinal's thoughts. He longed to keep Aisha close, a sentiment that masked a deeper scepticism about her long-term commitment and a persistent worry about the hefty price tag of an international cducation.

Their differing viewpoints often led to hushed evening debates, with Mrinal voicing concerns about the financial expense. Anu, however, remained steadfast in her conviction to provide Aisha with the best. Having encountered numerous obstacles in her own student life, she was not one to easily give up and was determined to proceed with Aisha's chosen path.

Anu often recalled Aisha's tendency for last-minute rushes, a trait that had even earned her the label of a procrastinator from her teachers. Yet Anu had always seen past it, confident in Aisha's sharp intellect and quick learning. Time and again, her daughter's brilliance had placed her at the top of her class, a fact Anu held onto tightly. Mrinal, however, couldn't rely on such a leap of faith. His doubts about Aisha's self-discipline sparked arguments every evening, but Anu's faith in their daughter held firm, even as the practicalities loomed large.

She knew that without the support of a teaching or graduate assistantship, the financial strain on Mrinal would be considerable. The thought caused a familiar knot of anxiety to tighten in her stomach. Yet, as always, Anu was ready to face the challenge head-on.

The farewell at Delhi's Indira Gandhi International Airport was a bittersweet moment. Anu clutched Aisha fiercely, deeply aware of the significance of this step towards her daughter's dreams across continents. But as the initial excitement of Aisha's college life settled, a gnawing anxiety soon began to haunt Anu's nights. Sleeplessness became her companion as she envisioned the dreaded phone call, the one where insufficient funds would shatter Aisha's aspirations and compel her return.

A month into college, the silent countdown in Anu's mind was unexpectedly shattered by a late-night call. Aisha's voice, crackling with excitement, exclaimed, "Mamma, I got the GA! I mean, the graduate assistantship!"

A wave of profound relief washed over Anu, so powerful it made her lightheaded. When she broke the news to Mrinal, his only response was a reluctant nod. "Hm. Looks like her luck held out."

The elation from the phone call faded, replaced by a familiar knot of unease. Since Aisha's departure, a new fear had taken root. Her daughter was adrift in a vast, unfamiliar world, and Anu pictured her navigating an alien landscape and fending for herself. Just as this persistent worry began to settle in, a promising opportunity emerged. An invitation to a conference in Washington, D.C., arrived, and in that moment, Anu saw a chance to not only attend a valuable professional event, but also to ease her anxieties.

Following the conference, the reunion with Aisha on George Washington University's Foggy Bottom campus was filled with long talks and shared meals. As they walked the campus's brick pathways, Anu watched Aisha's comfortable interactions with her roommate and her confident navigation of campus life. With each passing hour, a measure of reassurance finally settled within her.

The conference in D.C. introduced Anu to David Johnson, a thoughtful gentleman with a background in financial economics, working with the D.C. Public Service Commission. Their initial conversation, sparked by a shared interest in urban development, blossomed into a comfortable friendship. Dave, with his insightful explanations of the Commission's plans to modernize the district's power grid and its potential impact on local utilities, captivated Anu's interest. His perspectives offered a fresh lens on complex systems, subtly broadening her world.

Beyond professional discussions, Dave extended a hand of support to Aisha, offering her advice on navigating university life in a new country. Anu's gratitude for his presence as a guiding figure in this unfamiliar land grew steadily. Their connection continued through regular emails, with Dave always offering a patient ear and thoughtful responses whenever Anu reached out. In turn, Anu found herself confiding in him, sharing anecdotes about her life and family.

He would often say, "Anu, your life is an interesting story; you should capture it in a memoir."

Anu would laugh. "Maybe someday, Dave. When I have a moment to myself."

Dave became another cherished and dependable member of Anu's circle. His friendship, a new comfort in a foreign land, was soon mirrored by a reunion with familiar faces.

Anu's time in the States also allowed her to reconnect with Rose and Velvet, two spirited American women she and Aisha had befriended during their earlier trip to Italy. Rose, who lived in Bowie, possessed a genuine warmth that drew Anu in; their shared memories from their Italian vacation quickly rekindled their bond. Rose delighted in playing host, taking Anu on scenic drives to see the autumn leaves and insisting she try exclusive American delicacies like a perfectly barbecued rack of ribs or a slice of authentic key lime pie. It was a simple joy, but it resonated deeply.

These encounters revealed a comforting reality; beyond the familiar bonds of family already in the USA, Anu was creating a network of reliable friendships. Their genuine warmth, unpretentious manner, and willingness to assist struck a deep chord within her, making her feel less like a visitor and more at home.

*

Mrinal and Anu boarded the flight, their excitement palpable as they traveled to attend Aisha's graduation. It was a truly momentous event for the parents, seeing their daughter achieve this milestone at an American university.

A day before the ceremony, Aisha returned from college with her grade card. Mrinal held it in his hands, a mixture of disbelief and grudging admiration in his eyes.

"Well," he conceded, a wry smile playing on his lips. "I have to admit, your mother's stubbornness paid off again. This time, she won." He shook his head, looking from the card to Aisha. "I honestly didn't think you'd make it through, especially with our financial constraints. It was her unwavering resolve that ultimately swayed me, despite my deep concerns."

He paused, then added, his tone more serious, "A good memory alone doesn't help, Aish. You need to apply yourself."

Aisha chuckled, leaning over to hug Anu tightly. "Mamma always knows best. She's my 'kick-ass mom'; I love her to the moon and back!" She pulled away and pointed at the grade card in her father's hand. "Check out my grades, Papa. Then tell me I don't apply myself. You're so skeptical about everything."

Mrinal's wasn't swayed by this comment. He focused on Aisha's grade card, and then he exclaimed. "Aish," a hint of playful exasperation in his voice, "it feels like a miracle that you manage these A's and A+s when you seem to be perpetually socialising. I graduated with honours too, but I was hardly the social butterfly you are. I actually dedicated time to studying, not flitting about like you."

Aisha grinned. "Papa, you were a classic nerd. I, on the other hand, embrace life and absorb information when the mood strikes, often at the eleventh hour. But I get the results, don't I? Perhaps I've inherited a touch of your much-vaunted photographic memory."

Later, Aisha's graduation, marked by an impressive GPA of 3.97 out of 4, was a shared triumph. Anu especially reveled in it, while Mrinal remained silently skeptical, still wondering how his daughter managed to pull it off.

Anu often felt Mrinal hadn't learned to truly appreciate their family's achievements. Yet, in moments of quiet reflection, a wave of gratitude washed over her, encompassing even Mrinal. *"Despite our differences,"* she would muse, *"he is the co-creator of this girl who fills me with such pride."* She acknowledged his role, however grudgingly given.

Then she remembered her own mother, who would often say, "Anu's world revolves around her daughter."

Reflecting on her own life experiences, Anu recognized that her mother's words, once a simple observation, had become a defining truth. Anu realised that the challenges she went through had shaped her understanding of what truly mattered.

Aisha's graduation was marked by a series of celebratory dinners. The first was a quiet dinner with her family. Then, to everyone's surprise, Rose made the drive from Bowie to D.C. to celebrate. David also hosted a celebratory dinner, raising a toast to Aisha's achievement.

A few weeks later back in India, a thoughtful expression settled on Anu's face. She was touched by her new friends and the ease with which they embraced life, their directness, their willingness to connect. "There is much to learn from these Americans," she mused.

A sense of profound thankfulness would often lead Anu to hum her beloved tune from *The Sound of Music*, a quiet expression of her inner peace. "Nothing comes from nothing as nothing ever could. Somewhere in my youth or childhood, I must have done something good"—the lyrics echoed the sentiment in her heart.

55

Bridges Across Borders

On a trip to Kolkata, Anu's professor friend, Runa, invited her and Mrinal to join an excursion to the Sundarbans. Mrinal was initially reluctant, but eventually, he agreed. As they packed, Anu shot him a look that needed no words. He knew she expected him to keep his composure and, for once, not undermine her in front of her college friends, a habit he often resorted to.

Runa, a professor at Calcutta University, was leading the excursion with her postgraduate scholars specializing in algal cytology. The team was divided into two groups. The research of one group focused on bio-fuel extraction from the algal species Spirulina. The second was engaged in nanotechnology, specifically identifying arsenic belts and detecting arsenic using nanomaterial-algae hybrid biosensors. These efforts targeted regions with elevated levels of arsenic contamination, primarily in groundwater.

Anu and Mrinal joined the first group. As they swayed with the boat's gentle rhythm, Anu noticed a Danish couple, Ingrid and Jonas, who appeared somewhat overwhelmed by the rapid flow of Bengali conversation around them. Without hesitation, Anu approached them. Her warm smile and easy conversation quickly put them at ease as she translated key phrases and offered insights into the local culture. They exchanged laughter and stories amidst the dense mangrove forests, and a genuine friendship quickly took root.

Anu often reflected on the contrast she saw in Mrinal. While on vacation, he was a changed man, shedding his usual frugal nature. He enjoyed splurging, and Anu loved shopping as well. This gave Anu a different perspective on their life together, leading her to believe that everything in life happens for a reason.

When Mrinal retired, Anu suggested a trip to Scandinavia, challenging the notion that retirement meant being chained to the house. As was typical, her suggestion was met with countless excuses and a firm refusal. Convincing Mrinal to do anything in life was never easy for Anu.

*

Anu and Mrinal eventually made it to Scandinavia, finding themselves guests in Ingrid and Jonas's charming home in Svendborg, Denmark. They were deeply touched by their hosts' heartfelt hospitality, especially the cozy evenings by the fireplace and shared meals filled with unfamiliar yet comforting flavours.

As a token of their appreciation, Anu invited Ingrid and Jonas to experience the tranquility of Nainital, envisioning them amidst the Himalayan foothills. For Anu, these spontaneous connections felt as natural as breathing. She often marveled at her good fortune in finding kindred spirits scattered across the globe. Mrinal, however, was never quite comfortable around foreigners, preferring to stay in the background, quietly following Anu's lead as she effortlessly bridged cultures.

While they were vacationing in Scandinavia, Aisha prepared to leave Washington D.C. for her summer internship in Atlanta. Though miles apart, Anu's web of care extended across continents. Anu reached out to her good friend Indrani, a long-time U.S. resident, who immediately stepped in. Indrani reminded Anu of the Sen family, with whom they had bonded during their Bangalore days over lively discussions and filter coffee. Anu had lost touch with the

Sens after they moved to the U.S., but Indrani reconnected with them, and they immediately agreed to help.

True to form, Mr. Amit Sen and his wife, Mrs. Aruna Sen, were waiting at the airport when Aisha arrived, extending a warm welcome in Atlanta. They readily assumed the role of her local guardians, offering her Bengali cuisine, such as luchi, aloor dom, and payesh, and a comforting presence in a new city. For Aisha, it felt like coming home. For Anu and Mrinal, the relief was immeasurable, their gratitude a silent comfort from thousands of miles away.

Anu often reflected on her good fortune. The kindness of friends offered a quiet reassurance in a vast world. Later, during one of their trips to Atlanta, the Sens even welcomed Anu, Mrinal, and Aisha into their home. Their house, echoing with familiar Bengali melodies and lively conversation, left a lasting impression of their genuine hospitality.

After her internship, Aisha returned to Washington D.C. to complete her master's degree. Soon after, an exciting job offer from her former internship cemented her life in the bustling southern city of Atlanta.

*

With Aisha settled in Atlanta, Anu's visits often brought the familiar pang of a mother seeing her daughter establish a life far from home. During one such visit, Anu's cousin Piu shared the contact for her classmate, Vinee, who also resided in Atlanta. Vinee, a bright young woman with an infectious laugh and an open heart, quickly extended her warmth to both Anu and Aisha, introducing them to her diverse group of friends.

One day, Vinee excitedly introduced them to Francesca West, a vibrant and witty ninety-three-year-old. "You know, Anu," Vinee would often say with affection, "I found a mom in a foreign land." Then, hugging Francesca tightly, she would declare, "She is my foreign mom, my *pardesi* mom!"

Anu found a cherished companion in Francesca, whose zest for life and insightful observations always came with a twinkle in her eye. Their time together often involved cruising Atlanta's streets in Francesca's bright red Toyota, sharing laughter and stories that spanned Francesca's adventurous past and her sharp views on the present. Francesca also made sure Anu connected with her Indian friends in the city, like Rani, a dynamic entrepreneur with a remarkable collection of traditional Indian attire, offering Anu another glimpse into Atlanta's diverse cultural landscape.

Each day with Francesca brought new adventures and fresh perspectives. Anu grew deeply fond of Francesca, admiring her boundless enthusiasm and sharp intellect. Francesca often shared her philosophy, gleaned from a long and well-lived life: embracing challenges and pursuing one's dreams. Her unwavering mantra, "Life is good," echoed in Anu's mind.

One afternoon, over lunch, Francesca, intuitively sensing Anu's thoughtful nature, encouraged her to explore her memories. "Anu, you have stories to tell. Don't let them fade," she said.

Vinee, who had been quiet until then, suddenly seemed to perk up, "I've also started penning down my book, courtesy of my 'pardesi mom'."

"Go for it, girls. I'm looking forward to reading both your books," Francesca would cheer them on.

As Anu's friendship with Francesca deepened, the older woman's consistent encouragement to delve into her past and write her story became a significant catalyst, gently rekindling Anu's long-held wish to visit the land of her ancestors, a quiet yearning that had been growing within her for years.

Eventually, Vinee became Aisha's trusted local contact and support. These cherished connections, forged across cultures and continents, were more than just friendships;

they were the very threads of Anu's lifeline, each encounter enriching her understanding of the world and herself.

Aisha often observed her mother's effortless ability to make friends in a foreign land, a talent that sometimes sparked a touch of envy. "Mamma," she'd remark, "your knack for connecting with people across cultures is amazing, especially considering you grew up in India."

Anu would simply smile. "Maybe I didn't have the chance earlier, Aish, but when I did, it felt natural."

Aisha, looking impressed, would then suggest, "Maybe it's because you had so many pen pals in your school days. So you always had that bent."

"You got it, Aish. During our times, *Junior Statesman* had these pen pal columns. Now it's all memories," Anu said with a balmy look.

*

With her daughter now far away in a distant land, a quiet emptiness settled in Anu's heart, echoing with unspoken longings. The urge to reconnect with her roots became intense; Mihir, her Rangapishi, even frequented her dreams, hinting at a persistent unease and whispers of hidden stories.

Faint childhood memories surfaced, revealing a quiet respect for a faraway place and wistful smiles at specific names. Anu felt a deeper urge stirring within her—the past felt like an incomplete puzzle she was driven to piece together.

One day, seeking solace and a renewed sense of purpose, she turned to Mrinal. Her heart yearned to finally explore the land of her ancestors, a desire that had steadily grown into a profound need to reconnect with her heritage.

However, Mrinal met Anu's hopeful suggestion with a dismissive wave of his hand. "That's just a childish notion, Anu," he stated, his tone brooking no argument, his gaze fixed on the newspaper. His rejection felt like a sharp blow, leaving Anu with a profound sense of isolation, a sudden chill in the warmth of her memories.

While Anu wanted a companion, she feared that if she coaxed Mrinal, he might concede. However, she couldn't trust him; he had a habit of belittling her, especially in front of new acquaintances. Anu sensed Mrinal often struggled to accept her achievements.

Despite this, the pull towards her family legacy remained strong for Anu. There was an undeniable conviction that this exploration was a necessary part of her journey—a missing piece of her identity.

Turning the pages of an old family album, past narratives suddenly made sense. Each photograph, formal portraits and a grand, unfamiliar house, offered a silent hint. The words "Paksey", "Ratnaprobha Vidyapitha", and "Hardinge Bridge" resonated within her, pieces of a history she felt compelled to recover. This strong wish to link the scattered threads of her ancestry and grasp her true self ignited her resolve.

She would muse, *How do I make this happen?* The silent answer formed clearly in her mind; she must gather every ounce of courage and do it herself.

In those moments of doubt, the powerful melody and resolute words of Tagore's patriotic song would resonate within her, a guiding light in her determination: "*Jodi tor dak shune keu na ashee, tabe ekla chalo re*; if they answer not to thy call, walk alone."

56

The Secret of the Red Diary

The year was 2016. With a deep breath, Anu typed "Ratnaprobha Vidyapitha, Paksey" into the Google search bar. The familiar spinning wheel mirrored the frantic thrumming in her chest; a volatile mix of desperate hope and the familiar dread of a digital dead end.

Then, it stopped. Her breath hitched as a grainy image loaded—a yellowed, weathered wall with the school's name crudely etched like a forgotten tombstone. A wave of dizzying exhilaration washed over her, a tangible proof that this piece of her past wasn't just a story. Yet, a profound sense of detachment lingered; she was a silent observer across time and continents, witnessing a reality unknown to her, a past both hers and impossibly distant.

The image confirmed that her grandfather's school had existed, but its present reality remained an unanswered question, as below the image was written: "Image created on 8 January 2014, by Afzal Haq."

Intrigued by the grainy image and the possibility of a real connection, an unrest began to build, prompting her to consider ways to delve deeper. *But how?* the thought lingered. *There were no contact details.*

Months passed in contemplation. Then, one day, an idea struck. *Why not try Facebook?* She had reconnected with long-lost friends through its social media reach and decided to leverage the platform once more. This time, she typed: "Alumni Ratnaprobha Vidyapitha."

And there it was! The Facebook page for "Ratnaprobha Vidyapitha Praktony" stared back at her. The group, a surprising discovery, consisted of about 1,500 *praktony*, or alumni of RPVP. Swiftly, Anu typed, "Hello RPVP alumni. My name is Anurima Sensharma, and I am the eldest granddaughter of Amalendra Chandra Dasgupta, the founder of your school."

Anticipation mounted as Anu waited. The next day, her Messenger inbox was flooded with messages. Some were simple introductions; others expressed a mix of curiosity and awe, wanting to know more about this person from India who claimed to be the granddaughter of their school's revered founder, the late Amalendra Chandra Dasgupta.

Filled with triumphant excitement, Anu connected with the administrator of the page, Jamal-uddin Rohan, a professor of chemistry at Dhaka University. Professor Rohan, equally thrilled to meet a descendant of the founder, immediately called Anu on Messenger.

Their conversation was a flood of exchanged information and shared history. This significant day marked the beginning of Anu's journey to reconnect with her past, all triggered by a single Facebook page. Professor Rohan began sending pictures of her grandfather's house and the school, Ratnaprobha Vidyapitha. The images confirmed everything Anu had been dreaming of. She prepared for the unknown adventure that lay ahead, knowing she still needed to gather more information.

*

The year was 2016, and December marked Anu and Jay's annual trip to Kolkata. The sisters, along with their paternal cousins, gathered at their cousin Jhulan's house for a reunion. Among the elders were her paternal aunt Sarojubala and three of her five sons, Ranju, Biddhu, and Molu, who had come with their wives.

Ketoki, Jhulan's widow, was the eldest among them and the only one with memories of the family's past in Paksey and Comilla. As Anu looked around, she sensed a quiet history in the air, a story waiting to be told. She missed her mother, and a familiar question settled in her mind: *Why did she have to leave us so early when she was just a few years older than Ketoki?*

Ketoki watched Anu with a hint of a smile. Shifting slightly, she announced, "Anu, if you plan to write a book about your ancestors, I have something that might be useful."

Anu stared at her sister-in-law in disbelief, shocked by her uncanny intuition. Despite the surprise, she remained silent about her connection with the RPVP alumni and her planned trip to Bangladesh. Her curiosity was piqued as she watched her *Ketoki boudi* move away, a sense of elation filling her as she finally felt a part of this unfolding discovery.

Ketoki returned with a red diary. "Anu, you'll find what you're searching for here, and more," she declared. "This incredible relic, your grandfather's diary, was kept by my mother-in-law, Sarojubala, who is also your aunt, *Sejopishi*."

After meticulously dusting the book, she continued, "She had found it among her Baba's, your *Thakurda's*, belongings." She paused. "Take good care of it, Anu, and return it when you're finished."

Anu nodded, taking the diary. An envelope slid out. She lifted it, her eyes questioning.

"May I open it, *Boudi*?"" she asked.

Ketoki nodded. "Go ahead."

Anu unfolded a yellowed, age-dappled piece of paper. It read:

"Dear Sister, Swarnaprobha,

I hope this letter finds you well. Your brother-in-law Deben has passed away. In accordance with his last wish, I am sending his ashes to you. My daughter is now a grown lady and, like her father, works as a scientist in a laboratory.

With love and regards,

His loving wife,

Margaret Dasgupta."

Jay, who had been quiet until then, gasped. "Oh my gosh, what is this?"

Anu was dumbstruck. After a moment, she asked, "*Boudi*, could you tell us more about this letter?"

To their surprise, Ketoki revealed a long-buried family secret. "Years ago, after your Thakurma passed away, a parcel arrived with an urn and this letter," she began. "That's when the family discovered Deben had a daughter."

Ketoki looked at Anu and Jay. "Your grand-uncle, after going to Germany, earned his doctorate in Quantum Chemistry and worked as a scientist in a German lab. He married Margaret, a German woman."

"Yes!" Jay interjected. "Papa would say that when he was in Munich, he tried to find his uncle, his Mejokaka."

Anu nodded. "I remember Papa saying he looked into every science laboratory in Munich to no avail. He had left no stone unturned."

"Indeed, Anu. I heard that from my mother-in-law, Sarojubala, Ketoki said with a non-plussed expression. The letters from Germany had the Munich address, but he was untraceable. I had no idea my mother-in-law had kept this letter. After she passed away, I found the red diary and the letter in her trunk."

Anu's cousin Bidhu suddenly exclaimed, "I remember our maternal house on Kakulia Road. It was a huge mansion with a courtyard and rooms for every family member." He paused. "And Maa always talked about our grand-uncle

Deben. Later, growing up, he became a kind of role model for me."

Molu, sitting in the corner, chimed in, "Ma told me that our grandfather, Amalendra Chandra Dasgupta's name, is still in the Hall of Fame at B.E. College."

"Oh wow! We should go see it for ourselves," Jay exclaimed.

As the evening deepened, the past came alive, and Anu was spellbound. She uncovered a wealth of unknown facts about their legacy, including the story of their grandfather's house in Comilla, unclaimed for years and now a fire station in Bangladesh. Ketoki also shared stories of Amalendra's engineering brilliance. This surreal experience allowed Anu and Jay to delve into their family's rich past.

Then Ketoki suddenly blurted out, "I heard your grandfather used his entire provident fund of Rs 17,000 to rebuild Ratnaprobha."

"Rs 17,000 was a significant amount of money then," Jay commented.

"Yes, we knew he used his provident fund to build the school, but had no idea of the sum," Anu replied, her eyes distant. *People were selfless in those days, giving away their life savings at once . . . unbelievable.*

Jay added, "They prioritised philanthropic services, something rarely seen today."

Ketoki nodded. "One positive outcome is that despite the family's turmoil during the partition, all his children pursued higher education and secured good jobs."

Then Ketoki suddenly enquired, "Anu, are you by any chance planning a trip to Bangladesh? If so, take somebody with you. Will Mrinal go with you? Though knowing his nature, I don't think he would like to see your legacy."

"I thought as much," Anu replied. "Whenever I bring up the topic, he says it's all my imagination."

"I thought so too," Ketoki said with a knowing frown.

Having uncovered many ancestral facts, Anu picked up her *Thakurda's* diary. The yellowed, crisp pages crinkled as she turned them. She knew she held an invaluable gem, a portal to her past.

Clutching the red diary, Anu headed home. A sense of purpose settled within her as she crafted a dust jacket for the precious journal. Settling into a recliner, a growing curiosity drew her to the past. Carefully, she opened the first page and stared at the yellowed, handmade paper. In an old-fashioned slant, written with a black ink pen, it read:

Amalendra Chandra Dasgupta

Comilla, Paksey, 1910

Anu's grandfather, Amalendra, seemed to leap from the journal's pages as she turned them. He appeared to come to life, and she felt her past enveloping her like a mist, flooding her mind with ancestral memories. She recalled her great-grandfather's letters to her great-grandmother, Ratnaprobha Debi, and began to drift away to the land of her ancestors.

*

Later that week, as Anu continued to delve deeper into her family's history, a new opportunity arose. Mrinal received an invitation to his forty-year batch reunion. Anu's ears perked up; this was her chance to connect with her ancestral research in a tangible way. She remembered stories of Srimoyee and Srilata, two brave women from her lineage who had spent seven years in a momentous detention camp after their mission involving the District Magistrate of Comilla. Anu was determined to see that historical site for herself.

Mrinal, who preferred not to share much about his past, was initially uninterested in taking her along. But Anu was adamant; she couldn't let go of this chance. After repeated coaxing, he complied, and Anu, bubbling with excitement, accompanied him.

Upon reaching the campus, Mrinal took Anu around the place where the Hijli Detention Camp once stood. Anu saw that it had been converted into the Nehru Museum of Science and Technology.

"Why the Nehru Museum?" Anu asked.

With a hint of pride in his voice, Mrinal replied, "Because our first prime minister, Jawaharlal Nehru, converted this jail into the first technical institute of our country. And I am a proud alumnus of this institute."

Anu smiled. As she explored the area, Mrinal entered a room and suddenly remembered it was where some of their classes had been held.

"Really?" Anu shot Mrinal an exasperated glance, thinking, *What a character! Anyone else would have been flaunting that fact.*

Looking at him with reproach, she couldn't help but say, "You never told me this was a detention camp." A note of sadness entered her voice. "Then again, why would you, when you never believed me whenever I narrated the stories of my revolutionary aunts, Srimoyee and Srilata."

Mrinal merely shrugged, unfazed by her accusation.

As Anu wandered through the iconic structure, she felt goosebumps. *I hope I'm not dreaming,* she thought. *Because I can see I'm part of a rich history!* The stories of Jay, the Hijli Detention Camp, her grandfather's land—all of their history—stirred a fire in her belly, a sudden, fierce desire.

I need to see it. My dreamland awaits.

PART X
2017
Bangladesh

57

In Search of Her Roots

Anurima had grown up living in the shadow of her past, her ancestors clinging to her like an appendage. What had begun as a search for her long-lost roots quickly plunged her into a puzzling, uncharted chapter. She felt like a rudderless boat, more adrift and unnerved than by any past struggle, as she contemplated a voyage into the unknown.

But despite her discomfort with this newness, the allure of documenting her family's story fuelled her desire to experience it firsthand. Unearthing her grandfather's school, Ratnaprobha Vidyapitha, connecting with RPVP alumni, and finding his diary all lifted her spirits.

Things started falling into place when, the very next year in 2017, Jay mentioned her upcoming work trip to Bangladesh. Anu's aunt, Pinku mashi, also revealed that Anu's cousin Babai was there and had organised a trip for her during her previous visit. Anu saw an opportunity and began planning her trip with Jay, Babai, and the alumni from RPVP school. Jay and Anu had even booked their tickets.

However, at the last minute, Jay had to postpone her trip, leaving Anu unsure. Fortunately, Jay's colleague Poulomi was travelling on the same day, so Jay reassured Anu that she would have a travel companion.

*

Anu was at the Netaji Subhash Chandra Bose Airport in Kolkata when the sterile hum of the airport amplified her sudden sense of isolation. Pacing before the departure gate, clutching her boarding pass like a fragile key, she felt pressed against an invisible, cruel glass wall, able to see the hazy outline of her past but unable to touch it. The air hummed with a restless energy; rhythmic announcements echoed off the polished floors, punctuated by the squeak of trolley wheels and snippets of hurried conversations in a dozen tongues. A faint, lingering scent of jet fuel and something vaguely floral, perhaps from a duty-free perfume, hung in the air.

Boarding the Biman Bangladesh Airlines aeroplane, a different hum vibrated through the cabin, a lower, steady thrum. The ascent was a gentle push, and as the plane pierced the soft, white expanse of clouds, a hush fell. The world outside the small window dissolved into pure, silent light, and a sense of lightness bloomed within Anu, a primal stirring that felt like shedding a heavy skin. The waiting room, indeed, felt like a fading echo.

As Anu stepped onto the tarmac at Shahjalal International Airport in Bangladesh, the air was thick and warm, carrying a medley of unfamiliar scents, a sweetness both foreign and strangely familiar. An electric buzz pulsed through the crowd, an undercurrent of anticipation that resonated deep within Anu. This was it. She was standing on the soil of her ancestors.

A profound sense of release washed over her, and in the murmur of voices around her, she imagined she could almost hear the echoes of the past, a sweet, poignant melody that grew with each passing moment. The invisible glass wall that had separated her from her heritage had finally dissolved.

The clatter of luggage carts filled the air as Anu and Poulomi said their goodbyes. Pushing her own cart, its rubber wheels squeaking softly on the concrete, Anu's heart hammered against her ribs. The cordoned area buzzed with unfamiliar faces, their features a blur as she scanned the crowd, her gaze darting, searching. This was an unknown world to her; the only thing she knew they shared was language.

Then, she saw Babai waving from the midst of the crowded sidewalk. Anu sighed in relief and waved back. Babai seemed swallowed by the crowd, but he managed to make his way through and quickly took the cart from Anu.

Once inside the car, Anu told him about her evening invite to the Gulshan Club.

Babai looked curious. "Ah! Gulshan is a legendary club built during the Raj Era. But, who invited you there?"

"It's the RPVP alumni, from my late grandfather's school, Ratnaprobha Vidyapitha. You know, Babai, the mere existence of the school was a bolt from the blue. I thought it had perished with time."

"Okay, I get that. But if you don't mind, what is the real purpose of your visit? I'm sure it's not just to go to Gulshan Club?" asked Babai with a smug grin.

Anu looked at him. "I've come here to quench my thirst, to feel the land of my ancestors, especially the school my Thakurda built for the street urchins." She continued, "By a lucky chance, I connected with the alumni and I must confess, that is the reason I'm here in the land of my forefathers, the land of sweat and blood." She paused. "Today the RPVP alumni would like me to attend their annual alumni meet."

Babai grinned. "That is wonderful. Don't worry, I have a car ready for you."

"I couldn't thank you enough."

Babai smiled. "It's my pleasure, Anu di. And yes, I've chalked out your itinerary and organised an escort for you. You won't face any problems. Your safety is my top priority."

Anu leaned forward and hugged her cousin. She hadn't been expecting such thorough planning as she embarked on her seven-day tour. A sense of relief ran down her spine. *What a relief*, she mused, *to have family in an unknown land.*

*

Anu had been discouraged by her friends, who said she was travelling to a nation that had experienced a battle for freedom, a civil war, and a genocide that had left its imprint not only on the nation but also on the people within and beyond its borders. So, she was apprehensive and quite unsure of what awaited her in a place that had endured such tumultuous times.

The Dhaka traffic was a vibrant, honking beast, a stark contrast to the quiet hum of the airport. Through the car window, the city lights blurred into streaks of colour, each one a tiny spark in this vast, unknown place.

As the car approached the Gulshan Club, a nervous flutter danced in Anu's stomach, a mix of excitement and a tremor of the unfamiliar. What would these alumni be like? Would they understand the weight of her journey? These questions whispered quietly in the noisy car.

This evening felt pivotal, a chance to finally connect with the living legacy of her grandfather's work. The car stopped outside the main gate, and Anu alighted to be greeted by an assembly of RPVP alumni members, all dressed in their finest attire and evidently excited to welcome the granddaughter of their school's founder.

Professor Rohan's voice was a comforting anchor. He had been her main point of contact since she connected with the RPVP alumni Facebook group. But meeting them in person felt like stepping onto a tightrope. This wasn't just meeting people; it was touching a piece of her history, a history that felt both intimately hers and yet shrouded in a gentle mist of time.

Anu found herself at the centre of attention. She was pleasantly surprised to see the gate decorated with colourful festoons and balloons, but this was not all; more surprises awaited her. The president of the alumni, Mr. Abdul Motalaib, came forward and welcomed her with a rose, saying, "Anurima didi, you are younger than I expected.'

Anu laughed.

The photo sessions started, and everyone eagerly lined up to have their photograph taken with the founder's granddaughter. As Anu smiled for the cameras, she caught a glimpse of a familiar face in the crowd. It was Jay.

58

From Dust to Recognition

Jay stepped into the auditorium, her eyes wide with awe at the sprawling crowd. "Oh my God! I wasn't expecting anything like this," she muttered, her gaze sweeping over the sea of faces. She frantically scanned the room for Anu. This was a surprising turnout for what she'd imagined would be a fruitless trip. *I thought my didi would just be wasting her time here,* Jay thought, *as there was nothing left to see except the remnants of Thakurda's house in Paksey.* She gasped as her eyes scanned the hall, which was brimming with people. *Thakurda's school has an alumni association? Simply unbelievable.*

The hall was bustling with around a hundred alumni, all in attendance to honour their founder and his granddaughters. Anu had mentioned the event to Jayina but wasn't sure if she would make it on time, as her flight landed in Dhaka just a short while before the function. Luckily, Jayina arrived just before the main event, allowing Anu to introduce her to the alumni. Even though her unexpected appearance caught them off guard, they warmly welcomed her as another granddaughter of the founder.

The sisters looked spellbound as they took in the banner draped over the dais. "This event is to honour postbellum, founder of our school, Ratnaprobha Vidyapitha, Late Sri Amalendra Chandra Dasgupta, and his granddaughter Anurima Dasgupta Sensharma," it proclaimed. Then, the emcee took over the podium and invited Anu and Jay to be seated on the dais.

Anurima and Jayina were then escorted onto the dais. Before the alumni, they released a commemorative souvenir called "Protishthata" or "The Founder". The book with a portrait of their grandfather, Amalendra Chandra Dasgupta, on the cover paid homage to their benefactor who had passed away decades ago. The alumni then presented plaques and bouquets, commemorating him with heartfelt gratitude.

The emcee began, "We have the good fortune to chance upon the granddaughter of our honourable founder, whom we unfortunately have never had a chance to meet. After so many decades, let me take this opportunity to make this day memorable by showing our heartfelt gratitude to him and his family."

The sisters were overwhelmed. The alumni spoke fondly of their days at Ratnaprobha Vidyapitha and the memories they had made there. Jay and Anu sat mesmerized, transported back in time. They were struck by the deep gratitude the alumni still held for their founder, even seventy-two years after his passing.

After a while, Jay, unable to believe what she was witnessing, looked at her elder sister with an expression of disbelief. Anu gave a meaningful smile and whispered, "This is why I waited, Jay. I wanted my visit to be special. Something I could take back to my country with pride. I waited until I could find a good connection here, someone who may have heard of or known our Thakurda."

Jay nodded. "You've certainly done your research and homework, Didi."

Anu smiled. "Thanks to the digital age and Facebook."

Jay gave a thumbs up.

The alumni presented the sisters with plaques and books, honouring them with their traditional customs. Tears of happiness welled in Anurima's eyes as she was moved by the simplicity and humble nature of the people of Bangladesh. She could feel that the discovery of their founder's lineage had lifted a significant weight from the alumni.

In his speech, Professor Rohan highlighted the school's foundational role, noting that Ratnaprobha Vidyapitha had not only provided education but also served as a vital catalyst for social mobility in Paksey. Other alumni echoed his sentiment, passionately declaring, "Without the school, we would still be loitering on the streets." They called the school a guiding light, a 'lighthouse' for them.

Then, the sisters heard something unexpected. The host of the evening announced, "Many of you may not know, but this Dasgupta family was also part of the freedom struggle of the undivided Indian subcontinent." He continued, "Our founder, Amal babu's youngest brother, Satyen babu, was a freedom fighter, a revolutionary terrorist, and he died a martyr's death in an encounter."

"I was not aware of this?" Jay whispered.

Meanwhile, goosebumps rose on Anu's skin as she listened, mesmerized. She'd grown up hearing these stories, always believing them to be fables told by her Rangapishi. But now she knew the truth; her grand-uncle was truly a part of history.

A wave of heat flushed Anu's face, her breath catching in her throat. A freedom fighter. The word resonated deep within her, forging a new, powerful link to this land. The weight of the past, which had felt like a shackle, now seemed to transform into wings. While a flicker of understanding crossed Jay's face, a dawning realisation of the deep roots they shared in this land emerged.

After the main function, Jay leaned toward Anu and spoke in a hushed voice. "I have to go now. I have a dinner commitment with the organization I'm visiting in Bangladesh." She paused, her expression shifting. "But Didi,

I can see you really worked to make this trip a success. I'm truly proud of you."

Jay continued, her voice filled with newfound reflection. "I did visit Paksey and Comilla when I was younger, but I was too young to understand the vastness of our grandfather's philanthropy or the sacrifices he and our ancestors made during the freedom struggle. This event has been a real eye-opener for me too. If I hadn't come, I wouldn't have been able to appreciate the larger-than-life personality of our Thakurda and his school."

Anu nodded in understanding. "The people of Bangladesh truly know how to show gratitude. It's something worth learning."

"Indeed," Jay whispered back. "And Didi, is Comilla on your itinerary?"

Anu smiled. "How can I forget our ancestral home, our *adibari*? That's where all the action took place."

After Jay left, Anu spoke with each alumnus individually, delighted to hear about their success since graduating from the school. She was impressed by their varied backgrounds, which included civil servants, politicians, military personnel, authors, journalists, and professors, all of whom held important positions in Bangladesh. They all credited the school as a crucial stepping stone that helped them lead fulfilling lives. In that moment, Anu finally grasped the true significance of the school and why these individuals were so profoundly thankful to her grandfather.

59

My Golden Bengal

The rolling countryside blurred past the car window, and a wave of nostalgia washed over Anurima. Sun-drenched fields of marigolds and mustard sparked a melody in her mind: "*Amar shonar Bangla ami tomay bhalobashi*," she hummed softly, "My golden Bengal, I love you."

Anu remembered her Ma telling her that Rabindranath Tagore, the great Bengali polymath, wrote the song during the first partition of Bengal in 1905. The song evoked such strong feelings of nationalism among the middle class that, decades later, in 1972, it became the national anthem of Bangladesh. Its lyrics, which capture the beauty of Tagore's beloved motherland, the undivided Bengal, resonated just as deeply then as they did in the past.

Anu drank in the unfolding landscape, desolate yet beautiful in its pastoral quietude. Yellow stubble fields stretched under a pale golden sun as they drove towards Paksey, still five hours from Dhaka. A profound silence enveloped her, stirring a strange sense of déjà vu that intensified when she glimpsed a clay-banked creek, its stones like ancient jewels encrusted with blue-green moss.

This landscape vividly brought to life Tagore's poetic descriptions of his beloved Bengal, with its meandering *khal*, *beel*, *nadi*, and *nala*, the many canals that crisscross the country. During the dry season, the floodwaters recede and the *haors*, bowl-shaped shallow depressions, transform into fertile grasslands with isolated perennial water bodies known as *beels.* There was an unmistakable enchantment in the air.

Bangladesh lies in the floodplain of three great rivers, with one-third of the country being a wetland ecosystem. As Anu watched the landscape fly by, a stretch of reeds appeared, their slender stalks swaying as if beckoning her. Her heart swelled with a mix of excitement and anticipation as the wind blew against her face.

Yet, as she neared her destination, a sense of trepidation began to fill her. A knot of apprehension tightened in her stomach. What would it be like to finally confront the unknown? She was about to see the Paksey she had only heard about in stories from her childhood.

*

The Paksey railway gate appeared just as the clock edged towards 5 p.m. Against the waning evening sky, a lone figure stood silhouetted. As the car approached, the figure stepped forward, waving with an enthusiastic grin.

'Anurima didi, *ami Ripon jar shathe apni katha bolsen*!" he called out. "Anurima didi, it's Ripon here, the one you spoke to the other day!"

Ripon, an alumnus of Ratnaprobha Vidyapitha, had volunteered to take Anu to her grandfather's place. She invited him into the car, and they drove towards Paksey town. Anu felt a rush of excitement as they turned onto a side road from the highway.

Ripon remained quiet until he suddenly pointed to a wall. "*Didi, apnar Thakurdar shompotti ekhan theke shuru hoye,*" he said. "Didi, this is where your grandfather's property begins."

A wave of awe washed over Anurima as a seemingly endless boundary wall stretched beside the car. Then she heard Ripon exclaim, "*Eyita silo apnar Thakurdar shampottir pisoner gate*!" His voice brimming with excitement, he pulled Anu from her reverie. "This was the back gate of your grandpa's sprawling property!"

Anu nodded, still in a stupor. The car continued to roll forward until Ripon asked the driver to stop. She looked out of the window to see that the car had stopped in front of a towering gate, a mass of thorny wilderness with sculptures of lions atop each pillar.

Anu instantly recognised the 'Shingha Dwarja', the Lion Gate, which she had heard from her Ma that it led to Maa Kali's marble temple. Memories of Rangapishi's stories about their Paksey house then flooded her mind, and Anu sensed a joyous tingle.

The car drove around the tall boundary wall and entered through a small rear entrance. Anurima observed whispering paddy fields on one side, and on the other was a small *masjid*, a mosque, along with green-coloured dwellings for the *imams*, the religious leaders.

As the car moved along a dusty path, memories of her childhood stories came flooding back. With wide eyes, Anu tried to take in the sheer vastness of the estate. The trees seemed to reach out to her, and the ground held the dilapidated remains of what was once a noble household.

The car rolled to a halt, and Anu instantly recognized the building as Arohi Bhawan. Emotions stirred within her as she saw a gentleman standing in the doorway. Ripon introduced him as Raheem Punjabi, popularly known to the locals as Raheem chacha, or Uncle Raheem, the current owner of the house. The female members of his family were waiting inside.

Anurima was escorted in by some RPVP alumni. She climbed the stairs and entered a room that Raheem chacha said was her grandfather's study, the *adhyayan kakkho*. Raheem then pointed to another building across the main house. He explained it was her grandfather's *baithak khana*, a drawing room where he would entertain his formal guests.

It had a large hall with a sit-out. Anu could see that it was no longer in use and looked rundown.

Anu tried to imagine the past, feeling as though she had stepped into a time capsule. The house stood as a solitary outpost, a relic of a bygone era amidst the present civilisation.

Anu had plans to spend the night at her grandfather's house. She wanted to experience a bygone era and get to know the current family who owned the property. During their conversation, Anu learned more about Raheem and his family. Raheem's father was popularly known to locals as Arif Punjabi, but his real name was Mohammad Arif Chowdhury.

According to the family, Arif Punjabi, who had moved from West Pakistan before the Partition, was her grandfather's colleague. Raheem was his youngest son; his elder brother, Iqbal, had passed away. The family later narrated Arif Punjabi's brutal killing during the Bangladesh Liberation War, a story Anu had heard from Jay, who learned it from Iqbal years ago during her own visit to Paksey.

As dusk settled in, former students, staff, and the ex-principal of Ratnaprobha Vidyapitha all began to arrive to pay their respects to Anurima. For them, she was the revered granddaughter of their school's founder. Anu felt both embarrassed and deeply touched by their gesture.

However, conscious of her time, Anu excused herself. Eager to glimpse the fairy-tale town of her ancestors, she got into the car, accompanied by the alumni boys. They took her to the well-known BBC Bazaar, a place seemingly untouched by time, where she was told people once gathered to listen to the news on the radio.

As the car came to a halt, the boys excitedly told Anu that a few former students were eager to meet the founder's family. Surprised, Anu followed them to a small, rundown clubroom where men from the age of forty to seventy had gathered. With every passing minute, Anu felt herself shrinking back into the past.

The meeting concluded with tea and snacks. As Anu stepped out of the room, she noticed two men with shy demeanours standing beside their rickshaws. One of them came forward.

"Didi, *adab*," he said, his voice hesitant but proud. "*Amio Ratnaprobhar chatro, amiyo porsi class fibe obdhi.*" He continued in English, "Didi, greetings, I am a student of Ratnaprobha too. I also studied there till class five."

His pride and gratitude were clearly visible in his eyes, and Anu was overwhelmed by the experience. The serenity and simplicity of Paksey had already left their mark on her. As the lingering light of the day faded, she made her way back to the house that was once Arohi Bhawan, now renamed 'Ujjwala'.

The night was serene as she arrived, the moonlight gleaming off the silver sky. Anu had a fulfilling day and enjoyed a delicious dinner of her favourite Bengali dish, *shorshe ilish*; hilsa fish in mustard sauce, a fresh catch from the river Padma.

After a long day, Anu retired to her room, which featured a comfortable double bed adorned with fresh linen. As she lay there, she was enthralled by the shadows dancing on the ceiling. A strange scent filled the room, and in her mind's eye, she could hear a chandelier softly chiming as she drifted off to sleep.

The following morning, the sun's warm rays roused her. Quickly getting out of bed and grabbing her iPad, she set out to explore her grandfather's property. She had learned from Jay that it still technically belonged to the Dasgupta family and was now in the care of the Punjabi family.

Walking around, Anu observed the landscape and various fruit trees stretching tall against the sky. She then made her way to her Thakurma's bathing pond and continued to stroll through the vast area that was once a grand estate.

The ruins held her captive: the crumbling quarters of the house priests and the silent remnants of the domestic help's dwellings. Then she found it, a small area where the marble temple of Maa Kali had once stood. The adjacent meditation room was now open to the sky. A profound sense of connection washed over Anu; she could almost feel her Thakurda's presence in the stillness.

Anu was lost in her own world, taking in the remains of what was once a bustling household, when she suddenly realized she had company. Arif Punjabi's granddaughter, Abida, had joined her quietly. She always wore her hijab, which made her look like a doll.

Turning to Abida, Anu said, "I want to capture all of this on video."

"That would be very nice, Didi," Abida replied promptly, her eyes bright. "Back home, you can show it to everyone."

Anu smiled, a knowing look in her eyes. "Yes, Abida," she said, pausing for emphasis. "Seeing is believing."

Abida kept pointing to the trees, drooping with seasonal fruits, while Anu thought to herself that these had all stood the test of time, still retaining their majestic selves.

Anu was taken aback by the beauty of the rose garden and the sprawling vegetable patches. She saw crops swaying in unison, sugarcane, rice, and wheat which once again took her back to the stories she had heard as a child.

Then, she spotted Arif Punjabi's grandson, Aadil. He came forward. "Did you have a good night's sleep?"

"Yes, I was very tired," Anu nodded.

Aadil went on, "To be honest with you, there's hardly anything left now from the times of your Thakurdada moshai."

Anu nodded solemnly, as she could see that the vast property was now only a relic of a glorious past. They walked amidst the fields that smelled of damp straw while the large corn fields swayed in the wind. The pumpkins and gourds squatted together on their wigwams.

Anu carefully navigated around the large hose pipe, absorbing the landscape around her. At the edge of the field, a deserted brackish pond reflected the shadows of the trees with their dead leaves. She imagined how different it must have been 100 years ago when the property was thriving.

Anu pondered, *The splendid days have all gone with the wind!*

Anu quickly changed into a straight A-line dress for a breakfast invitation and went with Abida and her aunt to Nasreen's house, Arif Punjabi's sister. The warm hospitality and impressive spread of food were a pleasant surprise. After breakfast, Anu was keen to move on, as a visit to her grandfather's school, Ratnaprobha Vidyapitha, was next on her itinerary.

She returned swiftly to Arohi Bhawan, wanting to change into a sari. Abida told Anu to take it easy.

"No, Abida, I can't," Anu said. "I've come all this way because of the RPVP alumni." She paused. "Without their encouragement, I wouldn't be here. They are my inspiration."

Abida looked at Anu. "*Shekorer shandhane*? In search of your roots?"

Anurima nodded slowly, a sense of wonder still clinging to her. She gave her arm a small pinch. *Please, let this not be a dream.*

60

The Lighthouse

The car stopped in front of a huge iron gate, and Anurima looked out, seeing the large sign-board: "Ratnaprobha Vidyapitha, 1924." Anu could hardly believe her eyes.

Am I really standing in front of my Thakurda's school? she wondered.

Then what followed took her breath away. As Anu stepped out of the car, she was startled to find the entire school erupting in cheers. They greeted her with a Bengali catchphrase: "*Protishtathatar natni ke swagatam, swagatam*! We welcome the granddaughter of our founder. Welcome! Welcome!"

Anu was taken aback, embarrassment engulfing her. *They are treating me as if I were some minister coming to visit their school!* she thought.

As Anu walked down the driveway, students stood on high platforms, raining flower petals down on her. It felt as if a shower of flowers was falling from the sky in honour of the school's beloved founder's granddaughter. She felt overwhelmed, yet humbled by the display of affection and surprised by the grandeur of the event.

Then, as Anu entered the principal's office, she was amazed to see her grandfather's photo hanging alongside that of the Prime Minister of Bangladesh, Sheikh Hasina. The office was bustling with railway officers and political leaders who were all alumni of the school.

The principal of the school, Mr Rasheed, told Anu, "Didi, your grandfather was employed with the railways. Thus, after the partition of the Indian subcontinent, the school was taken over by the Pakistan Railways, and later by the Bangladesh Railways."

Anu immediately recalled as she had stepped out of the car, her eyes had immediately drawn on the school's sign board. The letters "Rly" were painted on it, a familiar abbreviation that brught back a flood of memories.

After the principal's welcome speech, a selection of snacks and tea was served. Anurima glanced at the elaborate spread of sweets, snacks, and fruits, feeling a little overwhelmed. *I'm already so full from the morning breakfast*, she mused, politely declining offers to sample the sweets. Instead, she contented herself with some tea and a few small treats, knowing she couldn't possibly do justice to the lavish display.

With the reception winding down, a teacher guided her to the school's playground. She was immediately engrossed in the impressive drill and physical training demonstration. But as the students' routine concluded, a sense of urgency dawned on her. People were waiting for her in the auditorium.

As she made her way inside, a palpable excitement filled the air. Eager faces and twinkling eyes turned towards her, everyone waiting for a glimpse of the founder's descendant. Moments later, Anu was escorted to the dais and seated among community leaders, railway school board members, and other respected guests. The program began with a flurry of tributes. As bouquets and plaques began to pile up in front of her, tears sprang to her eyes. She was so touched by the outpouring of love and respect that she looked around in a daze, overwhelmed by the heartfelt gesture.

The event host, Raju, guided the proceedings with impressive competence. As each alumnus's name echoed through the hushed hall, their felicitations a crisp rustle of paper against the microphone, a wave of warmth washed over Anu.

Mr. Sahil's presentation, his voice tinged with a familiar warmth, resonated deeply within her, stirring a gentle wave of nostalgia that lapped the shores of her present. The vibrant colors and lively sounds of her Rangapishi's stories flickered like old movie reels in her mind. She closed her eyes for a moment, the soft murmur of the audience a comforting backdrop, and savored the weight of each shared memory.

A quiet kinship settled over her, a feeling of roots running deep. Then a subtle shift in the atmosphere made her acutely aware of her Thakurda's presence—a feeling of quiet observation, as if from a silent guardian she had never met, yet whose spirit felt undeniably close. As she witnessed her grandfather's former students honouring and celebrating him, a warm pride enveloped her. Unexpectedly, a deep feeling of responsibility for his school washed over her, tinged with a profound sadness. It was like a king mourning a lost crown.

She reflected on the alumni's sentiment, acknowledging that *Thakurda's school had indeed been a lighthouse of knowledge for the people of Paksey.*

After the grand event, Anu strolled around and explored the school grounds. The rectangular playground was surrounded by classrooms, with the fourth side open to reveal a beautiful line of bungalows on the far side of the school building. When she asked Mr. Rasheed about them, she learned her grandfather had built the charming cottages as homes for resident teachers. The sight of the dilapidated buildings filled her with remorse. *Thakurda must have made them to attract teachers from far, she mused, and now they lie neglected.*

A sudden wave of emotion broke inside her as she longed for a new beginning. She felt utterly alone and helpless, a deep sense of loss washing over her. As she made her way to the car, a dull ache settled in her heart, for this was more than just a school. It was a lost legacy.

Their next stop, the alumni said, would be the Bangladesh Railway Office. Her mind numb, she stared out at the countryside, her heart heavy as the car pulled to a stop outside the main gate. The railways' chief engineer, Mr. Raheem, who was in the car with Anu, quickly went to procure the entry pass.

*

The air around the Paksey railway office hung heavy with the scent of damp earth and aged brick, a subtle mustiness clinging to the red clay that had witnessed generations of railway workers come and go. A faint, oily tang from some forgotten corner where machinery once hummed mingled with the drier, almost papery aroma of old documents and bound ledgers stored within.

Anurima stepped out of the car, her feet touching the same ground where her grandfather, Amalendra, had once worked until his retirement. The red brick buildings stood the test of time, a stoic reminder of the past when Paksey was the bustling headquarters of Eastern Bengal Railways of British India. Accompanied by Mr. Raheem, she walked past the imposing structures and entered the office premises, feeling the weight of history in every step.

Walking along the veranda, Anu felt a phantom presence. The echo of her own footsteps on the concrete seemed to layer with the distinct, familiar cadence of her Thakurda's walk, a reverberation not just of sound but of memory itself. It was as if the very stones held the subtle auditory imprint of his past presence, left by years of dedicated service.

Mr. Raheem stopped at a door, opening it to reveal a modest office. "Didi, please sit in that chair and get a feel of your Thakurda," he said, his voice laced with an underlying excitement. He gestured to the worn leather chair behind a desk. "This was the assistant engineer's office. Your Thakurda held this position during the construction of our monumental bridge."

Anu could not believe her ears. She nodded and gingerly sat down in the legendary chair. The worn leather yielded beneath her, a soft sigh escaping its aged depths as she settled into its contours. A faint, familiar scent of old wood rose to meet her, a comforting, almost ghostly embrace. The smooth, cool touch of the armrests, polished by years of her Thakurda's touch, sent a shiver of connection up her arms. *Am I dreaming?* she mused, pinching herself.

Meanwhile, the chief engineer got busy introducing the staff. Just then, a voice broke the quiet; "I think, sir, let's take Didi to the Drawing and Design section."

Anu was led into a hall lined with humongous concrete shelves reaching the ceiling. She could see brown files with sheaves of timeworn yellow pages peering out—the archival records, they said, that had been there since the bridge's construction. The staff, all wearing face masks, looked at her with a clear sense of admiration. They knew she was the granddaughter of one of the engineers who worked on their legendary Hardinge Bridge. The room also had large drawing boards and high stools. A lazy ceiling fan whirred overhead, its rhythmic swoosh a constant presence.

Mr. Raheem pointed at the drawing boards. "Didi, your Thakurda spent hours here," he said, his voice full of pride. "Amal babu played a big role in the planning and construction of our legendary Hardinge Bridge." By then she knew her Thakurda was popularly known as Amal babu in Paksey.

She looked at Mr. Raheem with a sense of reverence, her mind struggling to process the reality of all she had just seen. *Can all this be real?* she wondered.

As they returned to the assistant engineer's office, Anu found Mr. Raheem giving instructions to a colleague in a hushed tone. She looked around confused. Moments later, a gentleman walked in, carrying an enormous album. He placed it carefully in front of her, and Anu gasped, a small, involuntary sound hanging in the suddenly still air.

Her eyes widened, fixed on the title embossed on the aged cover: "Making of the Hardinge Bridge". Her heart hammered against her ribs as she reached out to touch it. It wasn't just an album; it was a tangible link to the stories she had grown up hearing, a key to unlocking a past she had only imagined.

She cautiously began to turn the pages, taking in the detailed instructions next to each diagram. Captivated by the events, Anu leaned closer to peer at the meticulous details of the design and drawings of each span of the legendary bridge. Mr. Raheem pointed to a drawing with millimeter precision. "Didi, look at the meticulousness and dedication of the drawings," he said.

A strange moisture flooded her eyes, a mixture of pride and unspoken sadness. She was amazed at how this history had trickled down through generations, still alive as if it were just the other day. *The people of this country have preserved every bit of the past,* she thought. Then a sudden, blinding knowledge engulfed her; *Thakurda had indeed left his footprints on the sands of time.*

As she was leaving the railway office, Anu was surprised when Mr. Raheem handed her a bag. "I hope you like it, Anurima didi. A memento from the railways," he said. Her breath hitched in surprise. Peering inside, she found an exquisite Dhakai Jamdani sari. A wave of warmth and genuine emotion washed over her, and her eyes softened with gratitude. A small, heartfelt smile graced her lips as she was clearly touched by the unexpected kindness and thoughtfulness of the gesture.

61

The Legendary Bridge

Anu was accompanied throughout the day by two women from the Punjabi family, Abida and her sister-in-law Nazneen, along with Nazneen's young daughter, Nazia. After visiting the railway office, the four of them got back into the car with Raju, the host of the morning's event. They were now on the final stretch, heading toward the day's destination. The other old boys followed on their motorcycles.

As the car moved through the delightful little town of Paksey, Anu was captivated. The lively sounds of the marketplace, snippets of conversations and the clatter of metal, drifted into the car. Sunlight glinted off the slate roofs of quaint buildings, and then, unexpectedly, she saw rows of identical, charming bungalows. They were so picture-perfect they seemed unreal.

Intrigued, Anu leaned forward, pointing at a row of bungalows. "Raju bhai, *oyee gulo ki,* what are those?"

A wide smile spread across Raju's face. "*Oguli* British *amoler* Naval quarters *silo,*" he beamed, his voice full of pride. "Those were the naval quarters from the British era. Now they lie vacant and run-down, just a reminder of our picturesque town."

Soon, the car entered the forest. The lively sounds faded into a quiet stillness, and the air smelled distinctly of damp earth. A subtle shift occurred within Anu as she watched the dense green foliage blur past the window.

"Didi, you know," Raju began, his voice tinged with reverence, "this enchanting town, our Paksey, *ekta jongol silo.* It was a jungle cleared by the English." A shadow fell across Anu's features as she listened, a faint note of something lost lingering in his words.

"Didi," Raju began, turning slightly towards Anu as the car continued, "Paksey is a unique rail *nagari.* It's the only railway town of its kind in Bangladesh."

Anu smiled. "It sounds beautiful. You must be very proud of it."

"Oh yes, very much," Raju said. He paused for a moment, his voice softening. "Here, one can hear the *Padma nadir kulkul shabdo*; the gentle murmur of the Padma River. You know, it's the pride of our country." His voice hitched slightly.

"The resonance of the waves against the trestles," he continued, his gaze lost in thought, "the sailing fishing boats… the charming bungalows." His words trailed off, a deep emotion hanging in the air.

Anu watched him, a feeling of deep understanding settling over her. "I see now why my grandfather chose this little town for his retirement instead of Calcutta." A strange feeling of kinship settled in her. "You know, Raju, I've also chosen to make my home in the lovely hill town of Nainital. Most Bengalis prefer Kolkata."

"Really, Didi?" Raju's eyebrows rose in surprise. "You've certainly inherited your grandfather's inclinations."

Anu nodded, a small smile playing on her lips. "Perhaps. It seems to run in the family."

Abida then chimed in, her voice tinged with melancholy. "Anu didi, your grandfather built such a beautiful house. We absolutely love it." Her gaze drifted to the passing jungle. "It's a shame your family couldn't experience your grandfather's wonderful property."

"Indeed," Nazneen murmured, her voice soft. "When I first arrived here as a newlywed, I was consistently impressed by the extensive grounds. It was so richly endowed with flowers, fruit-bearing trees, and fields of grain. A real zamindar-house feel."

A thoughtful silence fell over the car. Anu's smile faded as she considered their words. Just then, the car sharply turned uphill, and Raju pointed toward a small hillock. "That's our Paksey Railway Station," he remarked. "Isn't it cute?"

"The height is fascinating," Anu observed.

"Yes, it must be around forty-five feet above ground level," Raju replied.

Perched atop the raised mound, Anu saw a quaint little station, its red brick architecture a clear reminder of the Raj era. They got out of the car and began walking uphill toward it.

Anu's heart quickened with anticipation. *The Hardinge Bridge... I've heard so much about its grandeur. Will it truly be as magnificent as they say? A relic of a bygone era, a testament to engineering prowess.*

As the path cleared, the fabulous Hardinge Bridge revealed itself in its majestic glory. Anu gasped softly, a wave of awe washing over her. *It's breathtaking. The sheer scale of it, those towering piers... it feels like a connection to history itself.*

Raju went ahead and whispered something to the guard. Anu watched the exchange, her gaze lingering on the man. *Ratnaprobha... a name that carries so much weight in this little town,* she mused.

The uniformed man stood up, a respectful smile spreading across his face. He bowed slightly and said that he, too, was a student of Ratnaprobha.

Anu acknowledged him with a nod. The group then strode along the railway track, with Raju leading, while Anu marveled at the bridge's breathtaking design. Her thoughts were interrupted by Raju, who said with an air of confidence, "Didi, I don't think Hardinge Bridge has any rival. It is a unique structure. It is one of the historical attractions of our country."

A wave of awe washed over Anu as she gazed at the colossal structure of the bridge. *So, this is it,* she mused, *the bridge I've heard so much about and Thakurda's involvement in it.* She inhaled the air and looked up. "This place feels like a deep connection to our family," she murmured.

Breaking into her contemplation, Raju spoke. "They say a total of 24,000 construction workers worked two long years to complete this mighty bridge. Back then, this line was under the Eastern Bengal Railways." He blurted this out in one breath, then stopped abruptly, as if his duty were done.

Overwhelmed, Anu simply nodded. She was now standing in front of the Hardinge Bridge. The late autumn sunset cast a strange, mysterious radiance on her face as she stared in disbelief. A sense of wonder washed over her. Was this truly the fabled bridge of her childhood, the pride of the Dasgupta family, standing before her?

As she inhaled the damp air, her gaze drifted across the landscape, and she thought, *With an immense bore... like a rifle... my venerated grandfather must have had a powerful presence in this town.*

She walked up the bridge, her thoughts swirling. Then, with folded hands, she said aloud, "Thakurda, wherever you are, *tomake ami shato koti pronam janai*—I offer you my deepest respects."

She looked around. "I feel proud, *gorbo bodh hochhe,* to be your granddaughter," she whispered, staring up at the autumn sky with the gurgling of waves below. As they made their way out of the railway station toward the waiting car, the RPVP alumni gathered to bid Anu a fond farewell. A chorus of wishes and warm smiles surrounded her.

Though Anu offered her heartfelt thanks, her inner gratitude was far greater. *This genuine warmth, this connection... they didn't have to do this*, she thought. *Their welcome has truly touched me; I won't forget it. This profound feeling is a memory more precious than words.*

Anu looked at them, and the words tumbled out. "You made this day extra special for me. I'm carrying home memories I will treasure for life." She took a deep breath of fresh air. "I'm also so glad I came. I wouldn't have known the unwavering gratitude you still bear in your hearts for the founder of your lighthouse, Ratnaprobha Vidyapitha."

Anu settled into the car. As twilight deepened, casting long shadows, they drove out of the city, leaving behind the last vestiges of daylight. Reflecting on her journey, Anu felt a profound sense of fulfilment. Discovering this part of her heritage had added a new dimension to her being. She now understood the value of the obstacles she'd overcome, recognizing how life had taught her the power of unwavering perseverance.

62

The Fire Station

As Anurima and Poulami journeyed towards Comilla, a persistent doubt, thick as the morning fog, enveloped Anu. The information Ketoki boudi had shared was frustratingly meager.

As the car sped through the countryside, Anu confided in Poulami. "I'm going to Comilla on very limited information. All I know is that my grandfather's property has been unclaimed for many years."

"Then what happened to it?" Poulami frowned.

"Well, from the sparse details I have, it lay unclaimed in East Pakistan. Then, after the Liberation War, the Bangladesh government eventually took it over and built the Comilla fire station."

"Oh, I see. Let's hope they allow us inside the premises," said Poulami.

"I am literally groping in the dark," Anu admitted. "Let's hope for the best."

By midday, the bustle of Comilla town gave way to quieter lanes. As the car turned onto a road flanked by slender, towering *Polyalthia longifolia* trees, a sudden stillness settled over Anu. It wasn't logic, but a deep, inexplicable pull that whispered, *This is it.* The sight of two weathered pillars, stubbornly standing sentinel at the fire station's entrance, sent a shiver down her spine, a tangible link to a time she had never known.

As the car stopped, a burst of colour caught her eye; a sprawling rose garden, vibrant against the no-frills backdrop. A wave of exhilaration washed over Anu. The stories of her grandfather's passion for roses weren't just tales; they were real.

Getting out of the car, Anu and Poulami climbed a flight of stairs and found themselves in front of a door with a nameplate: Mr. P.K. Das, Officer-in-Charge. At the far end of the room, they saw a man in a crisp khaki uniform peering over a stack of documents. The afternoon sun, penetrating through a slit in the drapes, made his sun-tanned body glow.

Anu cleared her throat. "Excuse me, sir, *ami ki bhitore ashte pari*? May I come in?"

The officer glanced up, his voice curt. "Yes, come in, *kintu ki chayi?* But what do you want?"

"We just want to meet you, sir," Anu replied.

Anu and Poulami walked in and sat across from the officer. He eyed them suspiciously, his posture rigid.

Anu fumbled for her words. "I am Anurima Dasgupta Sensharma, the granddaughter of Mr. A.C. Dasgupta." She trailed off, watching his expression. His brows crinkled and his face darkened in a flash of defiance, as if her name had struck a nerve.

He leaned forward, his voice a low growl. "But why are you here? Is it to claim the property?"

The officer's question hung in the air. "Mr. Dasgupta was an engineer with the railways, am I right?"

A wave of disbelief washed over Anu. *Had she heard correctly? This stranger, in this unexpected place, knew something so fundamental about her family.* The realization hit her with the force of a physical blow and she was here. This was it. She was standing on her grandfather's land, and she felt the long threads of her heritage pull her back, resurrecting her past.

Anu assured the officer that she had come in search of her roots, not property. Her words seemed to disarm him. The tension visibly drained from his shoulders, and a genuine smile replaced his guarded expression. He then summoned a few staff members whose fathers or grandfathers had known her ancestor, Amalendra.

Anu understood his initial defensiveness now. Her mention of 'roots' had triggered a shared sense of history within him, removing the immediate threat he perceived, that she had come to lay a claim.

Anu's cup was full. She felt her life had a purpose, and the challenges she had faced now seemed insignificant against the backdrop of the precious memories she had carved during her journey. She reflected on her family's history, the courage and resilience, especially of the women. This was a stark contrast to the personal struggles she had navigated.

*

"Hey, just got an invitation from another alumni group," Anu told Poulomi over the phone. "They're organising a small get-together at a restaurant."

"Another one?" Poulomi laughed.

"Yes," Anu said. "This group couldn't make it to the Gulshan Club meet, so they're having their own."

Aariz Khan and Bidhan had invited Anu to join them, assuring her the gathering would be of close-knit RPVP alumni. Poulomi accompanied her. The murmur of conversation and the soft glow of the restaurant created a welcoming atmosphere. As Anu settled into her seat, she noticed the mixture of curiosity and genuine warmth in the alumni's eyes, a silent acknowledgment of her connection to their school's beginnings.

The dinner revolved around lively and engaging conversations, leaving a delightful aftertaste that uplifted Anu's spirits. Toward the end of the evening, Anu was pleasantly surprised when she received yet another beautiful Dhakai Jamdani sari.

A burst of childlike glee came over Anu as she accepted the gift. Her smile widened with an almost innocent delight, knowing the gift's rarity and artistry. It was a traditional Bangladeshi cultural symbol, and welcoming another exquisite piece into her wardrobe felt like a singular treat.

Anu had a memorable time in Bangladesh. The weight of finally standing on her ancestral land settled deep within her, a profound feeling of being home.

*

The flight back to India felt surreal. Anu was adrift in a sea of emotions—gratitude, wonder, a profound sense of connection. For weeks afterward, the world around her seemed muted, her responses delayed as she replayed the moments of her journey. The RPVP alumni had helped her discover her true identity, a concept that had previously lived only in the wistful narratives of her paternal aunt, her Rangapishi. Her tales of their ancestral home and the vibrant life they once knew in Comilla and Paksey were often tinged with the melancholy of displacement, yet they always carried an undercurrent of fierce pride in their heritage and the family's standing.

Anu's cup was full. She felt her life had a purpose, and the challenges she had faced now seemed insignificant against the backdrop of the precious memories she had carved during her journey. She reflected on her family's history, the courage and resilience, especially of the women—a stark contrast to the personal struggles she had navigated.

This journey, she realised with a quiet understanding, had been her own slow, determined effort to reclaim a part of herself, a reclaiming that resonated with a deep, almost instinctual recognition of what had been lost and what she was now finding.

Anu returned to Kolkata with a valuable experience, a collection of photographs and videos from her family's heritage. She then arranged a gathering with her paternal relatives to show them proof of their ancestral land that still existed, albeit in another country.

As Anu projected the videos and photos onto the wall, all her relatives watched, captivated. They saw the flowers that showered down on her as she entered her grandfather's school. They also saw Anu walking through the corridor of the railway office, entering the assistant engineer's office, and sitting in the chair where her Thakurda once sat, flipping through the historic album "Making of the Hardinge Bridge". The videos and photos told the story.

Mrinal remained silent throughout the gathering, then spoke up, surprising everyone. "Now I have to give credit to my wife. I never took her stories seriously, but today, I'm not ashamed to admit that I'm impressed by her courage and strength of will. I can see she has the mental fortitude to stand behind her words."

A stunned silence descended upon the gathering, all eyes turning to Mrinal in disbelief. Then cousin Bidhu looked at him. "I didn't know this part of your nature," he said. "I think out of all my brothers, I am the only one who has interacted with you." Mrinal nodded, his gaze falling.

Anu watched, astounded, as the evidence of her trip—the photographs, plaques, and books—visibly shifted the atmosphere. These tangible pieces from her ancestral home validated the stories she had so often shared with Mrinal. In that moment, she quietly mused *that his disregard for her stories had unknowingly served as a catalyst, igniting her determination to uncover the truth.*

Finally, Mrinal looked at her with a beaming smile. "Anu, I have to admit, I often doubted your pursuits and pulled you down, but you crossed all hurdles. Your determination is undeniable."

Anu's eyes widened in surprise as she looked at Mrinal. A single thought bloomed in her mind, *These are those rare moments!* Her gaze, brimming with unsaid gratitude, eloquently thanked him for acknowledging her accomplishments before her family.

A quiet melancholy then settled over her as she pondered the reality of a society where men seldom encourage their wives to establish their own paths and thrive. When, she frowned, will this patriarchal mindset finally release its grip? A fleeting thought crossed her mind, *Perhaps, without life's challenges, a comfortable existence would never have compelled me to leave my comfort zone and engage with the wider world.*

Ultimately, the emotional battles she had endured had taught her a profound truth: her current sense of identity was not freely given. It was a treasure she had meticulously forged through vulnerability and relentless perseverance.

A soft warmth spread through Anu's chest, a familiar sensation settling like a comforting hand on her shoulder. She heard an inner voice, clear and loving. It was her Rangapishi telling her, "Well done, Anu, I am so proud of you. You made it!" The pride resonated outwards, and as the echoes of Rangapishi's words faded, a quote by Kaci Diane filled the air, a quiet affirmation: "I love the person I have become, because I fought to become her." Indeed, all's well that ends well.

Epilogue

Toronto, Canada

2025

Retirement years for Mrinal were a comfortable rhythm of gardening, cooking, and TV, his mobile glued to his hand. Anu wasn't surprised when, true to his nature, he waved off her request to join her in Toronto for her book launch.

The flight was long. Anurima, weary from travel, stood in Toronto Pearson International Airport, her eyes repeatedly straying to her watch as she awaited her daughter, Aisha. "Late as usual," she murmured to herself the moment her phone chimed. "Mamma, sorry I'm late. I'll be with you in a minute."

Aisha then appeared, a tall young woman with a light complexion, expressive almond eyes, and long, straight black hair cascading down her back. She was dressed in fitted blue jeans and an elbow-length top with side slits, accessorised with a metallic ribbon belt. A Louis Vuitton tote, flat ballet shoes with a Tory Burch emblem, and a beaded brass bracelet completed her outfit, reflecting her strong interest in fashion.

Anu embraced her daughter. As Aisha loaded the luggage into the trunk and started the car, Anu felt an inner glow sitting next to her. A wave of satisfaction washed over her as she mused that she had raised her well.

Aisha, now a Canadian citizen, was doing well for herself. They chatted happily during the long drive to

Aisha's apartment, making the journey feel quick. Aisha told her mamma about her new friends in Toronto and her excitement to show her mom her new home.

Finally, they reached the building and took the elevator to the fifty-first floor. Aisha had splurged on a penthouse. Anurima was amazed, finding it hard to believe. Standing on the balcony of the apartment, taking in the view, she felt like she was floating through the clouds.

*

Anu was visiting her daughter, who had organised a book launch of her mamma's debut novel. Anu's excitement knew no bounds as she got ready, with Aisha accompanying her. She arrived early, allowing time to mingle before the event. The emcee was already at the podium, and Anu went up to the dais to join the moderator of her session.

That's when she saw him. She couldn't believe her eyes. *Is it Richard? Hope I'm not dreaming*, she mused.

He was looking at her with a big smile, his eyes sparkling. Their gazes met for a moment. He cast an approving look at her while a teasing grin flickered on his face. Anu's spectacles helped camouflage her inner self, rendering a superficially sagacious expression, while a lively flutter began in her chest. Lost in the moment's thrill, her senses buzzing, she lowered her eyes.

After an intense book discussion, reading, and question-and-answer session, Anu looked around. Richard was nowhere to be seen. Her eyes darted, too overwrought to let reason exert any influence. As she took her seat, a faint tremor crossed her mind. Had she lost him again?

She found the organisers guiding her to the book-signing table. She was amidst a sea of bubbly faces. The crowd had thinned, leaving only a small group of eager people waiting to have their books signed. Then she spotted him. He was standing patiently, skimming through her book. A powerful impulse urged her to abandon everything and go to him. She averted her gaze and focused on the new line of people.

Then she heard his voice, "Hi Anu."

Startled, Anu looked up. Seeing Richard standing before her, she hurriedly stood up.

"Hi Richard, what a pleasant surprise! What brings you here?" the words gushed out in a torrent.

Richard smiled. "Why? Won't you sign the book for me? Today is your day."

Anu blushed. "That sure can wait." She immediately got up, gesturing to the host to direct the crowd towards the tea area.

Meanwhile, Aisha had also spotted Richard. They chatted over tea and snacks. Richard explained he was in Toronto for work. Then, looking at Anu, he said, "Your Facebook post said you were in Toronto for your book launch, so I decided to surprise you. If you're free, can we catch up at my hotel over dinner tomorrow? Aish could join too."

Aisha promptly replied, "Sorry Richard, as much as I would have loved to, I already have a dinner invite." She dug into her bag and handed Richard her business card. "Where are you staying? I can drop Mom at your hotel and pick her up after dinner. Will that be okay with you?"

Richard looked at Anu. "Sure, that would be brilliant."

Clutching Anurima's debut, *Inheritors of Silence,* Richard headed back to his hotel, his curiosity growing with every step. He plunged into the pages immediately, reading late into the night, his thoughts swirling. *Are these characters based on real people?* he wondered, a frown creasing his brow. Then, a smug grin spread across his face. *This woman definitely has what it takes.*

The next day, as Anu walked inside the foyer, she spotted Richard sitting in one corner, engrossed in a book. From a distance, she could see the familiar cover.

The sudden, unexpected encounter with Richard had touched a deep chord within her. The feeling ripened as she slowly walked towards him.

Seeing Anu, Richard closed the book, and shaking his head with dour amusement, stood up and stretched out his arms. He looked at Anurima with unashamed affection.

Anu hugged him.

"You know, Anu, whenever I bump into an Indian or fly over India, you instantly come into my thoughts."

Anu smiled. "So Anurima Sensharma still finds a spot in your mind?"

"It's hard to forget some people."

Richard then sported his signature impish smile and picked up Anu's book, its pages fluttering like a caged bird. One of his bright blue eyes closed in a huge wink, and then he asked, "Is the Richard of your book the same one that's in front of you?"

The amusement showed plainly on his face. Anu shrugged animatedly.

Richard's face lit up with understanding, a brilliant sunrise of realization. The subtle lift of Anu's eyebrow spoke volumes, and he instantly knew.

As they sat down, Anu felt a profound shift. The mental chain—the long-held internal struggle and doubt she'd harboured about her feelings for Richard—began to loosen its grip. A burden that had weighed on her for so long lifted, leaving her feeling suddenly, wonderfully free.

A deep sense of fulfilment washed over Anurima. Her conscience was finally at ease as she quietly reminisced: *she was now able to recognise her mentor, the person who had been her guiding light.*

Acknowledgements

While writing is often a solitary pursuit, it is profoundly shaped by the encouragement and insights of many individuals. These acknowledgements reflect how various people have helped me shape my writing experience and bring this story to life.

I want to begin by extending my deepest gratitude to my literary agent, Hubhawks, and their incredible Editorial and Design teams. Your invaluable editing expertise, honest critiques, and insightful suggestions were truly pivotal in transforming and polishing the rough edges of my novel, while your beautiful design work gave it a compelling visual identity. My sincere thanks also go to Nu Voice press, partnering with Penguin Random House, for their invaluable support in distributing and marketing this story, ultimately bringing it to fruition.

In the nascent days of my writing journey, my American friend, Daniel Cleverdon, significantly influenced my growth. Thank you for meticulously going through drafts and providing timely input. Your time and care meant the world to me. You encouraged me to share my work, and through that process, I gained invaluable feedback.

I am grateful to my friend and editor, Priyakshi Rajguru Goswami, for her initial edits and guidance on structuring the dual timeline.

I would also like to thank my friend, Usha Guha, for her constant encouragement when I needed it the most.

Interacting with fellow writers has also been a crucial part of this process. The pandemic brought new avenues of support. Author Sweta Samota's online forums provided crucial direction for debut writers. I'm also thankful to Bijoya Sawian for her patient ear during the early chapter readings and for the compelling quote she provided for this book. My thanks also go to Aashray Raizada for his inputs during the initial writing of the chapters, and to Ratna Manucha for her valuable input on a couple of chapters.

Thanks to acclaimed author and editor Madhulika Liddle, who provided a fresh perspective on my manuscript. Your patience and insightful feedback transformed this story from its early drafts and helped me navigate the often-turbulent waters. Thanks for your support, insightful feedback, and the compelling quote for the book.

I am profoundly grateful for the generous advance praise from internationally acclaimed author Moin Mir, bestselling author and columnist Kiran Manral, former MP, author, and political activist Brinda Karat, former MP and actress Moon Moon Sen, and bestselling author Aloke Lal. Your words of encouragement and support are invaluable, and I am deeply honoured by your endorsements.

I am indebted to inspiring educators who instilled in me a passion for writing, including the late Sri Sudarshan Agarwal, former Governor of Uttarakhand. Thank you, Sir, for your encouragement.

My Support System

A special thanks to my family and friends for their unwavering support.

Krishna Deb, my Krishna-boudi, thank you for your invaluable contribution of the ancestral details that profoundly shaped this story. Thanks to my Mashi, Bithi Sen, for your continuous encouragement. To my sister, Montuli (Jashodhara), your patient listening and valuable suggestions for a few crucial chapters were an eye-opener. My cousin,

Khuku (Sriparna Bose), your constant encouragement and unwavering belief in my dream sustained me.

Thank you to Tutul (Manideepa Chaudhury) for your valuable input as we read the chapters together.

Finally, to my friends, Dr Anjana Sen and Bonani Chatterjee, thank you for your constant encouragement and motivation.

As I reminisce, my deepest gratitude goes out to my high school English teacher, Mrs Arati Sen, for not only teaching me the mechanics of writing but also for encouraging my creativity. Her support boosted my confidence and helped me see writing as a powerful means of self-expression.

Last but not least, getting inspired by fellow writers and their works has undoubtedly helped me grow and explore new styles, significantly enriching my writing process.

To the Reader

Finally, to you, the reader, thank you for picking up this book and embarking on this journey with me. I sincerely hope this story resonates with you.

About the Author

Aloka Dasgupta Niyogi is a debut novelist, an accomplished educationist, a motivational speaker, freelance writer, and social entrepreneur. Her diverse talents are also evident in her captivating travel blog and other published works. With postgraduate degrees in Science and HR Management, Aloka is the driving force behind Arogya Wellbeing Trust. The organization not only serves underprivileged children and women, but also supports literary arts through The Literary Table (TLT), an author-reader initiative. She also acts as the festival director of an annual literature and arts festival, actively fostering connections among authors nationwide.

Aloka's personal passions include reading, singing, and travelling. As a true globe-trotter, she loves exploring new cultures and destinations. She lives in the serene city of Dehradun, nestled in the foothills of the Himalayas, India, with her husband, Kunal. Her daughter, Ishanie, resides in Toronto, Canada.